First Bite

Or:
Confessions of Scarlett Wharton,
Vampire

L.E. Gibler

BlytheLea
PUBLISHING

Published by BlytheLea Publishing

Tumwater, WA - USA

www.blytheleabooks.com

Library of Congress Control Number: 2021921854

ISBN: 1-7371281-2-0
ISBN-13: 978-1-7371281-2-0

DEDICATION

To my friends on the wet side. This couldn't have happened without you.

And my family, that's always a given.

ONE

I have a confession to make: I'm a vampire. Or, to be completely honest, I'm half-vampire and half...no one knows and there lies my problem. You see, to be a vampire, or a werewolf, or any other of the supernatural creatures humans call Immortals is easy. There are schools, jobs, communities, but to be a half-blood, to be a hybrid, leaves someone out in the cold. There are rules to follow as a pureblood, regulations to help deal with humans. But if our blood is tainted, we are sent away, to the furthest outskirts our families can find. There, we are left to become whatever monsters we were born to be.

Luckily for me, there were enough hybrids to warrant some form of schooling. In the entire United States, there were exactly two schools. One was based in an undisclosed location in New England, which I sadly thought was a state for years. The other was moved to the foothills of the

Cascade Mountains in Washington State. This school, Hybrid High, is unto itself a rather interesting melting pot. For, you see, Immortals are not destined to mingle. Werewolves and werecats are still at war every few years. Vampires prefer vampires, and elves, the pale, cold, classically beautiful and incredibly powerful elves, prefer to live alone, searching enlightenment without contamination. Try to imagine, if you can, a mingling of hybrids and their parents, imagine the tense silences and the overwhelming feeling of fear and hostility. That was orientation for you.

While, for the most part, matings stay within species, the small percentage that do not, face issues all around. If their parents can overlook their own differences to stay together through the raising of their child, for rarely does a hybrid have any siblings, the mercurial effect of the crossbreeding makes even one child rather rare, then those parents are truly meant to be. However, just because one couple of crossbreeds can live in relative harmony and accept each other's differences, does not mean that said couple can accept other cross breed couples. I hear graduations at Hybrid High are quite the thing to watch. The founders of the school and their leading doctor, the renowned Daphne Lennox, had finally, after years of trial and error, found that if the elves and the vampires and the humans separated the werewolves from the werecats, some form of peace existed. By nature werewolves and werecats were meant to fight. Does a cat love a dog? A panther love a wolf? In case the answer is not overwhelming obvious, that answer is no. Vampires and elves had once had a similar feud, for while elves are Immortals with greater strength than any of the others of our kind, they have no craving for blood. Werewolves and werecats must bite, but for a vampire it is their way of life. Elves, in their infinite wisdom, excused the transformers, allowing them the weakness of their animal side, but felt that vampires, who had lost the ability to shift to bat form centuries ago, should be held to a higher standard. After all, without the ability to shift, they were, in essence, human. Elves, and this is what caused a great deal of conflict, conveniently overlooked the fact that while vampires could no longer shift, they had evolved to survive off blood.

There was a fifth Immortal, one talked about sparingly and often in hushed voices: shadow creatures. These mysterious beings lived in another realm. It had been decreed nearly one hundred years ago by their elders and by the Board of Immortals, that they could not live amongst humans, and while vampires might crave blood, it could be controlled, especially since the invention of blood banks, and werecats and werewolves, by transforming into animals could be explained away, and elves, despite their prowess in fighting and their pointed ears never drew attention to themselves anyway. Shadow creatures however, or, as they once were called, refractors for their apparent ability to move light, were not content to live amongst their own kind. Their ability to hide in broad daylight by shifting into particles of light made such things as bank robberies easy pickings. Museums, businesses, treasuries were all fair game. By the time the refractors reached their full potential, nothing was safe, and the entire Immortal community was at risk of detection. The irony of this is that despite common human myth, only an Immortal could kill another Immortal. Crucifixes, silver daggers through the heart, while painful, were not necessarily deadly. The only way a human could kill an Immortal was if they did not stop trying. A single bullet wound, even if through the heart, *could* be regenerated. Only a firing squad, a fire, a machine gun, you get the picture. It was difficult to kill an Immortal, so the fear of detection was somewhat weak, at least in my mind. How could I have known when I was a child what weapons humans had the ingenuity to invent?

These shadow creatures, as I said, were confined to their own realm, a place that humans and Immortals never traversed. However, it was felt necessary to patrol, and so an outpost was created on all sides of this mysterious forested realm to watch for beings no longer welcome in the mortal realm.

For much of my youth, my mother worked at one of these outposts. I was raised within a half hour's journey of the Other Realm. Our house was on the outskirts of the community that had grown around the outpost. The northern outpost was patrolled by werewolves, the southern by werecats, the western by elves, and the eastern by vampires. My mother's pure blood allowed us to live in the vampire encampment; indeed, these encampments often had crossovers of species, as it was vital for all of them to stay on top of what was going on both within and without.

It should also be noted that all Immortal children are born, well, normal. We do not manifest our powers until adolescence. For the first fourteen years of my life, I attended human schools, knowing I was different, but not knowing precisely why. Many Immortal children were raised this way, despite an abundance of Immortal schools. After all, we lived in the humans' realm, and it was a common belief that we should be raised to understand them. This not only protected us later, but it protected the humans as well. To understand one's enemy or something like that. Perhaps it was more of an environmentalist's job: understand the environment we live in to better protect it.

When I turned fourteen, despite a lack of manifesting an abundance of Immortal abilities, my mother had sent me off to Hybrid High. My mother thought the name was funny. Queer sense of humor my mother has, after all she is a vampire and she names her half-blood daughter Scarlett. Maybe she thought a name like Red of Blood was just too boring. I'm not sure I inherited the sense of humor. In fact, I'm not sure what I inherited, for I am seventeen and without any signs of blood cravings. I have, up to this point in my life, been, well, human. The only problem is: I am far from human. What exactly my father is or was is unknown to even my mother, but he was most definitely one of the Immortals.

It was not uncommon for hybrids to develop late. It was a genetics problem. Which set of genes would win out was a mystery to even our scientists. A child could grow up looking like their mother and have the Immortal characteristics of their father. Sometimes the blood in a hybrid was able to merge harmoniously and the hybrid child was able to combine her parents' powers. This was rare though. It was more common for the dominant genes to win out, but if one set of characteristics could not dominate the other, and harmony could not be achieved, the hybrid often died. Sometimes it was quick, one set of genetics would rise up and in a cataclysmic moment the body would fight itself in a roaring battle. Oftentimes, though, the death was slow, drawn out and painful. Every hybrid grew up knowing the risks of their heritage. The cold hard facts went something like this: sixty seven percent of hybrids survived with one set of parental characteristics winning out, eleven percent never manifested a power of any kind, another eleven percent were able to merge their powers, and the final eleven could not overcome the damage the body created.

Imagine, if you can, a school full of a little over one hundred hybrids, for, as I said, it was rare enough for a child to even be born from cross breeding, and to think that one in ten students would not survive the transformation. My class was thirty-three students, by those odds, only thirty of us would survive to maturity.

I'm a terrible downer aren't I? I have to confess to spending a lot of time researching these scenarios, for, you see, I don't know my other half. Vampires were the most compatible with the other species for hybrid survival, but not knowing my other half made me paranoid. I know, I know, I shouldn't be sharing this paranoia and bringing everyone else down, believe me, I get that lecture every Christmas when Mum and I visit relatives. Among other unpleasant dinner small talk. My mother's family was old world vampires who lived in Romania. My grandparents had come over at the turn of the century to help with the containment of shadow creatures, a time known as the Control. They had stayed, raised my mother, and promptly fled back to what they deemed civilization. It bothered them that my mother not only remained, but adapted. They had found a proper vampire husband for her back in Romania. When my mother had gone for Christmas that year and had been pregnant with me, well, let's just say that was the beginning of my problems with my extended family.

My last summer had been uncomfortable. As loving and caring as my mother had been all my life, especially in the face of her parents' and grandmother's opposition, she still wanted to believe I was like her. Seventeen years and all I had to show for myself was an ability to regenerate from nearly any injury. Every summer, my mom took me to her outpost and had me help out. This last summer, I was even paid for my efforts. Still, proximity to all things Immortal didn't equate to any change in me.

My mom and I didn't have a lot to say to each other my last week before school. I spent my time in my room, talking, texting, and emailing my friends I so longed to see. We lived a little over two hours from Hybrid High if one was an Immortal and ran as the crow flies. By human roads, the trip was three hours with coffee breaks. Orientation was August 22nd in the evening, and even though there were buses- charter not yellow- sent to several meet points, one just twenty minutes from home, my mom refused to send me in it. She had always driven me to school and this year would be no different. So, bright and early Monday morning, we loaded my two suitcases and bookbag into her car and set off. Please understand my definition of early may not be the same as a mortals. All Immortals share a natural aversion to morning, but not because we are necessarily harmed by sunlight. I promptly fell back asleep, and that saved nearly two hours of conversation. I awoke to find it was approaching noon.

"I'm hungry," I said as I straightened myself. My neck had an unpleasant crick in it. I twisted it each way and was satisfied to hear it pop. My mother grimaced at the sound. She hated it when I popped joints. For good measure, and just to be difficult, I slowly popped every knuckle, my wrists, elbows, and arching like a cat, I got my back, too.

"We'll be in Packwood soon; we'll stop there."

A very silent thirty minutes later, we were again on the road with food in our stomachs. My mother was nursing one of her revolting bottles of blood. She made sure to eat because I did, but food always gave her an upset stomach. She had been raised by old-school vampires who didn't see the point in accustoming their children to ordinary food. She had forced herself much later to eat solid foods, but she always had to wash it down with a bottle of O positive.

When the signs announcing Elixir Factory appeared, white with green moss growing over giving a wanted look of decay, I felt a burden begin to lift. The founders of Hybrid High had found an old building off the beaten path, the mansion of a very wealthy vampire. Miles from the actual building, they had built prison like fences bristling with electric voltage. Rusted signs posted everywhere warning of the danger of the fence, and by the time you found the first set of cast iron gates, most people were frightened enough not to proceed further. All appearances were to deter unsuspecting humans, and, as far as I knew, they had been successful. There were two dilapidated buildings within the first set of fencing that were in fact equipped with the newest observation technology. My mother came up to the one on the left and pulled out her work badge. Every Immortal carried identification of some sort acknowledging their Immortality. We didn't get drivers licenses or passports in the strictest sense. We got credentials. The computer accepted my mother, and the rusted guard rail rose up to allow us in. The second set of gates were more solid and manned by actual beings. An elven guard took my mother's information as well as my school pass, issued every summer for incoming students. He handed them back impassively.

"Welcome back to Hybrid High," he intoned. My mother smiled and drove us further in. The drive was quite long, and when it finally opened on a bend, my school was before us. The building was enormous, looking like a Tudor remodeled in the Gothic age. Gargoyles had been added, and the exterior had turned somber. It was a giant C shaped building, but the greatest oddity was the entirely modern addition in front of the great hall. A state of the art two story hospital was attached by a beautiful stone arched walk way. There had been a great deal of discussion on the hospital, but the owner of the school had been away and many who valued the older architecture blamed her for her absence and the decision of the school board.

"I've left two phone cards in your bag. It would be nice if you would give me an update every once in awhile."

I rolled my eyes and looked out the window as we pulled into the parking lot. Cell phones weren't allowed on campus. We were relegated to house phones. As all Immortals were deemed dangerous to some degree, all private schools had their own restrictions. Hybrid High worked hard to balance everyone, make us all equal, so that our natural differences of species might never be brought to the fore. There was no television at Hybrid High. We had movie nights in our cafeteria, but the point was to avoid conflict over material objects.

"Of course I'll call, Mother. I wouldn't want you to think something had actually happened."

"Scarlett Amelia Wharton, whether we are arguing or not, you can remain polite. Be happy I don't just call your teachers for an update."

I scrunched down in my seat, arms crossed. "You aren't likely to be getting any updates, Mom. It might be easier if you just accept that now."

"I don't know but that you want to be normal."

"Of course I want to be normal. I can't be like you so why not be normal? Why not be human?"

She flinched like I had struck her. "Maybe it was a mistake to send you to human schools for so long. My parents certainly thought so, and maybe they were right after all." She looked so weary and sad, I wavered, but then I remembered the anger of my grandparents.

"Grandma and Grandpa think I shouldn't have been born anyway, so what do I care what they think about my education?"

"Scarlett that isn't true and you know it!"

"You're right, it's just great-grandmother who flinches at the sight of me."

She sighed. "My parents have accepted my decision. My grandparents do try, but it isn't as though you make it easy for them."

"Because they make it so easy to love them."

"I have come to terms with the life I chose to live. You need to come to your own terms and decide how it is you want to live. As your mother, I will do everything in my power to support you."

I just scrunched lower. "I don't want to go to Romania for Christmas."

I could tell this hurt her, but she was coming to take my petulance in stride. "Fine, I'll tell my parents you aren't coming, but I'm not going to stop doing something I've done for forty-three years because you've decided to rebel."

"Fine, I'll just stay here. And I don't want my great- grandma at my graduation."

"It's too late to change that, you've already invited them."

I let out a great, petulant sigh. "Fine."

"Fine." She gripped the steering wheel tightly as we pulled into a parking space. The hospital on

Hybrid High's grounds served not just students, but was in fact the premier hybrid facility in the United States. As they only specialized in hybrids, though, their clientele was limited, but in order to deal with us cross breeds, the technology had to be cutting edge. The parking had been extended to incorporate the hospital.

We both climbed out of the car and took a moment to stretch long immobile limbs. Silently, we unloaded my luggage. She drug out the bigger of the two suitcases as I strapped my books to my back and lugged the other suitcase forward. We smiled socially at other parents and students, but no one stopped to make conversation. Walking in under the archway to the double doors, there was relative quiet. We had beat the rush in. The double doors opened into the entry hall. Branching left led to classrooms and further down the library before it turned into the additions of a swimming pool and gymnasium. We branched left, past more classes and into the openness that had become the cafeteria, with a kitchen added onto the outside. Straight through the cafeteria were the newest dorms, reserved for the boys. Keeping with the original building plan, the girls' dorms had become the rooms in the south branch, once family rooms and upstairs, servants' rooms. The larger rooms housed up to three students. Upstairs, my room held me and one other. My mom and I silently contemplated all sixteen stairs leading to my room. I looked back at her and seventeen years of living together paid off in silent accordance. I grabbed the handle of the suitcase she carried. Hefting my smaller, wheeled bag over my free shoulder, we carried my belongings up the stairs. We were both short of breath at the top. Neither of us moved for several moments. Ask the burro how he feels at the top of the Grand Canyon. Eventually, we moved on, down to the third room on the left. I opened the door and kicked my suitcase through. Two twin beds sat on opposite walls. Two bare desks with shelves and one empty closet greeted me. I moved off to my right and dumped everything on the bed. I had had this room for three years, had the same bed, the same roommate.

"Do you want help unpacking?" asked my mom.

"Nah, I'll save that for later. No rush, all I have to have ready for tomorrow is the uniform." I paused. "Thanks, though."

She started slightly at my change. "Of course. Well, if you don't need anything, I guess I'd better be heading back." She turned and started to leave.

"Mom?" She stopped in the open doorway.
"Yes?"

I walked over and hugged her. It was a bit awkward, but I just couldn't let her leave like that. She stroked my long black hair, the complete opposite of her golden bob.

"I love you, Scarlett, and I will miss you."

"I love you too, Mom." I pulled back. "But I still don't want to go to Romania for Christmas.

Her lips twitched for the first time in weeks. "You had to grow up sometime. You don't mind staying here for the holidays?"

"I'll be fine. Maybe I'll actually do something productive."

She laughed weakly. "You'll end up saving it all to the last minute, as you always do. Take care, my love." She kissed the top of my head. "Say hi to Sam and Maya for me. Oh, and Ben and Douglas too, I suppose."

"I will." She left then, and it hurt to watch her go. We had grown apart since my lack of abnormalities became glaringly apparent. Most of my friends had at least grown fangs. The only thing that set me apart from the average high school senior was my ability to heal. When I was five, I had fallen from my bike and before some very surprised on lookers, when the blood was washed away, nothing remained. Eleven years later, and nothing else had happened. Of course, I wasn't the only hybrid to display few Immortal traits, but it was frustrating to see so many around me changing.

I emptied my bag of books all over my desk and made a half-hearted attempt to organize it. I just rolled my overly large suitcase to the foot of my bed for later. I made sure I had my slightly rumpled uniforms hanging from the closet pole, then I left looking for amusement. While Hybrid High didn't have a strict dress code, we were given suggestions and encouraged to follow them.

The two forks of the dorms had a glass connection to form a triangle room in-between. This was our Group Room. I went down, but apart from seeing a couple classmates, I didn't see anyone I wanted to talk to. I wound my way out to the courtyard, a hedge-rowed lawn complete with a fountain. I gently trailed a finger along the upper tier. I glanced up as I finished my circuit and saw Ben, one of my best friends in the world. Grinning with the glee of a satisfied idiot, I ran over and hugged him.

"Hey Ben! It's so good to see you!"

Ben, being a half mortal elven cross, had been the first of my friends to mature. He had the keenest eyesight I had ever known, and I have met full blooded elves. He was tall and slender with powerful shoulders he utilized best in the pool. He was the Immortal Regional record holder for the freestyle and the medley. He shook his honeyed hair from his face when I released him.

"It's good to see you, too Lettie. How was your summer?" he asked with humor rampant in his soft voice, using my nickname. He had been privy to my heartache, as had my other friends, Maya, Sam, and Douglas.

"Dismal and you know it." I stuck my tongue out at him.

"Have no fear, I am now here and everything's bound to get better."

I laughed. "You missed your calling. Are you sure you don't want to sign up for theater?"

He looked around, and seeing we had no company, he grabbed me roughly by the shoulders and held me as though I might faint. We had played this game for years, as Ben was a movie buff and, well, I was named Scarlett. I knew how to play along. Weakly, I grasped his jacket lapels.

"Frankly, my dear, I don't give a damn," he said in a perfect Rhett Butler drawl.

"Ben, darling, stop man handling poor Scarlett. She has to go save Tara."

Ben let me up and we erupted in laughter.

"Hi Sam!" I called between laughs. The beautiful blonde vampire-werecat came over to greet us. She exuded grace with a new found sex appeal in every step. Sam had always liked boys, but I had a feeling she was going to be busy with all of the reciprocation this year. She sauntered up to me and gave me a quick hug.

"Scarlett, dear, you left our room a mess," she drawled.

I raised my eyebrows. "And you were able to notice?"

She held her curly head at a haughty angle a second longer before laughing. "We promised we would try this year to be organized!" she cried in amused agony.

I looped my arm around her waist. "We can start tomorrow."

Ben snorted. "You'll just wait for Maya to organize it as you do every year. You two don't deserve that girl."

Sam swatted Ben's arm. "Neither do you Benjamin Martin, but I don't see us bothering you about it."

"Besides," I said soberly, "she came down with a cold a few weeks ago and she hasn't been getting better like she should. Her parents are bringing her here for treatment. She wasn't sure when she could join us in class."

The other two sobered as well. Maya was an elven-werewolf cross. Ever since our second year, she had been having problems with her health. It seemed that her body could not decide what it wanted to be and anytime it had to fight an outside force, it tried to shut down in order to solve the problem. Maya was our all important glue. She could temper Sam, brighten me, compete with Ben, and she had been the first to include Douglas Green in our group.

"What a somber bunch you all are," came Doug's laughing voice from the stairs behind us. "I know school is bad, but it isn't as though I've died." He was a rare vampire-elven cross, but early on the vampire side had asserted itself. He had bright green eyes and fangs that twinkled when he smiled, with a mop of tight curls that he kept trying to push dress code to grow into dreadlocks like his dad had. He hadn't come to Hybrid High until his sophomore year. His parents were constantly traveling scientists, a bit disturbed to be raising an energetic athlete. Despite his good nature, he had been shy when he first arrived, until Maya had coaxed her science partner to join our band of misfits.

"We'd all be celebrating at your funeral," Ben said as they exchanged good natured blows. When they were finished, Doug bowed to Sam and me.

Due to rarity of hybrids, the students at Hybrid High came from all over the United States. There was another school on the east coast, but anyone from Kansas west made the trek to Washington State. Roughly, we estimated there were two students from every state who actually attended. I'm not joking when I say we're rare. Doug was from Texas, Ben from Montana, Sam from California, and Maya was from Alaska. I was the only homebred one of the bunch, born and raised in Washington State. We were hidden away in the foothills of the Cascades, and a blank spot on the map.

"Ladies, a pleasure to see you." He looked up and sniffed the air. "Is it dinner time yet? I'm starved."

"You're always hungry," I said, rolling my eyes.

"What's wrong with that?"

"Well, you don't really have to tell us if we already know."

He seemed to contemplate this with due consideration. "No, you just might forget and just once would be devastating."

Sam disengaged herself from me and took Doug's arm. "Come, if you're so desirous of getting food, you can find me something as well. Preferably rare."

Ben and I exchanged grimaces as they walked off.

"I hope I never crave blood," I said emphatically.

"I'm with you there. Though, in my case, I would have to be pretty depraved to crave anything other than one of the five food groups."

"Spoil sport. I've still got years to develop a craving."

He shrugged nonchalantly. "Research shows that most hybrids will display their predominant characteristics by their 18th birthday."

"So I've got eight months to decide what I want to be?"

"Yep. Which means I've got two, Sam's got ten, and Doug has four." We didn't touch on Maya. Being pragmatic was one thing, but accepting something that might still be fixed was another.

"Besides, the one thing hybrids are is-"

"Unpredictable." I finished for him for if there was one solid, valuable lesson to be learned at Hybrid High, it was that no matter what you thought you knew about yourself, you could always, *always* be wrong

TWO

By five the school was full of students and parents. This made for a lot of awkward moments. Werecats would run into werewolves and if it hadn't been for third, fourth, and fifth parties, I felt certain blood would have been shed. Not that vampires running into elves went much better. There were many reasons we hybrids were so incredibly rare. Not only were we genetically improbable, but species interaction made a match near impossible. Sam and I had gone up to our room to straighten a few more things out. Very few parents of fourth years remained. For the most part, nervous first years were surrounded by their parents. No matter how much our parents might love us, there was just too much tension to be comfortable or even safe for long periods of time. In cases such as these, self preservation often won out over parental affection. For uncertain first and second years, parents braved their own kind for an evening. By our third year, our parents usually just helped us to our rooms and left.

Right around five, the intercom crackled to life.

"Attention. Orientation will be taking place in the gymnasium in fifteen minutes. Please make your way there now. Remember, we are all here for the education of our hybrid children. Please leave your personal issues at the door." Our principal had the same sense of humor my mother did, and it was obvious in his voice.

Sam, Ben, Doug, and I made our way to the gym. Minor scuffles, pushing, tripping, etc, ran rampant. We found an unoccupied spot at the top of the bleachers. It took awhile for everyone to come in and settle. The teachers were stressed and harried by the time everyone was down and settled. Jackson Daniels, our stately vampire-werewolf principal stepped up to the microphone.

"Welcome to Hybrid High. Those who have been here before, welcome back. The purpose of this school is, and always has been, peaceful cooperation amongst species for the betterment of our children. Everyone here has managed to look past differences, and we ask that you continue to do so.

Now, for those whose first year this is, welcome! It is our purpose to help you understand what makes you different. To understand is to begin to accept. To accept is the first step towards growth. This will be new for you, but we have mentors to help ease this transition. You have been sorted based on the information that was provided over the summer. If you find something not to your liking, let us know, but this is first and foremost a school, and no one expects you to like everything. For all you returning students, please try not to torment the new students too badly. Remember you were young once too." This gathered a few chuckles from the crowd.

"On a more serious note, no student is to leave the grounds without at least three or more companions. When visiting Brimstone, as I know you all will, you must notify an adult before doing so. There have been rumors of creatures in the far woods, creatures no young hybrid is fit to meet. There are safe, beaten paths to follow. Unlike years gone past, these rules will be strictly enforced. Those who have been caught before, please share your experiences."

Dead, edgy silence greeted this. The four of us exchanged nervous glances. Douglas shuddered. He had been one of the unlucky ones caught going out of bounds. Torture was unacceptable, but locking us in one of the maximum security medical rooms was not. Imagine being in a padded room for hours on end, alone with your thoughts and urges. We Immortals have an enormous need to be outdoors or to at least be able to see the world. It is in our wiring, so to confine us so severely was a recipe for madness. Detention usually meant work in the kitchens, sorting and preparing blood meals.

If you think learning about what goes in hot dogs is bad, come spend a day in our kitchen.

"Now, fourth years, if you would please come down, Mr. Hansen and Miss Montgomery will have your class assignments." We were still a little stunned at his earlier speech, but eventually all the fourth years made it down. Mr. Hansen, our vampire-human History teacher, and Miss Montgomery, a rare fully balanced vampire-werecat, moved us into the far corner of the gym as Principal Daniels called the third years down. The teachers began barking out names. I was one of the last to be called of the thirty-three fourth years.

I came forward and took my schedule from Mr. Hansen. I moved away and scanned my class selection. It went something like this:

History (Hansen)
Biology II (Dawson)
Trigonometry (Austen)
English IV (Frost)
Bloodology (Montgomery)
Art (Peters)

Sam peaked over my shoulder and compared notes. "Eugh, why did you take Trig?" she wrinkled her nose at the prospect. "And Biology II? Where is the fun in learning about our transformations?"

Ben looked over my other shoulder. "Well, we've got the first four together."

Sam frowned at him. "You were the one who talked her into those study classes weren't you?"

He smiled crookedly. "I had help. It isn't as though Maya or I could make Scarlett do anything she didn't want to." He took her schedule. "Home Ec, aka Underwater Basket Weaving, and Theater Arts?" He looked over Doug's schedule. "And who convinced whom into Home Ec?"

"Hey," said Doug, looking slightly sheepish, "free food, man." He took Ben's and shrugged. Well, we've all got History and English. We blood suckers all have Bloodology. Not too bad." He looked around at the mingling students. "Think the class rooms are empty?"'

"Why?" I asked skeptically.

He looked at me with mischief in his green eyes. "First dibs on new books." It was such a universally accepted idea, we all looked around us at the same time, made sure no one was watching, and slipped out. Mr. Hansen's History was on the first floor, but we all had our history tomes. Immortals have to take four years of history. We first learn human history, then we learn our own. Our finals were always about how our worlds colliding led to catastrophic issues. Ben and I would need Biology II books. Biology was just what it sounded like. Biology II delved deeper into Immortal evolution and our transformations. Doug, for all he had been caught and punished before, was always up for a little bit of mischief. Everyone but Ben was also going to need a

Bloodology book. Add on Trig, which Doug had surprisingly elected to take, and we were up for quite the evening of mischief.

Biology was on the second floor, as were Bloodology and Trig. We ignored the ground floor and climbed the great center staircase. The upper level was split into two wings, but we felt safety in numbers was preferable, so we all went down to the Biology lab. The lab itself was locked, but the class room was open. The books were all stacked on the far table. Trust Mr. Dawson to be organized for tomorrow and then forget to lock his door. Ben and I took lesser used copies before going in search of Trig books. Mrs. Austen, a tame but intelligent elven-human cross, also had a few books out, but they were for Algebra. Ben found one in the far back, but Doug and I were out of luck. By the time we moved onto Miss Montgomery's room, we weren't the only fourth years on the prowl. Sarah Hart and Jessica Willms, fellow soccer teammates, came out of the Spanish class room.

"We traded ours in," Sarah whispered conspiratorially before they moved on.

Unfortunately, Miss Montgomery seemed prepared for us. Her office was locked and short of having someone break the door in, we were out of luck.

"Do we need anything else?" asked Doug, a bit forlorn at our lack of total success. Ben had given him the Trig book to make him feel better.

"I don't think so. I still have my History and English books. Art doesn't need one, so for right now I'm done."

Sam tossed her corkscrew curls. "I doubt Home Ec or Theater will need a book. You know we all finished our prerequisites last year. Why aren't you all taking relaxing electives?"

The three of us exchanged glances. Simultaneously, we shrugged. "Seemed like a good idea at the time," I replied.

"Something like that," added Doug.

Ben looked indignant. "I happen to like studying."

We all rolled our eyes at him.

"Yeah, you are a regular bookworm," said Sam.

"So when does soccer season start?" I asked, hastily changing the subject, as we all played.

"Thursday. I saw Coach Abrams before I found you all. Girls start at four, boys at five, with the field at five0 thirty," answered Douglas.

"How about a game of two on two?" I suggested. "Half field, till dinner?"

"Sounds good to me," said Ben.

"Meet you out there in fifteen minutes?" asked Doug, already running down the stairs.

"Come on!" Sam drug me to our room. We made it outside in under ten. We had geared up and Ben had brought the ball. Boys vs. Girls. Several of our teammates had followed us out and by the time dinner was served, we were full teams and full field, though not everyone had changed to shorts and cleats. It was so good to be back. We horse played all the way back in. Even though we weren't all fourth years, we all sat together that night. Together for the first time in months, it was a wonderful feeling to be back amongst my own kind.

The first day of class dawned a bit too brightly. Most Immortals were nocturnal. However, classes still started at 8:30 every morning. To make sure everyone was awake on time, the intercom would sound out like a bell, tolling three times at seven. It repeated itself, tolling six times at 7:30, nine times at 8:00, and then a remarkable twelve times at 8:25. It had been known for students to leave their bed and make it to class in those last five minutes. I was not one of them. It took me the full hour and a half to get ready. I had nearly three feet of hair, I had to get up that early. Sam, on the other hand, for all her vanity, ignored the first bell, and often the second. Our first year, I had gone back after my shower to wake her up. This worked until the spring day she first morphed. She still didn't have full werecat abilities, but when she had swung her hand out to ward me off, her cat like claws had torn right through my skin. My own powers of regeneration had made the gouges minor cuts in no time, but I had learned my lesson, and Sam was on her own.

My process of getting ready in the morning consisted of standing with my hair inverted over the blow dryer. Sometimes my classmates would add their dryers to speed the process up. Why didn't I just cut my hair? Because it punished me if I did by growing back thicker. It was as if the hairs on my head were their own form of Immortal being, with a personality all their own. When it was nearly dry, I threw it all back in a pony tail or braided it, or whatever worked for it that day. I swear it had opinions on how it wanted to be every day. I never left it down for it had the tendency to get caught in things, like door or lab equipment. Another painful lesson learned. I was down in the cafeteria before anyone else. The boys waited until the second or third bell, too. I took some cornflakes and orange juice and sat down. Nervous first years traded uncomfortable glances. Some had already made friends, but most were still too new. From personal experience, that newness lasted up to two weeks.

Ben and Doug came down with fifteen minutes to spare. Sam sauntered in shortly after. Sam yawned and stretched like a cat before examining her food. She nibbled experimentally on the blood porridge and finished her fruit salad. She had developed very eclectic tastes. We were all basically done when a loud crash sounded from the door closest to the girls' dorm. One of the first years sat sobbing in a heap of broken plates.

Every school had their queen bee. Ours was a vampire-werewolf Aryn Dorsett. She was the captain of the volleyball team, tall, slender, with a predator's personality. She had sleek brown hair and cold hazel eyes. She looked down her elegant nose at the quivering first year who had bumped into her.

"Stay out of my way," she hissed, walking right through the mess. She came to a table and stood there until one of her underlings rose.

"That was unnecessary," I muttered. Ben and I simultaneously rose and went to help the poor girl who was desperately trying to gather the broken remnants of her breakfast. I knelt down to help.

"Don't worry about it," I said softly. "Just avoid her at all costs." I smiled reassuringly at the blond, blue eyed elven-cross.

"And be happy she graduates in nine months," added Ben.

The first year kept glancing between the both of us, still frightened.

"I'm Scarlett," I picked up the last scrap and gave it to her.

"Ben Martin, at your service." He held out his hand and forced her numb fingers to shake his.

"Michelle," she whispered. Everything was gathered, so we all rose. "Why are you helping me?"

"Sometimes people just do the right thing," said Ben, patting her on the shoulder. "Get used to it."

She smiled weakly and went to deposit her broken meal.

Ben and I shrugged to each other and turned back to our table, only to come face to face with Aryn.

"What were you doing?" she asked bitingly. "You can't make them feel comfortable. Pain makes us strong."

"You don't have to be so mean," I replied warily, knowing she could best me before I could count to ten.

"How on Earth will they learn respect if you keep undermining me?"

"That isn't respect," Ben shot back coldly. "That's fear."

She curled her lip at him. "Do you want a reeducation?"

"That won't be necessary," Sam slid in between us. She had the same level of development as Aryn, and stood the best chance if we came to blows. Doug moved in beside her. If nothing else, we had numbers on our side.

"You always were an easy buy, Samantha. This do-gooding group doesn't suite you."

"Well, being a bitch certainly fits you. Howled at the moon lately?"

Violence was about to erupt on us when the five minute bell rang. I grabbed Sam and drug her away.

"Come on, Sam, there's no sense in fighting an already won battle. She knows you'd win, you always have."

"I don't know," said Doug smugly. "Four years running would be a pretty impressive record to hold."

Sam grinned with confidence. "Power is such a wonderful feeling. If only I was the sort to use it."

"We all have our failings," consoled Doug.

We filed into Mr. Hansen's room for our first day as fourth years. Ben and I left Sam and Doug at the Home Ec room before filing down to our Biology. I had heard the first quarter of Home Ec was dedicated entirely to blood preparation and how to test quality, type, and freshness. Honestly, Ben and Maya didn't have to work hard to talk me into Biology II. It was a rather mellow crowd Ben and I ran in. Hybrids were, by nature, athletic with powerful amounts of energy. Nearly every single student played a sport to deal with this need to be in motion. It was how we were able to field multiple teams for all seasons. The fall had soccer, volleyball, and lacrosse. The boys' soccer team ran their season during the fall. The girls ran an exhibition season. We played the five teams in our realm once rather than twice. The top two teams for the full season played for championship honors. Even in our mock season, expectations ran high. We had lost top honors in a shootout last spring, and most of our team had returned. Girls who didn't play soccer fielded a volleyball team. Boys had field hockey. The popular sport of football was deemed too dangerous for all Immortals. It had been attempted, but though we played with strict instructions to play without utilizing our abilities, we could not be trusted with a sport that often consisted of hitting people. We also could not be trusted playing mortals. Except for few and far between exhibition matches, we played our own kind.

I have to admit I was disappointed in my first day back. Biology II, the delving into the Immortal DNA, hadn't delved into anything. Mr. Dawson had spoiled all of my expectations by explaining that we had to recover our Biology I knowledge before delving into the fun stuff. Trig wasn't hybrid exclusive, neither was English. All four of us had English together, so we all made our way to lunch together. Considering the range of food available, I had developed a rather strong stomach, but with no craving for blood, I usually opted for salad bar.

We had shared nearly all our classes, so there was no need to trade stories, and conversation was limited to the three of us, as Ben already had his homework from History out. None of us commented on this bit of dedication. We had three years of experience.

"So are we looking forward to Bloodology?" I asked.

Doug wasn't paying attention to me. He was busy twisting Sam's corkscrew curls into knots. Sam twisted to look at me and had her hair pulled.

"Doug!" she cried. Turning back around, she punched him in the arm. "How would you like it if I did it to you?"

He was rubbing his arm, but he never failed to smile. "Well, it's kind of nice that my hair's so short."

"So," I said loudly, overriding the inevitable argument. "How about Bloodology?" My raised voice popped Ben's head up. He rolled his eyes at the scene and went back to work.

Sam shrugged. "I'm not sure how I feel about learning why I like blood. It might spoil the experience."

"At least you and I like blood," said Doug. "Poor Scarlett has to study the class and she can't stand the stuff. Remember Biology? She nearly fainted during every dissection."

I stuck my tongue out at him. "Like I haven't heard that before. I helped with the dissection, just ask Daniel."

"Daniel Livingstone and Brandon Hotchkiss worship the ground you walk on," Sam sniffed disdainfully. "They'd lie to their own mothers if you asked them."

I frowned, but since it was the truth, I couldn't very well deny it. Sighing forlornly, I went back to my food. Funny, isn't it, a near vegan vampire? Suddenly, a large commotion broke out at the table furthest from us. We all looked up, including Ben, to see Aryn and the leader of the third years, Miranda Jones, in a cat fight. Somebody's tray was on the floor, so though we had missed the initial action, a hypothesis wasn't hard to come by.

"Pick it up," growled Aryn.

"No," replied Miranda with an arrogant tilt to her head. "It was your fault. This is my place. You took it."

"Your place?" Aryn was near speechless at the sheer audacity. "This has been my place for three years. You can have it when I'm gone." Considering, I think this might have been the single most magnanimous statement I had ever heard Aryn utter.

"I want it now." And then all hell broke loose. Aryn struck the first blow, but Miranda was quick to retaliate. This was no mere female squabble. Aryn was a developed hybrid and to even think to take her on, Miranda had to have developed some powers over the summer.

"Ah," said Sam, leaning back in ease. "The yearly battle of domination. Every year, same time, same place."

"Power," agreed Doug. "Terribly difficult for those who don't have it."

The level of intensity in the skirmish was escalating. Before, when one struck, it had the power of a trained boxer. Now, they were flying back several feet. The climax would find someone going through a wall. Hence, the new entry to the girls' dorms. Like Sam said, it happened every year.

"Sam, don't you think it's about time?" I asked warily, watching Aryn slide down the length of one of the cafeteria's tables.

Sam stood up with great resignation. "Fine, since you insist." In one great leap, she crossed from our table to theirs. She whipped Aryn around by the shoulder. Aryn fell to the ground, too disorganized to regain her balance in time. Before Miranda could strike, Sam had her outstretched arm behind her back. "Ladies, we all know there can only be one queen here, and as hard as you might try, that person is me." She released Miranda with a slight push to her back. "Any further disagreements you care to air, leave me a message and my secretary will be sure to get back to you."

Aryn spat at Sam. "Your secretary couldn't harm a fly. My problems are with you, not powerless Scarlett Wharton."

Sam put a deadly hand on Aryn's throat, extending her cat claws enough to prick the skin. "You know full well if you hurt Scarlett, you answer to me. Isn't this public humiliation enough for you? I could do more." She turned her sharp eyes on Miranda. "That goes for you too." Rising, she dusted her hands and straightened her skirt with a bored air. "Nice talking to you." Calmly, she came back to our table. The entire cafeteria rose and applauded. She hopped up on our table and flourished a bow before hopping back down to grab her bag.

"Wow," I said in awe. "You couldn't do all of that last year."

Sam smiled smugly. "I did gain a little control." Her smile dropped a hitch. "Violent mood swings, though. Poor Mathias finally left for Russia with Chad to escape me."

Doug straightened. "He's in Russia?"

Ben looked at me. "When did he become such friends with Chad?"

Sam sauntered up to Ben and ran a finger down his cheek. "I apparently have that affect on a lot of boys, Benjamin, just because you're not one of them doesn't mean they don't exist."

Ben glanced wryly at Doug before looking back at her. "That doesn't answer why he went to Russia with Scarlett's boyfriend."

"Ex-boyfriend," I supplied. All eyes turned on me.

"Since when?" asked Sam.

I shrugged. "It just didn't work out this summer. We all knew he was going to Russia to work with hybrids there. My mom had me at the post all summer working, so it was just easier to be friends." Absolute silence greeted this. Finally, Doug let out a low whistle.

"So what the two of you are saying is that your scorned lovers are brooding in Siberia?"

"Something like that," I said meekly. "And we do mean lovers in the general sense, right? As much as I like Chad, well, I don't know why I'm trying to explain myself." I shut my mouth quickly before I could say anything else stupid. My traitorous friends were laughing at me.

Sam patted my hand and Doug my shoulder.

"Scarlett, darling, you were the last person we would have ever expected to have such a *loving* relationship."

"Samantha, on the other hand," said Doug with an evil glint. She looked coldly at him.

"That's quite enough of that," she purred. "I very much doubt you would want me to share all my secrets."

"I quite agree," Ben rose and gathered his books, looking bemusedly at the lot of us. "It's about time for your blood sucker course, anyway."

Ben had a frightening sense of time. He was swinging his bag across his shoulder when the bell rang.

"How do you do it?" I asked, pulling my bag from under that table.

He smiled crookedly. "I'm not going to share all of my secrets either."

Sam's demonstrations at lunch had brought balance back. For the most part, teachers did not like to interfere. Not only was it dangerous, but it was easier if this territorial war was won early. Teachers forgave Sam for her errant behavior because she brought balance to the ranks.

Sam and I had not started off as such good friends. We were dormmates, being of relatively compatible blood lines. However, in the first few months, I gravitated towards those who were more reserved, Ben and Maya, and Sam fell in with the faster crowd of were-crosses, including Aryn. We were civil, but hardly social. We didn't really start to bond until the day she tore my arm open. It had been the first time I had ever been harmed by an Immortal, but her powers were as yet so weak, my own had been up to the task. Despite what Doug says about my squeamishness over dissection, I hadn't panicked when Sam struck me. I had calmly, after the initial hysteria of pain, focused on healing the wounds. This in itself raised me in Sam's estimation. She made a point of inviting me with her, but for all our growing friendship, her friends and I just didn't click.

As I've mentioned before, we hybrids are very athletic. Even as first years, we turn out for sports and can often make a roster spot. That spring, we were both working for a starting spot on the soccer team. I was fast and efficient, and my work ethic gained some support amongst the older players, but Sam was a natural athlete in the breed of athletes. I had a roster spot, but it was Sam who started.

The same month Sam first sported her claws, she had a bit of an outbreak. Rather than a face riddled with acne, hers was riddled with fur. She is a very vain creature, and had manically waxed it all away, but the result was truly awful. Her face was red and blotchy with an all over five o'clock shadow. However, Sam was a born competitor, and though she wouldn't have been caught dead looking as she did on any other day, she was going to play. Her appearance gathered a lot of startled expressions, from our teammates and a couple hastily caught giggles. Unfortunately for Sam, rather than play a were-team, one who would understand her appearance, we were playing the Riverdale Elves. Elves never had to deal with fur, claws, or fangs. They were born with their lightly tapered ears and a beauty that defied description. Elves did not know how to look bad.

"Are you sure you're fine to play?" asked Coach Snow, rare concern evident in her voice. Coach Olivia Snow was the hardest of hard asses. She had coached for thirty odd years, though, and she knew how difficult it was to mature as a hybrid. Her one weakness was the safety of her team. And winning. The woman was obsessed with winning.

"It just looks bad," Sam replied lightly.

Coach Snow looked unconvinced. "If you aren't feeling well out there, you let me know. Don't take it personally if I send Scarlett in to replace you."

Sam nodded resolutely, but she was firm and she played exceptionally for the first half. There were fifteen of us that year. I paced the sidelines with two other first years and a second year. Coach

Snow had a pretty regular substitution. None. If one of the midfielders became a step slow, one of us was sent in, but the defense was never substituted. They were the best in the state, and Coach Snow made sure we were rarely tired through grueling practice. Of the four of us on the sidelines, I was the only one who actually liked playing midfield. It was a punishing, basically thankless job. Sam, though extraordinary, was a starting midfielder. The three forwards were all fourth years and while Coach Snow made a point of always playing the best, the three of them would have mutinied. I had been pacing some time when Sash Bard, a fourth year midfielder, had tired. I had been pulled back out when she was rested, but not without missing the growing nastiness of the game. No one had scored, and the game was nearing its conclusion. Frustration was running rampant on both sides, and if an opportunity happened to present itself to take someone out, it was done. The elven referee was busy using her super speed to keep up with the growing issues. One of their forwards nearly took our goalie out. One of our midfielders ran right over their sweeper. It might have looked like a regular game, but everyone knew better. Sam benefited from a loose ball and was running it up field, handedly working around two defenders, when, out of nowhere, she was plowed over by the striker. She got up a little unsteadily as the ref called the game to a halt. When the ref angrily asked the elf what she thought she was doing, she shrugged an elegant shoulder.

"It was so hard to tell where the human ended and the animal began."

Furious, Sam nearly made it past the referee, fledgling claws extended. The adult elf grabbed Sam. "Enough! I won't penalize either of you, neither is overly rosy right now, but I suggest you sit down, Number Nine," she pulled Sam towards the sidelines. The elf looked coldly at Coach Snow. "You know better than to play a morphing hybrid, Olivia."

Coach Snow gathered Sam to her. "So good of you not to call that penalty," she replied with heavy sarcasm. "Scarlett! You're up!" She looked back at the ref. "I trust you'll allow me the substitution?"

The elf nodded as though bestowing a favor. I came up as the ref moved off, but Coach Snow caught me. "Make them suffer, Scarlett. If you're ejected, don't worry, you'll still have a place on this team."

I looked to see if she was in earnest. She caught my eye and winked. I would love to say I was able to go out and save the day, but the best I managed was to innocently slide tackle the elf responsible for Sam's unofficial ejection. After 60 minutes, the game was still tied at zero. We moved to a shootout. The game had taken a lot out of Sam and though she had a place in the lineup, she took me aside.

"Can you make it?"

I was amazed that she was even asking. "Yes." I wouldn't let her faith in me be for nothing.

She nodded. "Go on, then."

My arrival in the lineup was not greeted with a standing ovation, but no one denied my right to be there. Hannah, our Captain, was set to go last. I was just in front of her. Riverdale scored, we scored. Riverdale missed, we missed. I came up and arced it through the left side. I was ecstatic! My first goal at Hybrid High. But the shootout wasn't over. The elf following me missed, so it was up to Hannah. If she made it…and she did! We all screamed and hugged. It was a wonderful feeling to finally be a part of the celebrations, knowing I had done my part. Sam made a point of sitting with me on the bus ride home.

"You know, Scarlett, I liked you before, but when you took that elf out, you got yourself a friend for life. It was exactly the thing I would have done." She dropped her head into her coat for a nap. "Oh, and nice shot, too."

As odd as it may sound, that was the day Sam became my friend. She never did things in halves, and when she became my friend, she did it whole heartedly. When Aryn had made a snide comment about Sam's choice of friends, Sam had her pinned to the ground in the Group Room faster than you could say werewolf. Samantha was known as the female power of our year. She simply has to remind everyone once. Every year. Among other things, it seems we hybrids have short attention spans.

THREE

We were all sitting down for breakfast on a Monday morning about three weeks into school when Ben came excitedly up to our table. Three tired, decidedly un-morning people looked up at his unwanted enthusiasm. Even I had overslept the first two bells.

"Why are you so chipper?" asked Sam grumpily.

"I had to go return Principal Daniels' <u>Historia Immortalis</u> this morning and I saw Maya's parents! They brought her back last night and they're optimistic that she'll be able to come back to class in a couple of weeks." He was smiling delightedly with his news. Sadly, the wonderful monument of the moment was lost on his audience. I finally shook myself from my sleep induced stupor.

"That's great! We'll all have to go see her at lunch." The other two nodded. Sam gave herself a little shake.

"It'll be nice to be able to depend on someone for answers again. It's been an absolute bear having to learn history on my own," she sighed. We all looked at her askance. She smiled a slow, satisfied, entirely cat-like smile. "Well, Ben is so stingy about sharing and no one else takes any better notes."

Doug shook his head in amusement. "Only you would look at it that way. I, on the other hand, am eagerly anticipating Maya's return. After all, Sam's the only one who shares her answers with me."

At lunch, the four of us went to the medical ward. The walkway between the buildings led to a sliding glass door. Directly within was a receiving desk. It looked like a game show. Sparkling white doors held four different destinations. Even through rumor, we all knew what the door to the right led to. To the right was what we all called the Psych Ward, where the rooms were padded squares with pressure sealed doors. There was only one way in and only one way out. One of the middle doors led the offices, the other was the long term care. The door to the left was for trauma and treatable problems.

"Purpose?" asked the receptionist.

"We're here to see Maya Duval," I said.

"Second door from the left, Room 206." She buzzed the door opened. Obediently, we went through.

"She gets paid to do that?" asked Doug incredulously.

We went through the open door and counted down to Room 206. The door was left open, and I nearly went by, still trying to look for numbers, when I realized I knew who was inside.

Sam and I ran forward to hug her. Maya was a werewolf-elven cross. She had slightly exotic features, with chameleon eyes and wavy black hair. Her skin was pale, as all Immortals, but she looked even paler now and her brilliant eyes were dulled, though they certainly sparkled at the sight of us.

"Hey!" she cried warmly, returning our hugs. "I'm so glad you all came down to see me."

"What else would we have done, silly?" asked Sam, snuggling in beside her.

"Well, you were always one for a social life, Samantha."

"Bah, that's all in the past." Sam straightened Maya's hair and otherwise groomed her. I had the sneaking suspicion Sam treated us all like a cat treats her kittens. She was always grooming something, usually herself.

Maya just smiled serenely. "That's what you say every year."

Sam's lips twitched. "A person can change."

Everyone else began to find ways to hide their smiles. Doug had to change his chuckle to a cough when she looked his way.

"I'm just happy to be back. I love my parents, but they can be quite suffocating. All I heard all summer long was: 'But the doctor says this', and I live so far away, none of you could visit."

I sat down on her other side and put my arms around her. "We're here now, and Sam will be by everyday for help with her homework."

Maya laughed softly. "How about study sessions until I can come back? I know you've all got soccer practice, but after?"

"Of course, we'll come!" I cried passionately.

"We'll be here every evening," said Ben calmly. "Though I'm not sure how much homework Home Ec, Theater, and Art will get you."

Sam sniffed disdainfully. "I did all of my requirements, same as you Ben. If I choose to spend my last year enjoying myself, what's it to you?"

I took a chance to look around while Ben and Sam argued over their classes. Maya had been given one of the better hospital rooms. It looked as though her mother had decorated. The rich green quilt on the bed, the green and gold curtains all held an elf's taste. A rich cherry wood desk had been squeezed in as well as an extra chair. Basically, Maya's room was as decorated as Sam and my dorm. It was even complete with her stuffed pony, Glitter. We stayed chatting for almost half an hour before the nurse ushered us out.

"I'm sorry, but it's time for your medicine, Maya." She ushered us towards the door. "And the four of you are going to be late for class." I held onto the doorway to stop from being herded out.

"Can we come back in the evening?"

The nurse pursed her lips. "I suppose." She looked at Maya's hopeful face. "Just an hour at first. I'll keep you updated as we go."

"Thank you!" I let myself be pushed out then, and I could just hear the school bell calling us to class. "We'll be back this evening Maya!" I sprinted off to catch Sam and Doug as we all slipped into class before the bell.

"It's amazing isn't it?" asked Sam as we sat at our duel desk. "How she can find such happiness."

Doug sat down in front of us with a sigh. "As long as I've known her, I've wished I could be more like her."

We joined him in brooding silence. The second bell rang and Miss Montgomery brought us all to order.

"Not exactly like her, though," said Sam quietly. "She's slipping away."

"She'll make it," I argued staunchly. "The best minds in the field work from here."

Sam just looked at me sadly. "I hope you're right."

I hoped I was too. The alternative didn't bear consideration. I didn't want Maya to become just another statistic in an otherwise harsh reality.

And then came Wednesday. I hate Wednesdays. The only redeeming quality of a Wednesday is that when it is over, there are only two days left until Saturday. I also hate Mondays, and Tuesdays, and even, on a bad day, Thursdays, but Wednesdays are like the last hill to climb until the finish line. However, that particular Wednesday would forever be remembered as *that* Wednesday. As I went about my morning routine, stumbling out of bed for the shower, drying my long black hair, brushing my teeth, I happened to notice something extraordinary. I am not a morning person, but even I had to notice that the teeth I brushed Tuesday were not the teeth I brushed on *that* Wednesday. My canines had grown to full vampire length and they tingled. Oh dear.

I sat alone that morning, trying to eat without biting my lip. Sam was, as usual, sleeping through the bells, and I couldn't fathom where the boys were. It was tricky work to eat around longer teeth, and I knew if any of my friends were to watch me, they would notice the abnormality. I didn't want anyone noticing this latest development. Lately, I had rather hoped on remaining normal all my life. The bacon and eggs were overdone and I was frightened that I could tell. Before, when Mrs. Baffert, our cook, happened to overdo something, it was all just food. With a sick feeling, I looked over at the vending machines. Given that the patrons of the cafeteria were likely to need blood to survive, the vending machines along the hallways offered regular junk food and blood food. I sidled up to one of the said vending machines and inserted my quarters for a can of, well, blood. I snuck outside to try this new beverage. Lucky for me I did, for though I might have grown fangs overnight, blood was still blood, and I spewed my first sip all over the marble patio. I ended up upending my breakfast with it and dropping the can far away. There were school counselors to help with these problems, but I knew that with the enigma that was my father, no one would have the slightest clue what to do with me.

Samantha joined me just before our first class, Mr. Hansen's History.

"I hate mornings," she muttered as we sat down in history.

"Tell me about it. And Wednesdays too." Unfortunately for me, I lisped a bit as I spoke. Luckily for me, Samantha was too tired to notice.

"Tell me why we go to class again?" she asked as our teacher walked in and began to gather our attention.

"Because we have to?"

Bloodology frightened me that day. We were learning the process of how blood vitalized the system, but, except to get a passing grade, I had never cared much for how this happened. Today, I was engrossed. I was also petrified. I took frantic notes, and asked questions, but I had three years of lack of attention to make up for it. My teacher, Miss Anne Montgomery, a very rare, fully blended hybrid, watched me with shrewd eyes, but when the bell rang I didn't linger.

I spoke little for the rest of the day. This wasn't, on the whole, a total rarity. With four other friends, there is always someone willing to do the talking. Not to mention, there wasn't a whole lot of time with soccer practice and study sessions with Maya. I mastered the art of eating over dinner, and no one noticed when I stumbled over a few words.

The next morning, Samantha and I sat chatting in History when a rare silence descended upon the classroom. Mr. Hansen had left for a brief moment, hence the noise, only to return with the most handsome boy to ever cross Hybrid High's threshold. He moved with the grace of a werecat, but with a werewolf's keen sense of smell, as he had identified everyone with just the flick of his nostrils. Mr. Hansen led the boy the front of the class, and for once, he didn't have to ask for our attention.

"Class, this is Marcus Shepherd. He will be joining the rest of you fourth years."

Calli, a very preppy blond vampire-human cross, was never one for tact, and while the rest of us just watched this hybrid in silent fascination, she asked the question we all longed to hear the answer to.

"What is he?"

Piercing blue eyes fell upon her, and Marcus spoke for the first time. "I am a full were-cross."

There were a series of oohs, as a full were cross was all but unheard of, but Mr. Hansen was quick to regain control.

"Please take a seat, Marcus, and we will continue in a moment. Scarlett, if you would be so kind as to share a book with Samantha so that our new student might borrow yours?"

Those blue eyes turned to me, as if he knew without asking who I was. I saw the nostrils twitch, and I knew from experience that werewolves were capable of remembering a person on a sniff alone. I mutely handed my book over without so much as a squeak, as a squeak would have been all I could have managed. With catlike grace, he moved to sit between Ben and Doug, who had the front row to themselves. I was never more aware of my fangs until that moment. I was embarrassed to feel a desire to bite, and I couldn't make eye contact with anyone, let alone the stranger in front of me.

Samantha, for all her lack of desire to converse in the morning, was shrewd about a great many things, and while it was hard to have popularity groups where anyone might become anything, the key to success on any given day was to be friends with the most intriguing half-blood. Marcus fit this bill and then some, so it was a stroke of masterminding only Samantha could achieve as she slid herself in beside Doug and the newcomer over lunch. I sighed at my friend's antics, and took a seat on the other side of the table beside Ben, who was busy with his Biology II homework that wasn't due until the next day. He barely looked up when I sat down. I looked over at what he was doing.

"The purpose of transfusion in regards to a hybrid's change, Ben, is to supplant any harmful effects upon a hybrid that may occur in ingesting another hybrid's blood."

He looked up in surprise. "Did you just volunteer an answer, Scarlett?"

I smiled weakly, but kept my lips tight. "Hey, we all have to study sometime." He looked back at the book. "Page 87, if it helps."

He dutifully flipped to that page and two paragraphs down found the answer he was looking for. Ben was pale and his sandy blond hair always stood out at odd angles as though he just woke up. He also had the keenest eyesight of any hybrid here, even though he was half mortal. Like everyone stressed, we were unpredictable no matter the genetics. Ben and I had been friends since we came to Hybrid High four years previously. However, until yesterday, he had always been the studier in our group of friends when Maya was absent. I had, sad to say, stayed up late into the night doing a week's worth of homework in the hopes of finding out something about myself. It hadn't exactly worked, but I was, for once, ahead of the curve.

When Ben finished his homework, and I had no more excuse to be helpful, we both turned our attention to the other three. Samantha was curled seductively towards Marcus, with her golden eyes focused intently on him. Douglas, for his part, was busy making knots in her hair. When he caught me watching him, he sheepishly stopped.

"Why did it take you so long to come here, Marcus," asked Sam in a purr. She was very good at that purr, but the werewolf part of Marcus appeared to be sensing her werecat half in overdrive, for he showed her teeth in a near snarl when she asked and the twitch of his nostrils was noticeable.

"This is a last resort," he spoke with finality, and while Sam realized it, she wasn't entirely deterred.

"A last resort for all of us, Marcus. There is nothing left for us to do when we are hybrids, but go where we can be monitored."

"Like rats in a lab, my dear Samantha."

"Hardly," said Ben with a quicksilver smile. "Rats go for cheese. Here we mostly go for blood, unless you're Scarlett or me."

"What are you, Ben?"

"Half elven, the meekest of the bunch. I have no desire for blood by nature, but even half elves can be unpredictable when they mature."

"And Scarlett?" Those eyes moved to me.

"Half vampire," I replied as coolly as I could, with my pulse skittering every which way.

His eyebrows rose. "And yet you don't crave blood?"

"Lucky for me, that seems to be something I missed in the genetic gene pool," I replied, feeling this need to combat him. His suave arrogance was grating.

"And yet you have the teeth to drink." He said, focusing on the canines I tried so hard to hide. Doug, Ben, and Sam looked sharply at me.

"Scarlett? You didn't have teeth yesterday." Ben took my chin in his hand to look at me more closely. I closed my eyes in pain, but dutifully bared my teeth. Ben's hand dropped as though he had been burned. "You have finally changed," he said in a neutral voice.

"No," I replied pitifully, refusing to look at my friends, the first people I should have told of my change. "I still don't crave blood."

"Just the teeth?" asked Doug, leaning across the table to get a better look. I nodded meekly.

"Why didn't you tell us?" demanded Sam.

I turned my sad eyes back to her. "It only happened yesterday, Sam. You know how we all wish we could just be normal. Why would I want everyone to know I'm morphing? Look at Maya. Every time her body tries to change, she ends up hospitalized."

"I am sorry," came the velvet soft voice of Marcus, "for bringing it up, but we are all bound to be something, are we not?"

"We half bloods are known to be only one thing: unpredictable." The pain I had focused on this newcomer and shifted to anger. "Some of us do not make our transformations into whatever it is we become. Even the bravest live with some fear of what we will be when we leave here."

"To live with fear is folly," replied Marcus coolly.

"To live without fear is inhuman," I returned hotly.

"But, my dear Scarlett, we aren't human."

My mouth snapped shut as the bell rang. I hurried myself out of there, hoping my interactions with this new hybrid were over for the day. If only I could be so lucky.

I went to visit Maya by myself that evening, as the boys and Sam had wanted to give Marcus a full tour. She was sitting up in bed reading when I came in. She looked up to see me with a smile.

"Hey, Scarlett. I hear there is a new boy in town." She put her book aside and patted the spot next to her for me to join. Her beautiful face was paler than usual, and her usually sharp eyes were flat.

"Who told you?" I asked, taking my seat.

"Sam ran up before Bloodolgy to tell me. She positively purrs when she talks about him."

"Samantha positively purrs over any guy with werecat blood in him."

Maya smiled. "I suppose so, but this was almost as bad as last year when she set her feline sights on Mathias."

I shuddered theatrically, and it brought a tinkle of laughter from Maya.

"I suppose, from a werecats point of view he is astoundingly handsome. Even a werewolf, such as yourself, would be interested, but a lowly vampire like myself is destined to want the blood first and the relationship later."

Her green eyes focused upon me. "I noticed yesterday that your teeth have grown. You didn't mention it, so I didn't, but are you having blood cravings?"

I startled for a moment. "No, I suppose your sharp elven eyes noticed?"

"What's the point in being half elven if you can't see well?"

"Yes, well thank you for your discretion. No, I haven't had any blood cravings, but my teeth itch every once in awhile. Marcus doesn't have your manners, by the way."

"Ratted you out did he? I suppose Ben was broken- hearted."

My eyes focused on my friend. "What you mean by that?"

"Ben always likes to be the first to notice these sort of things. It goes with the eyes. And to be bested by a were-cross. Poor Ben."

I had to laugh, but when I left some time later, I was far from being in a congenial mood. Maya faded more every day, and I felt that I should know how to help her, that something in my blood should do the trick to her recovery, but I was as lost today as I was any other day.

FOUR

Everyone at Hybrid High had been the new kid. The trick to survival is how quickly you can adapt. I had never seen anyone adapt as quickly as Marcus did in those coming days. He had obvious advantages of course. He was handsome and a rare hybrid. No one could think of knowing a full were-cross. The species rarely interacted, much less started families. In those first few days, everyone wanted to be his friend; however, with perfect equanimity, he disdained anyone except our group.

I was sitting down to lunch, but for some reason, I was alone. Ben had run off to visit Maya, who had been promised she could return soon. Sam had convinced Doug to go outside with her, and I just hadn't felt welcome there. This left me alone with my Bloodology book out, reading for class. I was surprised when someone sat down across from me.

"I felt you needed company," Marcus said with a cocky grin. "I assure you, I'm better company than any of those textbooks."

I smiled in return. "I don't know, textbooks can be quite good companions." I marked my spot and closed my book. He raised his eyebrows.

"Must be better than that one."

"I suppose I'm just not in the mood for blood."

"You don't crave blood, right?"

"It doesn't mean there isn't some appeal. Obviously, though, you far surpass it," I said sarcastically.

He laughed. "It's good to find someone who fights back. I think I just might like you, Scarlett."

I rolled my eyes. "Oh, I feel honored." But my lips twitched, and we both knew I meant it.

Sadly, my nice meal was rudely interrupted. Marcus was still considered fair game, and so the hunting season was on.

"Marcus," drawled Aryn, placing a hand on his shoulder nonchalantly. "Why don't you come sit with us?" she used her other hand to encompass her crowd of were-crosses.

Marcus looked up at her. "No thanks, I'm fine here." He turned back to his meal, obviously shutting her out. She looked at me in contempt.

"Come now, Marcus, we're far more interesting than Scarlett Wharton. You hardly strike me as the studious type." She curled her lip at me. Her attitude didn't bother me overly much. Aryn had never liked me, and it had infuriated her when Sam left her clique. However, I felt the need to keep Marcus with me. All I could do, though, was hopelessly watch and pray he chose me.

"I said I'm fine, Aryn. Thank you for the invitation, but I decline." He bared his teeth as he spoke, a faint growl to his words. Aryn's were-half tensed in response. Her eyes darkened and her teeth showed.

"Fine," she said curtly. "My door is always open to you."

He didn't bother to acknowledge her as she stalked back to her seat. I released the breath I hadn't realized I was holding. He had gone back to his lunch, but I couldn't.

"Why did you do that? You could be sitting amongst any number of people. Aryn is probably the most popular fourth year."

He looked up at me, those brilliant blue eyes bearing into mine. "What makes you think I don't like your company? Or do you wish me to leave?"

"No!" I caught myself, a bit surprised at my outburst. "It's just that I know what it's like to want to be liked." I shrugged helplessly, knowing I wasn't doing justice to what I was trying to articulate.

"You are plenty popular enough for me, Scarlett." He looked back at Aryn and her crowd. "I can smell her dishonesty. It amazes me she cannot." He looked at me with a faint smile. "You are honest. Even Samantha does not mean to be dishonest."

I mulled this over for a moment. "So you couldn't be friends with me if I lied? What if I said my favorite color was yellow and my favorite food was haggis?"

He laughed quietly. "You do not live for deception. Believe me, everyone is deceiving in some way or another, but I cannot sense that much. A naturally decent person smells differently than a naturally bad one."

"That's amazing. I've never known anyone who could do all that, but I guess I haven't known all that many werewolves either, and I certainly wouldn't have dared to ask those that I do know."

He winked at me. "I told you I was more interesting than a textbook."

Ben joined us when we were finishing up. He slid in beside me. "Guess what, Lettie," he smiled joyfully and shook his head. "You never will, so I'll have to tell you. The doctor's think this treatment might just do the trick. Maya can come back to class next week!" He looked across the table. "Oh, hi, Marcus. How are you?" His demeanor went aloof when he addressed my companion.

"Just, fine, thanks," replied Marcus evenly.

"That's wonderful news, Ben!" I exclaimed, ignoring their interchange. "She and I will be in every class except Art. It's like a free homework pass." I smiled wryly at my attempt at humor. Sadly, it was lost.

"We should be doing the homework for her," admonished Ben. "She hasn't been able to freely socialize in six months."

"Why the obsession with homework anyway?" asked Marcus. "Samantha and Douglas don't seem all that into it, and they get along fine."

"There is life after high school," replied Ben coldly. "Scarlett and I happen to be going to college."

"It's not an obsession, not really," I tried to interrupt their sparring. "It's just that I never did my own work. For the last three years, Maya was my savior."

"Scarlett, you don't need to defend yourself for actually doing your homework. Surely Marcus can understand the need to finish something."

"Why start now?" The two seemed to be waging their own war, and ignoring me for the most part.

"Regardless, it's wonderful Maya is coming back," I said forcefully.

"Yes, it will be lovely to see how she adds to your *fascinating* dynamics," added Marcus lazily. The bell rang and I stood in rush, eager to leave this odd struggle. Both boys rose with haste.

"Are we going to see her this evening?" asked Ben, placing a hand on my arm.

"Ben, we go every evening."

"I didn't know if you had made other plans." His gaze flicked to Marcus and back to me.

"Even when I relied solely on you and Maya to finish my homework, I never went anywhere on a school night."

"I promise I've made no plans to monopolize all of her time," drawled Marcus. "But the next hour, I fear, is mine. Come Scarlett, I might get lost."

Of all the things to say! "Do you need a map and a compass?" I asked tightly.

"No," he replied with velvet softness. "Just a guide."

I wasn't sure which of us was going to kill him. Ben was simply speechless. I swung my bag across my shoulders and started off. "Try to keep up."

When we reached Miss Montgomery's class, I was dismayed to see Doug and Sam sitting together. Knowing if I looked back, I would see a smug Marcus, I sat down in Doug's usual seat with a huff. He slid in next to me much more calmly. I glared at him.

"Why do you have to bait Ben? He's your roommate, surely you would prefer an equitable relationship rather than antagonistic."

He smiled with no warmth in it. "Oh, Ben and I get along just fine the rest of the time. And I like him, but he is so sensitive about certain things, I suppose I can't resist."

"It's not nice to tease someone just because they take their studies seriously," I said, conveniently forgetting how I had once done the same thing.

He just raised his eyebrows. "It has nothing to do with his, yours, or my study habits, Scarlett, and if you don't know what his weak point is, I'm not going to tell you." And the infuriating boy didn't say anything else all hour. I tried to follow along, but my notes were sporadic and I kept looking at Marcus in consternation. He looked innocently at Miss Montgomery the whole time. When class was over and homework assigned, he gathered his things to leave. He stopped and turned back. "If you ever want to know, Scarlett, all you need to do is ask."

Hah! He must think I was easy. He watched me with mocking eyes, but I tossed my head back in defiance.

"Well, if I'm ever dying of curiosity, I'll certainly know who to ask." I felt my victory was shallow and short lived, because all he did was smile.

Oddly enough, soccer became a comfort. Being run until it hurt was an improvement to the chess matches going on within the school. At least when I was on the field, I knew what I was supposed to be doing at any given moment. I was never left feeling as though I had missed something of importance, and conversation wasn't really important. Coach Olivia Snow made sure we were all running too hard to spare the breath.

The first game of our exhibition season was a week before the boys' first home game. The opponent was the Brimstone Vampires, our closest competitor. Many of the students found amusement in the fact that their mascot was their species. When they played the rare exhibition game against humans, they always referred to it as the Burbank Humans, or Goldendale Humans rather than their mascots, Coyotes and Eagles respectively. My mom, who had been a varsity tennis player for Brimstone, laughed to this day over the pure confusion on the faces of the local human athletes. Poor, oblivious creatures that they were, they never once made the correct assumption that their opponents were, in fact, vampires.

Friday evening at four o'clock saw all fourteen of us hybrids on the field. We had to play in daylight, as light dulled our super human powers. We vampires did not die in sunlight, but we lost a great deal of our power and we sunburned something awful. Think SPF 100. Jess Willms and I stood in the middle of the field across from the captains of Brimstone. The elven referee, all refs were elven as they were strong enough to separate us and in the heat of anger would not bite, calmly had us acknowledge the rules.

"And I'm sure I don't have to remind you ladies there is to be NO use of any abilities," he sounded like a butler discussing dirt on the mantle with a scullery maid. "This is to be a good clean game. Brimstone, as the guest, you choose heads or tails."

The pale redhead called for heads.

"Heads it is. Do you—"

"We want the ball," said the brunette, curling her lip at us. Pure bloods could be like that. In every school rivalry there was bad blood, but in our case it could be downright life threatening. Pure blooded vampires, werewolves, werecats, and elves were known to frown upon matches outside their species. Most, like the redhead, were ambivalent about us. We were different, they were different. We all faced difficulties humans couldn't even imagine. We neither loved nor hated, but coexisted. The brunette on the other hand, no doubt had a cross alliance somewhere in the family and had been raised knowing how utterly unsuitable such alliances were. Some find it hard to believe such elitism exists, but, honestly, how would the Rockefellers feel if one of their own married a waitress, or, worse yet, a vampire? Of all the species, werewolves were the most accepting. I think it went with the pack mentality. Dogs can come to like cats, but cats can only come to tolerate dogs.

"Very well," said the elf with supreme dignity. "Which side do you wish to defend?" He looked at Jess and me.

Jess pointed to where we had warmed up. "We'll take that side." She lifted her chin at the snobby vampire.

The referee nodded. "One last reminder for a fair game. Good luck ladies." I bared my teeth at the brunette and saw her bristle. I was flaunting our shared heritage and she knew it. Ah well, despite the elf's efforts, our games were never clean.

We assembled on the field, with all the contained energy of a storm and the dignity of fighting troops. Immortals were evolved to win battles, if that meant world war or exhibition games; we left our personalities at the door.

Brimstone led the charge down, but Jess and Sam made quick work of reversing the field. I followed as our forwards moved up the field, crossing it all over, from Jess to Sam to Lilly to Sarah, our other midfielders and back to me. Their defense held firm, though, and I found myself sprinting back down the field. The redhead was a midfielder like me. The brunette was their center forward. Coach Snow had pounded into us teamwork, and even though we had our fair share of divas, Sam being among them, when we stepped onto that field, no one person was better than the next. If she ever felt that way, she was benched. Apparently, the brunette had missed the memo. I arced back, following the ball, but when one of her teammates was open, she ignored her. Once could be understandable so early in the first game of the season. It took us all awhile to settle in, but the second, third, and fourth opportunities decided my unfavorable opinion. Our sweeper, Tina, boomed the ball back past midfield on our opponent's mistake. I trapped it low and swung it out to my right, to Sarah who toyed with the defender, egging her closer. When the vampire bit, relatively speaking, Sarah popped it back to where I was waiting. I had a clean shot up the sideline and I made for the opening. Sam came open and I prepared to cross to her, but not before the redhead caught up with me. I found myself on the turf, tangled with my opponent, the ball puttering away and out of bounds as the ref blew his whistle. I rose to my feet and smiled to the redhead who was grinning back.

"I do love a good slide tackle," I told her good-naturedly.

"Good," she replied with equal warmth.

There was some tension on my team, as the difference between success and failure was often a matter of inches. I scanned the defense as everyone set up for the throw-in, as the ball had made for the sidelines with no direction. Taking the ball, I backed up, ball in hand. I made eye contact with Sarah, Sam, and Jess, but I waited a half second longer. As I unleashed my throw, Lilly came sprinting up into an empty space, trapped it, controlled it, and shot. Sam was quick in for the rebound, but there was no need. Lilly's kick was true. Twenty minutes in and we were up 1-0. We jogged back to our side of the field, patting Lilly on the back.

As the game wore on, the pushing got worse. The forwards for Brimstone were not strong enough to break our defense, and half time was called with no change to the score.

Coach Snow, as usual, had few words of encouragement.

"Nice job, Wharton, Jones, but Scarlett, stop chatting with the enemy. We're here to win, not make friends." That was my half time pep talk. Emma and Katie started for Lilly and me. We watched as the vampires attacked our new additions, but they didn't get very far. However, the lack of success was beginning to wear on the forwards, the brunette in particular. When her left wing was stripped of the ball by Tina on defense, the brunette ran in for it. Tina, seeing the danger, passed it left to Corey, our striker, who kept it going, but that didn't stop Number 18. The ball was leaving Corey when the brunette slid low, taking Corey down. Yes, sometimes we miss the ball in a slide tackle, but this blatant miss was not to be tolerated. Lilly, the hot blooded werecat cross, was screaming for a red card. Coach Snow, also screaming, put a restraining hand on her, effectively silencing her for six seconds. We were awarded a yellow card. Tina, however, was slow to get up. Coach Snow barked for a substitution.

"Scarlett, get in there now!" I ran out. Tina was gamely hobbling off. She smiled grimly at me.

"Take her out for me, Lettie." We patted each other. I took the free kick, but as everyone was expecting a booming kick, I lightly tapped it out to the right defender, Lizzy. She, Corey, and I brought the ball up the field. I could have called Emma back to switch, but I didn't feel too horribly out of my element. The glory was in offense, and I had shared in that as a midfielder, but I had had a taste of the glory once today, and I was totally okay with sharing it.

The brunette's blatant penalty made us all edgy. Both sides were a whisper away from violence, but it was kept in check by common sense and a super fast elf. Wherever players were showing rising tension, he was suddenly there. Though dulled, his speed was still remarkable. The vampire's coach, a graying man with granite eyes, hadn't pulled Number 18. Cattiness aside, she was good, by far their best forward, but she knew it and refused to share.

The redhead managed to strip Sam of the ball, and she nimbly moved up the field. Faced with the unfortunate dual onset of Sarah and Elizabeth, or as we all called her, Lizzy, she cleared it to the brunette who had an open field. I swore at Lizzy under my breath and pelted after the vampire. Corey was running in for middle ground, but I was the only one with a chance to stop her before Wendy, our goalie. I had seen her near misses that Wendy had managed to save, and knew it was a near thing to a sudden tie. I reached her side and we ran parallel for several strides. Our elbows became locked as we battled for domination. She was pushing me in, closer to the goal net and in one strong thrust, she pushed me loose. She paused to set up and I took my last opportunity. Sliding down, I took her out, but the ball squirted safely into Wendy's waiting arms as the rest of the field crowded towards us. The vampire and I each traded subtle blows as we rose to our feet.

"Foul!" she cried, hissing in breath. I noticed her dilated pupils and retreated a step. "That was blatant."

"Oh, that's rich coming from you," I snarled back.

Teammates from both sides were gathering, but the elf was there in flash. He stood separating us.

"That was uncalled for from both of you. Eighteen," he addressed the vampire, "if you don't settle down, I'll eject you. Eleven, the same goes for you. Do it again, and you'll both be gone."

I nodded, but it was not a nod of contrition. So what if my second foot had followed through to clear the ball? It looked clean and even elven eyes aren't all seeing. He called for everyone to back up, and Wendy dropped kicked the ball back up the field. The offense played ball control for the next few minutes, running their defense ragged, but keeping the ball on the other side of the field. A good thing they did too, for Number 18 was looking for blood, and I mean that in the literal sense. A scant few minutes later, the referee blew the game over. We gathered forces before leading back out for end of the game congratulations.

Our team ran one captain first and the other last, to lead by example and make sure everyone followed. I was the trailer. The redhead led with the brunette behind her. There was friendly warmth in the redhead's congratulation, but the brunette pulled her hand away from me. She pulled her lips back to show her fangs.

"Filthy half-breed," she hissed.

I turned to retaliate, but Coach Snow put a vise grip on my shoulder and turned me. "Be smart, Scarlett," she hissed through clenched teeth. I angrily shook off her hand and turned back to good-gaming the vampires. The coach met with Coach Snow and I slowed to eavesdrop a bit.

"Quite the talented bunch you have there, Olivia," he said with a drawl.

"Thank you, Ivan, I appreciate the compliment," replied Coach Snow with ice dripping from her words. "But?"

"Your Number 11 needs to clean up her game and your defense is scattered."

I was so angry I nearly missed her response.

"Oh really? Is that why you couldn't score on them?"

"Don't listen to him," whispered a voice beside me. I turned to see the redhead standing beside me. "He's all bark and no bite, honestly. When you reach a certain age, the ability to bite becomes weakened. He won't admit it, but he's hit that certain age."

I looked at her with hostility, but as her words began to sink in, I smiled. "Ah, to be three hundred."

She grinned in return. "Yeah, he's been around since my great grandmother's time."

"Don't you mean great-great-grandmother?"

"Great-great-great!" she laughed, before sobering. "From me to you, nice job on Sylvia. We all secretly wish it was one of us, but she's so good we kind of have to deal with her."

I held out my hand. "I'm Scarlett."

She took my hand, but started at my name. "Did your vampire parent name you?"

"Yeah, how did you know?"

"My younger sister is named Scarlett. My dad thought it would be great to name us all after the color red or something to do with blood. My mom won with me, I'm Jennifer, but Dad calls me Red and my brother is Garnett."

My lips twitched in sympathy. "Let your sister know she has my sympathy." Her team was leaving the pitch without her. She noticed and jogged after them. Turning while running, she called out: "It was nice to meet you!"

"And you!"

FIVE

After our first game, we all felt a bit high on victory. These exhibition seasons meant little in the whole scheme of things, but to have a winning season regardless was great.

I was rather astounded to find myself tutoring someone in school. I had always gone to Maya or Ben for help with my own, but for some reason, Marcus felt that I needed to help him understand the complex and foreign principles of Bloodology. We all went to Maya's for study sessions in the evening, after our practices, but we never got around to the class that all but one of us had. Ben was our main study aid, so in that brief time with Maya, we studied with his help for History, English, and once in awhile, Trig. He, Maya, and I had Biology II, but Sam, Doug, and Marc became bored if we spent too much time on that. So, after our allotted hour, we adjourned to the library. I might have mentioned Ben's slightly obsessive study habits. He often did half of his work before class was even over. Three out of five days that week, I found myself alone with Marcus in the library. It would have been uncomfortable if it hadn't been for my ostrich in the sand habits and must study attitude. I can be very good at avoidance when I want to be.

Saturday was the boys' first home game and nothing for me or Sam. The boys were set to play Mountain Line Werecats and I was set to enjoy being a spectator. I went down to the game with Sam. We were both bundled up to handle the damp chill for long periods time. We sat with our teammates and chatted before the game began. I looked around for Marcus, but he was nowhere to be seen. He had seemed surprised at our selection of sports.

"You mean there's no football?" he had asked upon learning his four new friends all played soccer.

"Nah," answered Douglas, our sports guru, "they tried it years ago, but we just can't be trusted with contact sports. Amongst Immortals, there have been documented fatalities in football."

"Too bad, I was really looking forward to hitting someone."

"You played football amongst humans?" Ben was in shocked awe.

"Yeah, I suppose it was a good thing I was found before I hurt anyone. It was a very therapeutic sport for me."

Our boys' team was fairly decent. They had been out of the playoffs by one penalty shot last year. They were playing the team who had edged them out of that coveted spot and each team had the same record. Sam and Brittany, our free spirited left forward, got quite into the cheering business. They were up on their feet screaming encouragement every time one of our team had the ball. They were in good spirits at half, though both were showing signs of losing their voices.

"Well," said Sam with deep satisfaction, "that went well. I'm not sure Joshua would have seen Ben was open without the heads up we gave."

I caught Wendy's eye on the other side of Brittany and we both smiled. "I'm sure if they win, they'll have you to thank."

Sam cast me an annoyed glance. "You should try to show some team spirit."

"No thanks," I replied, leaning back against the bleachers, "you have plenty enough for the both of us."

"Between you and Britt, there's enough for the whole team," added Wendy.

"We're just not appreciated," sniffed Sam.

Brittany put her arm through Sam's. "We know our own worth."

All twelve of us, from Corey and Emma- our first years- to me and Jess had a hard time not laughing. We all resolutely fixed our eyes on the field, for to catch anyone's eye was to break the silence. Jess was the first one to break our vigilance.

"Scarlett, isn't that Maya?" She pointed towards the foot of the bleachers.

"With Marcus," added Wendy.

I rose to see better and sure enough, Maya stood huddled deep into her pea coat on Marcus's arm. When she saw me, she waved enthusiastically. She separated herself from Marcus and hurried up the steps. The whole soccer team was watching.

"Hey girls!" said Maya. She slipped in next to me. "It's so wonderful to be out here."

"Should you be?" asked Sam sharply, her protective instincts overriding her social skills.

Maya just smiled serenely at her as Marcus settled in behind me. "It isn't as though the doctors would have let me out without consent, Samantha. Marcus asked them this morning, and they agreed." As one, fifteen girls looked at Marcus. He smiled blandly back at us.

"You surprise me," I said slowly.

"Why?" he asked mockingly. "Didn't think I had it in me?"

"No, but you did this for a complete stranger. It was very good of you, Marcus. Thank you."

He seemed a bit startled at my thanks. Behind us, the boys were taking the field again and most of the girls turned back to watch.

"It was very good of him," said Maya. "I know none of you would have thought of arguing with my doctors."

I frowned, but Maya merely laughed at me.

"It isn't an insult, Lettie. You of all people would have been concerned for my safety. Ben would bundle me up in cotton wool, and Sam and Doug would pick me up and carry me back to my bed. Sometimes it's nice to have a fresh perspective." She put her arm through mine and promptly started to watch the game. She was the happiest I had seen her in a long time. I couldn't think of the last time she had been able to come outside with us. She had been sick since the spring of last year. Her body just wasn't handling her morphing well. I turned to look at Marcus. He was watching the both of us, not the game.

"Thank you," I mouthed. He nodded, but went to watching the game. Frustrated by his change, I turned back to the game as well, when, suddenly, I felt a humming in my veins. His breath tickled my ear as he leaned in close to whisper.

"I did it for you, Scarlett." His voice reminded me of rich, dark chocolate, and I couldn't help the shiver I felt. I turned again, but he was back to watching the game, and I was left to wonder if I had imagined the whole thing.

The game was tied, and despite valiant efforts by Ben and the rest of the forwards, it remained that way for the final minutes. They set up for their shootout. The first four to go all scored, as did the four werecats. Ben, as captain was the last to go. He shot a perfect arc into the upper right hand corner of the net. It now came down to Douglas. Doug had made the team his first year at Hybrid High simply on the lack of willing goalies. This isn't to say he isn't an exceptional goalie, there just weren't any to challenge his dominance. Even Sam and Britt were silent as the final werecat came to shoot. The entire girls' soccer team, plus Maya, were on their feet. We were all clasping hands with baited breath. We Immortals even take spectating seriously. The redheaded werecat sighted, set off, and kicked. The ball was set to exactly where Ben's had. Doug lunged to his left and his outstretched hands punched the ball wide. All fifteen of us were screaming. Most were jumping up and down. I hugged Maya, turned and hugged Sam. I glanced back for Marcus, but he was already gone. I looked around to see him at the foot of the bleachers exchanging a few words with Ben. Ben looked up and saw Maya. He went back to his team to congratulate the losers. As they were coming back off the field, he caught Doug and both boys separated from their team to come to us. They hopped over the edge of the bleachers and ran up the stairs.

"Maya!" cried Doug, the first to greet us. He picked her up and squeezed her tight.

"Let me — oof--- down, Doug! I can't breathe!" But she was laughing.

He gently lowered her down and Ben promptly hugged her.

"Did you enjoy the game?" asked Doug.

"You won, of course I enjoyed the game. I especially like that my two friends helped to win it. I haven't seen a game in six months. Come to think of it, I haven't really been outside in six months."

"Should you be getting back?" asked Ben. Both boys made to carry her. She laughed and shoved them both away.

"The doctors said I could be out so long as I didn't overextend myself. I've hardly done that by sitting here."

Sam frowned. "You should still be taking it easy, Maya."

For the first time, Maya's exotic features gathered in a frown. "I thank you all for the concern, but I don't need to be locked up for the rest of my life. Marcus gave me a moment of freedom and you are all trying to suffocate it."

I put my arm around her and forced the embrace she tried to shake off. "We're sorry Maya. You're absolutely right. We are being overbearing, so, in the spirit of celebration, who's up for coffee?"

I was met by total silence. Even Maya looked doubtful.

"I know my own limitations, Scarlett, and walking three miles to Brimstone falls into that category."

I sighed in annoyance. "What is the point of having three super strong friends if they can't carry you? It's my treat."

The four looked amongst themselves. As one, they shrugged.

"Hey, if you're paying, I'll carry the both of you," said Doug.

We made our way out of the now deserted bleachers. Sam moved to take Maya for the first run, but Maya held up a hand.

"What about Marcus? He is the one who made this all possible."

Ben's lips compressed. "He didn't want to stick around. I say we just bring something back."

Maya looked affronted. "It would be cold."

"He probably left to give us time together. He's oddly sensitive," said Sam.

"And insensitive," I muttered. Sighing, I realized my opinion didn't matter. "Someone needs to go find him."

"I'll do it," volunteered Doug. "The four of you get a head start. We can easily catch up to you." He tweaked my nose. "A turtle could keep up with Scarlett." He turned and sprinted back towards the school. It took him a few strides to build up to his Immortal speed, but he was soon out of sight.

"Come on, Maya," said Sam. She gently scooped Maya up. It took her a moment to gather her strength before she moved on. Ben and I followed.

"This feels so funny," complained Maya.

"You feel funny?" queried Sam. "Imagine how I feel. This should be done by a big brawny he-man, but there's none about."

"Hey!" Ben was affronted.

"Darling, you are not brawny. It was not an insult to your masculinity." Sam was too focused to turn and confront him.

"Was that a hint you wanted me to carry her?" asked Ben, still miffed.

"Hey, I'm right here!"

I had been following the conversation, but the ridiculousness of the situation overwhelmed me. I started laughing. All three glared at me, but it was all just too funny.

"It was your suggestion," bit off Sam.

"I didn't think you'd all take it so badly." By now, we were approaching the outer grounds. Hybrid High had been placed off the beaten path, accessible from only one direction by vehicles, but to the south, there was a short cut through the forest. We were on a hilltop, and had to descend three miles to get to Brimstone. The true test was going to be in coming back, but there was usually some willing person to help us out. When you are a teenager and confined to your school grounds, you tend to find ways of making sure you get back to where you're supposed to be. The vampires of Brimstone, a community started as a family gathering for the workers of my mom's observation post, were not necessarily overjoyed to be so near to us hybrids, but we were always a good source of income, especially on the weekends. The more understanding vampires were willing to give us rides back to our gates or to the foot of the hill that was our back road.

"Sam, put Maya down," said Ben, oddly edgy.

Sam did as she was told, but we were confused by the edict. Ben held up a hand, looking and listening intently. Even being half mortal, he had the keenest senses of all of us.

"We need to wait for the others. There is a check point 102 yards southwest from here. If we let them know, it will count as adult consent. However, it would be unwise for them to see Maya being carried."

I looked around, trying to see what Ben was talking about. I felt an odd shiver of apprehension.

"I don't think we're alone," I whispered. Everyone looked sharply at me. I heard a soft whistling above me. Ben's gaze shot up.

"Sam, guard Maya." He moved closer to me. The dreariness of the day began to seep through our psyches as well as our clothes, creating a feeling of deep unease.

I heard an odd sort of humming. I moved away from Ben, searching for the source.

"Scarlett!" Ben started after me, clearly torn between who to protect. I ignored him. The humming was growing louder. "Scarlett! Come back!"

By then, I had moved beyond them and the mistiness was surrounding me. Whatever it was, it was in pain. I moved through the underbrush, called by some sort of beacon. "Don't you hear it?" I called over my shoulder, not sure if they could hear me, as I could no longer see them. "Someone is hurt!"

"Scarlett! You're going past student bounds!" called Sam. "You have to come back!"

"It's right here! I can hear it!" Suddenly, I stumbled upon a crumpled form. I nearly screamed, but the hum of pain I could hear stopped me. I had known he was here. I could hear the three of them coming after me, but it didn't matter. Leaning down I moved a fallen tree limb to see what it was I had tripped over. Whatever it was mature. And naked. I crouched nearer. Nearly black eyes popped open as I hesitantly touched one burned shoulder. His pale skin was riddled with what looked like burns. He bared his teeth at me and I realized he was a full blooded vampire.

"What happened to you?" I asked.

"The demons of hell have been loosed." He closed his eyes and shuddered in pain and recollection. Weakly, he raised himself up on an elbow. "Do you know what the forest holds, child?"

I shook my head, too frightened to speak.

"Neither did I until last night. I suspected, but never could I have imagined." He collapsed back down in pain. "Do you know how to perform a Healing Bite, hybrid?"

"N-no."

He groaned in pain. "I didn't think so." In the distance, my friends seemed to be getting farther not nearer. "Do your friends?"

"Not that I know of."

In a flash, he grasped my wrist and bit. He pulled back with my blood on his fangs. I tried to escape then, a severely delayed reaction, but he held me firm.

"You'll do. When I tell you where to bite, I need you to trust and act on that thought. When you draw my blood, focus on something strong. I'll have to do the directing myself, but you have enough vampire characteristics to start the process." He sat up. At my blush, he pulled my scarf from around my neck and wrapped it around his waist. "Poor child, you certainly didn't ask for this." I could see that it caused him great pain to move as he did. His blood was now howling in my ears. He grasped my shoulders. "You must bit just below my neck and just above my heart. I don't mean to put undue stress on you, child, but we have only one chance at this." His eyes fluttered closed. Blearily, determinedly, he opened them again. "Focus on strength." His head rolled back, exposing his neck for the bite. "Now."

I was too terrified, but something was keeping my common sense at bay. Leaning in to where he had indicated, I bit. The taste of blood was nauseating. Imagine drinking blood. Revolting, right? I was as yet no different. His blood tasted toxic and the metallic tinge was almost unbearable, but I forced my thoughts to something strong. With my very soul, I thought of my mother carrying me seven miles on foot to the hospital the day I fell from our balcony. I had broken more bones than I could count, and had spent the next year in and out of the hospital, as my powers of regeneration were as yet still fledging. My mother had been there every day, my rock. Gradually, I felt my need to bite weaken.

"That should do it," he murmured. I detached my fangs and looked at him. He looked much improved, and he was watching me with the oddest expression.

"You are a fast learner," he said, a bit dazedly. "I've had that bite performed seven times in my 97 years, but never have I had such drastic results. You have saved my life, young one. I owe you a debt of gratitude."

"It was nothing. I'm sure anyone would have done the same."

"No, I don't think so." He was watching me intently, searching for something.

"Are we done?" I asked, growing uncomfortable under his scrutiny.

"Yes, of course." He sat back on his haunches, steadying himself to stand.

"Good." And I promptly threw up. He patted my back comfortingly.

"Was I your first bite, child?"

"Yes." I retched once more before sitting back. He was looking at me in sympathy.

"Poor thing. It was horrible of me to ask so much." He was a bit unsteady on his feet. "We must get you out of here." Taking my arm, he started to guide me out. We walked a little ways before running into a very tall, very imposing elven guard. The tall Immortal looked coldly at the vampire.

"Maxim Rochester, what an honor." The elf's impassive face made me nervous. "I thought it was made quite clear to you that you were no longer welcome here. In fact, unless I am mistaken, I am supposed to take you into custody if I should see you." The elf looked at me and frowned dark enough to make a small child cry.

"Captain Mortensen, so nice to see you here now. Where have you been?"

"If you were lost in those woods, Rochester, it was your own business. It isn't my job to look after you anymore." An iron grip snatched my other arm. "Students, however, are not only forbidden beyond this point, it is considered a punishable offense to lead them astray."

The vampire tightened his hold on my other arm. I was stuck in a tug of war. "This student just did your job for you, Mortensen. If not for her, I would be dead on your watch."

The elf pulled me towards him. "You are not my concern anymore. In fact, it would have helped me immeasurably if you had vanished, then I wouldn't be facing any difficult choices."

"Do you have any idea what they're keeping back there, Blake? They have them in energy cages! One of them got loose. That is no way to protect the children!"

A flicker of surprise flickered across the elf's features. "Surely you're mistaken."

Maxim showed his scorched body. "Does this look like a joke? You need to reinforce the power fields. This girl shouldn't have been able to cross to find me. I shouldn't have been able to get back without my passportal."

The security captain looked momentarily frightened. "You say one got loose?" His free hand went to his holster.

"Don't worry about that one. It was weak. I was able to kill it, but I nearly died in the process. Come on, Blake, think. These grounds are sealed off from students for what reason? They must be fully sealed! Isn't your son a student here?'

Both had gone slack on my arms, but I was too absorbed to leave.

"It's best if you left immediately, Maxim," said the elf in a much altered tone. "It doesn't matter whether I believe you or not, or whether I might, out of loyalty, let you go. You made this place unsafe for you fourteen years ago." He looked at me. "We'd best be getting her back to her friends.'"

"Are they all right?" I asked.

"They're fine, but worried. One of them came for me and my partner. These grounds are off limits."

Maxim's hand tightened again. "She did it to save me."

"So you said, Maxim, but how did she hear you when no one else could?"

"I'm not going to question fate, Blake."

"I heard his blood," I said somewhat shyly. "I could hear his pain."

Both me looked sharply at me.

"You're a fourth year, aren't you? A vampire and what?" The elf's hand tightened again.

I looked at my feet, shifting between their grips. "I don't know. I never knew my father."

The vampire finally dropped my arm in shock. "Great gods, no wonder I healed so quickly, child —"

The elf held up a hand and turned quickly. "Go now, Maxim. Child, give him your coat." The elf rapidly removed his and draped it across my shoulders. "Hurry, Maxim. Peter called for reinforcements to find her. You're not safe here."

The vampire donned my pea coat, still wearing my scarf like a kilt. I riffled through my purse. I pulled out my monthly spending allowance, what had been meant for the coffee. I stuffed it into his hands.

"I can't accept this," he tried to give it back, but Blake was pushing him away from the approaching noise.

"Buy some pants," I called out. He stopped and looked back at me.

"To whom am I indebted?"

"My name is Scarlett."

"And my name is Blake Mortensen, and you'll not have the chance to be indebted to anyone if you don't leave now." He shoved the vampire away. Maxim finally got the message, for he was gone in a flash, needing little more than two strides to build up his speed. The elf came up to me and steered me back the way I had come. "It would be best if you mentioned this to no one, not even your friends."

"Is he a criminal?"

The elf smiled for the first time. "Hardly. He was once the heir to this estate, but he very publicly disagreed with his father over what to do with it. The estate was deeded to his illegitimate hybrid sister. Then, fourteen years ago, he found out that the caretaker of the estate wasn't doing everything he was supposed to. When Principal Daniels forbids this forest, he means it. There are only a select few who truly know what goes on out there, but exposure now could mean the end of your school."

I was well and truly terrified at this point. In the distance, I could see the rest of my rescue party.

"How was I able to cross?"

"The boarder is weak right now. The recent storms have downed power lines. Now, truly, it is best if you don't know anymore. There is nothing more either of us can do. You know too much as it is." He turned his attention to the coming crowd. "Don't worry, Peter, I found her."

One of the uniforms came up to me. Painfully, he grasped my jaw. "It is a punishable offense to cross, half-blood. Shall we report you?"

"Leave her be, Johnson," barked Captain Mortensen. "The boarder is down. She got lost."

The other elf didn't listen. He grasped my jaw even tighter. An elf's grip can be lethal, and I winced at the pain. His hand was suddenly wrenched from me. He let out a howl of pain as Marcus stood there, grasping the elf's wrist with bone crushing strength.

"You're breaking my wrist!" he cried, trying to twist away.

"You were breaking her jaw," Marcus replied with a low growl. Captain Mortensen stepped forward and pried them apart.

"That's enough. Your wrist will regenerate, Johnson." He turned to look at me. "Are you all right?"

I nodded mutely. Marcus was still glowering at the guard. Cautiously, I approached him and gently laid a hand on his shoulder. He startled me with the abruptness of his turn. Protectively, he encircled my waist.

"We have to have the boarders repaired by this evening," barked Blake. "As for the rest of you," he addressed me and my friends. "You'd best be on your way. Come, I'll drive you. We'll be needing parts from Brimstone for all the repairs anyway. You were going to Brimstone, I trust?"

We all nodded.

"Captain," complained another of the guards. "It isn't necessary."

Mortensen looked back coldly. "I beg to disagree. It is never a pleasant experience to be lost in these woods. The girl deserves a chance to enjoy what she can of her day. No student is to be punished for trespassing until those boarders are all repaired. Do I make myself clear?" They all nodded, even I found myself nodding. "Well, get to it!" He looked back at me. "Come along, the lot of you. The van is this way." Silently we all followed, though all five of my friends were bursting with questions. I took shotgun, and the ride was silent, but full of bound to be disappointed expectations. Outside of the coffee shop, Captain Mortensen pulled up to the curb and let us all out. I waited until they were all out before turning.

"Captain, I hate to ask, but I gave all my money to Mr. Rochester. And this was my suggestion to come down."

The stoic elf's lips curved ever so slightly. Reaching into his pocket, he pulled out his wallet. "You are an extraordinary creature, Scarlett." He handed me a $20. "It is my belief that everything happens for a reason, a result of all my time with Maxim, no doubt. He was incredibly lucky to be rescued by you." I put my hand on the handle.

"When you have graduated, if you want to know more, I'll explain all that I can, but so long as you stay within their walls, it is best you know as little as possible."

"Will you be in trouble for any of this?" I was beginning to feel the overwhelming fear and paranoia of being involved in something 100 times bigger than me.

"No one knows and even the wildest imaginations could not grasp what has happened to you today. Good luck."

It was a new form of torture to sit there with my friends and not be able to share my day. Every one of them knew I was hiding something. I came out and admitted it rather than try to lie plausibly, which was never one of my strong points, but it didn't make it any easier. In the coming weeks, they all grew tired of trying to pry answers from me. As they stopped asking, I grew to forget. Not everything, that was impossible, but day to day activities replaced my fear and uncertainty. Surviving school and soccer became my priorities again, and that was fine with me.

SIX

Everything was slowly shifting back to normal until another would-be ordinary day came along to change my not so well ordered life. I came to a halt in the middle of the hallway on my way to class. Dread filled my every pore as I stared into the colorful array of one of my greatest nemeses.

"Oh no." It was more a curse than a statement. Sam had kept on walking. All around me, students kept walking. After all, there were only four minutes to get to our first hour. Sam had made it to the door of History when she realized she was alone. Turning back, she found me transfixed. Douglas and Marcus followed her.

"Scarlett, what is it?" Sam turned to see what I was staring at, but rather than consol her friend in my time of need, she started laughing. By then, Maya and Ben had joined us as well. When they saw the sign, Ben and Doug let out a helpless laugh, and Maya came to pat me consolingly. Marcus looked at the sign and then back at me.

"I don't get it," he said bluntly. "What's so funny about a dance?"

"Oh it isn't the dance, Marcus darling," said Sam with tears in her eyes. "It's what will happen to poor Scarlett." She just couldn't help herself, and she began laughing again.

Maya gently steered my frozen form towards History. "Every year, when one of the organizations like Honor Society or the Science Club needs money, they host a dance."

"Why don't they just stay with working concessions?" I muttered helplessly.

"I know why," said Marcus impatiently, ignoring my mumbling, "but what does this have to do with Scarlett?"

"Brandon Hotchkiss." All five of us spoke at once. Three in amusement, one in pity, one in dread.

"Who?"

"You know, pale kind of dorky vampire cross. Sits behind us in computer tech?" said Doug.

"The redhead?"

"Nah, the one with sandy brown hair that always looks mussed," clarified Ben.

"And every year," chimed in Sam, "as soon as one of those signs goes up, he asks Scarlett."

"Lucky for you, Lettie, we don't have more than three in a year."

I bared my teeth at Douglas. "Oh I don't know," I said with heavy sarcasm, "the idea is just so appealing." Seeing Marcus's continued confusion, I began to elaborate as we took our seats. The bell was about to ring, but we never paid much attention during the morning announcements. "We generally don't have dances," I explained. "Teachers hate to have to chaperone, and in years past simple disagreements over anything from beverages to dance partners have escalated into full scale violence. I'm told all Immortals have too mercurial hormones to be safe. Every year, though, we're told we can have one dance if we behave, with the promise of another if all goes well. I think the record is three in one year."

"Last year Ben was going to ask her," said Sam.

"But he beat me to it."

"He has like a sixth sense when it comes to Scarlett," added Doug.

"Why not say no if you don't want to go?" asked Marcus, clearly growing frustrated with our combined lack of clarity.

I gave him a look full of pain. "I can't be rude." I could tell he didn't understand. However, lucky for me class had begun. I took diligent notes rather than continue this discussion. When the bell rang, I was ready for it, and had skipped out for Biology II before my classmates had even grabbed their bags. I was nearly to Mr. Dawson's class when I was stopped. I didn't have to turn to know who it was.

"This isn't even your class, Marcus." I turned to look at him. "You're at the opposite end of the building, how are you going to make it on time?"

He just smiled devilishly. "I'll take care of myself. Now, since this is an issue for you, as your friend, I have two options for you. Option # 1: Say no."

"And Option #2?" I asked with raised brows.

He hesitated, uncertain for a moment, and in that moment, disaster struck.

"Scarlett?" I turned to see Brandon Hotchkiss behind me.

"Hey, Brandon," I said weakly. I knew what was coming, knew my answer, knew every dreaded minute.

"I was wondering if you would like to go to the dance with me?"

And then something in me changed. "I'm sorry Brandon, I can't."

"Oh," he seemed so crushed, so certain had he been of our pattern. "Why?"

I was startled by the bluntness. Too startled to formulate a response. I opened my mouth several times but nothing came out.

"Because she's going with me," Marcus's voice drawled. It had a hint of animal assertiveness that frightened poor Brandon.

"Oh, okay," he squeaked, too rattled by Marcus, who he didn't seem to have seen upon approaching me, to be heartbroken. He looked once more at me before he fled.

"I'll save you a dance!" I called out in pity.

Marcus snorted behind me. "I do you a favor and how do you repay me? 'I'll save you a dance!'" he mocked me in a sing song tone. All I could do was glower.

"There is no need to be rude, Marcus. Not everyone can be popular like you."

"There are plenty of reasons to be rude, if it gets you what you want."

"No," I snapped. "You're plenty rude for the both of us." I turned on my heel and stalked into Biology. I was still fuming all through English and Math. I had cooled down enough to sit with everyone for lunch; however, I made sure to sit as far away from Marcus as possible. I sat there fiddling with my salad bar, organized the toppings into pile, periodically eating. I was happy, in an absent sort of way, that I didn't have to drink blood. It certainly wouldn't have gone well with my croutons.

Sam sat down, the last to do so. "Ben, can you ask Scarlett? She looks so miserable."

Ben smiled somewhat shyly. "Sorry, Lettie, but since this is Maya's first time down with us all year, I asked her."

Sam snorted inelegantly. "Doug already asked me. I'm sorry, Lettie."

I just shrugged, deciding eating was safer than talking.

"Don't worry," said Marcus smoothly, "she's going with me."

"Really?" came Sam's delighted purr, loud enough and excited enough to ruin my leaning tower of croutons. "Well, that's just wonderful. Maybe Scarlett can finally enjoy herself this year."

I looked up to see everyone staring at me. Marcus was looking so smug, I could have slapped him. I stood sharply, taking my half eaten lunch. "You never actually asked, Marcus, and who's to say I said yes?"

Regrettably, my lunch was now ruined. I managed to save my roll, but I refused to stay in the cafeteria. I jumped the half wall out into the courtyard and made my brooding way out towards the forest grove. I was not the only student out, but I appeared to be the only one out solo. I made my way to the duck pond and threw my remaining crumbs at the ducks. They happily quacked their way up the slope to this unexpected snack. There was a bench made of broken branches with one full plank to sit on. It wasn't the most stable looking structure, but I was happy to see I didn't fall through to the mud below. I tried to find what was upsetting me the most as I sat there, ducks quacking at my feet for more food. Unfortunately, the list was so long that it was rather, well, upsetting. I finally accepted that life wasn't going to be improving anytime soon, so with a huge sigh, I got to my feet. Turning back to school, I saw Maya waiting for me.

"Hey," I said in way of greeting. I didn't wait, but she fell in step beside me.

"I realize I haven't been a part of our teenage angst much lately, but I just wanted you to know if you need someone sympathetic to talk to, I'm always here."

I paused a half step and looked at her. The pain I felt for my friend out weighed my own problems. I put my arm around her. "I know, Maya, and I love you for it." We walked back in quiet harmony. Sam always had to be in motion. The wonderfulness of Maya was that silence could often be golden. As we reached the courtyard, I broke the silence. "However, if you tell Marcus that he owes me an apology, it won't be the same thing at all."

She laughed softly. "You know me too well. What if Sam?"

"No. Same difference."

"The boys?"

"Wouldn't even think about it."

Maya paused, true confusion marring her pretty face. "Would you rather go with Brandon?"

"I would rather have been asked and then accept. For all that I dread Brandon asking me every year, at least he treats me with respect. A little too much respect, bordering on reverence that might be termed as frightening, but still."

Maya sighed for me. "Boys are the bane to our existence, aren't they?"

"Not Sam's." We both laughed and that was an end to that.

Soccer practice began with Coach Snow telling us if we even appeared distracted for the dance, it would be two-a-day practices until December. It ended on the same note, in addition to running two extra laps for extra measure. Sam and I were exhausted as we made our way back to our rooms and the promise of a shower. The boys had warmed up on the baseball field and were taking the pitch after us. I waved to my friends, but the shower was all that mattered to me. Sam, however, was always one for a distraction. I paused for her as she tossed her curly pony tail, still amazingly sexy for being so sweaty and dirty. Douglas and his teammate Joshua stopped as well. I caught the eye of Ben, who just rolled his eyes and jogged onto the field. I didn't know how long the flirting would go on, but it had never been my forte, and homework awaited. Trudging up to my room, I stopped at the base of the stairs. Senses tingling, I knew something was wrong. I dropped my bag and sprinted in the direction my senses were taking me. My cleats made an odd, eerie noise on the floor as I sprinted past classrooms and up the great staircase. My exhaustion from practice seemed forgotten, as I came to a halt in front of the science lab. I tried the door. Oddly enough, it was locked. Usually the classrooms were left open for our uses in studying. In fact, Mr. Dawson was known for staying up late experimenting. I backed up, desperate to open this barrier. Giving myself a running start, I threw my shoulder into the door. It took me three attempts before it finally gave way. Throwing the door open, it flew back, tilting drunkenly on its hinges. A small part of my brain registered this Immortal display of strength, but there was a much greater issue at hand. My pupils adjusted to the darkness, and I managed to find the light switch. The second the lights came on, I wished they hadn't. Destruction reined in the classroom. Logic should have been screaming for me to turn tail and run, but I could feel someone in pain. Somewhere amongst overturned tables and broken beakers was a creature in need. Moving shattered tables, I found someone curled into a ball, whining in pain. Slowly, I lowered myself and began to crab step towards him.

"Are you okay?" I asked, trying to sound calming and reassuring myself at the same time. "Do you need me to call for a doctor?" I had edged close enough for my outstretched hand to touch his trembling leg. Suddenly, in a whirl of motion, animal teeth nearly snapped my face off. I screamed in pure panic. Reflexively, I sprang backwards, landing on one of the still upright tables, another inhuman trait. Anyone with an ounce of sense would have left then. Apparently, though, I have no sense.

"Easy," I crooned, "I don't want to hurt you." The hybrid growled in response. I finally recognized him, my lab partner, Daniel Livingstone, Brandon's best friend. "Daniel," I called again, softening my voice into a melody, "Daniel, do you know who I am? It's me, Scarlett Wharton, you're lab partner. You had to dissect the frog, I couldn't bring myself to touch it, do you remember?" The low growl changed back to the painful whining. I felt I was beginning to get somewhere. "Last week we turned in our report on chrysalis with our models of the butterfly. Can you hear me, Daniel?" I made my way back to his side, and this time when I touched him, he didn't try to rip my face off. He let out a low howl full of excruciating pain. I could well understand. His transformation was a hodgepodge. One hand was a paw, one ear had grown out, his muzzle was the only full wolf part of him. And those teeth were real too. "I'm going to call for help, Daniel, just wait a moment longer, okay?" He whined and tried to follow me. I couldn't bear to watch, and was instantly struck with a conundrum. I closed my eyes, slowed my erratic heartbeat and called for help. We Immortals are not telepaths, but if you have shared enough of your soul, in times of great crisis, it has been documented that our blood can call for another. Some of the more skeptical members of my world compare this to faith healing. My mother swears I would not have survived falling from our balcony when I was seven if she hadn't heard me call for her. She was fifteen miles away at work when it happened. I had just gotten home from school and I had wanted to test the theory of flight. Usually the thirty to sixty minutes I spent at home were uneventful. Not so much that day.

Daniel continued to whine in agony. I stroked his mottled head, speaking calming nonsense. He curled his hodgepodge body into my side, seeking comfort. Finally, after what seemed like an eternity, I heard footsteps. I looked up to see Maya, illuminated in the door way.

"Scarlett?" she called. "Are you okay?"

"Call for a doctor, Maya, Daniel needs help."

"Daniel Livingstone? She took in the destroyed classroom. "Are you sure you're safe?"

The half wolf whined again, laying his miserable head on my lap. "I'm fine, but I don't know where the panic switch is."

She looked around helplessly, still hovering near the doorway. "Me neither. If you're positive?"

"I am."

"I'll run for help." She turned and bumped into someone. "Marcus!"

"Scarlett?" he called, looking around Maya for me. "Are you all right?"

I felt Daniel stiffening. Apparently, his turf was being crossed. "Marcus, go for help, Maya can stay."

I could see Marcus stiffen, and edge of hostility creeping into his posture. "Are you protected from whatever did this?"

"Yes," I said in panicked exasperation. "Now just go, you're making him uncomfortable."

"*I'm* making *him* uncomfortable?"

Maya wisely pushed him out. She came in towards me. "Is he okay?"

"I don't know. He's in pretty bad shape right now."

"How did you know? I saw your bag at the foot of the stairs and came looking for you."

"You didn't hear me?"

"I heard you scream and found the broken door."

"Oh," I was kind of disappointed in my ruined moment of faith healing. "I don't know, I could feel someone in pain."

"Lettie, you broke the door down." She sounded slightly awed and it made me blush.

"I guess I did."

"Did you know you could do that?" She was now beside the table I had escaped onto during Daniel's outburst.

"No, I don't know that I can do anything."

"Well," she finally caught sight of Daniel, "someone is certainly grateful you can do something special." Her eyes darkened in sympathy. "Poor Daniel."

Help was prompt in arriving, but when all was said and done, I found it hard to focus. One of the doctor's shook me slightly. "You should come down to the medical ward. It looks as though he caught you."

"Sure," I said absently. I watched them guide poor Daniel to some form of help. Absently, I raised my hand to my face and came away with blood. Turning to get better light on my hand, I heard a simultaneous gasp.

"Scarlett, your face!" Maya came to examine me. She tipped my face towards the light. "You need to have this checked out."

I frowned. "Why isn't my face regenerating? That was my one Immortal trait."

"An Immortal did this to you. I suppose if only an Immortal can kill an Immortal without a tool, we can scar as well."

There was a growing commotion in the hall. I could hear Sam's voice. "Maya," I asked urgently, "can you distract Samantha and anyone else? No one else needs to know."

"You'll see a doctor?"

"I'll make sure she does," said Marcus, nearly forgotten in the melee.

Maya nodded. "Give me a few minutes." She switched the lights off as she left through the broken door and headed Sam off. What she found to distract Sam eludes me to this day. It would have been beyond my abilities. When the hallways quieted, Marcus led me out of the carnage. I tried to ignore the tingling where his hand met mine. I tried to convince myself it was just the after effects of the entire experience, but I had proven I wasn't all that great at listening to my inner voices. Yes, plural. In vain did I try to rekindle my anger and indignation. We were halfway to the medical ward and quite alone when he stopped. It suddenly struck me how rigid he was. When he turned to look at me, I was genuinely frightened. Indeed, more so than I had been of Daniel.

"What on Earth possessed you to confront a morphing hybrid? Even I know how dangerous we can be." Each word was clipped and icy cold.

I shrugged helplessly. "He was in pain. I couldn't leave him."

He was too furious to immediately answer. "You could have been killed! Didn't you notice his destruction?"

"Actually," I said with my best attempt at levity, "the door was me."

He just stared at me uncomprehendingly. Finally, he dropped my hand that he had been grasping rather painfully to run both of his hands through his hair. "What am I going to do with you?" he asked in exasperation.

"You could ask me to the dance." I smiled tentatively.

He seemed jolted back to reality with my rather heartfelt suggestion. Turning, he continued towards the medical ward. "Come on." He didn't look back, assuming I was following. I frowned. To think I was subservient enough to follow without question just because he had shown me some tenderness. Okay, so I probably would have had it not been for my still present resentment to his earlier high handedness. He was at the bottom of the stairs before he realized I wasn't behind him. Looking back up, he sighed and I could feel it from my perch.

"Scarlett, will you go to the dance with me?"

I tried not to smile, honestly, I did, but I failed miserably. I trotted happily down the stairs, but as I passed him, he grabbed my arm.

"How did I hear you?" he asked in an agonized whisper. "I was in the library. How did I hear you from so far away?"

I was too startled to immediately respond. Then a grin spread across my face. "It does work!" I said ecstatically, trying to dance off towards the increasingly needed doctor.

"Scarlett," poor Marcus was sounding close to the end of his leash. I turned and place a consoling hand over his arm.

"My mother always told me if you can quiet your blood to a heartbeat, you can direct it. Most consider it voodoo hoodoo, but I have every reason to believe in it, especially now."

He just shook his head in a tired manner. "Will I ever understand just what it is that we are?"

"No." I replied blithely. "I mean, I've grown up knowing I was Immortal, and I still find things every day I didn't know about our kind. After all, we go to school for a reason."

He looked at me skeptically. "You really need to have that wound looked at."

"Why?" I asked innocently, beginning to feel light headed.

"Scarlett, how many fingers am I holding up?"

I tried to focus, but it wasn't working. Tilting my head to one side, I nearly fell over. He hurried in and righted me.

"You've lost a lot of blood. Come on, we just have a little further to go."

"Two?"

"What?" He was busy guiding me forward.

"Two fingers?"

"Nice try, come on, you're going to need some serious help."

"Hey!" I tried to back up in indignation. "I will be just fine. I can regenerate."

"I never said you couldn't," he replied consolingly.

"But you thought it," I retorted. "It's what everyone thinks. There's the powerless half breed." In retrospect, the words gushing from my mouth would have been better served staying in my mind with my mouth closed.

"Scarlett," he said kindly, "I've never thought that. Besides, you forget I was raised around humans all my life. Maybe I like your normalcy."

This statement startled me to a halt.

"Really?"

"Really, you don't have to be special to be liked. In fact, I like you just the way you are."

It is a sad, but true fact that I had to be reminded of this conversation years later. I guess I just wasn't aware of the amount of blood that had fallen from my cheek, not to mention a hybrid's first few transformations, even though all I had done was break a door down, were always exhausting. So, was it any surprise of what came next?

"Thank you, Marcus, I think I must like you too." And I then promptly fainted. Luckily, we were just a few feet from the infirmary. I came to as they were stitching my face. It was so unnerving to see a needle going in and out of my flesh, that I quickly passed out again. Oddly enough, I was not very good around blood. It was why Daniel had had to do all of our dissections. I was shaken back to conscience by Marcus. My eyes blurred as I took in Maya's worried frown behind him.

"How many stitches did she get?"

"Sixteen," replied Marcus.

"They sewed that much of me up?" I asked groggily. "No wonder I passed back out." I sat up tentatively. "When can I leave?"

"Well, they said you could be checked once you woke up. You should be fine to go after the nurse comes back."

I rubbed my hand carefully over my stitches. "How long till the stitches come out?"

"The doctor said they're dissolving stitches. As your body heals, the stitches will dissolve back into your skin. She said it shouldn't be more than three days with an Immortal's regeneration."

"Oh good, I'll just have to deal with stares for a few days then."

Maya patted me. "It isn't that bad, Lettie, and you did a good thing today."

I looked frankly at Marcus. "Really, how bad is it?"

He shifted in his chair. "Well, she's right, it isn't that bad."

I rolled back down. "Great! I must look like Frankenstein. You are both crap for lying, just so you know. It could be worse."

"Exactly," said Maya fervently.

"I don't know how," I continued, ignoring her. "But I'm sure somehow." I sobered instantly. "Of course, how stupid of me, how is Daniel?"

Maya frowned, searching for how to speak. "He's in Intensive Care. He seems to have stabilized, but they can't figure out how to fix what started."

"I feel like I should be able to do something for him," I was speaking to myself, but I still had an audience.

"You did help him, Scarlett," Maya said fiercely. "He might have died if you hadn't found him."

"He might still die," I replied quietly.

"Come on Captain Optimism, look on the bright side," said Marcus critically.

I sat up quickly, swinging my feet over the edge. My head swam a bit, and I was frustrated to see Marcus hovering over me. "Okay, bright side? I feel much better, and I want to go back to my room." Silently, Maya left to go get the nurse while Marcus and I glared at each other.

"How many fingers am I holding up?" He held up one hand, and I just couldn't hold onto my indignation.

"That's not fair!" I laughed as he switched his fingers continuously.

He smiled crookedly. "I never said I was fair."

I looked down at my clothes. The right side of my body was covered in blood. "Coach Snow isn't going to be very happy."

"You have nearly two weeks before your next game."

I brightened. "You're right. I should be fine by then. Good, I would hate to hear her take on what I did. She would be upset that my heroics weren't for the team's sake."

I was checked out sometime later. Maya and Marcus gave me a protective guard back to my room. I had to explain to Samantha sooner or later, but I did manage to leave off on all the details by the sheer need for rest and relaxation. It was all over the school by the next day that Daniel Livingstone hadn't made the transformation. Daniel had survived, but he had been a rarity. We had had students die before, and it was always a dark and somber time afterwards, full of unwanted introspection. No one wanted to face our own mortality so soon.

Sadly, if there is one thing we teenagers are, it is shallow. The thought of our upcoming dance replaced the fear of mortality in many. Maya and I made a point of visiting Daniel once a week. He was usually sedated, and I'm not certain he knew we were there, but it was as much for us as it was for him.

SEVEN

Luckily for my teammates and me, we had practiced well, and Coach Snow had been happy enough with our performance that we were allowed to take Friday off. We had won our exhibition game the previous week, and we could do no wrong.

Maya and I sat on Samantha's bed as we waited for her to finally decide on an outfit. Maya looked serene in a sage green chiffon blouse with a darker green sequined skirt. I had, in our free time waiting for Sam, piled her hair on top of her head and pinned it with a large leaf barrette. She looked like an elfin queen. In homage to my name, I wore a red scoop neck sweater with embroidery along the dip. Sam, having no elfin wisdom or namesake color, was stuck throwing every outfit she owned that wasn't her uniform, which was a lot, considering, on my bed. My shiny black hair fell down to my waist, the key reason I always wore it up. Three feet of hair was tricky to care for, unfortunately, in some sadistic way, my hair always fought me. Every time I tried for a new hair cut, it just grew back faster and thicker. It only took two tries for popular do's before I realized I was fighting a losing battle. I had to extract myself from my hair, as I was sitting on it, to go help Samantha. I plucked the golden blouse from the pile and handed it to her.

"Here, Sam. It matches your eyes. If you wait any longer, we'll be late. Besides, it isn't as though the boys never see us. We're all just goings as friends." I was greeted by a frightening amount of silence. "Aren't we?"

"Of course," said Maya, gracefully unfolding herself. "Anything else would be far too awkward."

Sam pulled the blouse on savagely. Flipping her golden curls out from the collar, she looked at us coldly. "You two are naïve if you think all those boys care about it friendship." She stalked towards the door. "I, for one, want more." And on that bombshell, she flounced out.

Maya and I looked at each other in alarm. It was Maya who prosaically lifted a shoulder. "The latest statistics do show that a lot of girls lose their virginity before leaving high school. I can't think of the exact number off the top of my head."

I shuddered. "I would be too afraid of what I might become."

Maya nodded. "Or what he might become."

Due to the forecasted rain, the dance had been moved indoors to the gymnasium. Due to a lack of aforementioned rain, the courtyard had been hastily decorated in lights. Maya and I made our way through the shining shrubbery, oohing and ahhing in nervous anticipation. The outer gym doors were open, allowing the music to waft gently out on the breeze. Okay, so it blared loudly, but I was trying to enjoy the moment. As Maya and I approached, we saw Sam take Douglas by the arm and steer him in. She gave one last defiant head toss before she was swallowed in glee. Ben and Marcus had been watching, joking amongst themselves at Douglas's expense, but they both turned to greet us, working for nonchalance. I caught Marcus's eye and blushed, embarrassed as much by the blush as anything else. I looked to Ben to see him smile genuinely at Maya before turning to me. I felt an unpleasant swoop in my belly to see the look he gave me. I glanced back at Marcus, helpless, but he had that predatory look of possessiveness that frightened me even more.

Graceful Maya swept up to Ben and took his arm. She smiled sweetly at the both of them. "Sorry we're late; we were waiting on Sam to decide an outfit."

Ben shook himself slightly and looked down at her, putting his hand over hers. "And then she beat you to the finish, how unsportsmanlike. But come, we are quite chivalrous enough to forgo complaining." He winked at Marcus before leading Maya inside.

As if my relationship with Marcus wasn't awkward enough, we were now left alone. Neither of us seemed willing to make the first move. In our silence, several laughing, easy-going couples made their way by. It just made these painfully long moments all the more excruciating. I finally dared to look at him and spoke before my fear got the better of me again.

"We should be going. They might begin to wonder."

He seemed to have been waiting for me to speak, leaning forward as though anticipating something of monument. When I spoke, he leaned back on his heels, and relaxed.

"Of course." He took a step back and made a sweeping motion with his arm. I preceded him in, aware that he stood only inches behind me, one hand on the small of my back, guiding me. I saw Maya and Ben at a table, laughing and clearly having a good time. Sam and Douglas were dancing, closely, even though the music was far from slow.

"You must have gone to dances when you went to human schools," I said, desperation beginning to seep into my voice.

"A few," he replied enigmatically. "It really couldn't be helped. The humans have these things every couple of weeks."

"Were they always this awkward?"

He looked at me as though startled by the question. After a moment's pause, he laughed. "I forget who gave you your experience." He took my hand for the first time all evening, and I had to firmly squash down my instincts. "Come on Scarlett, you are going to have your first genuine dance." He spun me onto the dance floor just as the band changed tunes. Dread and panic raged in me as the tempo slowed.

"I don't think this is a good idea."

"Scarlett, it's a dance," he said with exaggerated patience. "What else would we be doing?" He gathered me close and we moved, swaying to the music. I found myself slowly relaxing, bit by bit the tension began to ease. Deep within me, my blood called for his, as it always did. My fangs had their familiar itch, calling for the bite, but I forced myself not to panic. I could conquer my baser instincts. Breathing evenly, I laid my head on his chest, blocking out my inner nature to enjoy this moment. I felt him startle for a brief moment, but he too seemed to put his inner demons to rest. For four blissful minutes, I didn't think at all.

When the song was over, a scattering of applause broke out before a more general tune began.

"Now that wasn't so difficult, was it?"

"Trust you to ruin the moment," I muttered. "Just so you know, the last three years were not that bad."

"Admit it, Lettie," he leaned in whisper close, "I was better."

I punched his arm. "You know, Marc, I'd like you a lot better without the ego."

He grinned lopsidedly. "Ah, so you do like me then, it wasn't just the shock of all that blood loss."

I froze, trying desperately to remember just what I said when he was trying to take me to the infirmary. Recovering slowly, I rolled my eyes at him. "You are hopeless, Marcus, I hope you know that."

"That's what you're here for, to remind me."

I hate to admit it, but this was by far the best dance I had ever been to. Despite his protest, I managed to extract myself from Marcus's careful watchfulness and made good on my promise to Brandon. I stayed with him a little longer. After all, not only had I said no, but his best friend was still in the medical ward. He and fellow science geek Nina Sparrow had come together, and I sat with them for at least a quarter of an hour. Before Marcus could come and terrorize poor Brandon further, I left. I quietly slipped out to the courtyard. Sitting at the fountain, I gingerly removed my borrowed heels. It had been fun to stand next to the boys and nearly be their height, but my feet weren't cut out for the night life.

All in all, the evening had been so perfect, I would be content for it to end right then and there. I didn't want to risk Marcus ruining it in his form of a farewell. However, I knew that if I didn't go and find him he would come and find me. And with that nose of his, I would be easy to find. Feeling as though I was either going to finish off the perfect evening or ruin one, I rose, heels in hand.

I hadn't taken more than a step when I heard raised voices coming my way. I froze where I was, realizing that the fountain blocked me from view and if I moved I would be in an even more awkward situation. I recognized the voices as Sam and Doug and I prayed the ground would swallow me whole.

"I don't see what your problem is," came Sam's oddly pleading voice. "It isn't as if I slept with any of them."

"Any? You kissed my entire soccer squad!"

"That's not true and you know it!" she cried, and I could imagine her stomping her foot in protest.

"Oh really? Who missed out?"

I heard the sharp crack of her slap.

"Damn it, you used claws."

"You deserved it," she hissed. "Yes, I kissed Joshua, and Mike, but that was months ago. It isn't as if you've been exclusive."

"What about Marcus?"

I had to slap my hand across my mouth to stop my gasp.

"Who wouldn't want to kiss Marcus? Honestly, if Scarlett hasn't, I would be surprised. Besides you hateful boy, it is in my nature." I could hear the rise in her usual haughtiness, and could well imagine her tossing her curls.

Douglas laughed coldly. "Your nature? That's a low point, even for you. How would you feel if I kissed your best friend? Maybe we should go find Scarlett and find out."

"Go to hell, Doug." I heard her begin to move away. Douglas seemed to have a change of heart, for he moved after her.

"Sam, I want this to work, I do." Bravely, I peered around the fountain, trying to catch the rest of the conversation. Doug had Sam by the arm. I could tell even from this distance that she was reaching her volatile point again.

"Then trust me," she hissed.

"How?" he asked simply, and even I could hear his stark pain.

Something dark and hidden went off in Sam. Wildly, she grabbed him, kissing him in a way that would make the average person blush. I quickly pulled myself back behind the fountain, embarrassed to have witnessed something so personal. A bit unsteady, I sat back down.

"There," gasped Sam sometime later. "Compare that to how I kissed the others."

I felt this wasn't really the way to prove the matter, but I wasn't going to argue. However, for all my efforts to stay hidden from view, Sam's next words incited in me the fiercest desire to run.

"Or, better yet, go find Scarlett and see if she is even half the woman I am. You won't have to go far. She's hiding behind the fountain."

My desire to flee propelled me to my feet. Ironically, to avoid a direct confrontation all I had to do was choose the right direction. Instead, I walked right into Samantha. I had known her for over three years now. Never had I seen the anger I saw now. Her skin seemed to be like chiseled marble, cold and deadly.

"Did you enjoy your peep show, Scarlett? What, did Marcus tire of you so soon?"

My first inclination was to grovel for forgiveness, but no! The maturing hybrid in front of me had been my friend. I would not grovel for being found in the wrong place at the wrong time. Straightening my spine, I met her flashing eyes.

"While I consider you my friend, I would hardly go looking to eavesdrop on your personal life. Coincidences do have a tendency to happen."

She tore the shoes from my grasp. "You'll have to do better than that," she snarled. "You really are naïve if you think I would believe that."

"Well than I'll have to work on it," I said with more sass than I knew I possessed. "Any pointers?"

Her free hand shot towards me, but it never hit. Startled, I opened my eyes to look at Marcus. He stood there, still holding Sam's hand in his own. When she struggled, he bared his teeth.

"I don't think you want to continue in this vein," he said coldly. "It might get ugly."

She dropped the shoes as she struggled out of his grip. Both of her hands looked like weapons as she arched for a strike.

"Going to defend your weak lover?"

Marcus pushed me none too gently away. "I'm half werecat, too, Samantha. I know what you're going through. You'll regret your words in a few days' time and your actions even more."

"Had cause for repentance?" she taunted.

They had an odd sort of dance going on. One would approach, test the waters so to speak, then retreat. The other would imitate. Marcus, for his part, seemed reluctant to act, but he made sure every time Sam got near me, he shifted her off. Her fuse finally went off, and she launched herself through the air at him. They clashed for a brief moment. It was over in less than a minute. Sam lay on her back, Marcus's hand at her throat.

"Go and sleep it off, Samantha. Don't do anything else you'll regret." He released her and stood. She hissed before springing to her feet.

"You act so noble now, Marcus, but I've seen your uncivilized side. You're right we are alike, and you can't hide it from me." She savagely grabbed her shoes and headed off for who knew where.

I didn't realize I was shaking until Marcus put his arms around me, rubbing up and down my body, gentling my nerves. Doug approached us, looking apprehensive.

"What just happened?"

"Werecats have cycles." Marcus coughed uncomfortably. "I believe the term is being in heat. As Samantha matures, she is having to deal with more severe cycles until she finds her balance." My body began to tingle self consciously where Marcus was still touching me. The other part of me recalled what Doug had been upset about. Reluctantly, I pushed away from him.

"Does that mean I'm just a scratch for her itch?" asked Douglas.

Marcus shook his head sadly. "I haven't matured yet, Doug, I can hardly tell you. It passes within a few hours." He patted Doug's shoulder. He looked back at me with something like longing. "I don't think we can know anything for a few years yet. I think, Scarlett, you'll be safe to go to your room. Wherever she's gone, she won't be back soon."

I nodded mutely. As the first few moments began to fade, I felt my fear subside. I started off with an odd hitch of reluctance. This just wasn't the way to end my evening. Marcus stopped me as I made for the entrance. Leaning close, he looked at me with concern. "Would you like me to go with you?"

A new and frightening sensation swooped low and filled me with an overwhelming tingling sensation. At that moment, I wasn't sure I could trust myself alone with my protector. "I'll be okay," I replied, unwilling to look at him. This close, his blood was humming in my ears. Talk about being in heat. A gentle finger traced my fresh scar.

"Call me if you need anything," he whispered tenderly. In a moment's clarity, I knew I had to leave lest more than our friendship be ruined. I hurried to my room, not daring to look back.

Sam was not in our room when I arrived. I quickly hung all of her discarded clothes that littered my bed. Changing into my pajamas, I took my stuffed rabbit, Nibbles, and clutched him close. I crawled under my covers, yearning for my mother. Despite our rather fierce disagreements that had marred my summer, I longed for my parent's comfort. I fell asleep with silent tears on my pillow.

I awoke with a start sometime around dawn. Despite common belief, vampires do not see better in the dark. Dating back to our transforming ancestors, we hear better. When the eyes were useless, our ears worked as though with sonar. When I had broken curfew, my mom had known just what window I snuck back in through. As I lay there in the dark, the sound of the door opening sent sounds bouncing off objects in the room. I hummed, subconsciously and incredibly softly, sending out my own sonar. Sam had returned. I was too tired, still too close to dreams, to register my new found ability. I rolled away from her, hugging Nibbles closer. I heard the harsh thump of her shoes. Two more followed as she removed the pair she was wearing. Her clothes joined the pile before she crawled under her covers. Slowly, the sound of her sobs reached me. A part of me wanted to go and comfort her. She was obviously in pain, but memories of the evening flooded back. I could forgive her a great deal, but the fear and betrayal of her near attack kept me in bed. If not for Marcus, I might have born identical scars on my cheeks. As I stared at my wall, I wondered just how much of my reluctance to comfort her came from the fact that she had kissed Marcus, and shouldn't I hold that against Marcus as well? Angry at my own indecisiveness, I willed myself to sleep. My last thought was disappointment that Marcus hadn't kissed me, but was the desire for his blood the same as for his kiss? And if it wasn't, what did that make me?

EIGHT

Tuesday didn't flow any better than Monday. In fact, by the end of the week, I was quite convinced I had just endured the worst week of my life. I could talk to Ben and Maya freely, but Doug was still tense, Sam was hopeless, and there was a part of me that wouldn't let me look Marcus in the eye. I had come so close to utter weakness. I had wanted to bite, and that darkly seductive and newly awakened part of my being whispered constantly to take what I wanted. I now sat between him and Doug while Sam sat with Maya and Ben in History. For all of my new found study habits, I couldn't concentrate. My fangs would dig into my bottom lip in an effort to control these wanton wanderings. He wasn't exactly helping, either. While I could avoid him throughout the day, I spent meals on the move and refused to give up my seat beside Doug in Bloodology, he seemed to make a special effort to invade my senses in that first hour we spent together. I sat ramrod stiff, drawing blood from my lip in an effort to focus, and what would he do? It was painfully difficult to ignore the gentle hum of his blood and the bothersome itch of my teeth, but to make matters worse, every time my pen stilled, he would run a tantalizing finger down the back of my hand. I had to keep writing at all times, but I couldn't focus. That dark corner whispered that if I bit, just once, I could bear this wanting and waiting. But logic and fear continued to prevail. Not without effort, though. My tolerance was running low by Friday, and though I took notes just to have words across the page, I stopped frequently. Every gentle caress, for you can bet he wasn't paying a single ounce of attention to class, was stripping a little more of my defenses away. Three minutes to go and I very nearly snapped. There was a raging in my blood, being stoked and screaming for release, but at the last second I caught myself, snapping my pencil clean in two. This gathered some attention, but I gamely finished class with the bottom half and was out the door faster than any mortal feet could have carried me.

Needless to say, I was not at my best that day. My final class, Art, was the only class Sam and I shared without reinforcements. Mrs. Peters, a calm, earthy, leaves spectacles everywhere, sort of person had us working pottery with the wheel. I quite enjoyed this process. I could work the clay down and forget, for a time, the real world. I took my place at one of the pottery wheels and went to work. Some of the students, a combination of all four years, were on other projects. Some were creating clay creatures, so I wasn't in anyone's way. I let the wheel sooth my rattled psyche, but it couldn't last. I moved about, finishing my project, but wanting some more time. Mrs. Peters smiled indulgently and said I could stay a few minutes later if I wanted. I took another mound of clay and began again, but not two minutes in, a hand crushed down. Angrily, I looked up to see Sam.

"What did you do that for?"

"I wanted a turn. You're hogging the wheel."

I jumped up, covered in wet clay and water. "There was no need to ruin what I was working on! You could have just asked!"

"Oh, is that all? Fine, do you mind?" Students around us were beginning to look in our direction. Mrs. Peters was busy with the kiln and didn't immediately look our way.

"Well, now that you asked, yes I do."

"So why did I ask in the first place?"

Dimly, I was aware that the bell was ringing. Around us, our classmates took extra time to gather their stuff.

"You know what Samantha? If you would ask before taking or destroying something that is mine, this wouldn't be a problem."

"Marcus isn't yours, or did I need to ask your permission to snog him?"

"This isn't about Marcus! This is about you destroying my work and not trusting me to stay out of your private affairs!"

"Isn't it though? Admit it Scarlett, the real reason you've been avoiding me is because I got him first. And that just never happens. We're all so busy looking out for you, over compensating for your total inability to do anything."

I felt as though I had been slapped. Sam had never complained about my lack of abilities before. In fact, she often envied it.

"Better no powers than no control over them," I furiously shot back.

"I've had control over them when you needed it. And it's not just me. All three of us have to stick up for you, even dying Maya."

"Don't say that! She is not dying!"

"Open your eyes to reality, Scarlett. She won't make the transition and you'll never be anything but a half-breed, powerless bastard."

I gasped in anger. No one spoke to another hybrid like that.

"How dare you? Just because I don't know who my father is doesn't make me any different. And who's to say if we hybrids weren't sterile you wouldn't have a fatherless bastard of your own?"

Her eyes narrowed in anger, and her irises changed. Mrs. Peters had left, probably for reinforcements should our confrontation go sour. Sam turned to the work table and picked up the glazed bowl I had made for my mother. She cradled it lethally between her hands. When she spoke, her voice was low and dangerous.

"I could never expect you to understand. You have no powers, no inner demons to control. You don't have to work at being normal. I feel as if these three years were wasted." Her fangs were more pronounced, and her nails had grown. "In truth, you don't truly understand what it is to be helpless to your circumstances."

A cold tingle ran up my spine. I started to edge cautiously closer. "Sam, put the bowl down."

Those cat-like eyes met mine. "No. You need to be made to understand." And with furious force, she threw the bowl to the ground. I rushed forward, but I wasn't fast enough. This had been my masterpiece and she knew it!

"Damn it Sam! I try to understand. I never questioned your changes or treated you differently for them!" I was shaking in pain and fury as I helplessly tried to gather the shards of my work.

"You can never understand, Scarlett. That's the cold hard truth."

I rose with the pieces clutched in my apron. I was too angry to cry. I stood my ground despite her altered state. "I don't want you back in our room tonight. I don't want to see you until we load up on the bus for Wolfhaven tomorrow."

"Oh, is that right?" she smiled cruelly. "How are you going to stop me?"

There was a panic switch in every classroom in case a student should need immediate medical attention. Mrs. Peters was the only teacher who had actually shown her students where the button was. I turned from Sam and went to it. Flipping the outer casing open, I looked back at her with a taunt in my eyes.

"You were saying?" I asked coldly.

"You wouldn't dare!"

"We both know that if I push this button, it gains you a one way ticket to the Psych Ward. I can tell the responders I felt in danger."

"They wouldn't believe you," but there was a trace of fear in her voice.

"Oh really?" I pulled my sleeve back to expose three year old scars. "I never reported this, you know. I could have. Most other dorm mates do, but not me. If I see you again before six o'clock tomorrow morning, I will take it all back."

"It's not in you, Scarlett. You wouldn't want to hurt me."

"Why not? You've ripped my heart out and broken it into twenty pieces. Yes, I had no claim to Marcus, but you knew how I felt. You knew I would never intentionally interfere in your personal matters, but you nearly attacked me for being in the wrong place at the wrong time, and you destroyed my work! Tell me Samantha, when did you ever deserve my loyalty?"

She looked dangerously close to physical retaliation, but in an instant she calmed. "Fine, I'll just go get my stuff." She ground her heel down on a piece I missed.

"No," I said just as coldly, "I'll have it waiting for you. Go find someone more understanding than me to sleep with."

Her furious eyes met mine.

"I think that would be best," came Mrs. Peter's voice. "You might want to look into changing your dorm mates anyways." She was flanked by Miss Montgomery and Mr. Hansen.

"You two ladies might want to think about the wisdom of playing in tomorrow's game as well," said Miss Montgomery.

We both looked at her incredulously. For the first time all week, we agreed again. "What?" I asked.

"You're crazy!" exclaimed Sam.

Miss Montgomery shrugged. "Just a suggestion. Shouldn't you both be getting to practice anyway? If you can survive tonight, maybe you can survive tomorrow."

We mutely gathered our stuff and left under three watchful sets of eyes. We continued our stony silence all the way to the locker rooms. We had a light scrimmage to tune up, but for all the hostility Sam and I had, it was nothing to the squabble going on between Elizabeth and Isabelle, or, as we called them, Izzy and Lizzie. Rumor had it that when Lizzie found out Izzy had slept with her boyfriend, she had very nearly done the same with Izzy's at the dance. The reason no one had batted an eyelash at Sam and Marcus's confrontation was that every able body had been needed to keep these two apart. Lizzie and Izzy had grown up near each other, and became instant friends on their first day of kindergarten. They had weathered this sort of storm before, but it had always been a matter of first or second base, never before had it come to home runs. Coach Snow called practice after 45 minutes. She was screaming at Iz and Liz.

"Stop it! The both of you!! For goodness sake, we have a game tomorrow! As it stands, Katie will be starting. The both of you are benched. As for the rest of you, no one is to get tired or injured tomorrow. Save me the headache of these two playing together. Wharton, Bloom! Don't make me bench you too! Good night ladies," she said with resounding frustration. "Bus leaves at 6 sharp. If you're late, stay home. I am not waiting."

I walked off with Jess and Wendy.

"We all know she's lying through her teeth," Jess said good-naturedly. "She'd no more leave one of us than she would show her underwear in public."

"Ah, but remember how terrified we were our first year?" I asked.

"Were? What are you talking about? I'm still terrified," added Wendy, with a conspirator's smile.

"So," asked Jess conversationally, "What's up with you and Sam? Maya's not talking, and no one else is a credible source."

I grimaced. "Among other things, it turns out she kissed Marcus."

"No!" They both exclaimed.

"Not at the dance!" exclaimed Wendy. "He didn't let you out of his sight."

"I don't know when, and I would have let it go, but I only found out because I was eavesdropping on her and Doug. She caught me while I was out avoiding Marcus and Brandon."

"Was it intentional? The eavesdropping I mean," clarified Jess.

I shrugged. "I can't say I wasn't interested, but I hadn't gone out there looking for them. I've never wanted to be in the middle of Sam's affairs." I sighed heavily. "Besides, it isn't as if Marcus and I are actually or have ever dated. It's her business who she kisses, and if I hadn't been in the wrong place at the wrong time, it would have stayed that way."

"Scarlett, no one in the whole school goes near you when Marcus is around. And, besides this thing with Sam, I haven't heard of him leaving your side, so to speak." Jess was looking at me oddly.

"We all know he's taken," added Wendy. "Not that we blame you."

I shook my head, too embarrassed to continue. "How was the dance for the two of you?"

They both took the hint and left the controversial topic of Marcus to be.

When I went up to my room later that night, I fully expected to see Sam. I had forgotten my threat in lieu of three years worth of habit. A moment's surprise wore off and was replaced with relief. However, for all my anger, I was still dutiful. As I packed my uniform and gear, I packed Sam's as well. I packed it in one of her larger purses, as her gym bag was with her. Sam always made a point of packing protein bars. It was a game day ritual to eat one before every game. Sam always bought variety packs and had to weed out those with peanuts. When she ate peanuts, she had the habit of becoming red and splotchy with a horrid rash. Still doing what was right, I sectioned off two nut-less ones for her. After packing, I finished my homework and went to bed. I had a hard time falling asleep. Our conversation kept running through my head, and my beautiful pot! I was beginning to doze off when I suddenly flung myself from bed, ran to our closet, pulled out a nutty-chocolately breakfast bar and threw it in Sam's bag. Relieved, I promptly fell asleep.

I am sure I'm not the only one to make a rash decision and learn to regret it. Honestly, when I rolled out of bed Saturday morning, I had completely forgotten about my midnight impulse decision. I trudged down to the bus in my sweats. Wordlessly, I handed Sam's bag over. She was still wearing someone else's pjs. We loaded up and sat far apart. Wolfhaven was a nearly five hour drive, including our rest stop in Morton. As we rolled out, I fell back asleep. I slept through our first bus stop at a convenience store. When the bus lumbered on, I awoke in confusion. Shaking my head, I looked out the window for landmarks. The bus slowed for a stop light, and I swore I looked through a silver cloud just outside my window. The fragment seemed to move with us. Blearily, I rubbed my eyes and it was gone. It occurred to me that I might just be losing my mind.

We arrived at Wolfhaven just after eleven. As the bus rolled into their parking lot, Coach Snow stood to address us.

"Now, I'm aware that many of you are having issues. Let me remind you I do not care. Those issues remain on this bus or you do, it's your decision. Now, most of you know the drill, don't leave anyone behind." The bus had coasted to a stop. "Remember, no fighting, amongst yourselves or with them. We are here to win a soccer game."

I think I'll save a description of the first half. The entire game was a fiasco, but there were some mentionable low lights from halftime on.

We were down 1-0 when the ref blew the whistle for half. We jogged over to face Coach Snow's wrath.

"I've seen better play from junior varsity humans! Now, does anyone have any suggestions on how to improve—Samantha, what is wrong with your face?"

We all looked at Sam to see her covered in red patches. Her left eye was swelling shut. My stomach lurched to my feet. Now I remembered my petty moment. Even worse, I was trying to keep the horrified chuckle for escaping. Sam was absently rubbing an itch, but at Coach's question, she glared at me.

"There were peanuts in my protein bar. Somebody didn't pack the right ones and she knows it."

All those curious eyes turned to me, including Coach Snow's unfriendly ones. She looked about ready to kill me, but she forcefully shook herself from the impulse.

"Can you play?"

"Yes, I'm fine." She was obviously not fine, but Coach Snow took her at her word. After all, the alternative was still much worse.

"Good, I don't want to play Elizabeth or Isabelle unless I absolutely have to. Now, focus! I don't know how many times I have to tell you all that! Defense, shore up! Midfield, reinforce the defense. We will play defensively until we are able to do better. Now, go back in same as you started. Samantha, just let me know if you need to sit out."

Everything seemed to be going well after that. We quickly scored just three minutes into the second half, but that was the last good thing to happen that day. Katie, who had been starting right side defender, went down badly trying to get the ball from their star player. The werewolf scored as our whole team watched Katie writhing in agony. Tina and I carried her from the field. She was whimpering over the whole left leg. Immortals can regenerate, but it is harder when we're exhausted. With a look of disgusted resignation, Lizzie was sent in.

We were down again, but our team chemistry was horribly blighted. I cleared the ball up to Jess, but when she went to pass to Sam, Sam was too slow. On the next play, Sam just couldn't spot the ball. One eye was completely swollen shut. At the first available opportunity, Izzy was sent in. Unfortunately, Izzy's talent was not offense. Sarah ran up to switch with her, forgetting, for a moment, that the sheer proximity of now our right midfielder and right defender was currently lethal. The game was quickly spiraling out of control. Anytime Izzy or Lizzie had the ball, they were more concerned with hitting the other than in the game. I ran screaming over at them, pushing Izzy to the center of the field, where Lilly pulled her further. If only it could be that easy.

The werewolves were cunningly targeting our fracturing dynamics. Somehow they moved to the center, and were still targeting each other, leaving the sides unattended. Corey, Lilly, Tina, and I were nearly dead on our feet just trying to keep Wendy from being clobbered. I headed towards the dysfunctional pair, screaming at the top of my lungs in a brief respite with the ball with our offense. I got as far as "Pull it together!" before Izzy unleashed a kick that went right into my nose. Blood spurted out and the referee, conspicuously absent from our team's collapsing, had to call the play dead while I was substituted. Sam had to replace me, Emma was still battling chronic shin splints and Katie was still hobbling. So, one eyed Sam went in to defend the middle of the field. My nose bleed quickly stopped, but Coach Snow insisted I rehydrate before going back out. I took a swig from my bottle and Katie and I were ready to go back in. Unfortunately, in our absence, Wolfhaven had scored again. Twice. The score was now 4-1 and time was short. We ran in on our kick off, with Sam and Izzy coming out, but as I took my place, I felt a queer rolling in my stomach. Jess back passed to me and I swung the ball left to Brittany, but as the team started to move forward, I couldn't help the heaving. My breakfast came up. Gamely, I tried to continue on, but the pain of the gag reflexes was too much. I managed to slow one of their forwards, and I crossed it to Sarah, but then I leaned over and heaved again. Blessedly, the game ended soon after that, but I couldn't make it off the field. Even the werewolves were concerned. My team crowded around me, with Coach Snow coming to my side. She watched for a fraction of a second before barking:

"Bloom! What did you put in her water?"

Samantha, red and miserable came forward itching. I looked into her eyes and saw a flicker of guilt, but when she answered, it was with all her usual arrogance.

"Ipecac."

"What?!? You did what!?"

Sam twitched uncomfortably. "I didn't think she'd have it until after the game."

"And that makes it better? In all my years of coaching, I have never seen the sort of antics I saw here today. First Wharton gives Bloom an allergic reaction, then Chambers and Wood strike each other thirteen times in total, in which time they scored twice! And now this? Not only did you hurt each other, you broke Scarlett's nose and you destroyed our chances of winning. I have NEVER been more ashamed of a team than I am of you all right now. I want everyone on that bus in thirty minutes. Anyone not on it in that time will not only have to find a ride home, they will never be welcome on my team again."

Despite our nonchalance about being to the bus on time that morning, every single one of us was on that bus within twenty minutes. No one dared to talk on the very, very long ride home. Even the younger girls were subdued. Words simply could not describe just how far we had just fallen.

NINE

Coach Snow was so upset with us after our humiliating 4-1 loss to Wolfhaven, she cancelled Monday's practice. I heard it from Jess.

"She was shaking with anger when she saw me. 'Tell everyone there will be no practice today. I might do something rash and lose my job.' Those were her exact words."

I sighed. "I can't imagine what she would have said to me."

Jess patted my shoulder. "If I'd found out my best friend had made out with my boyfriend, I probably would have done the same. But no one could have known Lizzie and Izzy would go at it like that." She shook her head in bemusement. "You are feeling better aren't you?"

I smiled wryly. "Yeah, the ipecac only lasted for a little while. Sam was blotchy all night, though."

Jess snorted, and held her hand to her mouth to keep the laugh in. "Well, I bet we'll be going to two-a-days as soon as Coach can bear the sight of us."

"I'm sorry you and the rest of the team will have to suffer."

She shrugged prosaically. "It was just a matter of time before she insisted on two-a-days. Only one game left till winter sports, though, so we've only got three weeks left to endure. I'll be dreading March, though. She'll probably start us off with double practices."

"Her way of making sure the message sticks," I agreed.

"Well, good luck, Lettie. We were all happy to see you were alive this morning."

"Thanks, Jess, see you later." I made my way to Bloodology. There had been no smooth way to sort out our warring pairs. Sam and I couldn't sit together. Doug and Sam couldn't sit together. Sam and I had endured each other's company the previous week, keeping relative silence, but Friday night and Saturday had sealed our animosity. There was nothing like losing to make you want to be angry at someone else. I took Marcus's usual seat, and Doug accepted sitting beside me. Sam looked at us furiously before taking a seat in the very back. Marcus took this all in, but rather than avoid me entirely, he and Maya took the seat behind me. Miss Montgomery noticed the change, but didn't say anything. She knew what happened.

Everyone in the school knew. Izzy wasn't a blood sucker, so the horrid tension was absent from her and Lizzie to exacerbate an already uncomfortable class.

Tuesday's practice was just as miserable as could have been predicted. We started off with a half hour straight running laps. When those were finally over, Coach Snow had us split into pairs and play keep away for the next thirty minutes. This was exhausting, continual work. The boys were in the gym that evening. Coach Snow had been so furious, Coach Abrams had volunteered this aberration. After a scant water break, we split seven on seven full field with no goalies. We were all fit to be shot by the time Coach Snow finally called the game- I mean practice- over. We all collapsed where we were when the whistle finally blew.

"What are you all lazing about for? Two more laps before you're done!" A collective groan greeted her words. Sarah came over to help me up. Staggering, we all made the required laps. Finally free, we gathered our bags.

"Wharton, Bloom, Wood, Chambers! You're not done yet!"

The four of us froze. Reluctantly, I turned back to my furious coach.

"Sit!" she barked. We all dropped instantly. She looked around as though deciding which of us she wanted to lay into first. Lucky me.

"Scarlett, as a voted team captain, I expect you to lead by example. So, in that spirit, do you care to tell me just WHAT THE HELL YOU WERE THINKING?!?"

Fear forced me to speak. "I was angry. I knew Sam is allergic to peanuts so I swapped her breakfast bars. I am so sorry!" I was near tears in panic and guilt. "It was petty and ridiculously immature. I hurt the team and I promise to never, never do it again!"

Cold eyes watched me impassively. "What if I told you she had slept with your boyfriend?"

I met her eyes. "I would never try to hurt the team like that again. I wasn't thinking just how much it would affect everyone else. And it wasn't about the dance, not really."

She raised her eyebrows, but I refused to elaborate. The true reason I had snapped was known to Sam and Sam alone.

"Very well, the team has voted you captain, but that doesn't mean I can't kick you off this team. Consider yourself on probation. If you and Samantha can resolve your differences before our final game against Riverdale, you will play for me again in the spring." She turned her wrath on Sam. "As for you, I expect to hear nothing about your affairs again. Is that clear? Your personal life affects more people on this team than I ever could have imagined. If I could put you in a nunnery, I would." She sighed and regrouped. I watched in horrified fascination as her anger rose again. "As for the two of you," she pointed to Izzy and Lizzie. "I am tempted to cut you right here and now. If it hadn't been a game day, I couldn't have cared less what petty squabble the others were involved in. You two took the fight ONTO THE FIELD! I have NEVER been so ashamed. NEVER in my thirty-two years of coaching!" She turned away to regroup again. "I'm stuck in a bit of a quandary here. I want to win, but as it stands, I have only ten players. The four of you will show up here as soon as your class is out. I do not wish to punish your teammates. Wear your jerseys to class so I don't have to waste time waiting for you. You will run one lap for every minute I have to wait. All of you will be doing this until you can work together peacefully. Isabelle, Elizabeth, you are beyond probation. Consider yourselves the practice squad only. You'll have even further to go than Scarlett and Samantha. This is a team sport! Winning is about more than the moment. We have to win as a team, but we can lose as individuals. We have to become bigger than the moment!"

We were all listening in wretched silence. I dared to look up and saw the most spectacular sight. Two balls of light were streaking across the sky. They met above our heads. An eruption of noise momentarily deafened us. Coach Snow looked up. One ball of light had changed course and was now streaking towards us. She went pale and for an Immortal that's saying something. The second light, brighter, like white gold to the tarnished silver of the falling light, plummeted after the first and crashed into it before it could hit us. We were all too stupefied to move. What on Earth moved like that? We Immortals were used to more than humans, but we had never seen anything like this. The streaking lights plummeted into the ground at the end of the field. It sounded like an earthquake as dirt and turf sprayed everywhere.

"This is one of those moments you have to be bigger than!" screamed Coach Snow above the din and our ringing ears. "Run for the gym! GO!!!"

We sprang to life as these strange beings rose again. The darker light seemed obsessed with us. The brighter seemed to be trying to protect us. All five of us ran for our lives. The crater sized hole in the soccer field hinted at the possible destruction. Coach Snow outstripped us all, using her fully fledged inhuman speed to gather the onlookers inside. I was the only one who didn't possess this super speed, even if I was moving faster than I had ever known myself to do before. Even though it took some time to build up for Sam, she and everyone else had outstripped me. I stumbled on the lip of the field where it dipped down to the same level as the rest of the grounds. I crashed down the slope. My ankle throbbed where it had caught and twisted. Frantically, I looked up to see how close these creatures were and let out a scream of pure panic.

Ahead of me, Sam stopped. I could hear her calling out for me, but I couldn't move. My regeneration was slow because of the grueling practice. I was positive there was nothing left for me. The lights were moving too fast. Frozen in place, I raised my hands to offer some feeble protection, but as the seconds passed, nothing happened. I heard the deafening boom and felt burning particles on my skin but when I dared to open my eyes, a stranger was staring at me. She seemed to burn golden, from her wheaten hair to her peach skin.

"Go, child, get inside. You have a few moments until he will bounce back. You will be safe inside."

I opened my mouth silently. Finally, I managed: "What about you?"

She smiled kindly, but there was definite amusement in her eyes. "It is kind of you to ask, but this is my duty, now go." She was suddenly light again as she streaked upwards to meet the regrouping creature above her.

"Scarlett!" cried Sam, falling down beside me. "Are you okay? Come on, you've got to get up!" She stood and pulled me up beside her. I hobbled for several strides, hampering her progress, but I finally felt the warmth of the muscles healing in my leg, and put both feet down. We crashed through the gym doors and collapsed together. It was Douglas who had the doors open, and who now locked them, running a push broom through the handles as well as turning the key. Everyone was tense, and I heard frightened sobs. Confused, I sat up and saw Izzy and Lizzie huddling together, arms clasped around each other. Lizzie was crying into Izzy's shoulder. I looked around to meet Ben's gaze. He and Doug started for us when the intercom blared to life.

"All student report to your home rooms immediately. Use indoor walkways only. Teachers, this is a Code 23 emergency."

"All right everyone!" came Coach Abrams strong timbre. "Stay together and do not panic. To your home rooms!"

Sam and I supported each other, each of us still to rattled to do anything more than follow. Students were silent for the most part until we reached our designated room. Mr. Hansen was standing tensely braced at his desk, watching as we took our seats.

Lizzie and Izzy approached, still entwined like Siamese twins.

"Mr. Hansen?" quavered Lizzie.

"Yes, Elizabeth?"

"Can you call Miss Montgomery? Can I please stay here?" He looked between the two of them. Then his gaze switched to Sam and me. Everyone knew we all hadn't been speaking. This was turnabout.

"Of course, go ahead and sit down." He rose to use his phone. "Yes, Anne, Elizabeth Chambers is with me. Yes, you're welcome." He moved to the door and looked out. "Hurry up Shepherd!" Marcus trotted in, and he closed the door and locked it. "Seats please everyone." Those who weren't sitting did so. "Now, we are going to do a roll call, so if you'd all please be quiet, I will attempt to explain a Code 23." He gathered his clipboard. "Kelly Anderson?"

"Present." And on it went. I was the last called. Mr. Hansen put his board down and sighed.

"Since we're all here and accounted for," he trailed off, looking unnaturally exhausted. "A Code 23 is a Grade 1 lockdown. If there is deemed to be a threat from outside, all students must be accounted for, the grounds must be patrolled, and at least one additional hour is spent here until it is deemed safe to leave. After which, students are not allowed outside unless otherwise notified. You are to report directly to your bedrooms upon leaving here."

"What about dinner?" asked Douglas.

Mr. Hansen's lips twitched. "The school staff will bring you brown bags." There were several groans, including Doug's. "For the time being, try to amuse yourselves." He sat down to his desk and pulled out a manual."

"Mr. Hansen?" He looked up.

"Yes, Calli?"

"What just happened? All I heard was the thunder."

He looked at me and my teammates. "Ladies, would you care to tell us what was out there?"

"There were huge balls of light," said Izzy, quivering in her seat. "They tore up the soccer field."

"Every time they hit, it sounded like thunder," added Sam. "One of them took human form in front of Scarlett."

There were excited gasps all around and a deluge of questions. I ignored the questions and kept my eyes on Mr. Hansen.

He sighed heavily. "I don't want to unnecessarily frighten anyone. We all know there are things beyond our comprehension. Humans have not discovered us, it is only fair to assume we do not know everything that exists. The alternative does not bear mentioning." He looked intently at me. "All those who wish to call their parents, I will allow my office to be used for the remainder of our lockdown. Scarlett, you may go first." He rose and walked me to the door of his office. "Make sure she is all right first. I believe we may be facing a breach in her line of work."

I stopped at the door, worry began eating away at my insides. "Were those refractors?" I whispered.

He looked sadly sympathetic. "I was a student when the last was contained, but I know of no other creature who moves as lightness and darkness."

"But I didn't think they could direct their flight like that. My mom says they move more like clouds."

"They have been contained for over a century. Who knows what they are now capable of." He gently guided me in and shut the door. Feeling rather numb, I picked up the receiver and called.

"Hello?"

"Mom?"

"Scarlett! Is something wrong?" Her weary voice became panicked.

"Something happened at school today. I was wondering if everything was okay with you."

"With me? Darling, what happened?"

I briefly outlined my encounter, turning away from the avid faces of my classmates. Silence greeted my story.

"Oh my God. I can't believe it. Do your teachers know what they were? Has the RR been notified?" I referred to the Refractors Responders who were trained for what many viewed as an inevitability.

"I think some of the teachers suspect, but most are younger than the Control."

"Of course, I'm younger than the Control. Look, Lettie, if you have ever listened to me, listen now. Refractors are dangerous. Only full grown Immortals can handle them. If you leave the grounds, do so with protection."

"But what happened? No one has ever broken out, have they?"

"There was a horrible storm here two days ago. Lightening struck one of the generators and a tree went through the other. We thought we had two hours before the power was lost completely, but they must have been waiting. Four escaped before a response team was even on hand. I have no idea how many in total got loose. We're doing everything we can to control the situation, but they've grown strong. One stopped to talk to me. It seems they had an insurrection nearly twenty years ago and those who were for their exile were overthrown. Their powers fade in prolonged daylight, so what you saw was probably two fully charged refractors. The insurrectionists are being hunted by their own kind. It was our only option. We hoped they'd be back by now, but I fear the leak was more widespread than any of us imagined."

I was quiet for several moments. "Mom, are you going to be okay?"

"I'll be fine, Lettie. This is my job. I need you to promise to stay safe for me. I'm going to have to be working for as long as this takes. Until you hear otherwise, stay where you are safest."

"I promise. It's going to be okay, isn't it?"

"I hope so."

I looked back at the class. Other students would be wanting to talk to their families. "Mom, I've got to go."

"Of course. I love you, darling."

"I love you too."

Sam, Izzy, and Lizzie all took turns calling their parents. The rest of the students, though uneasy with the lockdown, didn't seem to know what to do. A few called, but most contented themselves with speculation. After that first onset of questions, I was left at peace. Marcus, Ben, and Doug all moved to surround me and Sam. Maya comforted the both of us, talking quite nonsense and stroking my hair until I at least began to relax. Listening to the rumors circling me, I realized that no one else in class had been raised on one of the Observation Posts. Some had heard natural rumors of shadow creatures, but I was the only one raised near where they lived. Suddenly, I sat bolt upright. What was it the vampire had said to me? The demons of hell had been loosed? Captain Mortensen had told me I didn't need to know what was in those woods. What if those Shadow creatures had not come from their realm but from Hybrid High's own grounds? The idea was terrifying, but who did I trust with the question?

Eventually, the intercom blared to life. "All students are to go directly to their rooms. All dorms will be in lockdown in thirty minutes. Dinner will be provided." The eerie static set us all on edge again.

"All right," called Mr. Hansen. "Off you go. Stay indoors!" Everyone began to file out, but I stayed in my seat. When the last student had left, Mr. Hansen looked at me. "Yes, Scarlett?"

"Those were refractors," I said without preamble.

He nodded sadly. "I suspected. I was a student when the Control came about. I'm sure I only saw a handful in my life. Is your mother all right?"

I nodded and rose to stand before him. "Mr. Hansen, what do you know of our forest? What happens beyond the student grounds?"

His face lost every ounce of color. "What do you know of that?"

"Nothing, really, but I have heard noises from there. What if what tried to attack me wasn't from the Other Realm, but from our own school?"

"Scarlett, whatever you do, don't share your suspicions with anyone. Most of the staff merely suspects, but the Board of Directors does not wish anyone to know. It is worth my job to even question. When you are free of this place, you can ask all you like, but do so with extreme caution. Extreme caution. Now, you'd best be getting to your room before they go into full lockdown. And, Scarlett, it would be best if you didn't mention your suspicions with anyone. Knowing what you saw were shadow creatures is not suspicion, and I suspect we will have an assembly tomorrow to discuss this. We cannot be the only who know. Now, if you'll excuse me, I'll need to see what I can do."

I was alone in the hallways and the eeriness of this made me pick up the pace. I jogged down the corridor and sprinted across the cafeteria. Taking the stairs two at a time, I skidded into my room.

"Scarlett!" Sam hugged me as I closed the door. "Where were you? We all got separated and I was worried."

I hugged her back. "I had to talk to Mr. Hansen. Sam, I know what those things were. They were refractors, shadow creatures."

Her eyes became as big as saucers. "Are you sure?"

"Positive. My mom says one of the generators went down a few days ago. No one knows how many got out."

"No wonder," said Sam, lost in thought. Suddenly, she grasped me. "It all makes sense! Those shadows were furious, at least one of them was. I could feel its anger. I'd be angry if I had been locked up for a hundred years."

"Do you know any stories from before the Control? I only know what my mom's told me."

Sam shook her head. "No, my parents are too young. All I know is that they are the most powerful of the Immortals. But hasn't Mr. Hansen mentioned them before in History? You take notes."

"All I know is that they were renowned for their thefts. I think the other Immortals have tried to erase them from our history. Even my mom's co-workers were reluctant to talk about what exactly it is that they guard and I worked there all summer. Mr. Hansen thinks we'll have an assembly about it tomorrow."

"I should think so! I mean, we could have died out there!" She had been up and pacing, but she turned to look directly at me and I saw pain flash across her features. "Lettie, I'm so sorry. For everything! For Marcus, for the dance, for the game. God! You nearly died and I never had the chance to tell you!" She started sobbing, and I had to go to her. We collapsed on her bed. I hugged her close, stroking her back.

"I'm sorry, too, Sam. I should have let you know I was there and I shouldn't have switched your breakfast bars. Are we good?"

She hiccupped with a smile. "Yes, we're good. You forgive me?"

"Of course I do." I patted her shoulder as she pulled away. "But if you ever put ipecac in my water again, I'll make a point of spewing the consequences on you."

She gave a watery laugh. "I don't deserve you, Lettie, I never did."

"Don't say that! If it weren't for you, I'd never have made it through our first year. If Aryn hadn't killed me, then Caroline Washburn would have. You and Maya are the best friends I ever had."

She hiccupped again. "We're the only friends you've ever had. Well, and the boys, I guess."

I glared at her in mock reproof. "The same goes for you, Samantha Bloom."

She glared back, but the animosity was gone and we both started laughing. "We're a sad bunch of misfits, aren't we?"

"Speak for yourself," I said blithely, flipping my pony tail. "I, for one, could fit in anywhere in any crowd."

She snorted. "Ah yes, and I rub shoulders with royalty."

"Had tea with the Queen lately?"

"No, but I did have lunch with the Prince."

It was wonderful to have the old Sam back. We joked around for some time, making up for the last few truly miserable weeks. Able, for the time being, to ignore the fright we had experienced that had brought us back together. About half an hour after I returned, there was a knock on our door. Cautiously, I went to open it.

"Who is it?"

"Room service," came the extremely caustic voice on the other side. I opened the door to see one of the lunch ladies. She looked ready to tear my head off, so I kept the door partially closed.

"Any blood cravers?" she asked.

I looked back at Sam. "Do you want regular or iron rich?"

"I'll take regular. I have my own booster packet and the blood cravers brown bag is basically what was left over from the cow."

"Two regulars, please," I said with forced cheerfulness. It didn't do any good. Two bags were shoved into my face.

"Enjoy." She hardly sounded like she meant it. I closed the door and brought the food over to Sam.

"You know hot dogs are basically what's left over," I told her.

"Hot dogs are at least processed. I brown bagged it once our 2nd year. I was sick for three days after."

"Was that what it was? I always wondered."

We dumped our meals on the bed. There were two bland looking turkey sandwiches, an apple, an orange, two types of chips, and two juice boxes.

"Do you ever feel like you've regressed to grade school when you get a lunch like this?" I asked.

Sam took the apple, and looking at me questioningly, took the BBQ chips. I reached out and took the Salt and Vinegar. It took her a moment longer to decide on the flavor of juice. I took the Berry Blast and saved her the decision.

"I often feel like we've regressed, and it has nothing to do with the lunch menu. I mean, honestly, we're stuck in our rooms every single night. We're only allowed off the grounds with permission and we're fed food a dog wouldn't touch."

"I don't know about you, but I'm okay with staying on school grounds for awhile. Though, as of today, even that's not safe."

Sam paused mid chew. "Wonder how long it'll take them to fix the field."

"Well, better hope it's sooner rather than later. The boys have a home game this weekend."

We ate in silence for several minutes. For flavor, I stuffed my chips in my sandwich. It also added a pleasant crunch. A knock sounded at the door. I paused from chewing and cocked my head. The knock repeated. Sam slid gracefully from the bed and swept up to the door with nary a sound.

"Who is it?"

"It's me," called Maya. "Can I come in?"

Sam opened the door and Maya slipped through. She was dressed in her PJs and she had a pillow under one arm and her stuffed pony under the other.

"Do you mind?" she asked.

"Of course not darling!" Sam guided her to the bed. " You're all alone in your room." We settled ourselves. Sam finished her food off quickly and got back up. "Come on, you two." She moved over to my bed and kicked her path clear. Setting her stance, she pushed the bed of the wall and towards the center of the room. Maya and I belatedly moved to help her. When she had positioned it where she wanted it, she moved to her own. The beds were iron frames, but with three morphing Immortals moving them, it wasn't any harder than moving the mattress frame. I was happy to realize I was gaining strength. I had had flashes before this, but to be able to have it when I needed it was a nice feeling. I still wasn't fast, I didn't crave blood, and I couldn't spring from one end of the room to another in a single bound, but we're talking baby steps.

While Sam and Maya made the new double bed comfortable, I took myself off to the showers. I went down to the far end of the hallway and looked out the window. The giant mound of destruction on the soccer field was foreboding. I shook my feelings of fright and headed in to wash the dirt and grime of the evening from my body. The warm water soothed my frazzled psyche, but even then I wasn't up for a full drying of my hair. I wanted my room, my bed, my friends, and Nibbles. I towel dried it as best as I could and gave it a few minutes with the blow dryer. Wendy and Tina came in and pulled out their own dryers to help. It was a sort of ritual amongst my teammates. Jess had once joked that it was my hair that made me captain. She often helped me in our four years together and she always referred to this as a team building exercise. When it was nearly dry, I thanked them and headed back to my room. It was nice of them not to ask what had happened. I think they realized that I was trying to forget.

Sam and Maya had our history homework scattered over the bed. I dropped my used soccer stuff and toiletries on my desk chair and grabbed my own books to join them. It took me a moment to realize they weren't actually doing the assigned questions. In fact, Sam was the most engrossed I had ever seen her with a textbook. I sat back baffled.

"What's going on?"

Maya raised her large hazel eyes to mine. "We're looking for information on shadow creatures."

Sam threw her book aside in disgust. "There's nothing worthwhile in there. All that book talks about is their ability to steal and their unwillingness to join the Board of Immortals. There is a single paragraph on the Control. One! How does a book cover over 2000 years of history and barely mention an entire race of immortals?"

Maya had flipped to the front of the book. "This was first published in 1876, but it was revised in 1909."

"So?" asked Sam.

"They must have revised the entire book after the Control."

I flipped to the same page. "And again after each World War. Nothing really happened in the humans' world in 1909 but all these other dates mark something considerable in the world."

"They erased history?" asked Sam incredulously.

"Edited is more like it," replied Maya.

"A total re-write. To the victors go the spoils." We sat in contemplative silence. "So, are we actually going to do our homework?" I asked.

"I don't see why," said Sam. "It isn't like the teachers will be able to focus any better than we are."

"I actually have to agree with Sam on this one," added Maya. "No one could focus after a lockdown." She shuddered. "And if anyone else has figured out what those were, we aren't the only ones up. I only hope the RR can contain them quickly. When I told my mom, she was panicked. Apparently, not everyone was for the Control. My mom says some of the elders fear they could be evolving in captivity."

"That's what Mr. Hansen was afraid of. And my mom's afraid there is an insurrection going on within their Realm."

"But that's what the Refractor Responders are for, isn't it?" asked Sam. "To find them and return them?'

"Yeah, let's just hope they can," I said.

Sam went off for her shower shortly after. When she came back, we all sandwiched together on our bed. I had Nibbles clutched closely.

"Maybe, if we're really lucky, this will all be over in the morning," I said hopefully.

"If we were really lucky," replied Sam, "we'd wake up and none of this would have happened.

TEN

I was the first one ready the next morning. Maya had to go back to her room for clothes and Sam was sleeping in. I trotted down the stairs to come face to face with a plexi glass wall separating me from the cafeteria. Several other girls were stuck in the same quandary.

"What is it?" I asked to no one in particular.

Emma Buckley, my teammate, looked back at me. "I think it's part of the lockdown. This looks to be unbreakable."

"Wow, when they said be in your rooms in half an hour, they weren't kidding."

Emma shook her head. "The only problem is how do we get it open?"

One of Emma's fellow first years came up to us. "I can't find an intercom or a panic switch. They'll have to know something's wrong by the time class starts."

By now there were about a dozen of us milling around the hallway. "What happens if we set of a panic switch in one of the rooms?" I asked.

"I don't know," said Jess as she joined us. "They don't take too well to false alarms, even if it is an accident." She reached the wall and extended her Immortal claws. She forced them down and all of us covered our ears in pain. Above and around us doors opened to see what the horrid noise was.

"Well," I said, trying to shake the pain away, "if that doesn't alert someone, nothing will."

It was another five minutes before the door retracted. On the other side was Miss Montgomery and Mrs. Peters.

"Our apologies, girls. There have been some glitches in the system," explained Miss Montgomery. We all began to file out. I said farewells to my teammates and went to sit down. I had just set my tray down when I was grabbed from behind.

"Oof! Good morning to you too Doug." I was passed to Ben without my feet touching the ground. I couldn't breathe by the time Ben was done. Gasping for air, I felt Marcus put an arm around me. He at least didn't try to squeeze the air from my lungs. "Hi to you too," I said weakly to the others.

"Lettie, we didn't see you in the hustle and when we tried to find you the entire boys' dormitory shut down." Ben was still looking a bit frantic, which was a surprise in itself. He was, after all, half stoic elf.

"Nothing happened," I assured them all. Making sure to reinforce my assurances with contact. "I just had to ask Mr. Hansen about what it was that attacked us last night."

"You," corrected Ben, "it tried to attack you."

I laughed at his over protectiveness and to cover my own fears on that matter. I would be having nightmares for some time to come. "It wasn't singling me out for any other reason than I was the slowest."

All three boys were still looking darkly at me.

"You aren't hurt in any way, are you?" asked Douglas.

"I'm fine," I stressed each word. Marcus took both of my hands in his. Gently, he pushed up the sleeves on both arms, inspecting for injuries. When my hands were given a clean bill of health, he touched my face, turning it each way. Finally, he let go.

"She looks fine," he said, leaning in front of me to address the two on my other side.

"I'm so happy you can listen to me," I groused, finally taking my spot and trying to eat my breakfast.

"So," said Ben sometime later, after all they were bound to be hungry too. "Do you know what they were?" I could hear the edge of smugness in his voice and knew that he knew.

"Sorry to burst your bubble, Ben, but my mother works on one of the Observation Posts. I may never have actually seen a refractor, but it doesn't mean I can't figure it out."

Ben did look deflated and I hear Marcus's deep chuckle. "I did warn you," he told his depressed dorm mate.

Ben just harrumphed. "Bet you Sam would have been surprised if she didn't live with Scarlett."

"Hey, now, that's not fair," interjected Doug. "To bring Sam in like that, everyone knows she and I don't pay attention to footnotes in history."

"Besides," said Marcus consolingly, "I had no idea, so that has to count for something, right?"

I snorted rudely. "Marcus, you were raised entirely amongst humans. It would have been a miracle if you knew what a refractor was. Ben, stop sulking, it's not flattering."

Maya came down then and saved us all. She took in my protective guard. Gracefully, she slid in across from me.

"I told them you would be fine," she said in a conspiratorial tone, "but would they listen to me? Of course not, but I had to ask myself if they listen to anyone."

"Other than themselves?"

"Exactly!" She bent down to her meal with a wink.

The three of them acted unduly offended. When the five minute bell rang, they rose as one.

"Well, since you have no need for us, we'll just see ourselves to class." Ben spoke with obscene dignity before leading the group away.

"What did I miss?" asked Sam, standing behind Maya absently chewing on one of her breakfast bars.

"The boys were being a bit overprotective of one of their own," replied Maya, effortlessly rising with tray in hand. "I told you all not to panic."

Sam chewed in silence, staring after the boys. I was scrabbling all my stuff together. Most of my dishes had wandered off my plate. Mysterious indeed, when surrounded by three teenage boys. The three of us made to go to history before Sam spoke again.

"What's it like to be so protected?" she asked.

"Annoying," I replied. "Especially by three overconfident, overbearing boys."

"She loves every minute of it," said Maya airily.

"I do not!"

Sam frowned. "I think I got the short end of the stick."

Maya patted her hand. "Sometimes, Sam, I envy you. You don't need protection. Scarlett and I may feel we don't, but the sad truth of the matter is that there are things in our world we need protection from."

Sam wrapped an arm around Maya's frail shoulders. "I'll always protect you Maya, even from those boys."

"What about me?" I asked, affronted.

"You're on your own, Lettie, unless you need protection from them, they are more than enough for you."

"Oh, thank you," I said sarcastically.

Sam and Maya flashed grins at me. "You're welcome," said Sam.

We all took our seats for History, but Mr. Hansen wasn't at desk. Someone I had never seen before sat on the edge, idly swinging one leg. I caught a glimpse of fangs, but her pant suit offset usual femininity of werecats and vampires. I scrunched my brown and picked up on a flaring nose: werewolf. She was well over six feet, with frizzy brown hair pulled into a tight bun. Her eyes were golden, more yellow than Sam's, and they followed us with a hunter's edge. When we were all ready, she raised a hand to gather our attention.

"Good morning, students. My name is Nichole Mason and I am here as one of Hybrid High's Board members, to talk to you about the troubling events that happened to you all yesterday." Her nostrils flared and her gaze shifted to me. "Are you the one who saw this being?"

"Yes," I replied, unreasonable anger stirring within me, "one of the refractors took form in front of me."

A faint lip curl greeted my words as did my classmates excited babble.

"I suppose many of you were able to decipher that those beings were refractors, otherwise known as shadow creatures. I am here to tell you this is nothing to be worried about." I bristled even more at this ridiculous statement. "The proper authorities were notified and the offending creatures of your unfortunate attack have been caught and dealt with. In a few hours time, your soccer field will be as it was and you all can count on going back to your day to day activities."

"But what are refractors?" asked Izzy.

Those cold hunter eyes turned to her. "A shadow creature is an Immortal who shifts into a being of light and darkness rather, than say a wolf or a cat. They were deemed a threat to not only the Immortal community but also to humans. One hundred years ago they were contained in the mountains. The term Control is often used to describe this time."

"But how did they get out?" asked Joshua, Doug and Ben's teammate.

"There was a mishap on the vampire's watch. Like I told you before, there is nothing to fear. They have been dealt with. It would be best if you all just put this behind you."

"Did they catch all of them?" I asked, the bile of indignation filling my mouth.

"I already answered that," she replied coldly.

"No, you said the offending creatures were captured, but there must have been more."

"What on Earth makes you think that?"

I thought a second longer to phrase this right. I didn't need Maya's hand on my sleeve or

Marcus's tensing in front of me to know I was in dangerous waters. "It seems logical," I began slowly, "for more than two to escape. If you left a door open, how many students would go outside?"

"None of you need to worry. The situation has been handled. It would be too terrible to imagine what might become of you if I were lying."

Every werewolf cross was on high alert. The full blood at the head of the class realized this and smiled with as much warmth as she seemed capable.

"It is my responsibility to guarantee the safety of you students. You all can recognize that as the truth. Trust that those who have your well being at heart are taking care of things beyond you. Now, since you have all been informed of the resolution to this crisis, I'll turn your class back over to your capable teacher. Remember you are all safe so long as the system remains intact. Have a good day." She stood and moved with powerful strides to the door. Opening it, I glimpsed Mr. Hansen on the other side. "They're all yours, Lee."

We were all silent until Mr. Hansen had settled himself. As one, we burst with questions. Wearily, and looking as though he hadn't slept at all, he raised his hand for silence.

"Miss Mason has done all of the explaining you will need."

"But she hardly answered any questions!" complained Calli, our spokesperson.

"She answered what will be answered. No!" He waved off a new flood of questions. "I cannot add anything. All I can do is stress that you all follow what has been told to you." He looked directly at me. "No matter what you suspect, it is no longer safe to voice any suspicions. I can hope it will be safe again soon, but let me add what I can.

"I was fourteen at the time of the Control. What your books still mention was nothing compared to what the times truly were. Yes, refractors were amazing thieves, but they are also extremely powerful. Their very nature made them objects of suspicion. One of their lesser known abilities is the ability to balance a hybrid's blood. You may not be aware that a fully balanced hybrid is more lethal than an ordinary Immortal. In fact a fully balanced hybrid is the only match for a Shadow creature."

"How does a refractor balance our blood?" I asked.

"By willing their own blood. Not all shadow creatures can make the transformation to their namesake. Only those who learn total control. Now, my time is running short before we get more company. I have to make you all understand. My first year as a student, at the predecessor to this place, was the year of the Control. The thought of an army of shadow creatures and hybrids was too terrifying for the other Immortals. Families turned against each other. The fear of something greater than us can be the most powerful weapon of all. I don't believe this is over, but please, for all our sakes, be quiet and be careful! I could lose my job for telling you what I just did."

The door opened and a new full blood entered. A pale, ethereal elf walked up to Mr. Hansen.

"Hello, DeWinter, I hear you are to be my assistant."

The elf looked disdainfully at our teacher. "I am here to assure these students there is no problem. I will simply sit in on your classes until the panic subsides."

"If the purpose is to assure us all is normal, doesn't your purpose negate that?" I asked coldly.

Fathomless eyes turned in my direction. "It is natural to fear what you don't understand, child. The Board has simply decided our teachers need our support."

I made to rise, but both Sam and Maya yanked me down.

"Scarlett, don't!" hissed Sam.

"I want proof," I shot off, ignoring my friends, my teacher, and all common sense. "I want proof I am as safe as you claim. In case you weren't aware, I was the one nearly destroyed by that refractor. If the other hadn't saved me, I would be another crater in our soccer field. How is your presence going to reassure me?"

Mr. Hansen was gesturing frantically and Sam was drawing blood. They didn't understand! I could have died and to hear these officious bureaucrats speak as though it was nothing was worse than Jess's nails on the plexi glass.

"Can you not respect the words of you elders and superiors child?" asked the elf with disdain dripping from his words.

I opened my mouth to say that he at least was not my superior when Marcus swung around and slapped a hand across my mouth. His blue eyes were blazing, but I saw fear in them as well. "Shut up, Scarlett," he growled low. "We can't protect you right now." Ben and Doug were looking at me with similar expressions. I shook myself free from his grasp and glared at them all before turning back to the elf.

"Of course my mother treated me to respect those worthy of it. And I suppose if you say we are safe, I should have no reason to doubt it unless I had proof. My apologies."

Elves are not stupid creatures. He watched the whole thing unfold, but he couldn't continue to berate me without a full scale insurrection on his hands. My friends were on edge, but the whole class was wanting an uprising. I would have made a nice martyr, right? His eyebrows fluttered up and then down again as he took in all of these factors. "Very well," he said with extreme dignity. "Like I said, I am here to reassure you, not to frighten you further. Let me reiterate what my colleague has already told you. You are all safe now." He looked back at Mr. Hansen before those chilling eyes came back to me. For all his impassiveness and all of my righteous indignation, I knew without words that I would be watched, and watched carefully. The elf drifted gracefully to the back of the classroom and sat down.

Mr. Hansen was still staring at me in horror. He finally shook himself back to the present. "I am sure none of you did your homework last night, so, let's review where we were. I'll expect your assignments tomorrow." He began talking about the War of 1812. Maya and Ben, for once, were not taking notes. Every student in class was torn between watching Mr. Hansen and watching the elf. The bell finally, blessedly, rang and we were left with more homework. I was on my way to Biology II when powerful hands grabbed me and spun me around. My back was pressed painfully into the staircase railing and I couldn't stop the cry of pain.

"What were you thinking?" asked Marcus furiously. "Couldn't you feel the threat they posed?"

I tried to free myself, but he was just too strong. His were traits must be surfacing for my fledging abilities were no match. "Let me go, Marcus." That didn't work either. I stopped struggling and looked back at him with equal fury. "I wanted answers, okay? I came within inches of becoming a crater on the field. My mother is panicking, and my mother never panics. I don't want someone telling me everything is all right when it isn't! It is far from all right!"

His grip loosened marginally. Between my friends, it was a wonder my upper arms weren't broken. "Lettie," he whispered, leaning his forehead against mine, "these people are more powerful than you or me. I cannot protect you if you cross them. None of us can."

"I want answers, Marcus."

He leaned back. "Answers can wait. Right now, those Board members are acting like caged animals. They might overreact if you push them right now. Please, Lettie, do it for me, and for Sam, Ben, Maya, and Doug. When this all settles, I'll help you find your answers, but I just can't right now."

The bell rang and we were alone in the entry hall. I sighed and collapsed against his chest. "I nearly died," I cried. "I knew there was nothing I could do, but then it all stopped. That darker creature, it wanted to kill me, me! Not Sam or Izzy or Lizzie. I may have been the slowest, but the others were still too far away from the building to be safe. Why? What did I do to it?" I burst into tears, feeling so totally hopeless. I couldn't find the answers because I couldn't even ask the questions. Marcus brought me closer, rubbing me gently.

"Don't cry, Lettie, please don't cry." His voice was cracking and I could feel his vulnerability. I snuggled closer, feeling this overwhelming need to comfort and be comforted. As my tears dried, I became aware of his steady heartbeat and it wasn't because my ear was pressed to his chest. His blood was calling to me. It was a haunting, alluring sound and I wanted to follow it so badly it hurt. My teeth ached to sink into his skin. Slowly, I pulled back, forgetting for a moment, where we were. All that mattered was the two of us.

"Miss Wharton, Mr. Shepherd, you're late for class."

Painfully, I turned away from Marcus to see Principal Daniels looking at us. He noticed my tears and Marcus's damp sweater. "Mr. Shepherd, Mrs. Usher is unlikely to notice your late arrival. Off you go."

Marcus looked questioningly at me. I nodded at him, telling him it was okay for him to leave. I numbly walked to the foot of the stairs.

"Miss Wharton." I turned back to Principal Daniels.

"Yes?"

"I understand that last night was difficult for you, but let me reiterate what I'm sure everyone has been telling you: be careful what you say. What happened to you was horrible, but sometimes the most dangerous people are those who do not own up to their own mistakes. If Mr. Dawson asks, tell him I stopped you. If he doubts you, I will vouch, now go."

I have to confess to some surprise when soccer practice was still held outdoors. Even Coach Abrams kept his boys inside, but not Coach Snow. There were six guards visible on the grounds, and several of the staff members were out as well. Miss

Mason hadn't been lying when she said the field would be repaired. It looked just as it had before the clash of the titans.

"I know you're all a little frazzled. It's understandable, but I trust we are all able to move forward. Offense, full team out against full defense, half field. Scarlett, Lilly, Katie with the offense. Izzy, Sarah, Emma, with the defense. Let's see if we can work together now!"

We put in one of our best practices. Coach Snow was so surprised, she called it over early.

"Well," she began, a little shocked, "I'm happy to see you were all able to put your differences aside. Remember, in two weeks we play our last game of the season. I shouldn't have to remind you how much this means. Anything would be better than Saturday's debacle. Keep up your level of play and I won't give you two-a-days. However, I still expect to see Wharton, Chambers, Bloom, and Wood early. I'll let today slide, but the four of you are still on probation."

Trust Olivia Snow to be the first to jump back to normal. Nothing could stop her in her pursuit of winning.

Considering everything that had happened lately, the next few weeks were a severe let down. At some time or another, every class was monitored by Board members. We were all secretly derogatory about their purpose. We were assured every day that all was safe, that everything was back to normal. I felt they were lying through their teeth, but I had been warned off enough to keep my mouth shut. I wanted to demand answers, but the fact that Maya and Marcus were always on alert always kept me in check. They were worried and where I could write Marcus off as being overbearing, Maya had never been worried without just cause.

Our final game fell on an uncharacteristic Friday. Coach Snow had asked Valley High for some more time, originally because of our disintegration as a team, but cleverly, she had forgotten to mention that our field had been repaired in a few scant days. Through her subterfuge, we had been given two weeks to get our acts together. However, our boys had the second best record amongst the Immortals, and they were set to play in the title game on the same day we were set to play. We had our game pushed forward to Friday so we could all travel to Mountain Line on Saturday. I'll summarize our game: We were a well trained machine, with all positions playing in sync, the elves didn't stand a chance. They were demolished by our angry and out to prove front line, and they couldn't break our determined defense. The final score was 4-0. Our record for the season was 4-1. If we had been playing a full season, we, too, would have been in the coveted title game.

When the freshness of victory wore off, and our plans for travel were solidified, I went off to find the only member of our band of misfits yet to be included. It was surprising difficult, for Marcus was in the library of all places. I took a seat at his table.

"The library?" I asked.

He looked up at me. "There wasn't much else for me to do."

My brow knit in confusion. "You could have stuck around with Ben and Doug."

Sighing, he put his book down. "Sometimes I cannot control my were-traits. I feel this overwhelming need to act out with animal force. Do you have any idea what that's like?"

"Yes," I replied slowly. "Sometimes, around certain people, I have the desire to bite." I stared at my hands rather than let him see the truth on my face. "But it isn't the blood I crave. I still can't stand the taste of the stuff."

He leaned back until two of the chair's feet we no longer touching the ground. "Do you think we mature beyond it?"

I looked up then. The extra distance was good for me. "I think we learn to control it. It is my nature to bite, yours to shift." I looked at his book, a manual on transformations. Gently, I removed it from his reach. "You don't need to dwell on it, Marc. No matter what we read, it won't help us transform. We might as well own up to the fact that we will have to face our changes when they come and enjoy ourselves until then."

He sat the chair back down on all four feet and grasped the book, but did not take it from me. "Is that what you're here for, Scarlett? To help me enjoy myself?" His words held a velvet promise that I tried to ignore.

"As a matter of fact, that's exactly what I'm here for. Sam, Maya, and I are going up to Mountain Line tomorrow and I came to invite you."

A flicker of his old self flashed in a roguish grin. "Are you sure you want to invite me along? Surely you would all enjoy yourself more if you didn't include a boy. After all, what are you going to talk about with me there?"

I frowned and smacked his hands with the book. "Believe it or not, we are capable of discussing more than just boys. But now that you mention it, I was planning on doing some Christmas shopping. A boy certainly wouldn't be interested in that, even if the shops are in a werecat town. I mean, you're sure to have seen everything worth seeing."

He grinned wolfishly and snatched the book from me. "I didn't realize you wanted my company so badly. Since you insist, I'll go." He frowned in thought. "Just when are you expecting to have free time?"

It was my turn to smile. "Well, since you asked. We might just have bribed the coordinating staff to let us leave a bit early, but I would hate to divulge all of our secrets."

Marcus looked wary. "What's a bit early?"

"Only half an hour, but if the girls play their cards right, we'll go straight through our rest stop and have roughly one hour in Mountain Line before our boys arrive."

"Do I want to know who arranged this?"

"For the most part, Sam and Brittany, but Maya added a more concrete battle plan." He looked to be second guessing his wisdom, so it was time for my final card. "You won't be the only boy, Marcus. Basically the entire lacrosse team is going too. It's called team spirit."

He curled his lip in a slight snarl. "Bah, but I'll still go on one condition."

It was my turn to look wary. "I didn't come here to make you go, Marcus." He smiled slowly, and as the smile grew I felt nails being pounded into my coffin. When Marcus smiled like that, it was dangerous for me.

"All I ask is that it be you, not Sam or Maya or anyone else on that bus, who is my tour guide. The broadening of my education lies solely in your hands."

I read once that snakes can hypnotize their prey. Well, at that moment, I felt like a mouse being charmed by the deadly snake. The worst part was knowing and being able to do nothing other than seal my fate.

"Fine," I said with an airiness I didn't feel. "If I knew you were that easy-" I trailed off, suddenly aware of how close he was and just what a bad choice of words I had used. Look left, little mousy, now right. I don't know how he closed the space between us, I mean, there was a table, but he was whisper close to me.

"You have no idea just how easy I can be, Scarlett." For one wild moment I thought he was going to kiss me, but in a flash it was gone and he was on his feet. Casually, he started to take his leave, but he turned a few steps from the door. "What time do we leave?"

I was still in a state of paralyzed shock. All my senses were in overdrive and it took me a delayed moment to realize he was speaking to me. I turned in my seat to look at him. "What?" I asked weakly.

The small, still functioning part of my brain was furious with his look of smugness. "What time do we leave?"

"Oh. 9:30."

He smiled crookedly. "See you then."

ELEVEN

At exactly 9:30 the next morning, I stood with Maya and Sam in line to get on the bus. I was talking in that airy way that screams I'm aware someone is watching but I refuse to give in. With an air of nonchalance, I climbed on the bus, but Sam and Maya, conspiratorial traitors, took a seat together. I glared at them, but they weren't looking at me. I knew he was standing behind me.

"You bribed them, didn't you?" I ground out, taking my seat and making room.

"Maybe," he replied, taking the seat next to me with a most annoyingly satisfied air. "But I don't think you really want to know."

I folded my arms across my chest and stared out the window as the bus departed. "Is this to assure I don't talk about you the whole way?"

"Oh, it's a bit bigger than that." He settled himself back in his seat. "I figured you could tell me about where we're going before we get there."

I sighed and turned away from the window. "What do you want to know?"

"Everything."

I shrugged. "I don't know that much. Mountain Line is a werecat community built off of a mining town in the Cascades. All of the schools we play are based in the woods. That way we're harder to find by humans. Wolfhaven and Brimstone are considered offshoots of the Observation Posts. It's considered normal to raise a family several hours from the Other Realm. My mom was one of the few who lived on post to keep her kid with her. Mountain Line, Riverdale, and Valley High are based in areas where human economy exists. They were here before the Control."

"Why did you grow up on post?"

"I think it's because my mom was a single parent. Even using her speed on foot, it's still over two hours to the closest houses in Brimstone. Most of the vampires go on foot in the summer but use cars in the colder months. Some also work one full week on, one full week off. My mom kept me within 20-30 minutes travel. It simplified one thing for her."

"You don't visit on weekends." It was a statement not a question, and I felt a familiar sense of guilt.

"I did my first year, but it's at least a two hour drive to my house and I can't super speed. We were always on a budget, so the miles really added up." I was still a bit on edge with my mom. I called her every Sunday, but I hadn't shared my fledging abilities because I didn't want to get her hopes up. Lately, she was incredibly tense. It seemed by all appearances that the shadow creatures had been returned, but my mom had her doubts. She was working overtime with a few of her closest colleagues trying to pin down their suspicions. So far, she was still planning on going to Romania for Christmas, which meant I was staying at school. Marcus wisely picked up on all of my unspoken unease and changed the topic.

Samantha was the field marshal for us and half an hour out from our usual stop, she moved to the front of the bus. She didn't stay long, but when she returned to her seat, Brittany went up. After Brittany went up, one of the Lacrosse players went. Success was measured by the fleeting glimpse of a gas station. The sweet smell of victory greeted our noses as we unloaded in Mountain Line.

The shop fronts looked like something from an old western. Flat fronts with rickety porches lined the main street. On one side there was a grocery, general store, beauty salon, nail salon (werecats were very into grooming), post office, and book store. On the side we unloaded was their main restaurant, a video store, a knick knack shop, a grooming parlor (again, for the inhabitants not pets), and at the end was the bar. Off on side streets were clothing, coffee, ice cream, and some shops that were disturbing to even step foot in.

The one thing that every werecat community had was a hunting range, and I don't mean like shooting at cutouts. They brought in prey and loosed it, allowing the transformed werecat to go chase it down. The werecat exclusive shops usually catered to this disturbing hobby. My mother had never mentioned them to me, and when I had found out about them my first year, she had politely curled her lip and said that I should be lucky I had none of the unrestrained animal in me.

I pointed this all out to Marcus as we got our bearings in the biting cold. He was turning around, nostrils flaring, taking it all in. Locals looked at us all in mild surprise. A few walked by muttering, others started talking about Mountain Lines chances in the game. For the most part, shop keepers were happy to see us. We were an expected source of income.

"Do you see anything that interests you?" I asked Marcus.

"It's all interesting. Do you have a favorite?"

"Come on, we'll eat lunch first. They have a great diner. It specializes in raw meat and pizza." I took his arm and led him across the street. The sign out front read Murphy's Diner with a picture of a cat sitting in front of a steak, fork and knife raised. Sam and Maya had already come over and were seated with Jess and the rest of the soccer team. Most of the lacrosse players were seated near the buffet. A few of the volleyball girls had come, but they were nowhere to be seen. I frowned at my surroundings. There was no way Marcus was going to be comfortable at a table full of girls, and I refused to sit at a table full of boys. Bravely, I led him to the bar seats.

"Just how much did you pay them?" I asked as I perused a menu.

"Do you really want to know how much you're worth?"

"Or how cheaply my friends can be bought?" He just smiled sympathetically. "I suppose it wouldn't be flattering either way. How long did you buy me for?"

"Oh, I paid for the whole day."

I groaned and raised my menu so I didn't have to look at him. A waitress came to take our order. I opened my mouth to order, but I was a second too late. He quickly ticked off our choices of salad dressing before continuing, and wasn't it just like him to know what I put on my salad every day.

"One medium pizza, Hawaiian on one side, meat lovers on the other."

The waitress sized him up and smiled. "Do you want your meat cooked?"

He leaned in conspiratorially. "Cooked, my friend doesn't have our affinity for raw."

I was speechless. When she left, I worked up my tirade only to be derailed right out of the gate.

"Your favorite is Hawaiian isn't it?"

"Yes, but-"

"And when you said they served great pizza, you meant you'd had it before and were insinuating you were going to eat it again."

"Well, yes, but-"

"So what's the problem? I simply took care of the hassle of ordering."

"Marcus," I said with frazzled patience, "I was perfectly capable of ordering for myself."

He raised his dark eyebrows. "Do you want to change your order? I'll call the waitress back over." He began to raise his hand, and I wrenched it back down.

"Let's cover some ground rules. Number One: I can make up my own mind and express it. Number Two: You are to respect rule Number One."

He looked expectant. When I didn't continue, he asked: "What's Number Three?"

"I can't think of one, but if I do, I'll let you know."

He smiled and took my hand off his wrist. With causal ease, he brought it to his lips and kissed the back. "I have no doubts you'll keep me in line." His lips whispered across my skin, sending ripples through me. He released my hand and the devilish twinkle in his eyes didn't bode well for me. "You know, if I pay for this, I think it gets to count as a date."

I sat bolt upright, eyes flashing. "Dates are usually mutually consenting. You bought me off my supposed friends."

He leaned in close, his lips inches from my ear. "Then leave."

I pushed him back, nerves skittering in twenty different directions. "That's not the point."

Regaining his seat with ease, he watched me carefully. "Isn't it?"

I sighed forcefully. "I didn't say I couldn't enjoy myself. But you never asked, I never said yes. This is not a date. We are friends and that's it."

His eyes narrowed. "Did you treat your last boyfriend like this?"'

"Chad was a gentleman. He always asked before taking." The smell of pizza was intoxicating. I looked up to see one go by. Our waitress came by with salads and breadsticks.

"It'll be just a few minutes more," she assured us.

The food seemed to distract Marcus. I watched him eat with surprise. He looked up at me, somewhat startled at my close scrutiny. "What?"

"Sorry, I'm just surprised at your gusto. Sam has to make herself heat human food, and my mom has to have a glass with blood with her meal."

He shrugged, still eating. "I was never given the chance to eat anything else. I simply eat whatever is put before me. Don't tell me you just noticed."

I started in on my salad. "I confess, I haven't really made a point of noticing your eating habits before now." Taking a couple of bites, I tried again. "What was it like growing up with humans?"

"The same as you, I think. I didn't know what I was so I never thought something was wrong." He was edgy, and I could feel his radiating hostility.

"What's going to be a safe topic?" I asked, trying to go back to neutral ground.

He paused from hovering to look at me. Really, how did I not notice his eating habits before? "I may not like to talk about some things, Scarlett, but I'll answer any question you ask of me."

That was dangerous and I didn't have the courage to test it. "Can I take a rain check? An offer like that needs a worthwhile question."

"All right," he said, finishing off his salad and eyeing mine. I pushed it over. "Thanks." He then proceeded to finish mine.

"Did you lick plates clean as a child?"

"Depends on what was for dinner."

"You're serious, aren't you?"

In response, he picked up my salad plate and proceeded to lick it clean.

"Stop! Oh that's just wrong!" I was laughing so hard, I nearly fell off my bar stool. He reached out to help steady me.

"It was really good dressing," he said innocently.

Our pizza appeared while I was drying the tears of laughter from my eyes.

"Do you need plates?" asked our waitress.

"No thank you," Marcus replied. He stopped and looked at me. "Unless you want one."

Shocked to be included, I set down the piece I had been attempting to devour. "No, I'm fine."

"Enjoy, then."

I looked at Marcus in wonderment. "Wow, I think that was a first."

He raised his eyebrows over his pizza. "I never said I couldn't learn."

I frowned, but it was hard to keep my mouth down turned. "Don't talk with food in your mouth."

He threw his head back and laughed. "I'm afraid I can only learn one thing a day. You're welcome to try again tomorrow."

I laughed quietly and picked up my abandoned slice. "Okay, one manner a day. I won't overburden you, will I?" I bit into that gooey, delectable slice, deliciously sweetened by pineapple before looking at him.

"You might stretch my capacities for polite society, but you're welcome to try." He reached for another slice. I looked at the pizza and did a double take. I was still on my first piece. He was currently finishing off number three. Abandoning manners, I ate faster. It was a matter of survival. It I didn't eat fast, there wouldn't be anything left. In the end, I lost anyway. He ended up getting one of my pieces. He did ask, though. I groused, but let him pay the bill.

"I suppose I owe you something now. Do you want to pick it out?"

He looked at me oddly, but didn't argue. "What do they have here that the humans wouldn't have?"

I looked around as we left the warmth of the diner. "You mean beside the restaurant that serves raw meat? How about the groomer? It serves all your feline needs."

"It does?"

"Read the sign. Come on, it's great if you have grooming issues." I took his hand and hauled him down the street. A bell jingled when we walked through. The shop owner came from the back.

"Can I help you?" He was several years past 300, and his fingernails seemed stuck in claw like form.

Marcus was picking up a brush big enough for a horse. "Just looking," he replied casually. "What sort of cat needs a brush this big? It's the size of a football."

The werecat tensed, and I figured he had to think we were very lost mortals. Gently plucking the brush, I put it back. "Just because you haven't transformed into a deadly predator doesn't mean you won't one day be big enough to bring down a wildebeest. I imagine this is for some caring person to groom you with when you're in cat form."

Marcus pulled the brush off again and I saw the older man relax. He started back towards his office. "You two kids let me know if you need any help."

Experimentally, Marcus ran the brush down his arm. "If I become a werecat, would you buy me one of these?"

"Sure, should I wrap it up and put it in your stocking with all the coal?"

He smiled and put the brush up. "I see I missed out staying home for all of those away games."

I laughed but kept going. There were all sorts of products. A fish aisle, full of sardines, tuna, and flavored treats the size of Ritz crackers. I picked up some tuna and salmon flavored treats for Sam, who, sadly, had a stash in our room.

"Scarlett! I found my perfect present!" I went over to him. He was holding a shirt up that read:

If you don't tell your kid about catnip, who will?

"What's so great is no one but an Immortal would get it! Oh, can I have it, please?" He was hamming it up for me, but it suddenly occurred to me that Marcus probably hadn't received very many presents in his life. I took the shirt and pursed my lips, trying for my best impression of my mother.

"Would you actually wear it?" I asked with mock seriousness.

"If it weren't near freezing outside, I'd wear it to the game."

I smiled and handed it to him. "All right, but we're even now and this no longer gets to be counted as a date."

"Can that be my present?"

"Of course," I replied, pulling my wallet from my purse. The salesman came out to ring us up. He chuckled at the shirt.

"I didn't mean the shirt," murmured Marcus.

I stiffened, but smiled for the werecat as I handed my money over. "I'm not going to answer that here," I whispered back.

He sighed mightily. "Outside?"

"No." I received my change and thanked the werecat. "Come on, we'll be late for the bus."

He hung along a half step behind me. I kept looking out of the corner of my eye. He looked just like a beat puppy. Before we crossed the street, I put my hand out.

"Look, Marc, I like you, but I don't want to ruin what we have by trying to go any further. If you're willing to be patient, I am willing to reconsider."

He reached up to touch my cheek. "I can be patient."

"Then I am willing to reconsider, but not now. Come on, we really are going to be stuck here if we miss the bus."

We were two of the last to get on. Sam and Maya smiled innocently as we took our seat.

"How was your trip?" asked Maya with angelic innocence.

"You two think you're so sneaky," I replied, flouncing onto my seat.

The bus began to rumble forward and both turned around to face us.

"No, really," said Sam, "how was it?"

"Well," I replied archly, "I certainly learned who my friends are."

Sam waved her hand dismissively at me. "How about you Marcus?"

Marcus contemplated me with all due consideration. "I'm learning patience."

Both girls looked disappointed and turned back around. "You're no fun Scarlett," groused Sam.

I stuck my tongue out at the back of their heads. "I didn't realize you were profiting from your amusement," I said dryly.

"Oh, he didn't pay us in cash," piped Maya.

Sam nudged her so hard she nearly fell into the middle aisle. When she righted herself, Marcus flicked her in the back of the head.

"Hey!" she turned to glare at Marcus. "If I knew I could bribe you for some time with Ben I would. Oops!" she looked truly terrified to have let this slip. Her pale face turned bright red and she hastily turned forward.

"Maya," I began, but Marcus put a hand over my mouth.

"Don't worry, Maya," he said quietly, with more sensitivity than I would have given him credit for, "none of us will say a thing."

"But you'll act differently. Don't you dare!"

"What?" I asked sarcastically. "Leave you alone with him? Wander off to our own table and leave the two of you to find your own spot? No, I wouldn't dream of it."

"Scarlett," Marcus said warningly, "leave it."

I rolled my eyes and stuck my tongue out at him. "Maya, you have my word I won't pull anything like you and Sam did. I cannot be bought."

Shyly, she looked at me. "Honestly?"

"Cross my heart and hope to die."

"Sam?"

"Of course I won't, Maya."

Maya relaxed down into her seat. "Thank you."

The game was well worth a three hour bus ride. Sam had found blue pom-poms, our colors were blue and gray, and she handed them out amongst everyone. Marcus looked at his with disgust.

"You want me to do what with it?" he asked, holding it away from him as though it would bite.

Sam sighed with exaggeration and took it from him. "You cheer with it. You show school spirit. See?" She waved it with enthusiasm before handing it back to him. He took it with extreme reluctance.

"So, you're saying we're the cheerleaders?"

"Something like that," she replied blithely.

Marcus looked at me for sympathy, but it was too funny to sympathize. Every time our boys had the ball, Sam was up waving hers with more school spirit than an entire cheering squad. Even her cohort in peppiness, Brittany, was subdued. She had come down with a bad cold on Thursday, and playing yesterday hadn't been good for her. I confess I'm a sucker for a pitiful face. Any number of strays found their way home when I was a child, but my mom had to find human homes for them. The threat of a hungry neighborly vampire snacking on one of them was more than she thought I could bear. So Sam, standing up and cheering all alone, was a bit too much for me. I rose to stand with her. I took Marcus's pom-pom and started screaming at the top of my lungs. Brittany, still sniffling, got up next, followed by Maya, Jess, and Wendy. Eventually every one of our soccer team and all of our friends were standing and screaming like maniacs.

The game was tied at two all and there were only a few minutes left in the game. Sam and I were nearly hoarse, our voices cracked at the oddest moments. Doug made a great save and Sam lost hers completely. She was still waving her pom-poms around with even greater enthusiasm as the minutes ticked away. I held my breath a moment as Joshua shot, but the werecat blocked it. The pom-pom was gently plucked from my fingers. Surprised, I turned to see that not only had Marcus stood to cheer, he had brought the entire lacrosse team with him. Most of the boys looked at me with wry amusement. We all knew each other, it was a small school, and for the most part, we hybrids learned to laugh at ourselves early in life. I handed over my pom-pom and witnessed one of the funniest moments of my life. Marc took the pom-pom back two rows to stand at the front of the lacrosse team, like a conductor before the orchestra. He raised his hand as though he was reading his orchestra and when he brought it down, the boys let out a giant cheer. It started as a rumble and grew to a roar. I had to slap my free hand over my mouth to stop the laugh that bubbled forth. Marcus reprovingly shook his head and gestured me forward. Obediently, overflowing with mirth, I went back to my own cheers.

Two minutes to go and Ben managed to fake past the werecat defending him. Streaking down the field with natural grace, he set up and scored! The ball curved beautifully into the left corner, past the goalie's outstretched hands. The team ran together, with masculine shows of affection, as they ran back to center field. I screamed with everything I had left, and felt my voice go. Now Sam and I were both hoarse. Everyone else was cheering with amazing enthusiasm, even the boys behind us were doing so without prompting. The werecats gathered for one last desperate surge. They moved with fury, sprinting and crossing a fraction faster than a mortal could, but Eddie Varlos, our striker, stopped the frantic charge. As he cleared the ball up the field, the referee called the game over. Pandemonium reigned. The boys all met at half field, hugging and slapping each other on the back, their celebrations finally climaxing in a giant pile of happy, dirty, immensely satisfied athletes.

In the stands, we were all jumping up and down and hugging each other. There were tears in Sam's eyes. She turned to look at the still standing lacrosse team and Marcus with his single pom-pom. She climbed up the two rows of bleachers and hugged the lacrosse captain, Davis, and Marcus. She mouthed the words of thanks, but nothing came out. Marcus patted her on the back when she tried again. Maya climbed up and gathered Sam back.

By then, the boys were starting to leave the field. Many of them waved at us, joking around amongst themselves and throwing well meant sarcasm at the boys cheering squad. Sam shook herself free of Maya and leaped down, landing on her feet, naturally. She hugged Ben fiercely before turning to Douglas. Then, in front of half of the school, she kissed him. I stared in horrified shock, embarrassed to be witnessing such an intimate moment. I managed to break contact to find Maya staring with her jaw slightly ajar. Uncomfortably, I gathered Sam's discarded pom-pom and went to gently shake Maya. I could hear her jaw snap shut.

I tried to suggest we head back to the bus, but all that came out were a series of croaks, vaguely similar to the words. She nodded, understanding what I was trying to say.

"Sounds like a plan." She took my arm and led us out of the bleachers. We joined the procession of our classmates, but I couldn't see Marcus or Davis. Ben came to greet us as we touched ground.

"Great game, Ben!" said Maya. He smiled ecstatically as he hugged first her and then me. "You couldn't have planned a more perfect game if you tried."

"Thanks, Maya." He put an arm around both of us, as I took his duffel bag and put it over my outside shoulder. "Great cheering, all of you. I have to admit I nearly fell over in shock when I saw the boys leading their own cheers. Davis said he was coming for his teammates on the swim team, but I never imagined he would bring the rest of the lacrosse team, let alone Marcus. Man, that was priceless."

"Weren't they great?" asked Maya. "And to see Marcus conducting them."

"It certainly was unexpected," laughed Ben. "I mean, he rarely sticks around for the whole game. I personally believe he finds soccer boring."

"Well," I croaked, "you can't hit anyone in soccer."

Ben laughed at me. "Did you and Sam lose your voices, Lettie?"

I nodded my head rather than try speech again.

He squeezed my shoulder. "Well, I appreciate it, and I'm sure Doug does too, just for a different reason."

We all looked back to see if Sam and Doug were even coming with us. They were entwined, but moving in the right direction.

"Yeah," said Maya, a hint of wistfulness in her voice, "he does certainly seem to be appreciating the moment."

We made it to our two buses, and Ben had to leave. "We need to go down to Brimstone to celebrate," he said, as he took his bag back. "I'm looking forward to pizza and ice cream."

Valiantly, I hid my guilt. Maya caught my eye and safely spoke for us. "I think it should be my treat, at least the ice cream. Scarlett can cover the food."

Well, I thought prosaically, I was always up for more pizza.

Ben stopped to look at us both. "Thanks," he said with warmth, "to the both of you. I really appreciate this." He loaded up, and I could gratefully load onto mine, where I could recover my voice.

Marcus rose to let me have the window seat. I just smiled, and he sympathetically patted me on the back. "Your voice should be back by the time we get home."

"School." I corrected weakly.

"Yeah, that too."

Sam was the last one on the bus. She sat with an air of divine happiness. Maya and I exchanged glances, but since only two of our group could talk, it was a quiet sort of ride home.

Ben didn't get his pizza. We stopped at a McDonalds on our way back. Maya did buy everyone their choice of dessert, but I put off my end of her devil made bargain for later. It wasn't like we didn't go down to Brimstone whenever we could. And since I was the one who had had a job during the summer, I was the expendable source of income.

TWELVE

When Soccer season ended, I found myself at loose ends. Unlike Sam, who played basketball, I had no winter sport. I became the camp follower. Where Maya followed our games in the fall, I was left to follow in the winter. In years past, Maya had been a talented point guard, but with her weakened body, she had asked to take my place as stats keeper. I could no more deny her that than I could deny myself chocolate. Doug and Sam, the true athletes were starters for basketball. I had fully expected Marcus to turn out for basketball. His desire to hit people could kind of be utilized under the basket, but he just shook his head when I asked.

"I have hidden talents," he had said, with a usual hint of seductiveness.

I had just rolled my eyes. "Flirting isn't a sport."

He smiled in response. "It wouldn't be fair to you if it was."

Ben was an excellent swimmer. He had brought home several trophies for our school and he was even allowed to compete in human events periodically. In years past, I had followed Sam and Maya around, but this year, in fairness, I first went to Ben's swim meet. For once in my life, I had been too busy studying for quarter finals to follow the social tide of school. The first meet was held at Hybrid High. I settled myself in the bleachers, fully prepared to cheer Ben on in his events, mainly anything involving the freestyle. I was not expected for what greeted me at the sight of the relay team. I had brought my very important Biology II research with me to pass the time when Ben wasn't swimming. Books and papers fell lifelessly from my lap when I saw Marcus standing beside Ben. There were quite a few good looking swimmers. Wolfhaven Werewolves, Valley High Vampires as well as Brimstone, Riverdale Elves, and Mountain Line Werecats all had their fair share of titter worthy boys, but the breath was ripped from my numb chest as I watched Marcus readying for his swim. Had I missed him earlier? I had made sure to watch every freestyle event, but the Biology II was due on Monday and my partner was still in the infirmary. I had opted to do my own project rather than join Ben or Maya's teams. I had been engrossed in the breakdown of my own genetics, but surely I could have spared enough time to notice Marcus. Well, I was noticing now.

Davis Wheeler, a vampire-werewolf cross, was the lead off. He kept good pace with the other back-strokers before Wes Cooper went in for the breast stroke. A fellow Trig student, Wes was a slight redheaded vampire-werecat cross. Oddly enough, despite their polar opposite halves, Wes and Davis both seemed predominantly vampirish and were close friends. The instant Wes came in, Marcus dove off. I might have figured all of his power would be harnessed into the powerful butterfly. Wes and Davis had done well. Our team was in the top three, but Marcus put them all to shame. My last summer at home, I had watched the summer Olympics. Michael Phelps had nothing on Marcus Shepherd. Where Michael was talent and grace, Marcus was talent and power. He came back over three body lengths in front of the next closest team, the Riverdale Elves. Ben slipped into the water like a dolphin, but it was no contest. Ben had won every single freestyle event he competed in, the 100m, 200m, and 400m. With the daylight Marcus had opened up, all Ben had to do was finish.

I was speechless as Ben touched the wall and came up for air. Numbly, I applauded with the rest of the audience. Several girls around me were tittering amongst themselves. I was too stunned to be angry at their empty effusions of my two friends. The relay had been the last of the day, and people began to move as the athletes left for the locker rooms. No medals would be awarded. The winning school of the meet received a trophy and I figured with two power horses, we were bound to get every trophy for the year.

I managed to finally shake myself back to reality. I dismally took in the state of my research. Lowering myself down, I gathered my fallen supplies. I stuffed everything back in my bag and stood. Two boys were coming my way, but there were still many students left, and other swimmers, including the girls who had swam earlier in the day. There was little interaction across cultures. Ambivalent, I swung my bag across my shoulder. Only then did I realize Ben and Marcus were watching me with unrestrained glee.

"I told you I had hidden talents," said Marcus laughingly.

Ben grinned like an idiot all at my expense. "I wouldn't trade these elven eyes for anything. That look of pure shock was so totally priceless!"

I frowned at their cockiness. "The real reason you had Maya ask for my help with the stats books." I snorted in disgust. "All of you were laughing at me."

"Nah, Sam and Doug are as out of the loop as you were."

"Oh, that makes me feel sooo much better."

Marcus hopped over the railing, gathering some attention. He took my chin in gentle, chlorinated hands. "Bet you never imagined I could find happiness without hitting anyone." He leaned in devilishly close. "Was it surprise of seeing me, or seeing me half naked?"

I jumped back, frowning even deeper. "Humph! See if I come to another swim meet this year." I turned on my heel and stormed off. Marcus was the last person I would tell about *those* sort of thoughts.

Ben found me later in the library. Okay, so half of my absorption in my homework was my natural procrastination, but I still had a new found need to understand. Ben took the seat beside me. He whistled at the stack of books I had accumulated.

"You know, I've been the good student for years, but you're putting me to shame here, Lettie."

I marked my page and looked at him. I politely raised my eyebrows. "Can I help you?"

"I've come to ask your forgiveness. I can't control Marcus, but I hope you won't hold him against me."

"Are you trying to say that this was all his idea?"

"Well, maybe, does it work?"

I melted into a smile. "I guess I understand where it was amusing for the both of you. You and I did something similar to Sam with Douglas in our second year, but that was for Halloween. And I did promise I would go to at least two of your swim meets."

He nodded happily. "Well, you know that we will have meets after the first of the year."

I laughed softly. "Thanks, I can keep my word then."

He looked intently at me and something flickered in my awareness. "I'm glad he hasn't ruined our friendship."

I was startled at the seriousness in his tone. The alarm began to grow in intensity. I removed my hand that I just now realized he had placed his over. Resolutely, I opened my book. "That would be giving him far too much credit."

"Are you going to be studying all night?" I refused to look at him when he took that tone.

"It is due on Monday," I replied, making a concerted effort to take notes. I heard him sigh and push back in his chair.

"Sadly, I finished Thursday while you were working with Maya. I suppose there's no point in asking what you're doing tomorrow?"

"Well, if you're volunteering to proof read my paper, I accept," I said blithely. It took him a moment to respond. He seemed to have to shake the words from his body.

"Of course, I'll always help you when you need it Scarlett." He pushed himself out of his chair. "Well, I'd best let you get back to your studies." I watched him leave with a heavy heart. In that moment I passionately wished we never had to grow up.

I had ample opportunity in the weeks to come to wish none of us had started the inevitable process towards maturation. Sam and Doug, though considered an item, were on again off again for much of the month of November. It wasn't until just before mid-winter finals that they found some accord. I had no idea what sort of accord it was, I did not want details. Maya did, and whenever I made an offhanded comment, she would smile smugly and ask if I wanted to know more.

"No!" I replied, forcing my attention back to studying.

Maya and I were alone, as the other four were at their respective practices. "It's not so bad, Lettie, and you know you want to know."

"No, I don't. So long as we are all speaking to each other again, I am okay without knowing the how's and whys."

She sighed. "Is that what your problem with Marcus is? You want us to all be speaking all the time?"

Frowning, I looked back at her. "Is that such a bad thing?"

"Well, it seems a bit impossible to accomplish, if you ask me."

"Which is why I don't ask," I replied tersely.

She just shook her head. "Have you never wanted to take a leap of faith?"

My otherwise distracted brain slowly began to process a great many outside factors. Of course Maya would want me to care, and she followed Sam because she had always had to live vicariously through us. I stretched a hand out to her. "What about you, Maya? Why don't you take a leap?"

She pulled away from me. Distancing herself in every way she could. "Unlike you, I know that if I tried, I would be rebuffed. Soundly."

She sounded so broken, so fragile, I wanted to hug her, but she was making it quite clear that she wanted nothing of the sort. "Well then," I replied in a lighter tone, making us both realize it was best to move on, "we shall both have to remain single."

Her hazel eyes met mine and I saw a hauntedness that frightened me. "What if I don't want to remain single for the rest of my life? What if I want to be kissed just once before I die?"

"Stop it, Maya! We have years ahead of us. Years to find someone truly special who appreciates you, worships the very ground you walk on. Don't think that we are stuck at school. Besides, doesn't everyone mention that college guys are way cuter? And with a few more years, they're bound to be more mature."

She had to shake herself. "Right, college. Are we all going to the same place?"

"Well, you and I are going to Transylvania Tech, I don't think Sam or Doug has any inclination for anything after high school, and Ben was thinking of Harvard."

Sighing, she settled more comfortably in her chair. "All right, you and I will just have to make a point of finding worthy guys when we go off to college." She looked up at me through her lashes, and her look was warmer than it had been. Cunning, but warmer. "What about Marcus? Where is he going?"

I shrugged. "Beats me. I'm sure Ben mentioned every opportunity after high school to him when he was new, but he's never mentioned what he's going to do."

Her smile became almost Machiavellian. "I don't think you need to worry over much, Lettie. He'll follow you wherever you choose to go."

Sadly, I couldn't keep the blush or the stutter from hindering me and letting her know just how right she was. "It doesn't signify," I muttered. "So, about tangents…" I forced her back to the homework at hand.

That Thursday and Friday were our finals. Three classes on Thursday, three on Friday. When all was said and done, we were free for two whole weeks. Saturday morning, the buses filed in to take my classmates off to their families. I had made sure to give everyone their Christmas presents Friday night, so I slept through their departure. No one minded, it was considered odd to wake up for something so early if one didn't have to.

There were very few people who remained for the holidays. Students and teachers alike returned home, but some, like myself, remained. Some had no home to go to, others were still in the depths of their transformations and were not allowed away from the help they needed.

On the first day of vacation, I sat in the library with my Bloodolgy book open in front of me, having nothing better to do, really, than homework. Someone came to sit beside me.

"You know our homework isn't due until after vacation," came a slightly drawling voice. I looked up into Marcus's blue eyes.

"But if I get it done now, I won't have to do it later," I said with exaggerated patience.

He simply smiled. "Show me a student who actually thinks that way, and I'll happily sing Christmas carols in the middle of the library."

"I hope you sing well," I replied, bending my head back to my homework, but I couldn't quite gather the attention I had had a moment earlier. He simply sat there and waited. I sighed in frustration and shut my book. "Fine, you win."

He laughed as he sat back in his chair with all the grace of a full grown werecat. "So, tell me Scarlett, what leaves you here for the joyous holidays?" He was very good at smoothing the rancor in his voice, but I detected his bitterness, perhaps because I shared a bit of it.

"My mother and I decided it was best if I didn't come home this time."

He raised an eyebrow. "And I suppose it's too personal a question to wonder why?"

"We had quite the heated argument before I came here this year. She is a full blooded vampire and I have yet to display any Immortal characteristics."

"I thought I heard that half human crosses sometimes never display Immortal powers."

"That's the problem. Whatever my father was, my mother is positive it isn't human."

His nose twitched and I had to laugh.

"Can you smell what my other half is?"

He looked slightly sheepish. "I'm trying."

I just shook my head. "I have a talent of sensing what others are. I can't sense what I am, but you are welcome to try."

He leaned closer, his nostrils flaring, and I closed my eyes for an instant, feeling that familiar urge to bite him. I threw myself back in my chair, my eyes flying open. "And you, Marcus, why are you here?" I was embarrassed to hear the breathlessness in my voice.

He sat back in his chair, his eyes becoming hooded. "I thought that would be quite obvious."

"What would be obvious?"

"I have no family to go to, Scarlett. I'm an orphan."

"Then how do you know what you are?"

He smiled coldly, and he didn't meet my eyes as he answered. "I was in human foster homes most of my life. I was in three over eleven years, for though humans could not sense what I was, they knew I was different and it frightened them. I was lucky to be found a year ago by a full blooded werewolf who just happened to be searching for hybrids in human homes. Lucas, the werewolf who found me took me in for several months, explaining what I was and arranging for me to be brought here. It wasn't easy for him."

"Or you," I said softly, knowing the hurt that lay beneath his cold monotone. "I suppose we're just the opposite. You, growing up with normal people and being different, and me growing up with a vampire and being normal." I hesitated for a moment but gradually laid my hand on his arm. The contact roused him out of revere. Those sharp eyes focused in on me.

"Yes, I suppose we fit the outcast mold better than most." He looked down at my hand and I hastily removed it. "So, I suppose it's just you and me here for the holidays, then?"

I shrugged my shoulders. "I guess it is."

"Well, then, there are much better things to be doing than studying." He grabbed my hand and my book bag and drug me out of the library.

I was moderately worried about what Marcus might consider better than studying. Our first stop was to drop my bag of books. We passed by the doors to the courtyard on our way to my room. Outside the snow was falling softly. He looked out at it and then back at me.

"Come on and get dressed, we'll go build snowmen." He had such an odd enthusiasm that I was reminded strongly of his fractured childhood.

"Marcus, I am dressed," I said with amusement. He turned to look directly at me and his gaze made me catch my breath.

"More the pity," I thought I heard him murmur. "Coat, gloves, scarf," he ticked off on his hand. "Honestly, I thought you were smart."

"Oh, I feel so insulted," I returned, making my way up the back stairs to my room, tall, untamed shadow in tow. Grabbing my parka, I shouldered into it while exchanging my slippers for lined boots. "What about you?" I asked as I pulled my hat over my ears. He had been standing in my doorway, looking a bit imposing and watching me with a guarded expression. He started slightly at being addressed.

"What about me?"

"Coat, gloves, scarf?" I ticked the items off on my hand.

"Well, I've made sure you're ready. I'll meet you out there." And in a flash he was gone. My whole life was spent around Immortals, but I still was caught off guard when they moved like that. At my more sedate pace, I went down to wait for him. I had just reached the cafeteria when he appeared beside me, slightly winded.

"I told you."

I just rolled my eyes. He was in rare form. Springing in front of me, he graciously opened the door for me. Vaguely surprised at this courtesy, I walked through and into the frozen winter land with a word of thanks. The fountain was amusingly covered in snow and icicles. It looked as though it had frozen in motion. We cleared the upper level and paused.

"So where to?"

He stood still, one hand shielding his face as he surveyed our surroundings. "No one's gone near the woods, we should have good snow there." He headed off and I hurried to keep up. I was sinking in the snow as I walked at it was tiring work. Marcus found his clear, untouched space and walked around before finally decided on a starting spot.

"I'll make the bottom and you can do the middle," he said over his shoulder.

"Oh thank you," I said with heavy sarcasm. He turned to look back at me.

"What? Did you have a better idea?"

"No, but you're back to telling me what to do. You'd made such progress."

"Scarlett," he said with exaggerated patience, "do you want to build the top bottom or middle of the snowman?"

I bit my lip to keep from smiling. "I'll make the middle, thank you for asking."

He just grunted and proceeded to ignore me while he rolled snow. I waited for him to acknowledge me, but he didn't even look in my direction. He was wholeheartedly committed to his project. Sighing, I bent to my own work.

"You done yet?" he called sometime later.

I turned to see what he had done. His mound was nearly waist high. My eyes widened. "How big do you plan this thing to be?" I rolled more snow into mine to compensate. "I don't think we'll be able to lift this. Well, maybe you, definitely not me." He came over shaking his head.

"Scarlett, you really need to stop viewing yourself as weaker than the rest of us. I've seen you do amazing things when you think no one is watching. So, go on, pretend I'm not here."

I glared at him. "Right, that'll be easy."

He stepped away from me. "Try."

Muttering to myself about how annoying he was, I bent down and squared myself to lift. It was utterly hopeless. Closing my eyes, I quoted some movie wisdom to myself about doing and not trying. I was totally amazed when the large ball of snow lifted in my grasp. It was tricky to hold it though, as ball was very wide and my fingers couldn't grip it. I was about to lose it when the other side balanced. Opening my eyes, I saw Marcus on the other side. He was smiling with something like pride in his eyes.

"What did I tell you?" he asked, but his usual cocky tone was missing.

"You?" I asked, smiling softly. "It was all Yoda. 'Do or do not, there is not try.'"

I could feel his laughter through the snow. "I didn't take you for the Star Wars type, Lettie."

"Oh?" I replied archly as we awkwardly crab stepped towards his base. "What did you take me for then?"

He looked a little bit guilty and waited until the middle mound was placed. "Chick flicks," he muttered.

I patted him on the arm. "If it helps, you didn't really strike me as the Star Wars type either. More Die Hard, Jason Bourne."

We both turned to look at our creation.

"It needs a head," I remarked.

"Do you want to make it?"

"No, you're much better at this than I am. I'll go find a face and arms. We should have found a carrot from the kitchen before we came out."

"Be creative," he replied, kneeling back down to gather the head. I ventured off to find what I could. I came back with some rocks from by the pond and some different branches. He stood face to face with his creation, trimming off uneven parts like a sculptor. Dropping my collection at his feet, I looked up.

"It has to be well over six feet," I said in awe.

"Roughly six four," he replied absently, still sculpting. I realized it was only two inches taller than he was.

"I feel short." I was five seven, which was decent, but most people would feel short around over six feet of snow.

"You're the perfect height," he said absently. I had to stifle the laugh that bubbled forth. Even distracted he was still a flirt. When he finally stepped back, I put rocks for its face, with some left over to run as buttons down its middle. I let him choose the branches for arms. Stepping back, he viewed his creation with pride.

"It's missing something," he mused, more to himself than to me.

"Well, no carrot so no nose, and no old fashioned pipe or hat." I trailed off when his gaze swung back around to me.

"No, that's not quite it," he said, still not entirely talking to me. He wasn't looking at me either. Instead, he gaze was fastened on my hat. I began to retreat when he abruptly snatched my hat from my head.

"Hey!" I tried to grab it from him, but I was too slow and too short. "Marcus!"

"Hmm?" he asked, adjusting the hat on his creation's head. He turned back. "Oh, yes, thank you for reminding me." Whereupon he took my scarf too.

"Marc! Give it back!"

He held his arms out to block me. "No, he's perfect now." Deliberately, he looked at me with that lost puppy expression I was so gullible for. "You wouldn't want to ruin my Christmas would you?"

I stopped struggling. "This is hardly all of your Christmas."

"But it's the best snowman ever and my snowman needs a hat and scarf. Please?"

I always was a sucker for a sad face and he did say please. "Will you promise to retrieve them before someone else does?"

"I promise to buy you a new hat and scarf if these go missing."

I frowned. "I don't mean to sound rude, but where do you get the money from?"

He shrugged. "Lucas sends me an allowance. He says the school has the funds for my clothes and books."

"That's nice of him," I said tentatively. Conversations about Marcus's past rarely went well if they lasted past the first question.

"Yeah, I think he feels responsible for me. Most of the hybrids who don't grow up with their family are found too late to save them."

It was such a horrible fact, but I knew Marcus wasn't ready to open up about it. "It's a miracle you turned out as normal as you did," I said, with forced lightness, but meaning every word.

"Yeah," he replied, working to forget the last few minutes, "makes me wonder where your mom went wrong." He trotted away laughing. My first impulse was to follow, but a half step in I realized, he had left my scarf and hat unattended. I stood on tiptoe to reach them when something hard and icy cold hit me from behind. I whirled around in time to have a second snowball land right below my chin.

"This is war!" I grabbed a handful of snow and ran after him, having to high step like some fancy show horse in the snow. I was hit two more times as I ran for shelter, but my aim was pretty good and we were soon even on hits. I took cover behind the bench by the frozen duck pond. Its unsteady structure still held up well to the onslaught. I popped up when the snow stopped coming and threw back at him.

"Come on, Scarlett!" he called. "You've got to move sometime!"

Instantly alarmed, I realized the voice was only a few feet from me. I dashed out and away, getting one right in the middle of my back. I dropped down behind a brush covered in icicles. I peeked up and scouted where he was before launching another snowball and dashing for new cover. I could hear him cursing as he got stuck in the shrubs. I turned back and pelted him mercilessly. The tree above him scattered snow on top too. He was swearing and laughing simultaneously.

"All right! All right! You win!" He bent to extract himself, and I came out of hiding.

"So, Pax?" I asked, nearing his position warily. I was watching his hands closely to see if he wasn't gathering any snow.

"Yeah, truce, pax, whatever." He finally got the offending branch off his pant leg, but before he straightened, I slipped up and dropped an icicle down his neck before high tailing it out of there.

"Scarlett!!!!"

I was half way back to safety when he caught me from behind. I was tackled into the snow. Coming up, spluttering, I laughed.

"You're very good at tackling people, aren't you?"

He leaned in and brushed noses. "You have no idea." Seductively, he leaned in even closer and for

once all I wanted was a kiss. I had no urge to bite.
His gloved hand reached to cup my head when an
icy shape slithered down my back.

"Ahh!!!" I shot up, arching away from the
freezing bit of torture sliding down my back. I
pulled the back of my layers away and finally it fell
out. "You fiend!" I cried. He had rolled over on his
back in laughter. He propped himself up on one
elbow.

"But Scarlett, all's fair in love and war."

"Bah! I'm freezing!" I scowled at him and
began the slow trudge back to my room.

"Where are you going?"

"I'm going to get warm!"

"Can I help?"

"No!"

Marcus and I were two of fourteen students
still at school. Every first year had gone to their
family. Five other fourth years, including Daniel
Livingstone, had to remain. Daniel still hadn't
healed, so his parents had come to him. There were
four third years and three second years. I knew the
other four fourth years. They were all were-crosses
that ran with Aryn's crowd, but I made a point of
having nothing to do with them. One of the third
years was in my art class, but besides that, I knew
the other kids by name and nothing else.

There was a signup sheet posted for a van ride
to Brimstone. The staff who remained wanted
some time away from us, so they had all drawn

straws on who would go to chaperone the remainder. Since the refractor attack, trips to Brimstone had been restricted to group ventures only. Captain Mortensen had seen to the restoration of the boarders and more security had been brought in. We were still reassured on a weekly basis that we had nothing to worry about by a visiting board member. Unfortunately, their continued presence had the opposite effect. Every student now began to wonder, some more than others, and I had heard others being told what I had been reminded, to not ask questions. Knowing you are surrounded by additional security forces 24/7 has the tendency to raise more than a few eyebrows.

I had finished my Christmas shopping early, so I had to contemplate the necessity of actually going to Brimstone. I spent some rare alone time mulling over just what to do to amuse myself for the next ten days, as Marcus was sure to find me the second I cracked a book open. However, after much pointless contemplation, I had a sudden inspiration to see to Marcus's Christmas education. There was one small problem with this. Marcus went everywhere with me. The only free time I had was when he swam, and there was no way I could totally pull one over on him and get him to go swim when the van left. I knew that if he saw my name on that list, he would sign up too. I wanted him to enjoy this Christmas, as I was sure he hadn't enjoyed many others, but I needed some space.

Desperate times call for desperate measures, and there were some questions I needed answered.

THIRTEEN

I set my alarm early for the next morning. Dressing warmly, I stuffed money in my pockets, grabbed a borrowed coat I had been meaning for some time to return, and slipped out the side entrance once used by servants. I took the wooded path, making sure to stay where other footprints had come before me. Since Marcus and I had built our snowman, several of the other students had traipsed the woods. When I got to where my tracks would show, I paused, looking for the electric boarder. The energy field created a wide berth on either side where the snow didn't stick. Hopping from inconspicuous snow patches, I edged up to the field and began to trace my way back to the guards' office. Industrious people that they were, they had shoveled a path all the way around the building and out to their vehicles. Slipping into the path, I peeked in one of the windows to see Captain Mortensen sitting around a set of papers with three other Immortals. Now, the intelligent thing to do would have been to walk in and ask to speak to him directly, return his coat, and hopefully ask for a favor. Like I said, though, I had ulterior motives. I wanted to know, with as much certainty as was in my power to ascertain, if refractors were held on our school grounds. Logically, if they were this power field humming behind me would react the same way as the one at my mother's work did. Back tracking a safe distance, I pulled out a small electromagnetic device commonly referred to as a passportal.

My summer job had taught me a great deal about the energy field that surrounded the Other Realm's inhabitants. If I was correct and the school's boarders were the same technology, then I could force my way through with a little ingenuity. Any disruption, an animal trying to fly through or a tree branch falling through the field, created an alarm and someone would be dispatched to investigate. The way to pass was tricky, though. A shadow creature could will their entire body, every single fiber, but a pulsating electromagnetic field was too difficult for them to match. When they tried, the energy forced their body to shift, and they couldn't control how they were shifting. The other Immortals were able to cross through with help because their body, even if they were a shape shifter, was always, at heart, solid. However, with no help, you would be shocked by enough energy to light up our school. It wasn't fatal, but it hurt.

Doug had ingeniously decided on a way to try and get through by shifting from one form to another in the process, thereby shifting the body make up to compensate for the shifting energy. The only problem was that Doug was a vampire-elf cross who couldn't shift. He had convinced someone more gullible to do it for him. Apparently, it had worked until the kid couldn't get back through the other way. Both perpetrators had been caught and punished in the Psych Ward. That had been an end to all of Douglas's brilliant ideas. He had promptly decided that if the school wasn't going to acknowledge his brilliance, he wasn't going to try and dazzle anyone.

The help needed to pass the barrier was a passportal. It was designed to match the frequency of the field and create a bubble around the wearer. However, the technology of the passportal was designed to create an undercurrent to disrupt shadow creatures should they ever come into possession of one. It just so happened that I had a passportal in my possession from my summer job. Technically, I was supposed to have returned it, but no one had thought to ask, and I had simply forgotten. As I've said, my interest in school and Immortals in general was severely limited until the day my fangs grew in.

I still wasn't a rocket scientist and it took a few minutes to remember how to work the blasted thing and get it aligned to this particular power field. I waited until I could feel the bubble around me. Cautiously, I extended one hand. Relief washed through me when I wasn't instantly sent back 50 feet by a painful electric shock. My mom, finally fed up with my attitude one day, had told me to try to get through without her help. For weeks I got cold sweats around any form of electricity. It *hurt.*

Slowly, cautiously, I walked through the barrier. It zapped my backside a bit as I stepped through, kind of like static electricity. Quickly, I made my way back to the guards' building. I had to dive into a bush to avoid being seen. Crouching, I waited as Captain Mortensen came out with a younger elf. They were just a few feet away from me, but we were separated by the power field.

"That was close," said the Captain, scanning his horizon.

"What do you think it is?" asked the younger elf.

Mortensen shrugged. "Could be a tree falling, but I don't see anything. We haven't had any issues in a month. It's probably just a power spike." He pulled up the collar of his coat. "Check the north side for anything, I'll check down south." Both guards left, hands on holsters. I waited for the other guard to leave before hurrying after Captain Mortensen. My progress was somewhat hidden by the hum of the field, but I saw him tense. He paused and scanned the field only to see me.

"Scarlett!" he ejaculated. "What in the name of heaven and hell are you doing on that side?" He sounded quite angry, so I hastily explained.

"I had to talk to you. I have a favor to ask."

"And you had to cross a forbidden boundary to do that?"

"Okay, so I was curious to see if this boarder was the same as on the Observation Posts." I held up the passportal that was around my neck. "They must be keeping refractors here." It belatedly occurred to me that I was now on the same side as the refractors. Quickly, I passed back through the barrier. The speed of my motion sent a more powerful shock through me. Passportals were not meant for any sudden movements. When I stood in front of him, I handed his jacket over. "And I wanted to return this to you."

He was horribly torn. Anger was palatable, but for some reason, he seemed to be fighting the urge to laugh.

"You set off the containment field to return my jacket? You could have just knocked on the door." He was pulling me away from the office in contradiction to his words.

"I had to know." I said simply, and he knew to what I referred.

"I heard about your attack," he said, still pulling me along. He didn't stop until we were out of sight of the guard building. "I suppose it is natural for you to be more concerned than your classmates. You've obviously worked on an

Observation Post, and you saw the damage done to Maxim. I don't approve of your methods, but I'll help you with this favor so long as it doesn't mean you'll be breaking more rules."

"I just need a ride to Brimstone." I was a little shocked at his attitude. Quite honestly, I had gone out this morning thinking I just might spend the rest of my vacation in detention.

"Why not just go with your classmates? I know they are scheduling another trip before Christmas."

I sighed, trying to find the words. "I just need to go and get some Christmas supplies without company. I really, really want to surprise someone."

The elf looked intently at me. "Very well. Stay here, hide as best you can, and wait for me to return."

I nodded and slipped in amongst the snow covered ground cover. I watched as he returned back to the office, but he went out of my sight for some time. My main focus was on ignoring the biting cold, and I was almost shocked out of my hiding spot when he returned.

"Follow me," he said curtly. I obediently did as I was told. He took the last vehicle in the line, the one positioned completely out of sight from any onlookers. I climbed in while he cleared the windows. We were some ways down the road before I dared to speak.

"Thank you, Captain, I really appreciate this."

"Tell me Scarlett, what was so important that you would risk punishment for?"

I sighed and chewed my lip while debating how to phrase my reason. "One of my friends, he's here for the holidays because he has no family. I have my mom, but we decided it was best if I didn't go to Romania with her this year. He doesn't have that and I want to surprise him by showing him everything Christmas can be."

He was silent for so long, I was worried he was going to change his mind. Finally, he spoke in a much less controlled voice than I was used to from him. "My son, Jordan, goes to his mother. We figured that was best since she can show him Christmas spirit that I can't." There was a hint of bitterness to his words and I wondered if all of those fated to suffer at Christmas were drawn to each other.

"Are you and his mother separated?"

"Yes, we have been for nearly all of Jordan's life."

"I'm so sorry."

"Don't be. It was a mutual decision and I get to spend most weekends with him while he is at school. So," he said in a much different tone, "you risked near expulsion to give your friend Christmas?" He paused a moment. "And of course you wanted to prove a point I'm sure the Board of Directors has been trying to deny for some time."

I nodded. "The refractor that tried to attack me, was it from the school?"

"No. Those two were from the Other Realm."

"But there are refractors on our grounds." It was a statement not a question.

"Unfortunately," he replied. "I don't fully comprehend why, but it has been the policy of the Board of Directors to fire those who ask such questions. I cannot imagine what they would do to a student.

I let this sink in before asking my next question. "My mom is worried that the escapees are beyond anyone's calculations. Do you know any more?"

"Not officially. Most everyone who can remember the Control are overly eager to believe that all of the shadow creatures were captured and returned."

"But you have your doubts?"

"Yes, but it is a dangerous time to have doubts, Scarlett. Shadow creatures are incredibly intelligent. If some escaped and evaded capture, they'll lay low for awhile. The darker, more hostile shadow creature largely responsible for the damage to your soccer field sounds like one of their own criminals. Every refractor found guilty of a high level of crime, if it was not deemed condemnable to death, was assigned a keeper."

"But why would they target our school?"

"I don't know, but I don't believe when the generators went down that every shadow creature was waiting. Some, I believe, were sucked out. When the energy grid at the school has gone down, anomalies pop up all over. I've seen tree branches sucked out of the containment field by the force of the power fluctuations." We drove in silence for a few minutes more. On foot, the three miles to Brimstone was straight, but Hybrid High was set on a hill, and the way down was a switchback. "It is possible that they were drawn here because of the similar power field. Please do me a favor, Scarlett, and don't get caught pursuing this."

I slouched low in my seat as I saw Brimstone coming into view. "There's nothing to pursue. All of the teachers are all too frightened to speak, what with the school board looking over their shoulders, and my mom doesn't want to frighten me so she won't say anything. It's just so frustrating to sit here and do nothing and know nothing!"

He smiled slightly. "I have a feeling that you'll get your answers sooner rather than later. So," He abruptly changed topics, slowing down to the city speed limit. "What are you planning on getting for your friend?"

"Well, I need marshmallows and hot chocolate. We have a microwave in the Group Room, but I want to make the kind my mom does. The kind that tastes like melted chocolate. I also want to do some decorating, but I'm not flush enough to buy the decorations. All my summer savings were spent on presents and pizza. I thought I'd be alone for Christmas and it wouldn't matter."

"What about sugar cookies and gingerbread?"

"I thought about it, but Mrs. Baffert, the cook, nearly took my head off for even suggesting she let students in her kitchen. And the Home Ec room is locked until after break."

The elf cleared his throat uncomfortably as we pulled into the parking lot for the grocery. "You're welcome to use my kitchen. Most of the guards live on the grounds in the teachers' area."

"Really? That would be wonderful! Do you have a tree?" I asked excitedly, words bubbling forth with little to no thought. "Cause if not, I'll have Marcus bring one in from the forest."

"Marcus? The full were-cross? The one who nearly broke Peter's jaw?" He sounded amused, so I felt comfortable enough to laugh.

"Yes, but I promise he's housebroken."

This elicited a smile. "I don't blame him. He was simply protecting what was his."

I couldn't bring myself to protest someone I owed a favor, much less a stately elf. I had always found their stoicism a bit unsettling. "So, do you need a tree?"

'No," he said a bit forcefully, "but you're welcome to add some decorations as long as you clean up afterwards and leave some food for me."

He was definitely amused, but his sense of humor was well hidden and a bit odd. "Well, with his appetite, we'll have to make double batches of everything, but my mom is a pretty good cook for all she had to learn to eat food late in life and I tried to learn, so it should be edible at least."

We were parked, and I double checked I had all my cash.

"I'll be back for you in about thirty minutes. I'm going to go get some equipment for the generator or risk someone noticing something is off."

"Thanks," I hopped out and waved as he pulled off. I ran, buried deep in my outermost layer into the grocery store. I quickly found the ingredients for hot chocolate, as well as some necessities for cookies. I stopped in their selection of Christmas and chose a few of their less expensive items. Some part of math classes had been ingrained on my brain along the way, for I knew when to say enough was enough. I made it outside with exactly $3.26 in change, asking for my supplies to be sent to Captain Mortnensen's house, as the school often called in orders. I didn't know where he lived, but the cashier didn't even raise an eyebrow, so I had a feeling they knew. With nearly the whole of my summer's earnings spent, I went next door to the novelty shop, coming out with a Santa hat and a mini pack of cookie cutters and four cents. I was happily swinging my little bag when Captain Mortensen pulled up.

"Where did you send everything?" he asked, seeing only my last stop.

"To the school. Don't be alarmed if you have groceries waiting for you."

He frowned at the window. "I work from 7 to 7 over the holidays. There aren't enough of us with these added security measures to do a full rotation. My spare key is under the second pot from the door. Let yourself in and lock up before you leave."

"Of course." And edge of awkwardness had enveloped the car and we rode back in silence.

"You might want to change your hat," he said with dry humor. I had swapped mine for the Santa hat.

"Oh! Of course!" I bent down to rifle through my bag. A firm hand pushed me back down.

"Stay down! It looks as though we have company." I could feel the car pulling into a parking space. Captain Mortensen swore under his breath, a rare slip by an elf. "It looks as though your power surge got some attention. That's the car of Paul Wisner, the Head Director himself."

"What are we going to do?" I asked miserably. "I didn't know it was going to be this bad, honestly."

"They must be bored," he replied. "How did you get here?"

"I followed the barrier, the snow doesn't fall there. Before that, I stayed on the student paths."

"Impressive. All right, when I get out, I'm going to walk straight up there and create a diversion. Get out, stay low, and make your way back south, do you understand? You'll have to go back down to the road and come back through the forest. It'll take you longer, and it will be freezing cold, but you can't go anywhere near that power field again."

"I'm so sorry I got you into this," I said miserably, trying to look up at him while bent in half.

"Don't think about it," he replied. "This just might be the most fun I've had in years. I probably shouldn't say this, but I enjoy bothering the Board. They sent me here after Maxim fought them and lost. This is to be my penance. Something tells me you're going to help me even the score."

"You won't get into any trouble will you, creating the diversion?"

He smiled. "All I'll be doing is talking, but if they find you out here with that passportal, there will be hell to pay. And in case anyone asks about why you're at my house, I worked with your mother twenty years ago in Montana." He took the keys out and reached for the handle. "What's your mother's name?"

I was too frightened of detection and cramped to laugh. "Katarina Wharton, but twenty years ago she would have been Katarina Conachi." She had changed her name when she realized she was expecting me. For some reason, single mothers were discriminated against more severely than one species married to another. It was a sad fact, but bastards, such as myself, were viewed worse than children of near impossible crosses. At least with marriage, so the reasoning went, the pair was giving their union a chance. My mother, having grown up in a very strict vampire community, had known what her child would face if not protected by a name. She had changed hers and moved back to Washington to work at the Observation Post.

"That should be enough for why you'll be breaking and entering into my house." Again, that odd humor. "Good luck, Scarlett."

I followed his directions, and though I was near panic most of the time, no one came after me. I slipped back into the school the way I had come in, freezing and wet, icicles hanging from parts of my hair. It was nearly ten and most everyone was awake. I opened my door and threw my bag on the bed. Unconcernedly, I started to strip out of my wet garments. I was pulling on a cream cashmere sweater when I felt a familiar hum in my blood. I whirled, half clad, to see Marcus in my still open doorway.

"Marcus! Get out!" His blue eyes were sparking dangerously and the next thing I knew he was lifting me off the ground. His fingers were crushing my arms. "Marc, you're hurting me."

"Where were you?"

"Put me down." I winced as he strengthened his grip. "I had to get some things, please, it hurts." I whimpered. Instantly, his expression changed to concern and he placed me gently back on the ground.

"Why didn't you tell me?" He was still staring at me, and I really wished I had more clothes on.

"Haven't you even been surprised before?" Uncomfortably, I turned and grabbed my dry jeans and pulled them on. I heard his intake of breath and I didn't dare turn around, lest my own weakness be seen. Forcing myself forward, I rummaged around my closet for the other hat I knew I had hidden in there. I had packed to amuse myself for Christmas. I grabbed the other from my shopping bag. Turning, I held one out to him. "Here, I've decided to educate you in the true spirit of Christmas."

He was looking at me in a way that made me tremble to my very toes. He reluctantly broke contact from an appraisal of my body and took the proffered hat. Only when it was gone did I notice how badly my hand was shaking. I crammed my hat on my head to hide my tension.

"So what's my surprise?" he asked, voice neutral as he examined the hat as though it was going to bite.

I rolled my eyes. "If I told you if wouldn't be a surprise, now would it?"

"Then when do I get my surprise?"

My lips twitched, catching on my fangs. I was dealing with an eager child wanting to know when Christmas was. "Have you had breakfast?"

"Yeah, bet it's all cold now."

Grimacing, I put my boots on and walked towards the door. "Well, I haven't. When you're done swimming, I'll take you over."

"Over where?"

I sighed. "That's part of the surprise, Marcus. Now, go swim your thousands of laps and come get me when you're done."

"You're not going to watch?"

I just looked at him askance. "Why? You won't be doing anything I haven't already seen you do before."

"You could always swim with me," he said, moving devilishly close. In a complete turnaround from earlier, he ran gentle hands up my arms. "I'm sure you could stay afloat."

"You always know how to make me feel good about myself," I replied sarcastically. "Maybe later I'll go swimming with you just to prove I can, but right now you need to go burn off all your extra energy and I need to gather the rest of the supplies." I pushed him towards the door. "Go on, I promise I won't wander off again."

"I'd have to come after you and I don't think you'd like that."

"Do you ever get tired of protecting me? I am a big girl, believe it or not I can take care of myself."

"Not as well as I can."

"You're impossible. Now, go." I shoved him out the door and closed it behind him, fully aware that if he had wanted to he could have just broken it down. I bagged some paper, ribbon, glue, scissors and glitter. I didn't know what we could accomplish in one day, but I'd try. I also packed my jacket and gloves before going off to Marcus's room to grab his. I took my load down to the cafeteria and waited. Dinner was still a full meal, but unless you could find Mrs. Baffert early, lunch was a brown bag affair. I occupied myself cutting out intricate snowflakes, making a mess I knew Mrs. Baffert would scream at me for. Someone sat down beside me and I looked up in surprise to see Audrey, my fellow art student.

"Hey, Scarlett."

"Hey, Audrey, how's it going?"

"Oh, pretty good. I just wanted to swing by and chat. Thought you'd appreciate some feminine conversation."

I looked at her a moment before bursting out laughing. I wiped a tear from my eye. "Thanks, Audrey. It certainly has been different having only Marcus for company."

She made a face. "I know how you feel. My parents are in Argentina for the holidays and if Rex, my cousin, weren't stuck here too, for the same reason, I'd have gone crazy from the lack of company. As much as I love him, though, he just can't understand why I want to do things like read."

"I think it's a rare and yet undiscovered breed of males who would understand. Where is your cousin now?"

"Oh, he and a couple of the other students went off to play basketball. Where's your watchdog?"

"Swimming. For once, I'm kind of happy I don't have a winter sport."

"Yeah, I can relate."

"Do you want to help me decorate tomorrow? I should have enough made to do your room too."

"Sure! After all, we girls have to stick together. Do you have another pair of scissors?"

We cut all sorts of shapes in all sorts of colors and just enjoyed ourselves. Audrey was incredibly talented at cutting chains. I brought out that glue and glitter, but a loud screech stopped me.

"Not in my dining room you don't!" Mrs. Baffert was coming at us with a raised broom. "Get out and take your mess with you!"

Audrey and I scrambled to gather everything and bolted to the Group Room. When we reached its safe walls, we fell into chairs laughing.

"Oh, I knew it had to be coming, but it was worth a ruined meal or two to see her face!" She gasped in helpless mirth.

"Yeah," I agreed, "but I'm glad we didn't find out what she can do with that broom!"

Audrey winced at the thought. "We can both regenerate, right?"

"Well, even my abilities might have been tested."

We popped popcorn and put aside our artwork for a game of pool. I had simply never got the hang of foosball and we couldn't find the puck for air hockey. Neither of us was great, but it was fun.

"Was I supposed to hit that ball in?" she asked as the striped 11 ball fell into a pocket.

I frowned in consternation. "I think we've both hit in so many we can't remember who's which."

"Oh well, we'll have to write it down next time."

I was setting up for my shot when I knew we weren't alone anymore. I closed out my inner voice and shot the purple 4 in. Unfortunately, the cue ball went in with it. I straightened.

"All done Marcus?" I asked without turning. Audrey, who had taken the cue ball out and was sighting her next shot startled and looked at the doorway. She looked back at me as I was defiantly not turning around.

"Wow, I didn't even hear you come in," she said to Marcus, still looking at me.

"Hello Audrey. Are the two of you about done?"

"Well, nearly," she seemed a little flustered. I sympathized.

Finally, I turned to look at Marcus. "You can wait a little longer, can't you?"

"I want my surprise," he said with a hint of petulance.

"I'm not going to just leave Audrey," I replied. "You can just wait your turn."

I turned back to the game in time to hear Audrey's quickly hidden terrified chuckle. She forced herself to take her shot, but it bounced wide.

"I could give pointers to help speed the game up," called Marcus.

"Sometimes half the fun is in trial and error. I brought your coat down, but I forgot your boots. Maybe you'd like to go change? We'll be going outside."

He let out a resigned sigh. I let out one of my own when I knew he was gone. I sighted and sunk the 10 ball.

"How do you do that?" asked Audrey in awe.

"Do what?"

"Take control. I would be too terrified to tell him what to do. I mean, he positively radiates power. I can barely think when he's in a room, let alone speak."

I frowned after him. "He can be kind of overwhelming sometimes, but I've never seen him harm anyone who wasn't threatening—" I paused in mid-sentence, "well, me." It was a worrisome revelation and brought back Captain Mortensen's words of Marcus protecting what was his.

Audrey sighed. "Sometimes I envy you, Scarlett. The only guy who has any sort of protective inclination towards me is related."

"Just so you know, it's not all it's cracked up to be." We finished off the last two balls, the 8 had long ago gone in. "If you want to come by my room around noon or so tomorrow, we'll decorate."

Marcus had materialized in the doorway. He gathered his coat and my bag of supplies. Silently demanding, he held my coat up.

"Sounds good. Is it just the two of us?"

"Well, you're welcome to invite someone, but there really isn't anyone else left here that I know."

"Yeah, I know what you mean. Okay, I'll see you tomorrow."

I let Marcus help me into my parka, but I shoved him away when he tried to zip it up. "See you later Audrey!" I waved to her before heading off with my watchdog.

"What are we doing around noon?" he asked as we made our way outside. The teachers' bungalows were on the east side, separated from the school by a few hundred feet of blessed space.

"You are going to be swimming. Audrey and I are going to be decorating."

"What if I want to decorate?"

"Then when you're done swimming, I'll help you do your room." It belatedly occurred to me the error of my words when his eyes became hooded.

"Really?" he purred. "You usually don't come to me."

Like I needed the signs screaming danger to realize my gaff. I sighed in exasperation. "Marcus, you really need to be on your best behavior if you're going to be getting any surprises." Every word coming out of my mouth was dangerous! I gesticulated helplessly. "Look, I want you to be able to enjoy this Christmas, but I mean that in the strictest sense. I bought your Christmas present, I arranged for your surprise, but there is nothing, well, sexual, about any of it. If you can't behave, I'm going back to my room and locking the door."

He just started laughing. "You are such an easy target, Lettie, but it is fun to tease you anyway."

My eyes widened and I punched his arm. "You are such a fiend!"

He put an arm around me and ruffled my hair. "I know, but you love it." He was so exasperating, but his humor was leagues less dangerous than his lethal smile and melting purr. I punched him in the stomach for good measure.

"Just try to be civilized, okay?"

"Right, what was I thinking?" I knew we had reached Captain Mortensen's bungalow when I noticed my groceries on the porch. I was vaguely surprise to see three shrub pines. Each had a row of lights spiraling up. I had honestly expected Captain Mortensen's house to be the only one undecorated, all Scrooge like. Bending down, I pulled the key from under the second pot. Marcus was watching all of this with impassive scrutiny. I put the key in the lock, but before I could open the door, we were interrupted.

"What do you two kids think you're doing?" I turned to see one of the guards staring at us in hostility.

"Captain Mortensen said I could use his kitchen," I replied as coolly as I could.

"Kitchen, is that what you call it?"

I blushed in anger. "I don't know what you're insinuating," I replied angrily, "but you can call him if you don't believe me."

"Besides," replied Marcus with deceptive ease, "we wouldn't be admitting to using anything, kitchen or otherwise, if it were for a nefarious purpose." He had casually hunched a shoulder against the porch pillar, but I could feel the tension radiating off of him.

The pompous guard, who I recognized as the one who had nearly broken my jaw all those months ago, pulled his radio from his back pocket. "Johnson to Mortensen."

"What is it Peter?" came the crackling voice of the Captain.

"Did you allow two students the use of your house?"

"Yes, I suggested Scarlett Wharton use my kitchen. Is there a problem?" Even over the static of the radio, I could hear the Captain's disdain.

"You do realize you've allowed the use of your house to two teenagers, don't you Blake?" replied Johnson, apparently oblivious to the attitude on the other end.

"I trust Scarlett to respect my property. Now, are we done? Because this is not only none of your business Peter, but you're wasting your lunch hour."

"I'll do you the favor of checking on them, Blake."

"And I do thank you." Straight static followed and I knew Mortensen had finished.

Johnson looked at us. "Don't think I won't be checking on the two of you."

Marcus saluted at him. "Just doing your duty, right?"

I have a feeling that if we had been off of school grounds, the elf would have gone for Marcus's throat. He looked daggers at the both of us before stalking off. I watched him go, and was a bit surprised when Marcus reached past me to open the door. He didn't move back, though, just remained there, crowding me until I moved.

The bungalow was a narrow two story dwelling. The front door opened up on the living room with a bar wall separating the kitchen. Stairs ran off the right hand side leading up to the rooms above. Elves loved to broaden their minds, and the topics of the books covered anything from Astronomy to Zen gardens. I took the bags from Marcus and put them on the counter.

"So," he asked, "is this my surprise?"

"Part of it," I replied, putting my groceries away. "Today, I'm going to make the best hot chocolate you've ever tasted. Tomorrow, we'll try sugar cookies and anything else I can think of."

He was looking at me oddly.

"What?"

"You never struck me as the Suzy Homemaker type."

I pulled out matching aprons that I had snuck from the kitchens. I draped his over his head and took the crumpled elf hat out of his pocket and tugged it over his head. "I'm making an exception."

He looked amusingly ridiculous in the hat and apron. "And what do I get out of this?'

I smiled brightly. "To experience Christmas."

His expression turned sour, so I stood on tiptoe and lightly kissed his cheek. "If you are absolutely miserable, you can go amuse yourself." I turned and headed into the kitchen. I pulled a copper pan from the cupboard and put it on the stove. I gathered my ingredients and tools. Glancing back, I realized he hadn't moved. Frowning, I started phase three of my Christmas plan, my brow knit in worry. I had figured this wouldn't be easy, but I had expected an ounce of enthusiasm. Working in silence, I hummed Christmas carols to myself. Popping marshmallows on top of my creation, I brought the mugs to the table.

"Here." I pushed the cup to him.

He was looking at me with fathomless eyes. "Why are you doing this?""

"Everyone deserves to enjoy themselves sooner or later. I can't change your past, but I can work with what I've got."

He didn't touch his chocolate, but continued to stare at me. It was making me nervous.

"Aren't you at least going to try it?" I asked tentatively.

"You aren't doing this out of pity are you?" he asked in a lethal voice that set the hair on the back of my neck on edge.

"No, I'm doing this as your friend. Besides, I don't have anyone to share Christmas with this year. Maybe I want a chance to be free from judgment." He started at my words. "If I had gone back, I'd be in Romania right now, hearing my great-grandmother belittling my mother and not even acknowledging me. Believe it or not, you're not the only one with family related issues."

"I'm sorry." He seemed to struggle with the words. "I've never had anyone who cared as much as you do. At least not someone who knew what I am."

I bowed my head at the praise. "So, are you going to try the chocolate?" I was staring at my mug, so I watched as his hand covered mine. Slowly, I raised my head to meet his gaze. Humor was warming his previously impassive face.

"I've certainly never known anyone like you before, Scarlett." Removing his hand he finally took a sip. "It *is* good."

I snorted. "You sound as though you were expecting otherwise."

"Well, you aren't taking Home Ec."

"Oh, so you're saying you think Sam is a better cook than I am?"

"No, but Doug might be." He was laughing at me and I couldn't help but join along.

When we finished the hot chocolate, Marcus helped me add some paper decorations to Captain Mortensen's Scrooge-like interior. I guess his idea of a Christmas tree was the shrubs out front. I left him a mug of chocolate in the fridge, put my dishes away, and we went back to the school. Johnson was not far away. Honestly, I thought as I looked over my shoulder, didn't he have a life?

FOURTEEN

Sugar cookies followed hot chocolate. I found a few cookbooks in the Captain's library and gave them to Marcus to find something for us to try. My supplies were hardly unlimited, so we were conservative. We made decorations, took fallen pine boughs, and fashioned wreaths. Audrey and her cousin Rex joined us for the decorating of our rooms. We ended up having a snowball fight after lunch, with most of the students coming out to join us. The four fourth year were-crosses always teamed up, and though I wanted to win, I refused to be on their side. My aversion to all four of them didn't go unnoticed by Marcus, who had been "one of the guys" and helped clobber the rest of us. When they finally deemed the game over, Rex had tried calling the game over and had been torpedoed for it, I stormed away from their self congratulations. I was so furious I was shaking.

Marcus ran after me. Catching me, he grasped my arm to stop my progress.

"Come on Lettie, it's just a game."

"It is never just a game with those monsters, Marcus." I twisted away.

"Let her go, Marc!" called the ringleader, a tall blonde werecat-vampire named Jeremy Walsh. When I say Sam saved my life in our second year, I mean it. Jeremy had made it a point to torment me, and he was vicious. He would trip me, twist my arms out of their sockets, but the most memorable occasion had nearly been my death. He had grabbed me from behind and while his clique verbally abused me, he had grasped my waist in a crushing embrace and extended his full claws into my flesh. If Sam hadn't attacked, heedless of her own safety, he might have pierced a vital organ. As it was, I had to visit the infirmary every day for a month to fully heal the damage. First thing third year, he had found me and apologized profusely, saying he had changed and was remorseful of the pain he had caused. No matter what he said, I couldn't forget the blinding agony of being pierced by three inch claws. It's just not the sort of thing to forget or forgive easily.

"Scarlett, wait." Marcus caught back up with me. "Why don't you come with us?"

I looked back at Jeremy and his clique and curled my lip. "I don't like the company. It's a challenge to be civil to bullies, let alone socialize with one."

"What's wrong with them?" he asked.

"I thought you could smell Aryn's dishonesty. Can't you smell their cruelty?" They had apparently thought enough of Marcus's company to come get him. I recognized only one from that day, but those wounds were far more than skin deep.

"Come on, Marc," said Jeremy, "you and your girlfriend will have the entire evening. What with Kevin playing, we need you to make it an even three on three."

"Tell me, Jeremy, do you play fair these days?" I snapped. "Or if Kevin doesn't have enough abilities, will he be clobbered too?"

His blue eyes flashed at me. "I told you I changed Scarlett."

"Then why not play fair at such a simple thing as a snowball fight?"

"Maybe I was hoping you might have changed since our last encounter."

"Once a bully, always a bully." I spun on my heel as well as I could in the snow.

"You don't need to take your frustrations out on me. It's not my fault you don't have any abilities."

I covered the distance in one swift move. "Just because I don't have your abilities doesn't make me worthy of torment." I vaguely acknowledged everyone's surprise at my speed. I was too angry to care. "And if it weren't for my ability to heal, you would be considered a murderer."

"Scarlett—"

"Stay out of this Marcus."

"I told you I had changed. I'm sorry for what I did, but if you had no ability to regenerate, what purpose would you have had to be here?"

My fury was bordering on uncontainable. Fury was literally sparking from my finger tips. "It's sad that we hybrids, discriminated against for our tainted blood, find a new form of elitism. I'd rather be a powerless hybrid than a gifted one who abused my talent."

"It's easy to be on a high horse when you have a safety net of talented hybrids to catch your fall."

"Go on then," I taunted, "take me down a peg." I saw fear flicker in his eyes. Uneasily, his gaze shifted to Marcus. "Don't worry, Marcus will stay out of this, won't you?"

"Scarlett, let it go," said Marcus. My gaze lashed to his. "He has changed."

Anger can do funny things to people. I was usually the pacifier. I tried to bring peace, but I felt like something in me had snapped free of its restraint. "Tell me, Jeremy, what would a gentleman do if I slapped you?"

Various protests burst forth, but neither Jeremy nor I paid them any heed.

"A gentleman would take the hit," replied Jeremy, struggling for calm.

"And what would a bully do? What would you have done two years ago?"

"You wouldn't have had the courage to hit me two years ago." There it was, the straw that broke the camel's back. My hand lashed out and the fury crackling in my fingertips scorched his skin. His hand went to touch his face, and I could see him battling hard to contain himself.

Marcus had wrapped my arms behind my back and rotated me away from retaliation. Everyone was watching with bated breath to see what Jeremy's reaction would be. I savagely separated myself from Marcus, prepared to take the retaliation.

"I suppose," he forced out, working with every fiber of his being to hold his temper in check, "that I deserved that." His gaze met mine and I nodded to him. He began to turn away, and Marcus came to take me away.

"You're going to let her get away with that?" asked the were-cross I barely remembered.

Marcus's grip on me had loosened, but I could feel his rock hard body and saw his nostril's flare. Maybe Jeremy had indeed changed, but this other hybrid was becoming a threat.

"Yes," replied Jeremy. "I suppose it is natural to want some retaliation. I was a monster for what I did to you Scarlett." He rubbed his face where the mark of my hand was now fading. "Do you forgive me now?"

I nodded mutely. My anger was fast fading and a natural fear began to penetrate. Jeremy might not have struck me, but the threat was not gone.

"Come on, Jer, she can obviously handle herself. No one hits us!" The other- Austin, I finally remembered his name- moved to stand a half step in front of Jeremy. I could see the claws on his finger tips. Jeremy looked at me and I could see that he saw me as an equal for the first time since we had met.

"Leave it, Austin. Come on, maybe we can find a second year to play." He, Kevin, and the other of his posse, Cody, turned. Austin, however, was coming to me.

"Do you think it was Jeremy's idea to torment you? All of you weak hybrids are an insult to the rest of us."

Marcus was growling low, and Austin simply smiled mockingly at him.

"I suppose some men find it chivalrous to defend a weakling. I really had thought better of you, Marc."

"Like anyone should care what you think," I hissed. "People like you are the reason our species are exaggerated into monsters."

Those claws rose up to strike me as his face contracted in a horrible snarl, but Marcus released me and pushed me aside. He met Austin's blow and threw his shoulder into him, plowing the other hybrid into the ground. Jeremy, Kevin, and Cody came hurrying back. The other students, from Audrey to Bethany, a second year, also came to us.

All of us watched the tableau in horror. No one wanted to stop the fight, but if they weren't stopped soon, they were going to tear each other to pieces.

"Austin stop!" called Jeremy. All the others chimed in, calling for the two to stop, but the animal side of a were can be hard to ignore.

I've never been overly religious, but I said a prayer before going in and pulling Marcus off. They had been rolling and pummeling, and when Marcus got on the top half of the pile, I used all my strength to pull him back. The flailing slashing hands of Austin sliced my arm, but I doggedly kept at my task. Jeremy and Cody had rushed in to pull Austin away. Rex came to help me, but for all of Marcus's problems, he recognized the need to protect me even from himself.

"Man, Marc," said Jeremy, inspecting Austin. "You can do some damage."

"Isn't a good thing he likely won't live through the change," spat Austin.

Everyone went silent and still. We might, when we are young, talk in hushed voices about our chances of survival. The fact that roughly ten percent of all hybrids who reached puberty never reached majority was a conversation killer. It was simply not discussed. Sam had mentioned her fears for Maya, but she knew better than to ever discuss it in front of Maya. Everyone did, except, apparently, Austin. Every one of us was staring at Marcus to see how he bore it. His body, only moments before tense with restrained power, had gone totally slack. I kept my full body grasp of him. It seemed I was now holding him up.

"What do you mean by that?" Quietly, deadly, the words slipped from his mouth.

Even Austin knew he had overstepped his bounds. He looked indecisive and unresponsive.

"What did you mean?" Marcus enunciated every word.

"Everyone knows werewolf-werecat crosses are the least likely to complete the change," he seemed pleading, and fear covered his face. "Come on, every Immortal knows it. It's a root conflict of the species."

"I was raised among humans," replied Marcus, and I was chilled to the bone at his tone. He sounded dead.

"I thought—I just knew you would know." Austin was backpedaling so fast he was tripping over his own tongue. Jeremy and Cody mirrored the horror of the situation. I wrapped my arms tighter around Marcus.

"Marcus, it doesn't matter," I said fiercely. He pulled my arms away. I was losing him and I couldn't stop it.

"Yes it does." He didn't look at me again, but turned and went back to the school. I stood watching him, feeling as though he had taken a part of me with him.

"I'm so sorry," muttered Austin. "Can you tell him I'm sorry?"

I looked over my shoulder and glared at him. "Maybe you should think before you speak. You might want to try thinking before you act too. We were all raised with the knowledge of our possible mortality. He was not. You'll have to apologize yourself when he is ready." I raised my head and went off in search of him.

It took me the better part of the evening to find him. In fact, I had spent the rest of my day looking for Marcus, wherever he had gone. I finally found him just before dinner, sitting alone in one of the lesser used stairwells. He twitched when my scent hit him, but he made no effort to leave. I cautiously approached him and sat a stair above him.

"Marcus?" I asked tentatively, afraid to touch him, but wanting to comfort.

He leaned his head back against the wall behind him, and with closed eyes, he asked: "Is it true?" His voice was brittle yet I still dared not to touch him.

"Yes," I replied quietly. "Werewolf-werecat crosses are the most volatile to transform, but it isn't as though they never survive the change." He turned his head away from me, and I now dared to reach out. "You're strong, Marcus, if ever anyone would be able to make a difficult change it would be you."

"He never told me," he said, as though I had never spoken.

"The werewolf who took you in?"

"Lucas told me that all hybrids were in danger, but he never said how dangerous I would become."

"Enough!" I grasped his face with both my hands, having to slide down a step to do it and forced him to look at me. "Yes, children born of a werewolf and werecat mating are the most likely to have problems making the change, but look at Maya. Do you think anyone would have ever suspected that a elven-werewolf cross would come so close to dying? We are unpredictable, Marcus. There is no right or wrong, no way of knowing what we will become. You can't just sit here in misery wondering when the worst will come if it ever does."

He looked quite shocked at my words, as though I had slapped him. He tried to pull away but I wouldn't let him. I forced him to hold my gaze, refusing to allow him to descend back into the dark place he had been. He finally relaxed his taut frame, only then did I release him. His whole body began to shake with the release of his tension, and when he looked back at me, I could see just how close he had come to breaking. My heart ached in response, and I put my arms around him, trying to block away the demons all hybrids were born with.

"Doesn't it frighten you, Scarlett, not knowing what you might become?" His voice was whisper soft and I had to strain to hear it.

"Of course it does, Marc, but we all have to live with that fear, even if we are inhuman."

He laughed bitterly. "I suppose I was a fool to say what I did that first day. You were right, I was wrong."

"Well, we're all going to be wrong sometime or another. At least you can admit to it."

He laughed with a bit more humor this time, but he made no move to leave and I made no offer to release him. I closed my eyes and I could hear our breathing, hear as his steadied, and then, softly, I could hear our heartbeats. That sound awakened in me that horrible sensation I had so often around him. Still unable to release him, I had the almost overwhelming desire to bite him, but even as my conscience battle with my instincts, my baser self comforted my inhibitions, telling me it wouldn't hurt him, that it would awaken in me everything I had ever wanted. The only problem as I weakened, was that the back of his head was hardly the place to bite. I gently stroked his head, an intimacy awakened within me, and as he tilted his head back to look at me my inner voice screamed to bite. He must have seen what I felt, for he looked slightly startled, and as he pulled back, my conscience slapped me. I dropped my arms, and clambered back several steps before I could get my feet under me to stand.

"Scarlett?" He tried to reach for me, but I was already backing up the stairwell.

"I believe it's time for dinner." And without any further explanation, I ran for the cafeteria. I was half an hour early, but I certainly wasn't going back down that road.

Dinner was a tentative and awkward affair. All total, about thirty members of Hybrid High- teachers, students, and staff- had remained. Mrs. Baffert always made a lavish meal, but neither Marcus nor I could do it justice. Captain Mortensen had come to the school that night with the rest of his shift, and Mrs. Baffert was positively fawning over them, forcing triple servings on all. I just had to speak to him, but I feared leaving Marcus alone. Yes, I had trouble trusting myself around him, but he was still in a very dark place. Jeremy made the first steps towards reconciliation, and I hurried to talk to the Captain.

"Captain Mortensen?" I asked quietly, separating him from his coworkers.

"Scarlett?" He rose and came to stand beside me. "Is something wrong?"

"I know I've asked a lot of you and you hardly have a reason to grant me anymore favors, but please, I have to ask."

"What is it, Scarlett?"

"Marcus found out about a full were-cross's chance of survival today and he isn't taking it well. Could you maybe let us come over tomorrow for the whole day? If I can just keep him occupied, maybe he'll be okay."

He looked at me sympathetically. "Of course. I'll see what I can do, but you can't make him deal with this and it might be best not to force it."

I nodded my head sadly. "It's just so hard to see him so miserable and be unable to do anything."

He patted my shoulder a bit awkwardly. "Do you know what I think?" I shook my head. "I think you've yet to make any gingerbread and I still don't have a tree."

I brightened. "You want one?"

The elf's gaze moved to Marcus. "Something tells me he needs Christmas more than anyone else here. Besides, carrying a tree will help keep his mind off himself for awhile. Just remember not to push him too hard. Oh, and Scarlett? The decorations are in the attic."

I went back to Marcus, who was leaving for his room. "Marcus." He stopped and looked back at me.

"I don't really want to do anything else right now, Scarlett."

I nearly flinched at his tone, but I gamely came to him. "That's fine, Marc, just let me know you'll still be here when I get up."

He looked at me without amusement. "Where would I be going?"

"I don't know, but I need you to be here." Tentatively, I put a hand on him.

"Have more surprises?" His voice was horribly caustic.

"Maybe I just want to know something will remain constant."

"If you're that worried, you're welcome to have Ben's bed." He untangled himself from my single hand, and walked off. Furious at the dismissal, but aching with sympathy, I stormed off to my own room.

I awoke much later in the night. I had tried to study and finally give up a little before midnight. Blearily, I looked at my clock to read it was only 2:30 in the morning. I rolled over and tried to go back to sleep, but I just couldn't. Finally fed up, I put my bathrobe on over my pajamas and set off for the boys' dorms. The empty corridors were unnerving in the extreme. A nearly full moon threw eerie shadows in. Eventually, I reached Ben and Marcus's room. Cautiously, I opened the door to see Marcus sprawled on top of his sheets. I tiptoed into the room and sat down on Ben's bed. Pulling my legs up under me, I sat there for the longest time just watching him breathe.

When I was certain he would be fine, I curled up under the sheets and fell asleep.

FIFTEEN

Snuggling deeper into the pillow, I awoke slowly to the gentle stroking of my long hair. I couldn't escape the satisfied sigh before my location penetrated my sleep fogged brain. My eyes popped open to see Marcus sitting beside me. His face was back to its normal level of expression and color. He smiled crookedly when I looked at him.

"You know, I wasn't entirely serious when I suggested you sleep here, but it does save a trip." He brushed some hairs away from my face. "Thank you."

Slowly, I sat up. "I just had to know you were all right."

"Sometimes I feel like you're mothering me, but if a little mothering means you'll come to my room at night, I'll take it."

I frowned and slid out of bed. "It's nice to see you're feeling better." I gathered my robe from the ground and put it back on. "So, do you have plans or do you want to be mothered some more?"

"Just as long as you're the one mothering. What's on the itinerary?"

"We're going searching for a Christmas tree for Captain Mortensen. You get to carry it."

"All righty then. Are you going Christmas tree hunting in your pjs? Not that I mind, after all, it would fall to me to keep you warm."

I opened the door and started walking down the hall. "Whatever, go run laps or something." I belatedly considered myself incredibly lucky no one saw me as I made my way back to my room. It didn't take anything more than a few hormones to assume what I had been doing.

It was rather amusing to watch Marcus get his perfect tree. We didn't have any tools except his incredible strength, and, honestly, I had only thought we'd be going to find the tree. Marcus had other ideas. We found a cute little tree a bit gangly and looking sad amongst so many taller siblings. When I suggested it was perfect, Marcus got up right next to it. I was turning away to go back for a formulated plan, when I heard a ripping sound coming from behind me. Turning, I stared aghast at Marcus. In a few pulls he had the whole tree. He was panting with the effort, but when it was finally free, he was grinning like the complete idiot he was. My mouth was moving but nothing was coming out.

"So where to?" He was very proud of himself. My mouth continued to gape like a fish out of water.

Finally, I managed some form of speech. "To Captain Mortensen's." I continued to stare flabbergasted as he hefted the five foot tree over one shoulder. "Are you going to be okay? We could always go get help."

He didn't even break stride. "Are you telling me that when you said we were going Christmas tree hunting, you only meant looking? That was rather short sighted of you." He was setting a brisk pace and I had to run to keep up. There were a few breaks when he shifted the tree to his other shoulder, but we still made extraordinary time to the bungalow.

"Where do you want it, boss?"

"Just in front of the door for now. We don't have a stand, and I don't want to pry into the Captain's possessions."

"So what's the itinerary for today? I mean besides the Christmas tree."

I let out an exasperated sigh and turned to look at him as he leaned the tree against the porch railing. "Do you want me to give you a day to day plan? Whatever happened to being spontaneous?"

"Scarlett, you're the least spontaneous person I know. You have to have a plan for everything that you do."

"That's not true!" Even though I knew it was.

He just raised his eyebrows. "Right, well, I'll let that one slide, otherwise we could be out here all day. Are you going to open the door?"

Honestly, sometimes that boy could be the most infuriating being on Earth. With exaggerated impatience, I wrenched the door open. The decorations we had already put up, paper snowflakes, colored cut outs of all things winter, were still up, but the house still lacked the total Christmas cheer. I knew that if we had some garlands and some lights we could really make a go out of it, but I knew we were already treading into deep waters just by being there. I hardly knew Captain Mortensen, and though he had thanked me for the food we had left him, I knew that I still didn't understand him and that I had absolutely no purpose invading into his life. The cookbooks we had been using were still stacked on the far end of the bar, and I grabbed the top one and flipped to the page on gingerbread.

"All right, Marcus, for your information, today is all about gingerbread. We are going to make gingerbread men and a gingerbread house. If Captain Mortensen doesn't want it, we'll take it up to the school for the rest of the students, carefully."

"And what about tomorrow?"

"You know, Marc, I honestly don't have tomorrow planned. Sometimes I really do wait until the day of to figure out how to amuse you."

His expression deadpanned, and I knew I had just overstepped an unspoken boundary. He was tricky to talk to on a good day, but that was usually just my boundaries, it was like talking to a cobra in the last twenty-four hours. One minute he was teasing and funny, the next he was distant and cold, and just a little bit deadly.

"You don't have to amuse me Scarlett, I am quite capable of doing so myself." He rigidly turned back towards the door.

"Marcus, don't leave. If you don't want to be entertained by me, if you want to go find someone or something else to occupy your time, I understand, but I would like your company." There, enough honesty to hold him. He turned back around, a slightly broken expression hiding in his ice blue eyes.

"There is no one I'd rather be entertained by, Scarlett. If I have to bake to be with you, I will put on the apron and that ridiculous hat. But I absolutely refuse to sing along with you."

I smiled hesitantly. "Okay, deal. Now, are you ready to bake? It's such a masculine past time and all."

He grinned lopsidedly as he put his apron on. "Ah yes, right up there with embroidery."

"That's just because you've never been allowed to grill. I'll try to do something about that this summer. You'll discover just how masculine cooking can be."

"And you would know all about this how? You were raised by a single mom."

"And you were raised by wolves," I shot back cheekily. "Just so you know, I did have a boyfriend once, and I stayed with him and his family for a weekend last year. He had all his cousins over, most of them male, and they all liked to grill things. For three straight days I ate food off the grill."

"Was that the first indication you wouldn't work?" He had that dangerous hint in his voice that usually warned me off.

"Oh yes, I just couldn't bear to be with a man who could cook," I replied with heavy sarcasm.

He backed away from the mixing bowl I had brought out and held up his hands. "Then I shouldn't be learning to cook."

I just rolled my eyes. "It's a little too late for that. Maybe the moral of the story is you need to cook like a woman, show your softer side."

He looked slightly affronted. "Bah, I don't have a softer side."

Grinning wickedly, I poked his ribs. "Somewhere, deep down, there is a romantic heart just waiting to be released. Otherwise, heaven help me, but I do believe I just wasted the last six months of both our lives."

"Scarlett-" that dangerously emotional tone was back, "what do you mean by that?" I was busy grabbing the candies I had bought in Brimstone, and I didn't immediately turn back around.

"Well," I began cautiously, "I did promise to reconsider, but if you're as unfeeling as you want me to believe, as suave and debonair without a true and caring heart in there, I absolutely refuse." I brushed past him. "Now, we have a lot to do in a short amount of time, so if you would just stand back a moment, and I'll include you in a moment."

Wisely, he left it alone, which actually surprised me. He might finally be learning tact. There might be hope for him yet. For my sake, I sincerely hoped so.

While the gingerbread men baked, I had Marcus make frosting while I created packets to decorate them with made out of wax paper. It was so hard not to fall just a little bit in love with someone entirely willing to cover himself in powdered sugar in the pursuit of the perfect frosting. However, subtlety was still not his greatest gift, and frosting gingerbread men did require at least a degree of subtlety. His gingerbread men looked like beggars in white tatters with crooked features and open buttons. He did give his best for one, and it was good enough to warrant being set aside. He quickly learned that those that failed my inspection were fair game, and it was impossible to get a good cookie from him after that. I set up the platform for the gingerbread house while he gorged himself, laughing to myself, and often at him, for not only was he covered from head to toe in powdered sugar and flour, but he had frosting all over his face and hands.

"You should take a look at yourself," I said, finally unable to hold it back. "You look like you fell into a barrel of flour and forgot to dust it off."

Looking down at himself, he laughed. "You can't say I don't have some feminine sensibilities. A man's man wouldn't be caught dead covered in sugar."

"Well, a man's man would be missing out on a lot of the good things in life."

He stood and dusted some of it off, but the case was helpless. "Any better?" he asked, after he had made a white cloud to surround him.

I just burst out laughing. "Not nearly! Not only did you get nowhere on your apron, but you're covered in frosting over every other part of yourself."

He raised an inspecting hand to his face and started to rub. It succeeded in smearing the frosting to make him look like an Indian with white face paint, or a soldier trying to camouflage for the arctic.

By then, I had collapsed against the counter with tears of laughter falling from my eyes. I leaned unsteadily into one of the bar stools, but I couldn't balance my shaking body, and I crashed to the floor, still laughing.

"Scarlett? Are you okay?" He came around to look at me, my big abominable snowman.

"Oh," I gasped, "I've never been better!" He stretched out a hand to help me up. With one abrupt tug, I was careening into his powdered chest. I pulled away and inspected the damage. "Thanks," I said lightly, "I was wanting to look like you."

He smeared frosting down my nose. "I could help with that."

"You know, when I said you looked bad, I never meant I wanted to look like you. I was kind of hoping you could neaten up not mess-en up."

He just shrugged. "It's hard to take you seriously when you're just as filthy as I am, besides, I didn't fall off a bar stool."

I frowned, but the smile that burst from within was hard to control. The buzzer started to go off and saved me from any open retaliation.

Marcus had wanted an elaborate house, but I was hardly a master baker, and I insisted we start small. The one story, ordinary roofed house was a disappointment to him until he realized he got to eat the candy decorations too.

"Tell me, Marcus, if I didn't feed you, would you still be so happy?"

He looked at me, and an air of seriousness fell about him.

"You know, Lettie, you don't have to try so hard to make me like you. I would have been quite content to just spend Christmas with you, but yes, the food does help."

I paused with my tube of frosting poised over the eaves. "What makes you say that?'

He smiled softly. "Why else would you go so out of your way to see to my happiness? Honestly, I hadn't expected this year to be any different than the other seventeen."

"Maybe I wanted to enjoy my holidays, Marcus. Maybe this has nothing to do with you."

He was leaning in close to me, his nostrils flaring faintly. "Darling, you always smell guilty when you do the slightest dishonest thing."

"Maybe," I whispered, my eyelids growing heavy, "I was tired of feeling inadequate. My family hardly accepts me, but if I could make you feel accepted, then it would be a good holiday."

He gently brushed his nose against mine. "That's more like it. Do you feel accepted, Scarlett?" It was so hard to concentrate. My breathing was labored and my whole body was humming. Could I even be trusted to speak?

"Yes," I exhaled against him.

"And are you happy?" My body was straining towards him. Every ounce of me wanted what he had been offering for months.

"Yes." I closed my eyes and leaned forward. His lips touched mine in a whisper and I arched closer, wanting more, but he was setting me aside and turning towards the door. I felt bereft, as though the breath had been sucked from my body, but I was still breathing.

"Good evening, Captain," Marcus said brusquely and I just wanted to kill him. Every cell in my body was still aching for more and he was capable of speech. I was scarcely capable of breath.

"Hello Marcus, Scarlett." He closed the door behind him and came into the kitchen. "Nice tree, I suppose you'd like something to put it in?"

A cold dose of reality washed over me then. Of course Marcus could adapt quickly. I was not his first, or second for that matter. I pulled away from him and smiled at the Captain.

"Do you like it?"

"I do, but it'll have to be decorated. Why don't you two finish the house while I go get what I can find? Oh good, you made extra. Whoever taught you to cook should be canonized." He took a gingerbread man and moved up the stairs.

I picked up the tube of frosting a bit awkwardly, remembering just when I had dropped it seconds earlier. Luckily, Marcus wasn't interested in continuing, for he was sifting through the grocery bag the elf had returned. With some confusion, he pulled out three Christmas videos.

"*A Christmas Carol, Miracle on 34th St*, and *Annabelle's Wish*? Captain Mortensen hardly seems the sappy Christmas movie type."

"Generally, I'm not, Marcus," came the Captain's voice, as he descended with two boxes stacked in his arms and a tree stand dangling from his fingers. "But, in the spirit of Christmas, *sappy* Christmas movies are a must. *Annabelle's Wish* was my son's favorite."

Marcus flushed slightly. "I'm sorry, sir, I didn't mean to be rude."

The elf just raised an eyebrow. "I imagine we often say things we don't mean, Marcus. You don't have to stay and watch. I was going to suggest I heat up some TV dinners and we watch one or two, but if you'd rather not…"

"Not at all. I'll go bring the tree in." He hastily turned and hurried outside. I looked questioningly at the Captain.

"Are you trying to prove he's fallible, Captain?"

"Call me Blake, and no, that wasn't entirely the idea, but he isn't the only one who doesn't appreciate the holidays. You seem to appreciate enough for the both of you, and he needs to appreciate it all on his own."

"Do you mind the tree? Truly?" As I asked, Marcus came back in with the tree, roots and all.

"No, Scarlett, I don't mind, and it might be nice to have a change this Christmas. Now, Marcus, why don't you help me put the tree up while Scarlett finishes her house?"

Captain Mortensen's decorations were indeed sparse, but while he and Marcus quibbled over where to put the tree, I ran out for some holly berries. One of the teachers had a holly tree on the side of their house, and I carefully chose branches that wouldn't be noticed missing. We put the two meager strands of lights on our little tree, with the few ornaments left, the holly berries, and some cut out snowflakes. It wasn't going to win any awards, but it was perfect. We all stood back to admire our work.

"Well, would the two of you like to stay? You don't have to, and I'm sure Mrs. Baffert is making something much better than microwavable meals up at the school."

I smiled graciously. "I would like to stay, Captain. If you don't mind, I'll get the movies ready."

"Not at all." He glided off in that strange, effortless elven motion of his, but turned to look back at Marcus when he was in the kitchen. "And you, Marcus?"

There was a vague edge of uneasiness in Marcus's frame, but he looked at me for a second before nodding. "Of course I'll stay. After all, what is Christmas without a sappy movie or two?"

Both the Captain and I ignored his sarcasm, but I had the feeling that Marcus's comfort zone was being pushed to its limits.

Marcus and I sat on the sofa, and Blake took the armchair as we watched *A Christmas Carol*. I brought out gingerbread, sugar cookies, and milk for *Miracle on 34th St*. We were all a little too tired to get up for *Annabelle's Wish*, and sometime towards the end, Marcus fell asleep, leaning onto my shoulder. I adjusted him to where he was flat on the sofa, head resting in my lap. Unconsciously, I stroked his tired head while I finished to movie. As the credits rolled, the Captain spoke for the first time in two hours.

"He obviously cares very much about you, Scarlett. It was good of you to do this for him."

"It hasn't been too much for you has it?"

"Not at all. He's lucky to have you." His voice seemed distracted.

I gently stroked Marcus's head in my lap. "And I'm lucky to have him, but I just can't be what he wants. He means too much to ruin our friendship."

"That's most likely a very wise decision, but be careful you don't create too much distance. He needs you now more than ever. These teenage years are the most difficult, physically and emotionally. You cannot go through life alone and expect to be happy. Believe me, I speak from experience."

I hesitated to immediately respond to such an honest statement. "So, are you saying I should give in?"

"No one should tell you what to do, least of all me. You know what's best for yourself and for awhile what is best for Marcus too."

With the Captain's help, we roused Marcus and got him back to his bed. I debated staying with him, but he was far too exhausted to be any trouble, so I sought the safety of my own bed.

SIXTEEN

Christmas morning came and went. Even in my earliest years, I had been unwilling to wake up early. For me, and basically every other hybrid, it was Christmas afternoon that we looked forward to. I wrapped my robe around me and put on slippers before trotting downstairs. The cafeteria was filled with food and people. Heavenly aromas wafted my way and I could tell that Mrs. Baffert had well and truly outdone herself. I walked as though pulled by some invisible force to the food line. There were hash browns, eggs Benedict, waffles, bacon, sausage, muffins, croissants, the list went on. Inhaling deeply, I selected foods by my nose alone. There were, in case anyone was worried, two blood casseroles and nearly raw steaks as well as the beverage selection being orange juice, milk, and blood. However, I was doing my best to enjoy the meal.

I took my full plate and sat down, ready to enjoy myself. Audrey bounded over with a filled stocking in her hands.

"You'll never guess Scarlett!"

"Never guess what?"

"Oh! I'm sorry, but you just have to see the Group Room."

My lips twitched. "Audrey, I'd like to finish my breakfast."

She finally looked down at the table. "Oh, okay." She sat down beside me. "I can wait."

As I continued to eat, she started to tell me of her Christmas presents. "I realize that I must be boring you, but I just had to talk to someone and Rex isn't up yet."

I smiled over at her. "It's quite all right, Audrey. I don't mind."

"No? Oh good. Now, do you see this stocking?" She held up a green stocking that I could see her name embroidered on.

"Yes."

"There's one for everyone in the Group Room. It's as though Santa really does exist."

I had to stuff food into my face to keep from smiling. "So," I said after a great swallow, "what' in it?"

"Hmm, looks like chocolates," she pulled bags out and examined the loot. "Cookies, an apple, a chocolate orange, and gum drops." She pulled that bag closer and dropped as though burned. "Eww, those get to go to Rex."

I picked up the offending package. "Huh. Blood flavored candies. Well, I guess I'll have to save mine for Sam. You don't do blood either?"'

"No, I take after my elven dad not my werecat mother."

"How are your Christmas family dinners?"

"Oh, well, they usually manage to be civil for one evening. This year, though, they all went to Argentina to see Rex and my mutual grandparents. I'm not sure how my dad or his mom will handle that. I mean, usually, we choose a nice neutral place like a hunting lodge. And my grandfather can be a bit rough on anyone not related, same species or not. Our parents thought it'd be safest if the two of us stayed here. What about you?"

I smiled without humor. "It's just easier for me to stay here."

Audrey nodded sagely. "I think everyone's Christmases must be a bit tense. I mean, most Immortals don't like to cross species and every single one of us is a testament to what they don't like."

"It's kind of funny, isn't it?" I asked, finishing off my plate. "I mean, we are all the minority on this planet, and yet we can't accept our own kind."

Audrey looked a bit perplexed for a moment. "You know, Scarlett, maybe that's what we hybrids have been missing. We've never had a voice like Martin Luther King or Castor DeVale (the vampire leader of the first Immortal council). We need someone to speak for us." She had an odd sort of fire burning in her eyes.

"Well, it won't be me. I'm terrified of public speaking."

She shook herself slightly. "Yeah, and anyway, it would probably have to be someone with a record of achievement. I wonder where I could find one."

"Sometimes circumstances make the person," I added, still watching her from the corner of my eye. "Shall we?"

"Maybe you have some peanut brittle in you stocking I could barter for. I love peanut brittle."

I put my tray back and followed her back to the Group Room. "My mom loves blood brittle. She says it's good for her teeth."

"Eww. My aunt made it for Christmas a couple years ago. She thought it'd be a bit more popular with all those werecats, but they seem to prefer things that feel like raw meat and taste like it."

"Have you ever been told you're missing out on the finer delicacies?"

She made a face. "All the time, but I argued they're the ones missing out. You and I get to eat anything from omelets to tiramisu and enjoy it for the texture and taste. My mom eats regular food because she has to, not because she wants to."

"My mom always makes sure to have a bottle of O Positive on hand. She always has trouble traveling by mortal means. They have all these check-ins. My grandparents flew back over here one year and believe me, my great-grandmother's antics made the national news."

"How horrible! I guess that's why my extended family never travels by air. The buses are much less conspicuous. It's a lot easier to hide a cow carcass on a bus than a blood bank on an airplane."

"Can you imagine how the in-flight meals would go? 'What do you mean it's cooked all the way through? I said rare!'"

"Are you trying to tell me you don't slaughter the beast in flight?"

"Guess you flight stewardesses will have to be our main course."

"And, by the way, what's your blood type?"

We were in peals of laughter as we entered the Group Room. Everyone else already there looked up with something like confusion. Rex, Audrey's vampire-werecat cousin, unfolded from his chair and came over to us.

"Can I have your gumdrops?" he said without preamble. Audrey looked at me and rolled her eyes.

"Sure, do you have anything I want?" She rummaged around and pulled out the bargained item.

"Yeah, I've got peanut brittle in here somewhere." He stuck his head in the bag while he searched. I figured now was as good a time as any to actually get mine. Only three stockings were left: mine, Marcus's, and Austin's, who had been least in sight since that memorable snowball fight. As it was approaching one o'clock in the afternoon, I was borderline worried about the lack of appearance from Marcus. The ten other students gathered in the Group Room were busy with the contents of their stockings. Some were wagering their candy on a game of pool or foosball. Audrey had been pulled in to partner her cousin again Jeremy and Kevin in pool. Taking my stocking and Marcus's, I climbed up to his room. Feeling rather cautions, I knocked lightly. No response. I knocked a bit harder.

"Marcus? Are you in there?" I hadn't lived with a werecat-cross for three and a half years without figuring that they could, at times, sleep through Armageddon. Finally feeling that my pounding and shouting was getting me nowhere, I tried the door handle. Nothing. By now, I was furious, with rage born of fear. He was so unpredictable he could be swimming or dead on the other side of that door and his severe mood swings into melancholy frightened me away from common sense. Wait, swimming. I should check the pool. Stopping just shy of breaking his door down, I ran off for the pool.

My panic evaporated when I saw the lone figure in the swimming pool. I was shaking in relief as the adrenaline left my system. Shakily, I sat down on one of the starting blocks. It took him several laps to notice me. By then, my relief had been replaced with aggravation. Was it justified? Probably not, but no one is ever perfectly rational.

"You could have told me you would prefer to spend your Christmas morning in the pool, but no, you let me assume the worst. You unfeeling, insufferable-" He splashed me. All my righteous anger choked me of speech.

"Merry Christmas to you too, Scarlett." He dipped below the water and came up sans goggles and swim cap.

"You splashed me!" I spluttered.

He smiled and sprayed water up at me like a dolphin. "You could always join me. Surely you have other pajamas."

I crossed my hands across my chest. "Hah." He simply splashed me again. "Stop it Marcus!" I backed out of his range.

"Come on, Lettie, be spontaneous." With his powerful arm, he sent a wave that soaked my lower legs.

"If I promise to swim later, with a swimsuit, will you stop?" I was busy trotting further out of his range.

"Where's the fun in that? Come on, prove you can be just as much fun as Sam. Even Maya would join in."

"What makes you say that?"

"Maybe she already has."

I was being baited and I knew it, but damn the torpedoes, right? Defiantly, I dropped my bathrobe, the stockings, and my pj bottoms.

Standing there in my cami and underwear, I glared at him before diving in.

"Happy?" I asked when I surfaced.

"More than you could imagine." The smokiness in his voice told me just how badly I'd been had. "Do I still get a Christmas present?"

I splashed water at him. "Is it wrapped? Is it sitting on your desk? Yes, so I suppose no matter how naughty you are you still get it. I'm afraid I didn't save the receipt."

He just smiled at me. "If I had known before…"

"Marcus, you couldn't have been any naughtier if you had tried." He started towards me and I flipped back. "No! That wasn't an invitation." I flicked water at him with my feet.

"Would it work if I told you to be more fun and easygoing?" he asked with deceptive innocence.

"I'm in the pool aren't I?" I gently backstroked away from him. "So, do you have any plans for today? You have your presents to open, and I brought you a stocking. Dinner is early, at six or so, and they're going to set up a projector in the cafeteria to watch movies we can all agree on."

"Sounds like you have it all planned out."

I flipped up to see he had caught up with me. "No," I said with exaggerated patience. "I haven't penciled anything in from 2:00 to 6:00."

"Oh, so I get some say in the matter?" He was hypnotizing me again. Not only was I a mouse, I was a drowning, hypnotized mouse.

"Of course," I said with bravado I didn't feel. "It's all yours, within reason." I was treading water as he approached, but really, it would have been better if I had just let myself drown.

"Well, I could tell you any number of things I would find entertaining, but within reason? Now that narrows it down a bit."

We were now circling each other, but the terror of being trapped closed out the humming of his blood. It was so close to the surface, I could feel my blood begin to pump in rhythm to his and it was a beautiful, terrifying thing. I couldn't do that! It was like descending down to the dark side of the Force, to embrace this longing, but oh the temptation!

"Marcus, please don't," I paddled away. "I can't do this."

He didn't follow, but I knew he wanted to. "Why, Scarlett? Tell me what it is that you fear."

"I-I can't explain," I said miserably.

"Is it me?'

"No, I don't know what I would become and it terrifies me. I couldn't live with myself if I hurt you."

He laughed humorously. "You? Lettie, dear, I'm the one you should be worried about."

I had backed into the wall, figuratively as well as literally. "No, I know you would never hurt me."

He was approaching again. "Then why do you fear yourself? I would never allow any harm to come to you. I would even save you from yourself if I could."

"But I don't know what I am, no one does. And I can feel this power in me, I don't know how to control it."

"Would you let me in if you could?"

He had me pinned, but I felt no more urge to flee. "Yes," I lisped over my teeth.

Bracing one hand on the swimming pool wall, he leaned in. "If I can find away to control myself, and if you can do the same, could we finally be together?"

Swallowing hard, I met his intense gaze. "Is that what you want, Marcus?"

"More than anything."

"And you won't forget about me or go chasing after Samantha if it should take longer than you might like?"

"Scarlett, have I left you since my first week? You once asked for patience. Haven't I shown you patience?"

"And I have reconsidered, over and over again, but I need to know who I am, I need to be able to trust myself."

He laughed softly. "I'm not going anywhere."

"Neither am I." He placed his second hand on the wall, fully corralling me. Gently, he kissed me. It was the oddest thing to be kissing while totally unsecured in a large swimming pool. Just as my senses faded to only one focus, I lost my hold and bobbed underwater. I'm pretty sure I've heard of fighting cats being stopped by being doused with cold water. A chlorinated dunking did much the same thing. I came up spluttering and Marcus was holding on the wall with the whole of his right arm and rubbing his forehead.

I shook my long black hair from my face, dislodged by the sudden and unexpected movement. "Are you all right?" I asked, seeing a faint red mark in the middle of his forehead. He must have crashed into the wall when I went under. He looked at me with a wry smile on his face.

"Never better. Do I still get presents? I mean, as much as I enjoyed it, I'm sure I just overstepped about every line for good behavior you drew."

I laughed softly at him. "I can hardly blame you. Come on, though, it would be best if we got those presents opened before you do anything else." I levered myself up on the side of the pool and sloshed over to my robe. Delicately picking my stuff up with my fingers extended far from my dripping body, I padded of to the locker rooms to wash some of the chlorine out. I heard a great swoosh that heralded Marcus following me. Then, a loud banging sounded behind me. Whirling, I saw half of the remaining students coming hot on our heels. I was two leaps and a bound from safety, and I did just that. Quivering, being cold and apprehensive, I listened from the entrance of the locker room as it curved back away from the pool.

"Hey Marcus!" greeted Cody. "We're all going out to have a full out snowball war. We were hoping you and Scarlett would come out. No Austin, so full teams of six."

"Of course, I'll have to dry off first," Marcus replied with perfect equanimity. "I'll let Scarlett know."

"Tell her she's been designated one of the captains. Audrey is the other," said Rex.

I hurried and showered, using liberal amounts of the shampoo dispenser and gym towels to try and give my hair some chance. It was impossible to wash quickly. I broke into Sam's locker and pulled out her basketball jersey. Pulling my pjs on, I cinched the robe closed and went out. Marcus was leaning negligently at the opening to the lockers.

"So, up for war?" he asked, expression daring me to say I'd eavesdropped.

"No," I muttered, not up to the challenge. "It'll take hours to dry my hair."

"Do you need help?"

"First off, you'd be no help whatsoever, and two, it takes at least 30 minutes to dry with a minimum of three blow dryers going. I'm going to freeze!" He swung an arm around me and handed me my stocking.

"We can warm you up later. I, for one, would like your hot chocolate and I'm sure Captain Mortensen would like some too."

I frowned. "You just want his leftovers."

"And your hot chocolate. Dessert."

I couldn't help the laugh or the eye roll. "I'll have to bundle up for a blizzard to survive. You're my watchdog. If I look like I'm going to come down with hypothermia, take me back, okay?"

"Sure thing, Lettie. So, are you going to pick me, Captain?"

Rex, Audrey, Jeremy, Nick, Bethany, and Ty fielded one team versus Marcus, Cody, Kevin, Brian, Cassy, and me. Well, let's just say it was a lot more evenly matched. We played capture the flag, full out war, and something like Risk. Audrey and I took to directing the troops to capture the other team's captain. Cody and Cassy, a 2nd year, finally got to Audrey, but in my moment of glory, Jeremy and Rex got me. We all called a truce and went in for a much needed dinner. My hair was still wet, but it was packed under a polar fleece hat, and I had to wear that hat through dinner. Marc and I hiked over to the Captain's house and made hot chocolate. He came down with us, but he had agreed to take the night shift for a week for a struggling co-worker.

"It doesn't matter, overly much. Elves can go days without sleep."

"You won't want us disturbing you, though."

"I would appreciate some sleep, yes, but if you need anything in the evenings, you are still welcome to use the kitchen. You'll need to restock on some of the essentials, though."

"Of course. Saturday is a trip to Brimstone. I wouldn't want to abuse your generosity."

"It was hardly generosity, Scarlett. You've done more for Christmas for this house than I have as long as I've lived here. Maybe I'll ask Jordan to stay next year. I mean, if two 'cool' fourth years can amuse themselves, I'm sure a 3rd year could."

I stood up on tiptoe and kissed the stately elf's cheek. "Merry Christmas."

He looked a bit taken aback by the gesture. "Thank you Scarlett."

Marcus had been busy collecting a thermos to transport our chocolate back with us. He came up to the two of us with the air of someone who has finished.

"Merry Christmas to the both of you," said the Captain. "I do appreciate all that you've done."

"And we appreciate the opportunity," replied Marcus with the utmost civility.

The elf allowed himself a smile as he showed us to the door. "Don't be strangers."

"We won't," I assured him before following Marcus back to school.

Finally, I was able to shower with full products and a blow dryer to help me. I had switched to my full flannel pjs as opposed to the cotton pants and cami I favored. All three of the remaining girls came in and pitched in a few minutes with their blow dryers until, at last, I was completely dry. I put on my bunny slippers, gathered the presents stashed in my closet and padded off to find Marcus. He wasn't in his room, but he had shortsightedly left his presents there. Balancing even more into my arms, I went awkwardly down to the Group Room. He had reserved two stuffed chairs by the fire for us. I dropped the entire pile onto his lap and sat down across from him.

"They're not all for me," he said, bewilderment strong on his features.

"Of course not, I get something too, but you can divvy them up."

I dropped my slippers and tucked my feet up. "Go on, I've never waited this long to open my presents before."

He slowly divided the gifts, but he still seemed surprised at his stack. I paused from unwrapping Sam's gift to look at him.

"Didn't you ever get presents?" I asked softly.

"Of course," he replied sharply.

"But?"

"It's nothing."

"Fine." I went back to my gift, a framed picture of our soccer team in a soccer themed frame. Smiling at the gift, I opened the rest, deciding that if Marcus wanted conversation, he got to start it. Ben gave me a beautiful planner, as it was tradition, Maya had given me a wonderful book about how to deal with crazy Immortals. She had a copy and had loaned it to me. It was full of how to get through things like Christmas dinner with relatives who wanted to drink your blood. It was totally tongue and cheek and absolutely perfect.

Douglas's gift made me laugh out loud. It was a full length poster of *that* scene in *Gone With the Wind* with the words: 'Frankly my dear, I don't give a damn', printed at the bottom. Douglas had been the one to start the tradition of tipping me over and doing the Rhett impersonation. He and Ben had, during our second year, battled constantly over who did it better. Sam and Maya had been the judges and I had been the dummy for all the purpose I had served.

My chuckle brought Marcus's attention, but he didn't ask, so I didn't elaborate. My mom had sent gifts from my grandparents, sent early and through Immortal couriers, as they were faster and cheaper than the alternative. My grandmother had sent a delicate shawl, embroidered by her own hands. To a vampire, it would be a beautiful work of art, but please remember, that side of my family was a bit off their communal rocker. Rather than embroidered flowers, it was bats with a red background that inspired thoughts of dripping blood. My mom had selected a deep red sweater overlaid with black roses. It was beautiful, and, more importantly, something I would actually wear.

Marcus had finished his unwrapping and wore a ball cap that had to be an inside joke amongst the boys, my t-shirt, with a pullover and a collection of books on his lap. Regardless of his gifts, he was watching me as I opened my last gift, the one from him. Inside the box was tissue wrapped heaven. I pulled out a midnight blue cashmere scarf, hat and gloves. It was a sensual pleasure to touch them. I ran the scarf against my cheek and broke our silence.

"It's exquisite, Marcus."

"Does it make up for the ones I left outside?" he asked with a wry smile.

I pretended to contemplate. "Not on principal, but otherwise, yes." I dropped off my chair to look at his books. "Wow, this is quite the selection."

"Yeah, Lucas is very thorough. When I ask about something, he makes sure every answer is available."

I held up a book entitled <u>Teen Heartache: Love for the Teenage Immortal.</u> "And this is from him?"

He flushed slightly. "No, that's from Samantha. It's a joke, right?"

I flipped over to the back and read the summary. "We can hope so, otherwise I'd have to be even more embarrassed than you are."

He removed the book from my fingers and put it behind him. "There, now all I have to worry about is her asking about it."

I patted his leg. "You've got a week to come up with something. Don't look at me for suggestions, though. That is one area Sam has always been the expert." I went back to thumbing through his books. Most were rare publications about transformation. As this was Marcus's first year with Immortals, he wasn't in advanced Biology, but his need to understand apparently exceeded class room expectations. One book fascinated me with genetic distinctions. I was absorbed when I started to feel Marcus's hand on my long, unbound mane.

"I'm sorry, Lettie, about earlier. I don't like to talk about my past."

I looked up. "I *knew* that."

He gave me a small smile. "I was an orphan for nearly as long as I can remember. I might have had Christmases, but they were never genuine. They were either forced or cold. Lucas found me about a month before Christmas last year. He took me in and cared for me when my foster family had parted ways, but I always felt as though I was a self made burden for him. He never discussed it, and after awhile I stopped asking. I've been different all my life, and I knew it, but not why. I was popular in school for my looks and my jock status, but no one ever stopped to look as hard as you have."

I felt tears begin to well in my eyes. Gently, I rested my head on his knee. "Thank you," I whispered.

"Why are you thanking me?"

"It's one of the best Christmases I ever had, too." I snuggled down and let my tears flow onto his knees.

"Scarlett, why are you crying?"

"Shut up, Marcus, and let me enjoy the moment." I reached over the top of my head and placed his hand back on my head. "Sometimes happiness doesn't have to make sense." We stayed like that, each comforting and healing the other well into the night. It was so wonderful to have helped someone enjoy the spirit of the holiday season. Our happiness might be tested in days to come, but I had that one perfect moment to look back on.

SEVENTEEN

The rest of our vacation was hardly noteworthy. I finally convinced Marcus that we really needed to finish our homework before January 2nd. Nearly all 13 of us began to trek back to the library towards the end. Marcus was drug by me, Rex was drug by Audrey, and Cody brought Jeremy and Kevin who brought…well, you get the picture.

By New Year's Eve, the others had to join us just to have company. Most moaned loudly, but, in my case, I simply suggested Marcus could go do something else, but that would mean doing his homework by himself. Four days of cramming allowed for New Year's to be all ours. Rex, with sources unknown, had procured fireworks. We all gathered outside to set them off. Audrey was given the first honor. As the rocket shot off and burst into a million tiny particles of light, panic sounded from inside. Every single teacher and staff member still at Hybrid High was outside by the time we set the second firework off.

"What is going on!" screeched Miss Montgomery.

We all turned to see seven teachers and staff members gathering, none dressed for the elements.

"They're fireworks, Miss Montgomery," replied Rex with a shrug.

"Aren't fireworks banned from student grounds?" cried Mrs. Baffert.

"Hey, it's not like I'd set something off that was illegal," said Rex petulantly.

"Unfortunately," came the dry voice of Mr. Hansen, "Mr. Cabrera is correct. Setting such things off inside is prohibited, but not outside."

"What's the big deal anyway?" asked Jeremy.

All the teachers stared at him. "Are you saying none of you, not even Miss Wharton, can recognize the similarities between a firework explosion and the attacks of the shadow creatures?" demanded Miss Montgomery.

I froze, my body beginning to tingle in fear. "No," I gasped. "It hardly sounded like thunder. Honestly!" I exclaimed, recovering from my moment of fear, "They're just fireworks!" Perhaps, in my desire to recover, I overreacted…

Marcus encircled me protectively and some of my tension eased.

"How was anyone indoors supposed to know they were just fireworks?" demanded Mrs. Baffert.

We all looked around each other for an answer.

"You mean I was supposed to tell someone?" asked Rex.

Audrey hid her face in her hands, but when I looked back at the adults, I realized several were trying very hard not to smile.

"I suppose," said Mr. Hansen, "we'll have to make some additions to the rule books. For now, go ahead and finish what you have."

"But-" Mrs. Baffert protested.

"Martha, why don't you call down to our security and let them know," overrode Mr. Hansen kindly. "I'm sure Captain Mortensen saw the display."

Mrs. Baffert huffed before storming back inside. The rest of us stood around a bit awkwardly. No one wanted to get in trouble now that the line had been pushed. Audrey was still too mortified to even look at us, and Rex appeared to be having a delayed attack of conscience.

"Well, aren't you going to light them?" asked Miss Montgomery.

"Or do you need one of us to do it for you?" added Mr. Hansen, and I was now positive both were laughing on the inside. The other four remaining staff members were trading looks of repressed amusement.

I have to say Rex was quite the talented agent for borderline illegal fireworks. They were remarkable. Bright greens, reds, golds, and even a few that shot off like flowers, with a purple exterior and gold interior. We had several Roman Candles, and there were enough for everyone to shoot off two apiece. Even the teachers joined in. Growing up, my mom and I had done sparklers, and that was about it. This isn't to say I hadn't seen the displays of others, but to see and be right there with it was truly amazing, and loud, very loud.

When the last firework was lit, Rex called out "Happy New Year!" It was our curtain call. I was happy our audience had grown, for Marcus and I had yet to firmly establish any boundaries. True, since Christmas we hadn't done anything but embrace or hold hands, but, well, New Year's did have its own traditions. I tried to console Audrey when all was said and done, for she still hadn't fully recovered from her embarrassment, even if it was not for herself she had been humbled.

"Scarlett." I stopped at the sound of Mr. Hansen's voice. I went back to him even as Marcus lingered.

"Yes?"

"I realize today was about the moment, but you, especially, need to be aware of the sounds of a refractor. You cannot afford to forget."

My brow knit in confusion. "Why me in particular?"

"You have seen one in both light and human form. We both know better than to assume the worst is over, at least I hope we do." Miss Montgomery came up and forcefully took his arm.

"Do you have a death wish?" she hissed as she pulled him away. I lost his response as she savagely pulled him indoors. I stared up at the night sky, exhaling and watching the fog of my breath. Holding my hand out for support, I felt Marcus grasp mine, firm and reassuring. For his benefit, I began to think aloud.

"Refractors blend, they don't disperse like fireworks except when they collide. They sound like thunder not whistles. I can't think of anything else." Exhaling again, this time in frustration, I turned to look at him. "I worked so hard to block it out. Was that wrong?"

He moved closer and began to stroke my back. "You did what you had to," he spoke softly as though gentling a wild animal. "We were basically told to forget, Lettie. I suppose Mr. Hansen asked you about it?"

I snuggled closer, trying to block my world out. "He doesn't think my attack was the only one and he isn't the alone. I tried after the attack to find what I could, but it seems that refractors have been systematically erased from every source and I dared not ask. Mr. Hansen is still nervous about what the Board could do, and Miss Montgomery was furious he spoke at all."

"As they should be. Those members who observed our classes, every single one of them was dangerous. Do you have any idea what it's like to smell that danger and be confined into doing nothing? Right now, they control our fate."

"It doesn't seem fair. Do you even know what they're keeping out there?" I asked, gesturing towards the woods.

"Scarlett, you need to listen to me." He held me away and forced me to meet his gaze. "Those Board members control us right now. If we fight too hard, there is the Psych Ward."

I was startled from my comfort zone. "How do you know about that?"

"Everyone knows about it, even a newbie like me. And believe it or not, after your brush with school bounds, Doug told me what they did to him. If you fight the Board, they won't set a release date."

I shook him off in anger, stalking back to the school. "In case no one noticed, I have stayed on the set path. I haven't even discussed with anyone what happened. It's suffocating! What do you want from me? A promise that'll I'll behave for as long as I'm here?"

His temper was beginning to rise as well. "Yes, that would be a start."

"Well, I won't promise something I can't keep."

"Then you'll simply be making my life a little more difficult. If I have to protect you from yourself, I will."

Indignation boiled over. "You're treating me like a child! Give me the credit for some self preservation. I won't go looking for trouble, but if it comes looking for me, I'm not going to just ignore it."

He lost some of his tension. "All right, I can handle that."

"You can handle that? What responsibility is it of yours?"

"Damn it, Scarlett, you are my responsibility!" He caught me in two strides and shook me. "Don't ask me why, but you always have been, so please, just stop arguing!" I set my lips in a mutinous line. "Thank you, now come on, I'm getting cold."

I knew I was being childish, but I stayed where I was as he left. It was just so infuriating to be treated as though I had no common sense. Okay, so maybe I didn't always show the greatest use of what I did posses, but still. My petulance wasn't hurting anyone but myself though. I had finally opened up my memories to that day and being alone away from safe walls made me edgy. The lack of sound on the cold winter night frightened me almost more than being alone. My growing fear made me want to run for the Group Room and the warm fire as well as the comforting presences. I could see Marcus in the distance, waiting for me by the courtyard doors. And though I was willing to admit my folly to myself, I was not willing to admit as much to Marcus.

It was a blessed day indeed when everyone began filing back from their vacation. I was coming back from the library when I saw Sam and

Maya. They dropped their bags and ran over to greet me.

"It is so good to see you!" I cried as I hugged Maya. "How was your vacation?"

"It was nice to go home," replied Maya.

"More importantly," said Sam with meaning, "how was *your* vacation?"

I looked at her blankly. Then her meaning hit me. "It was all right."

Sam frowned. "No, really, how were your two weeks alone with Marcus?"

"We were hardly the only students here, Sam."

She pulled me into an empty classroom with Maya following. "Are you trying to tell me that you spent two whole weeks with Marcus and *nothing happened*?"

I blushed furiously. "What exactly did you think would happen?"

"Something happened," said Maya, watching me intently, "but I think not enough for you to win the bet."

I felt cornered. "Bet?" I cried, my head ping ponging between the two.

Sam, though, wasn't finished with her interrogation. "Come on, Lettie, we've been waiting for two weeks for an answer."

I looked darkly at her. "Samantha, you were with your family. I'm sure you had better things to do than wonder about me and Marcus."

Sam and Maya exchanged a look. "No, not really, so come on, if you can't tell us, who can you tell?"

"There's hardly anything to tell."

"Did he kiss you?" asked Maya in a gentler tone.

"Yes," I whispered, unable to meet their inquisitive gazes.

"Finally," breathed Sam. "What else?"

"Nothing!"

Sam looked frustrated. "Absolutely nothing? No second base, no touch feely, maybe you're missing a bra moments?"

"Sam! What are you, my mother? I didn't sleep with him if that's what you're asking." And I hadn't, at least not as Sam was thinking.

"Hah," said Maya. "I win."

Sam glowered at her. "I need to go talk to Marcus."

"You do not!" I argued. "Are you two saying you really did bet on my personal life? How could you?"

"Like you and Maya didn't bet on me," Sam replied indifferently. "As infatuated as I was with Mathias, I wasn't that oblivious."

Maya shrugged sadly. "We seem to have issues as friends. It wasn't an insult to you, Scarlett, but you and Marcus just have so much chemistry, well…" she shrugged helplessly.

I ran a hand through the loose strands of hair at the top of my head. It was horrible, but the worst part was just how close I had come to proving them right. "And to think I missed you both," I grumbled.

Both came to embrace me. "We missed you, too," said Maya.

"But I still need to have a heart to heart with Marcus."

I glared half heartedly at her. "Why?"

She patted my shoulder. "Someone has to tell him the rules."

"Sam," I said warningly, "I can handle my own problems. Besides, as much as I'm sure this will disappoint you, we haven't been on *those* terms since Christmas. We are and will remain friends."

Both looked at me oddly. "Right, you keep telling yourself that," said Sam.

"How awkward would it have to be?" I asked sharply. "In a few months none of this will matter, but dating one of your friends who all your other friends like was just too uncomfortable the last time."

Sam sobered. "It really isn't that bad."

"No? Marcus and I may have chemistry, but we're too volatile. I don't want to lose my friends again this year."

Sam looked sheepish and Maya absently patted my shoulder.

"I think it's best," soothed Maya. "You know yourself better than we do, but have some pity on Marcus. He's hopeless for you."

I shifted uncomfortably. "It's not as though I'm his only choice."

Sam dropped herself in beside me. "Lettie, I kissed him, not the other way around. And while I respect your wisdom, I should probably follow it, I just can't. And, in some ways, Marcus and I are a lot alike, so I think I need to talk to him because, honestly, let's face it, you can be difficult to understand." She bumped into me playfully. I just rolled my eyes.

"Can I trust you to be subtle?"

Maya snorted into her hand. Sam looked offended.

"Of course you can, Lettie." She glared at Maya before flouncing out. The minute the door closed behind her, Maya started laughing.

"Subtle? Sam? Hah!"

"Hey, she's going to talk to Marcus. In comparison she is very subtle."

Maya thought about this for a moment. "I'd say they're about even."

We sat there a little longer, each imaging Sam trying for subtlety.

"So," I finally said, "did you bet money or what?"

"Money," replied Maya. "But we didn't figure it out that you two would be here until we were on the bus, so we could only bet what we had. Douglas was our book keeper."

"Douglas knows?"

"No, we just asked him to hold our money until after break. He and Ben aren't due until the evening though, so I'll have to wait."

"You owe me something."

"Why? Did you come that close to temptation?" Her large eyes looked at me in renewed curiosity.

My cheeks were red, but I refused to look away and spell my own guilt. "Maybe Marcus did more than Chad, but that was simply because Chad was a gentleman."

"You know, it's horribly sad that I have to live vicariously through Sam. Even with Chad you were horribly close mouthed."

I rolled my eyes. "If I ever have a noteworthy moment, you'll be the third to know."

"Third?"

"Well, I would know, he would know."

"Ah, I got it." She hopped off the desk and waited for me to do the same. "So, there really was nothing noteworthy for two weeks?"

"Maybe, I don't know what is noteworthy in your books, so I can't say."

Maya threw her hands up in despair. "Sam's right, you are hopeless."

EIGHTEEN

It took a little getting used to having everyone back. Classes started, and, for once, I was ahead of the game. However, neither Marcus nor I seemed to know just how to react with company. He would be fine for long periods of time, and then fall into a deep depression, a place so dark only the foolish dared to enter. Ben and Douglas couldn't understand what was up, no matter how they tried, so it was up to me to find him and save him from himself.

Every once in awhile, he would pull me away from the group and just talk, speaking like a caged animal about what was bothering him. Other times, usually after grueling exercise, he was back to his normal self, and I was having a hard time deciphering his quick-silver psyche.

Unfortunately, Marcus was only one of my problems. My attentiveness in class, which had before been taken for granted, became just a little too out of place when I came back from vacation prepared. While most of my teachers simply took my dedication in stride, Miss Montgomery, my very shrewd Bloodology teacher wasn't to be so fooled. Just two days back, she stopped me as class came to an end.

"Scarlett, a moment."

I stopped in the middle of the herd as people pushed past to enjoy the rest of their day. Miss Montgomery's voice told me all too much. First Marcus and now this. When the room was emptied, I came to stand by her desk.

"Yes, Miss Montgomery?"

Her shrewd eyes measured me up. "Can you tell me why you have gone from being an average student, satisfied with B's to a student obsessed with knowing every answer?"

"Maybe I decided school was worth the extra effort." "Scarlett, I have not been teaching for over a decade to be fooled by any student. Would you care to tell me the truth?"

I closed my eyes, accepting this moment had finally come. Without looking at her, I raised my upper lip.

"Ahh. So you're abilities are beginning to manifest. Of course it is natural to want to understand so much."

"But that's the problem; I haven't manifested anything but the teeth. Sometimes, around certain hybrids, I feel the need to bite, but it is not the blood I seek. I still can't stand the taste of blood."

She pursed her lips thoughtfully. "I teach this subject because I understand how it is that the process of maturation occurs. However, I would never presume to know everything. Have you told no one else?"

"Well, I mean my friends noticed the teeth, but, no, I haven't told anyone about my urges."

"There are councilors, of which I am not one, but I could make a recommendation."

"No! It really isn't necessary. I'm not having problems accepting who I am. I just want to know what's happening."

She pursed her lips again and idly began tapping her pen against her desk. "I knew your mother when I was younger. We were neighbors for years, so I hope you will not find my next question too forward, but do you know your father?"

"No."

She nodded as if expecting this answer. "I have been teaching hybrids for eleven years. In all that time, I have never seen your combination. Even the hidden traits can be seen by trained eyes. If you don't mind, I would like to contact a friend of mine, Daphne Lennox." At my sharp intake of breath, she raised an eyebrow. "You've heard of her?"

"Who hasn't?"

She chuckled softly. "Of course. She has seen things we could only imagine. I think you might be of interest to her. There are several students in your year that might attract her interest, but you just might seal the deal."

"Why me?"

She smiled, but it was more to herself. "Don't think I am unaware of what you have been up to. Daniel Livingstone, for one."

Too disconcerted, I decided to switch topics. "Do you think she could help?"

"It certainly couldn't hurt."

I nodded. I went on to Art, but this gnawing uneasiness followed me around for days afterwards. However, with Marcus being so unpredictable, something was bound to happen to pull me away from my self analysis. Two weeks back, and I found myself being pulled brutally away from my studies and into an empty classroom. He was even darker, edgier and more dangerous than usual. The only problem was, he wasn't making a lot of sense as he grumbled, swore, and waved a piece of mail about.

"I don't understand, Marcus, you're going to have to explain it to me," I finally forced him still for a moment.

He looked up at me with such an air of savagery and hostility, for a moment I thought he might refuse. Then, all at once, his face crumpled and he looked away.

"It's a Christmas card from my last foster home. Ellie Perkins was the closest to a mother I ever had, but I ruined it."

I slipped close to him, trying to comfort by my presence alone. "How?"

He shook his head and tried to distance himself. There was an inner battle going on and he was losing.

"Marcus, what happened?" I held onto him, struggling to keep him with me. He was shaking in pain, but he finally collapsed against the wall.

"It was a little over a year ago. We were driving home from a football game. It was Johnny, her son's, birthday and she had asked permission to take us herself. There were five of us total in the car, me, Ellie, Johnny, and his friends Clark and Pete. Johnny and I got along, but we weren't really friends. I was there because Ellie insisted. I had been with them for nearly three years and she made sure I was family. It was late and we were on a back road, just five minutes from home when it happened. A drunk driver had crossed over into our lane. Ellie swerved away, but he hit us. More specifically, he hit my side. I should have died, everyone said so, but I didn't. Nearly everything was broken, but I managed to get out. The other boys had been relatively unharmed and they made sure Ellie got out. She was unconscious and severely injured. I tried to crawl away, but I passed out just off the side of the road.

"I woke up a few hours later in a hospital and though I was covered in casts and wraps, I knew there was nothing wrong with me. However, I had apparently been a dangerous patient, as I was restrained, and I was still too weak to set myself free. It took me two days to get free. The doctors wouldn't release me, but I insisted. I went home, but no one was there. I went back to the hospital, still slightly delusional. I knew I would find Ellie there, but I never expected to find her like that." His voice broke and he looked away from me. I kept my hold on him. I refused to let go.

Finally, he spoke, but he still couldn't look back at me. "She had a broken leg, arm, and she had been in a coma for 24 hours. When I found her, Kenneth, her husband, was there. The door was open and they were arguing. They were arguing about me. Kenneth kept insisting that Ellie let me go. I was obviously not normal, he insisted, wasn't I well in two days after a crash that should have killed me? Apparently, no one had come to see me because it frightened them. Ellie insisted I was a miracle, that I should be comforted not ostracized for living. I had never heard her speak so harshly to anyone, let alone her husband. I was so shocked, I missed part of the conversation, but Kenneth kept stressing that Ellie let me be cared for by a Mr. Springer, who, he insisted, could understand me. I think if she had been stronger, she would have argued longer, but he stressed her weakness in being unable to care for me." He spat out the words and my heart wrenched for his pain.

She kept saying 'I need to talk to him, I need to explain we still care.' Then someone else said there would be no need, I had been listening to the whole thing. I hadn't even realized there was someone else in the room until he spoke. And when he did, his voice sounded like echoes of cold winter nights and it sounded so familiar. When he came to the door, I saw these golden eyes, just like a wolf's. I was forced to go in, this strange creature left me no choice. Ellie looked near tears and Kenneth was crimson. She called me to her side and she was so choked up she couldn't say the words. I patted her and tried to tell her it was okay, but I know I didn't lie very well. Lucas, for that was who had come for me, took me with him that night and started my education in the ways of our kind." His voice trailed off. I had listened to him in heart wrenching silence. If I could have taken some of the pain, I would have. And even as he stopped, I couldn't yet talk from my own tears.

"Marcus, it must have been the worst moment, but it wasn't your fault. Eventually your human family would have noticed you were different. All the love in the world couldn't help you become a full Immortal."

His harsh laughter felt like someone was stroking my hair backwards.

"Especially considering what I am. At least she never had to see me become a monster."

"You are not a monster! If you are, we all are, but we can move beyond it. We are different and unpredictable, but not monsters."

He looked at me in cold amusement. "You're so easy to aggravate. I could slit your throat in three seconds and you'd be none the wiser."

My eyes flashed. "Are you trying to make your point because you're failing miserably. I am sorry for the life you have lived. God, Marc, it's a wonder you survived at all, but if you think being nasty to me is going to get you anywhere, you are dead wrong."

"Oh, am I?" His eyes were brittle and the loving boy I was beginning to know was lost in their depths. He ran a gentle hand along my throat, finally grasping it. "What's to stop me?"

"Stop it," I hissed. "This isn't you." My throat vibrated against his hand. "Don't think I haven't been threatened before. I've nearly died from such threats, but you would never hurt me. No matter what you are feeling, remember that."

His fingers flexed and suddenly he released me, throwing himself away from me. He ran shaking fingers through his hair. "What have I done?" he whispered. "Scarlett, lock me up, please."

I unfolded and came up beside him. "Are you back, Marcus?" He looked at me and I saw the broken, not volatile side. "You're not going anywhere. I won't let you leave me."

He was shaking from head to toe. He took my face in both hands, rubbing his thumbs up and down. "I couldn't live with myself if I lost you too."

I smiled reassuringly. "I'm not going anywhere. Not unless I have to go save the world."

A ghost of a smile flitted about his lips. "You really aren't frightened of me are you? Why? When I'm frightened of myself?"

"I've never felt safer than when I'm with you. Even now, you didn't hurt me. How could I fear that?"

"But I don't know my own limitations, and what's to say next time I won't hurt you?"

It was my turn to trace his face. "You should try to trust again, Marcus. It can be very comforting to know you are cared for.'"

"So you do care for me?"

"Of course I care. Jeez, sometimes your obtuseness frightens me."

"Then why won't you date me?"

"Obtuse with a one track mind," I said to myself. "When the school year is done, I'll go anywhere with you."

He sighed and I felt the tension melt away. "Four months?" he asked piteously.

"Yes, four months. You've lasted four months already. You can do it."

"It's going to be hell." He pushed me back, but before releasing me, I saw his eyes begin to sparkle with their old mischief. "Dates are classified as what in your books?"

I frowned, trying to out think him. "Well, us going somewhere alone, spending quality time together, and I'm sure you'll have some displays of affection."

He smiled wickedly. "Scarlett?"

"Yes?" I asked warily.

"We're alone."

"Yes."

"And we're spending quality time together."

"Well, may —"

"So," he interrupted, "all that's needed is a display of affection." And so saying he swept me up in a Gone With the Wind embrace and kissed me. It took me several moments to push away.

"No," I gasped. "We've had this conversation. We were just having this conversation. We can't go there."

He just raised his eyebrows. "Why? Is it your friends? Half the school thinks we're a couple anyway."

I glared at him. "You're not helping your case. As much as I cared for Chad, I couldn't bear the scrutiny. As long as you and I stay friends, I'm left alone. Yes there are always questions, but I don't feel like a fish in a bowl all the time. Sam likes the attention."

He prowled up to me again. "So, let me get this straight. As long as no one knows, we can be together?"

I threw my hands up in the air. "How would they not know?"

"I wouldn't tell," he whispered in that velvety, abandon all senses tone.

"I would," I replied.

He leaned in and brushed my lips, but pulled away. "Let me know if you change your mind." And then he just took off. He stopped and looked back at me when he reached to door. "Thank you for being there for me, Lettie, every time I need it. Just remember, I'll be there too if you ever need me." Talk about double entendres and raging hormones. Damn if I didn't need him, but no! I wasn't going to fall again. Four months, Scarlett, four months.

Of course nothing is ever easy when you're a teenager. Marcus's severe mood swings shifted to slightly less volatile waters after his outburst. We managed to find some sort of middle ground, and I even went to a few swim meets. Spring was approaching, and I took to running the trails with some of my other teammates who likewise didn't have a winter sport. Everything seemed to be going according to plan, but in high school, all that can change in a second.

I had sought solitary in the library one day after class. Sam and Doug were bickering over some forgotten moment, Maya was in the infirmary for the next few hours getting her weekly check up, and Ben and Marcus were having a very masculine battle over superiority in the pool. A small, nagging part of my brain told me that I was the object being fought over, and I could barely stand to think of it. Only three weeks until the end of winter sports and the beginning of soccer. Thank goodness. I needed an outlet for all this tension and studying just wasn't cutting it.

Frustrated, I slammed my book shut and buried my head in my folded arms. But it was so difficult. It didn't help that for all my attraction to Marcus, my logical brain told me that Ben would be a far better choice. He was caring and could be quite selfless. Marcus on the other hand, well, let's just say that selfless was hardly his better trait. I couldn't talk to Sam. She'd suggest kissing both, or sleeping with them, to decide. Maya would be too heartbroken over the idea of me even caring for Ben to answer. Furiously, I wrenched the book open, determined to finish my homework. I was three problems from the end of my Trig when I felt Marcus enter the room. He couldn't actually help me by staying away, now could he?

I looked up in frustration and exasperation. However, the sarcastic words that I had hastily prepared, died on my lips when I saw just how happy he was. He looked askance at my books.

"Come on Lettie, I have something to tell you." Single minded as ever, he began to close and gather my books into my bag.

"Marcus," I hissed. "I'm not done!"

He just sighed, stopped gathering my stuff, and merely grabbed my arm, yanking me out of the quite sanctity of the library.

"Marcus!" I drug my heels, but he was stronger than I was, and I knew that if I argued too much, he would simply throw me over his shoulder and take me anyway. After all, we're talking about the boy who uprooted an entire tree for Christmas.

When we were safely down a school room corridor, he stopped and turned to look at me with boyish enthusiasm.

"Lettie, I've just solved my problem!"

I raised an eyebrow. "What problem would that be?"

He just sighed in frustration. "Think about it, Lettie. I was able to play football and hit mortals for three years. All I had to do was control my powers, even if I did it somewhat subconsciously. I've been worried for weeks about becoming some sort of uncontrollable monster, but it's simple. All I have to do is do what I've done before!"

No one emotion came to surface at his exclamation. Was I happy for him? Absolutely, but I knew it wasn't quite as easy as it sounded.

"Marcus," I said cautiously, slowly, "what if it isn't that easy? What if your body overpowers you?"

He looked intently at me and smiled that half cocked grin that always tugged at my heartstrings. Gently, he reached out and brushed the pad of his thumb against my cheek. "Don't worry, Lettie, I'll make sure that I never fail for you. I realize it's going to be difficult, I'm not a fool, but half of doing something is believing. I can believe in myself now, and I think it will be enough."

I smiled sadly in return. "I hope it is, too, Marcus. I really do."

His expressive mouth turned down. "I'm going to do this, Lettie, and then, you and I can be something more. With no fear between us."

I stepped back as though struck. "What makes you think that is what's wrong?" I rasped.

"Isn't it?" he asked softly.

"No! I was never afraid *of* you Marcus. I am afraid *for* you. And of myself. I don't have your faith. I don't even know what I am! What if I am half shadow creature? What will *I* become? You can be safe and control yourself Marcus, I have every faith in you to do so, but I have no faith in myself!"

He grabbed me and held me to where our faces were level. "I have faith in you, Scarlett."

I closed my eyes and drifted back down to the ground, almost as though I slipped through his fingers. "It isn't enough," I whispered, as my feet touched the ground.

He growled low in frustration. "Will it ever be enough?" he asked roughly. "Or are we both just wasting our time?"

I turned my face away in pain. "I don't feel as though it's been wasted," I whispered almost to myself, but I couldn't open my eyes to look at him either. When your blood calls for someone, you can feel their presence. I felt his as he began to draw away and it hurt like hell.

"You let me know when you decide, Scarlett." His voice was formal, almost detached, and it pierced my bleeding heart still further. As I felt him leave, I collapsed to my knees, and curled up in the fetal position. There was this aching in my chest and it just wouldn't go away.

What's it like to lose your best friend? In one year, I had lost three at separate times. First Maya to her illness, then Sam to our feud, and now Marcus to a quarrel. I don't know how I got through the following weeks. They were torture, acute and soul biting. I was not by nature an unsocial person, but I found myself very, very alone before soccer season began. I would go out and run the forest trails just to feel something, if only the burning of my lungs. I made a point of dropping in on Captain Mortensen at least once a week, and Audrey and I would get covered in charcoal and pastels after art class, but nothing was right without Marcus. Funny how someone I had never known six months earlier held so much of me now. Maya quietly accompanied me to and from classes, we studied with Ben, but there was so much unspoken tension that we couldn't discuss much of anything. Ben was angry with Marcus for whatever he had done to me. Maya was heartbroken at Ben's attentiveness to me, and I was heart sick about it all.

The first day of soccer practice, I was the first on the pitch. When Coach Snow told us all to warm up, I was the first one around the field three times. I was the fastest in every practice drill, and I was beating my lazing teammates to every ball. Everyone else was still in practice mode, warming up after a long winter, but I was in game mode, as much as it was wearing me down. No one took me aside and asked what was wrong. Sam just shook her head when Jess headed my way, and the distance this created just fueled my anger. For two straight weeks I ran my butt off, literally. I was losing weight with all my exercise, and I was losing sleep. I saw sympathetic glances from all my friends, but as much as I wanted someone to gather me up and comfort me, I didn't want to be pitied, so I just kept going.

Our first game, like always, was against Brimstone. The savage part of me that had possessed my better traits, was looking forward to meeting the brunette who had been so cutting in the fall. I wasn't disappointed, but she was no longer Captain. Jess and I shook hands with Jennifer and a shorter, younger blond vampire. Jennifer smiled at me, and for a moment, I forgot my agenda and smiled back, but from there it was all business.

I was playing sweeper, and I was all over the field, but even my savage need to punish myself was kept in check by my teammates. I couldn't steal the ball from them, and that was all that kept me from killing myself. Early on, I forgot for a moment and foolishly took the ball up the field with only one goal in mind. But Jennifer took me down when I wasn't looking, so focused was I. She offered to help me up, and I took her hand without thinking. She held on a second longer, forcing me to look at her.

"You're going to kill yourself at this pace, you know," she said quietly. "As much as I admire your dedication, I'd like to see you alive for the year end championship."

I shook myself slightly and in that moment my whole world came back to me with a resounding crash. I was being selfish, and half crazed, especially if a near stranger was noticing. From that point on, I played with a modicum of intelligence.

We were tied after half, when the brunette stole a pass from Brittany to me. I spun in my tracks and bolted after her. She evaded Tina, but the sidestep took her momentum, and I came up from behind. I rammed into her and her dark eyes registered me. She slammed back into me as we both fought for control of the ball. I could hear the referee moving in behind us, and I knew the fury the elf would unleash on the both of when this was done, but I was not going to fail. I pulled myself a step in front and took the ball. I crossed it across my body with my left foot out to Corey. We were still entangled when her foot shot though my legs, and I went down hard. Her cleats had smashed into my calf and my tired, overused muscles cramped hard. I was down in a second, rolling in agony, but I refused to give in. The ball was already up towards midfield, and the referee had had to turn back, but Sylvia was still looking down at me, a sadistic smile curving her lips. That smile stirred something deep within me akin to hatred and it brought me to my feet. Her expression flickered when I stood on both feet. I had the ability to regenerate, but I was exhausted from over a month of excessive exercise as well as this game. Gamely, if a bit stupidly, I turned to head back up the field.

I must have done a decent job, because I couldn't hear Coach Snow screaming for my replacement and Sylvia's ejection. Blessedly, not ten minutes later, Jess scored what proved to be the winning goal. In twelve minutes it was all over, but as everyone gathered on our sidelines, my body hesitated at midfield before giving out. I collapsed in a heap. I rolled over to see the sun peeking out from behind the clouds and it made me smile. I could hear frantic voices around me, and I felt someone lift me before I completely passed out.

Waking up was an odd affair. I remember hearing the dim, steady whirring of machines and the soft murmurs of voices, but it was a while later before I managed to open my eyes. My eyes were sluggish to open, and I felt as though I had been asleep for months. Cautiously lifting my head, I took in the IV attached to my arm the bright white lights, the nurse at the foot of my bed and my entire soccer team in the hall. I wanted to smile, laugh a little, and tell them it was okay, but I found it hard to move. I looked to my right and saw Maya talking quietly to my mother. Wow, I must have been out of it for some time if my mother was up here. It took a full Immortal at least two hours if they ran flat out to make it from my house to my school. Groggily, I shook my head, and finally caught someone's attention. My mother was quick to come to my side.

"Scarlett, how are you feeling, darling?" Gently, my mother pushed my long black hair from my face.

"Okay, I guess," I said, my voice stiff and croaky.

She smiled down at me. "You've given us all a scare, dear. I don't believe your teammates have even gone to change since they brought you in."

"How-" my voice gave out and I had to try again. "How long have I been here?"

"Nearly six hours."

I sighed and rested my head back against the pillows. "Am I going to be okay?"

"The doctor's say you'll be fine in a couple days, with rest." She stressed the last two words and I couldn't stop the groan that escaped me.

"But school and practice."

"They will all be there when you get better. But this was brought on because you exhausted yourself." Her tone was the righteous mother, and it was comforting to hear it.

"Are you going to stay?" I asked.

"I'll be here through tomorrow night unless you want me here longer."

I looked at her and knew what went unspoken. It had been over six months since we last saw each other, and though we were back to conversing without tension on the phone, memories of our last few days together crowded to the surface. "I think I'll be okay by tomorrow, but thanks for offering." I raised my head to look around me again. "Do I have to stay here?"

"Just for observation. You should be out by tomorrow." She sighed and gently traced the curve of my cheek. "You had us all worried, Lettie. Even Immortals can push themselves to hard, and with hybrids it's a tricky science to treat you all."

Maya came and sat down at the foot of my bed. "Luckily, they seem to have had a breakthrough on our medicine in recent months. I'm living proof." She patted my foot through the covers. "Mrs. Wharton, if you'd like to go get something to eat, I'll take you down to the cafeteria. I'm sure all of Lettie's teammates want to say hi."

My mom looked at the hallway full of tired, worried faces. "Of course, that would be very nice Maya."

Sam led the charge as all thirteen of my teammates rushed in. Sam took the stop closest to me while Jess, Wendy, Lizzie, and Izzy fought for the remaining places on my bed.

"You had us worried, Scarlett," said Sam earnestly. "Even the vampires were concerned."

"You just fainted dead away," explained Jess. "No one knew what had happened. We just saw you lying dead on the field."

"Well," corrected Wendy, "not exactly dead."

"Are you feeling better?" asked Brittany.

"Yeah, I guess," I replied, finally able to speak. "I feel as though someone set me in an oven and forgot about me though."

"Well," said Sam with a sniff of aplomb, "it's your own fault. I mean when a player on the other team realizes you've gone off your rocker, it should mean something."

"Lay off, Sam," Jess rebuked. "She's obviously still out of it. We can start ribbing her when she's back on her feet."

"Yeah," added Lizzie, "give her twenty four hours of well deserved peace first."

I was still a little woozy, but it felt good for them to care. "Maybe I'll rethink staying here overnight after all. If I leave, Sam will be able to rib me with no one to play interference on the poor invalid." My lips were twitching, and everyone else was laughing at me.

They all stayed until the nurse looked in and was horrified at the stress they must have been causing. I was sad to see them all go and to hear that my visitors were now limited to two at a time. Doug and Ben were the next to come in. Whereas my teammates had stood in the hall and waited for nearly eight hours, when Doug and Ben had heard the news, they had come to see if I would live before going off to feed themselves. Coming back sated, they walked in still in uniform, as they too had played, and sat on opposite ends of the bed.

"Are you feeling better, Lettie?" asked Ben with concern pouring from him.

"Sure, it was nice to be cared for though."

Doug tapped my foot. "Like we never take care of you?"

"Well, you never bring me breakfast, lunch, or dinner in bed. You don't offer to do my assignments if I'm still feeling too weak."

He perked up. "Really? Someone offered that? Wow, can I join you in the sick room?"

Ben glared reprovingly at him, but I just smiled. "Douglas, there are other ways of getting someone to do your work for you, as you well know. I wouldn't suggest joining me here though. I mean, look around, everything is white and sterile."

He did look around, as did Ben. "I can see what you mean," Douglas said after his inspection. "How did Maya last so long here?"

"She was in the recovery ward for most of it," replied Ben. "Don't tell me you didn't notice the difference."

Douglas just rolled his eyes. "Even I'm not that obtuse, Ben. But it's all the same really. You're surrounded by four walls and you have to wait to be told you can go somewhere. How long are you in for, Scarlett?"

"Hopefully just through tomorrow. My mom said they just wanted me for observation overnight."

"They'll probably make you into a guinea pig," said Doug prosaically.

"Don't be ridiculous," snapped Ben.

"What, a young hybrid who passed out needing to be kept overnight at the least? Don't tell me you don't suspect them."

"Our physicians are hardly going to keep Scarlett here as a lab rat."

"What's to say Maya wasn't one?"

They were both glaring at each other, and Ben was quivering in anger. "Ben! Doug! Stop it! There is no need for this! I will be fine and out of here tomorrow! Why don't you both go find Sam and compare notes? Besides, my mom's back and I'm only allowed two visitors at a time now."

They both stood, looking darkly at each other. "I hope you're feeling better soon, Scarlett," said Doug, coming to hug my recumbent form.

"We'll see you tomorrow," added Ben, kissing my forehead. "Don't go anywhere."

I smiled wanly at them, waving as they departed.

My mom greeted both boys as they left before taking the chair closest to my bed and pulling a newspaper out of her bag. Her silver eyes, the only trait I had obviously inherited, met mine for a moment as she opened the paper to the crossword. "So, Scarlett, Maya tells me you've been running yourself into this exhaustion. Even the doctors noticed you had lost a healthy bit of mass. Any particular reason why, dear?" She looked intently at me even as her hand filled in a clue.

I shrugged and tried to look unconcerned. "I don't know, I just felt like running a lot lately."

She didn't immediately answer, instead choosing to fill in a few more answers. "Do you know a four letter word for cat?" She wasn't really asking me, so I didn't need to answer. It was all rhetorical.

"Puma?" I suggested anyway, just to be different.

She seemed to contemplate this. "Yes, I suppose it does work." The silence dragged on to the point of discomfort. Apparently, my mom had found a new tactic in six months away.

"Mom? Do you have any idea what I am?"

She looked up then, even setting her pen down. "I know you are half vampire, my dear. However, when I met your father, it was in daylight, and you know how my senses are nearly worthless in the daytime. Now that I think about it, he always made sure we met in the light of day. My best guess to this day is that he was an elf. I could not smell his scent, as any Immortal could smell a werewolf or a werecat, but even then there was something different."

"Could he have been a shadow creature?" I asked in a whisper.

My mother startled as though struck. "Scarlett, there have been no documented cases of escaped refractors until this year. The odds of what happened last fall are so infinitesimal, no one thought of what might happen should both generators fail. I have had to explain this to the Board of Immortals seven times now. If your father was not an elf, I simply do not know what he was, but I don't see how he could be a refractor."

I shifted uncomfortably and looked away. "Then I shouldn't have anything to worry about, right? I mean, elves and vampires are pretty stable crosses."

I could hear her sigh. "Lettie, how many times have we been over this? Every hybrid is different. I should think you will be fine, even if you never manifest any powers."

My anger sparked to the surface. "Is that all that matters? My powers? Or lack thereof? But I can do things, I can!"

She unfolded herself from the chair and came to place her hand on me. "Darling, don't work yourself up about this. I still love you no matter what. It's what I was trying to tell you all summer, but you're stubborn little self wouldn't accept it. For all I know, your father could have been human or from another planet. I am sorry, Scarlett, for your sake, that I don't know more, but I don't."

I frowned petulantly. "You don't believe me that I can do things, do you? I've done a healing bite, surely that takes some talent."

She looked startled. "When did you need to give a healing bite? Surely this school is safer than that?"

It suddenly occurred to me that I had promised not to tell anyone of my encounter with Maxim Rochester. However, pride and filial duty wanted me to speak out, to prove that I was indeed Immortal. "It was just before the outbreak of the Other Realm. Someone was hurt on the school grounds. It was nothing really." But I had said too much. Those silver eyes bore into mine.

"Scarlett, why didn't you tell me about this? And just who was this person that couldn't wait to be treated by the very skilled staff here?"

If I could rewind time, I would. Pride must go before the fall, right? "Mom, I promised I wouldn't tell anyone." I couldn't keep the whine from my voice, but it didn't do much good.

"Who was it Scarlett Amelia Wharton?"

I looked down at my folded hands. "His name is Maxim Rochester and he was going to die if I didn't help him." My words were scarce more than a whisper.

My mother's gasp was more audible than my words. "Maxim Rochester was here?" She strode away from me, and I was startled enough to look up.

"You know him?" I asked in surprise.

"Of course I know him. I went to school with him. He insisted on public schooling even though his father could well afford private tutors. He had to leave, pressure from the Board of Directors, when he came back over ten years ago. The whole thing was a bit of a fiasco. You shouldn't even speak his name around here unless you really know your audience."

"But I haven't told anyone. You're the first person, Mom, I promise."

She looked at me, and she seemed to have aged in those few moments. "Good, and we should keep it that way. I don't want my baby becoming embroiled in something so soon." I wanted to protest that I wasn't a baby, but I stopped myself. "Even so, Scarlett, you need to be especially careful. If Max has come back, he must want to expose the school for something. He always has a motive. Just stay close to your friends, and let them keep you safe."

"Mom," I said in exasperation, "I can take care of myself."

"I'm not saying you can't, dear, but the ability to heal is not a good defense and besides, four is better than one. Or is it five now?

I was furious with her attitude towards my abilities, but I still felt so powerless, in so many ways, that I let her change the subject. It was easier this way, but I vowed then and there that someday everyone who thought I was helpless would be proven wrong. I didn't know how, but I was determined.

"What do you mean?" I asked with no inflection. It would take a moment or so longer to get past my anger.

"Well, you always mentioned someone named Marcus, especially over Christmas. I was just wondering if he was the young man I've seen prowling the halls with a furious expression on his face."

I blushed. "I don't know about that. We haven't been speaking lately."

My mother's eyebrows rose. "Ah, I see." And it seemed that she did. I blushed even more as I saw what she must have.

"It doesn't signify," I muttered. "Ben, Sam, Doug, and Maya are more than enough protection for whatever is going to happen to me."

"Of course." She seemed satisfied, though, for she sat back down to her crossword.

Sam, Maya, Ben, and Douglas took turns visiting me the next day. My mother kept me company until the early evening. We had found a safe middle ground to talk around, and we parted on much better terms than we had at the beginning of the school year. Unfortunately, I was not deemed well enough to be allowed back to my room. The doctor in charge of me, a middling age elf name Dr. Spitzer, came in and examined my pulse and vitals.

"You're still not quite there, Miss Wharton. I think we'll try you on something a little stronger than this IV." He smiled with no warmth, and I was more than a little concerned when he injected me with a silvery serum. Maya and Sam were there, and Maya patted me consolingly.

"Don't worry, Lettie, that's what they give me every month."

My nose twitched and my fangs itched, but I was silent until the doctor left. "What is it, Maya?"

She crinkled her brow in concentration. "I'm not certain. It's the latest technology, that's all I know. They've been experimenting for decades on hybrids to see if we can be cured. Who knows what they've finally found."

I was suddenly tired as the medicine began to seep in. Instead of leaving, my friends settled in around me.

"Don't worry, we'll get your homework for you," said Maya.

"And we'll come by at lunch with the boys. All of them," added Sam, but their voices sounded as though they were coming from a great distance.

"Even if we have to drag Marcus here with brute force."

My eyes began to flutter. "I miss him," I whispered, not sure if the words were audible.

"He misses you too, Lettie," said Sam sympathetically. "He's just being a stubborn ass. We'll make sure he's here tomorrow."

I don't remember speaking again, but I fell asleep with a smile.

I awoke to pure darkness but a deafening scream in my veins. Sitting bolt upright, my eyes searched vainly for something to sink me into reality, but I came up with nothing. I was sweating through my hospital gown, but that was the least of my worries. My blood was screaming in pain. It felt as though something cold was invading my veins. I gasped in pain, not wanting to cry out for fear of being heard. I didn't want to have to go through that whole three ring circus again. Falling out of my bed, I crawled towards the bathroom, whimpering in pain. Using the doorway to prop myself up, I turned on the switch. As I stumbled towards the sink, I expected to see a monster staring back at me, but all I saw was my own face. I looked down at my arms, staring intently at the veins I saw there, but whatever was happening to me was internal only. I felt this need to purge myself of whatever evil was wreaking havoc on my body, but how? It was in my blood, too deep to force out of my stomach. Desperately, I looked around me, but came up empty of ideas. A flash of myself in the mirror gave me my answer. Feeling as though I had gone over to a crazy realm, I steeled myself to bite. My fangs sunk into my wrist, and the taste of my own blood was revolting to my tongue. I forced myself to bite my other wrist, dimly aware that if anyone found me, it might look like a suicide attempt. I closed my eyes, holding both wrists out over the sink, and thought only of eradicating whatever invader was in me. Slowly, my blood ran down my hands and into the sink. It seemed like an eternity before I could feel my own blood beginning to assert control. Very slowly, I opened my eyes, to see a black blood running from my puncture wounds. Frightened, I turned on the sink and ran warm water over the wounds. Eventually my teeth marks faded. Feeling weak, additionally so with such a loss of blood, I stumbled to my bed. I crawled under my covers, cold and shivering. It was much later that I finally fell back asleep.

It was late Monday morning when I awoke. I was lying on my side, away from the door, but I could hear the nurse and doctor on the far side of me.

"She's just tired, I don't see why we can't just send her back," the nurse whispered.

"Don't you understand, Mary? She is another test subject to be monitored. Her recovery is very slow by comparison to the others. This is reason enough to keep her."

"She's tired and alone. I'm sure she just wants to go back to her normal life. You have plenty of test subjects, Doctor. She was simply over exhausted."

"Even so, the medicine should have sped her recovery, not slowed it."

"Not every hybrid is the same, you always say that. Her mother won't speculate on what the father was. You cannot treat her as a known hybrid cross."

The doctor sighed heavily. "Fine, I guess you're right. When she gets up, let her know she's free to go."

I waited for them to leave before turning over, only to see Marcus dozing in the corner.

"Marcus?" I asked, somewhat dazedly. "What are you doing here?"

He startled so sharply I thought he might fall out of his chair. It took him a moment to focus. Shaking himself, he came to stand beside me. He wouldn't quite meet my eyes when he took my hand. "I was an idiot to have stayed away," he said to the bed. "And last night, I knew you were in pain, so I came to see if I could help, but you had already gone back to sleep. I guess I just stayed."

"Aren't you missing class?" I asked.

His mouth crooked up in a lopsided grin. "Since when has that ever mattered to me?" Before I could say anything, he held up his hand. "While you may have been sleeping the morning away, it isn't nearly as late as you think. The second bell hasn't rung yet."

I smiled as his eyes finally met mine. "How did you know I was in pain?"

He looked uncomfortable, and began to pace. "I don't know, exactly. I woke up last night and just knew." He stopped and looked at me. "We seem hopeless, Lettie, you and I. No matter what I do, I keep coming back to you."

I smiled with tears in my eyes. "We're certainly hopeless, I'll give you that. Marcus, can I ask a favor?"

"Anything."

"Could you go get me some clothes? I heard them say I could be released, but I'm not going anywhere in this hospital gown."

He smiled with a trace of his old humor. "Can I choose the clothes?"

"No. I want my PJ's and a sweatshirt. And my bunny slippers."

"You take all the fun out of life, Scarlett Wharton. All right, I'll be back in a flash."

"You'll have to be fast," I warned. "Wouldn't want anyone to think you were *trying* to skip class."

He just saluted to me before dashing out.

NINETEEN

It took me two weeks until I was deemed healthy enough to begin my normal activities. The doctors were truly confused at my slow progress. Regardless of their urgings, however, I absolutely refused anymore of their miracle serum. It had been disastrous the first time. I didn't want to give it a second chance. Coach Snow was still reluctant to let me practice, and I missed a full month of starting on Saturdays. It frustrated me to no end, but it was frustrating her too, for she finally pulled me aside one night after a string of two ties, one loss, and one win to demand if I was feeling better. When I assured her I was, she sighed in relief.

"Thank God. Do me a favor, Wharton, and make sure we don't lose another game. If we're lucky, we could still make the championship game."

My mom now called on Wednesdays and Sundays. From the sounds on her end, she was being worked excessively. I had asked when she had stayed with me in the hospital if all the refractors had been caught. She simply gave me *the look* and told me it was best if I didn't ask questions like that around anyone I didn't trust. I believe she was under the impression the walls had eyes and ears. Every once and awhile, my mother goes off on these Great Aunt Marta streaks where she is overly paranoid, but her track record for being paranoid with reason was pretty good. With the exception of my one slip about Mr. Rochester, I didn't err again.

Marcus and I had progressed back to being friends. It might be seen as regression, since we were no longer friends with any sort of benefit. Now that he had mastered his fear of his powers, he wasn't in any need for my comfort, and I was still testing the waters of how far I could go on my own. It was an odd sort of feeling, but I was finally beginning to be independent.

Mr. Hansen was in the middle of drawing a diagram of the plan for the D-Day invasion when his phone rang. I was too busy catching up on my notes to notice that he looked at me. Samantha gave me a nudge.

"Scarlett, Marcus, you are wanted in the medical ward." His gaze was full of questions, clearly nothing had been expected.

I jumped when he called my name. Wordlessly, I gathered my book and bag. Marcus, too, was caught off guard. Confusedly, silently, we left together. We had cleared the class rooms before either of us spoke.

"Do you?"

"No." He was tense.

We walked in through the sliding doors. Walking up to the front desk, we came to stand before a bored and manicured blond.

"Shouldn't you be in class?" she asked nasally.

"We were called to come here. Scarlett Wharton and Marcus Shepherd?"

She looked down at some papers. "End of the hallway," she pointed behind her. "Last office on your left. Do me a favor and don't get lost."

Somewhat startled by this rudeness, I was a half step behind Marcus as he followed her directions.

"Werecats," he said sourly. "They think everything is about them. No doubt we disturbed her nap."

I snorted, not knowing if he was in earnest or jest. After all, he was half werecat. He looked back over his shoulder and smiled his wolfish grin.

"Well, she certainly grooms herself."

"Vanity does seem to be a problem for werecats."

"I'm not sure Sam would appreciate our conversation."

We had approached the end of the hall. He flashed his canines again. "I'm allowed to depreciate my own kind. You might be in trouble."

We both waited outside the door before it was buzzed open from within. Within the office, machines whirred from every side. Marcus went straight where his nose led him to. Belatedly, I looked at the stranger rising from the large mahogany desk in the center of the room. This had to be Daphne Lennox. Her auburn hair was pulled back into a sleek bun. She was dressed for business in a severe black skirt and jacket accented by a blood red scarf. Trust a vampire hybrid to have a weakness for red. I mean, speaking from experience and all. Her sharp green eyes met my wandering ones.

"Scarlett Wharton, Marcus Shepherd, it is so good to finally meet you." She came around her desk to shake our hands. "I am Daphne Lennox and I have made it a point of mine to meet the both of you."

Marcus was getting his caged vibe, and I moved to make contact with him. Soothingly, I ran a hand up and down his arm.

Daphne smiled in understanding. "You see, I have traveled the world seeking understanding of hybrids. It has been my life's goal to understand how we hybrids work so that I might help save hybrids from the effects of the transformation."

Marcus's nose flared several times, seeking to pin the doctor's scent. "You sent Lucas to find me," he said after his third nostril flare.

Daphne looked momentarily surprised. I didn't imagine it happened very often.

"Yes, I had been looking for you, for I knew of you. We won't discuss how, just yet, but I was desperately searching, knowing my time was running out before I could find you safely."

Marcus shifted uncomfortably. "Okay, so that might explain why I'm here, but what about Scarlett?" He had quietly and quickly moved himself into a protective position.

Daphne didn't miss much. As I noticed Marcus's protectiveness, so did she. One finely arched eyebrow rose a little more. "You needn't worry, Mr. Shepherd. My intentions towards the both of you are the same. You see, both of you are rare hybrids. I once did a survey of hybrids and found that nearly two thirds were vampires crossed with a transformer. If elves cross, it is usually with the more docile humans. As you must know, Mr. Shepherd, a double were-cross is exceedingly rare. The genetics are simply incompatible. As for Miss Wharton, I have a hypothesis, but it is simply that. If you would come with me?" She gestured us back out of her door and back into the hallway. "There is one other or your year, a friend and a third rarity, shall we say, and I would hate to have to repeat myself."

The problem with the medical ward was that due to the sometimes violent nature of our shifts, each room was sealed to protect those outside. It was similar to walking through a psych ward. Marcus and I followed Doctor Lennox to a laboratory room. Long tables held complex equipment. Seated at one table was Maya. I was so confused I forgot to move. Marcus ran into me with a grunt. Somehow, though, his usual gruffness was missing, and he simply propelled me in to the room. It belatedly occurred to me that she must have been missing for her weekly check up and Daphne Lennox had simply kept her.

"Despite the shortness of your education, Mr. Shepherd, I trust you are far enough along in Genetic Mutation to recognize cells in the transformation state?" Marcus gave a curt nod. "Good. Now, if you and Miss Wharton would be good enough to take a seat?" She went to the table and chose two syringes. I will be needing your blood for this lesson."

I unbuttoned the cuff of my blouse and rolled up the sleeve to free my elbow. Doctor Lennox quickly and efficiently drew my blood. She then turned and took Marcus's. When she was done, I looked at Maya questioningly, but she just shook her head. She was no further than we were. Doctor Lennox moved from place to place, arranging, prodding and clicking components into place. We were so intent on watching her, none of us spoke. In a few brief moments the projector attached to her computer whirred to life, casting blood work for us to see.

"Tell, me Maya, what do you see in this picture?"

Maya had always been the brains in our group; she was smarter than everyone and studied harder than Ben. "By the configuration and blood count, I would say a vampire with alien blood in the system, indicating feeding."

"Very good." The monitor whirred until a spiraling DNA strand appeared. "And now, Scarlett?"

I looked closely at the strand. I'm not sure what human technology is like, but we had to go so far into our genetics to understand ourselves, that we were by far on the leading edge. Immortals were able to differentiate the markers that indicated werecat, werewolf, elf, and vampire DNA. For ease of understanding, each species was given an indicator color.

"I see werecat markers. The blood is a vampire-werecat hybrid."

"Correct." She switched back to the blood count screen. "Mr. Shepherd, what do you notice about this sample?"

"It's compatible. There doesn't appear to be any agitation even with the alien blood."

"And Maya, what do you see in this one?" The screen changed to show the blood cells skittering about in on one direction with some dark substance in the sample.

"It looks like an incompatible host," said Maya quietly. "But how do you manage to keep the movement? I thought only blood still contained in the body moved like that."

Daphne smiled at her, her bottom lip catching on her teeth. "I've been a hybrid scientist for nearly fifteen years, if the technology did not exist, I invented it. Now, as you all know, unlike humans and pure bloods, a hybrid's blood, besides performing life functions, must also process for the genetic differences. A werecat's blood must process for a change. A vampire's must process for a bite. For when the very essence of the body changes, the blood must make the change as well as bones and tissues. We can see the blood, observe its changes and understand where we cannot watch bones shift on this level. But a hybrid's has a problem in deciding what it's supposed to process for. It is this instability that is so catastrophic." Another genetic sequence appeared on the screen. "What sort of hybrid am I looking at now?" The markers kept shifting. It was as though the being was unstable down to its most basic element.

"Me," came Marcus's frighteningly clipped voice. "That is a full were-cross."

"Close, Mr. Shepherd, but not quite. You see, humans cannot break the DNA as we can, but this computer allows me to do many things humans cannot. This is your DNA now," the markers stopped, but there was a pattern. "What I just showed you," and the DNA sped up again, "is what your transformation, your maturity, will look like." Another screen flickered on. This one showed a third marker, neither elven nor werewolf, dominating the DNA. Maya gasped in recognition.

"What's wrong with mine?"

"Just a moment if you please, Miss Duval." A new sequence appeared, this one holding the usual strands like those we share with humans, color coded red markers, yellow, and an orange. I leaned forward, unable to believe what I was seeing. This was simply projection. The computer assigned colors as it identified Immortal markers. Red for vampires. Yellow for werecats. Blue for werewolves. White for Elves. The merging of primary colors was certainly left out of textbooks.

"This is the genetic makeup of you Genetics teacher. She is one of the few whose genes merged with no outright domination. Yours, Miss Duvall, seem to be trying the same. It is common practice to check all students three times a year for stability. I have brought the three of you here because of all the students tested; you three have the most unstable systems. There are a dozen others, scattered through the years, who I feel the need to monitor, but in Miss Duvall's case, the transformation has already begun. I am a firm believer in the cultivating of new ideas. I believe that you might be able to help yourselves. In Scarlett's and Marcus's case, their transformation is on the verge. You might bring new ideas I would never consider." Despite her closing words, the three of us were struck silent at the death knell in our instability. We all knew the ratios. No one even moved. Daphne looked at us in sympathy. "I have seen miracles in my years studying we hybrids. I have every faith that we will find a solution"

"Do you truly believe that?" asked Maya, and I could hear the brokenness in her voice. I stretched my hand across to cover hers. She had endured so much, she needed every shred of hope she could get.

"It cannot hurt at the very least. I will be in residence here off and on for the rest of your final year. I shall do everything I can to help, but for right now, I urge you to stick together. Support each other. I shall be checking on you when I have something to report. Feel free to come to me, my office door will always be open. Now, I am sorry, but I have a great deal to do and a very short time to do it in. I'll call for you again when I have something. Unless someone has an idea now?"

We all shook our heads. Slowly, I rose, feeling as though someone had just walked over my grave. I looked at Marcus and Maya to see similar expressions. Marcus was shuttered, but Maya was empty. I shouldered my bag as we prepared to leave.

"Miss Wharton, a moment more." My friends looked back at me, but I just nodded them on. I turned back and rested my bag on the table.

"Yes?"

"Miss Montgomery asked me here especially for you. Please, sit down a moment." The projector whirred to life again. A DNA strand appeared, flickering, shifting, and trying to be white and red at the same time. "Don't be mistaken, Miss Wharton, the white you see is not elven. My best hypothesis is that your father was either a shadow creature or a hybrid himself. If the prior is true, you are truly rare and extremely gifted. If the latter is true, you are the first I have ever heard of hybrid producing an offspring from another out crossing with no tie in back to the original line. I was not sure how you felt about your lineage, which is why I asked you to remain. I understand you do not know your father?"

"No, but my mother, she works at the vampire outpost on the control, doesn't see how a refractor could have escaped so long ago. She says the recent break out was a combination of nearly impossible factors."

"Yes, she is absolutely right, but did you never think that not all of the shadow creatures were captured in the Control? Indeed, the Old World is still far more lenient with their kind then we are here."

I started. Of course, it made so much sense. "My mother, she took me to work this summer, but security is so tight. Is it possible they are still hunting refractors?"

She nodded her head. "I had hoped you would see. However, it is also possible your father was a hybrid. Your body has too much to process, but it wants to make sense of the madness. I think, and this is merely a hunch, that you are the key to solving the hybrid dilemma."

"Surely not," I protested.

"I didn't say I had proof, my dear, but my hunches are rarely wrong. Now, you must be wanting to get back to your friends. I shall let you all know when I have some news for you."

TWENTY

So now, on top of everything else, Marcus, Maya, and I were expected to spend time with Daphne Lennox in her free time, which didn't always correspond with ours. There was one advantage to this, though. Because she carried so much clout, we were freed from assignments if she had need for us. I began to dream in DNA sequencing, searching my subconscious for answers, but when I would wake, all I remembered was that I could help, not how.

We ran the tables in soccer, and closed the month of April out with four wins to land us in second behind Riverdale. Brimstone sat one game behind us and Coach Snow was growing panicked. We were up to two-a-days on Tuesdays and Thursdays, and for all the damage I had done to my body in the early spring, I was worried I might suffer a relapse. Lucky for me, I had Maya in my corner, who, with the help of Marcus, forced food on me on a regular basis. If anything, I *gained* weight in the next few weeks.

The six of us had all signed up to go down to Brimstone Friday night. We watched a movie, gorged ourselves on pizza, and otherwise created havoc where ever we went. I was sitting up sometime near two in the morning, knowing I had a very important soccer game in a few hours, but still feeling queasy from the excessive amount of pizza. Impatiently, I wrapped my rubber ducky bathrobe around me, put my bunny slippers on, and went downstairs. Feeling restless, I went outside to the courtyard and sat down, watching the stars overhead. It took me some time to realize I was not alone. Someone was pacing up the length of the encasement. I was too frightened to move until I realized it was Maya.

"Maya!" I called, laughing in release. "What are you doing up so late? Was it the pizza for you too?" I went to touch her, but she didn't turn. "Maya?"

Still no response, but she had found the stairs, and was making her way out of the courtyard. "Maya?" I was beginning to grow frightened. All the hairs on the back of my neck were standing on end as I followed her. "Maya, can you hear me?" I ran to be in front of her, but she just kept walking right past me. I waited a moment, torn between the need for support and the safety of my friend. She just kept going as I stood in quandary. If I hurried, I could get Sam and be back before she did herself any harm, right? She had made her way to the soccer field and was walking out to the student boundaries at an alarming pace, and I made my decision. Sprinting after her, I found it hard to catch up. She was moving in her sleep with the speed of an Immortal. It wasn't until I could feel the electric hum of the boundary that I caught up with her. "Maya! You need to wake up!" I tried to shake her, but it had no effect. "Maya! We have to get you back inside! It's dangerous out here!" I was scared out of my wits, but Maya was possessed. She reached out a hand to the barrier and let out a giggle.

"It tickles," she said dreamily.

"Tickles? That's mega watts of electricity, get away!" I wrenched her hand away, but she shoved me away.

"With a shapeshifter's body, I should be able to make the crossing," she said in a strange voice. Before my horrified eyes, she began to shift into a wolf. Half way through the transformation, she slid one hand through the barrier. Wolf or no, I remembered quite vividly the power of that barrier. I could see the electricity building around her, and I knew her body wouldn't make it, no matter what this alter ego said. Throwing myself in front of her, I felt the enormous charge pass from me to her, and we were both thrown backwards. The aftershocks vibrated along the lines, hopefully signaling help soon. I rolled over, in total agony, and crawled towards Maya. I came upon a silver wolf, moaning low in pain. Reaching out gingerly, if foolishly, I stroked her softly. Beneath my hands, she morphed back to human form, shivering and naked. Her hazel eyes looked up into mine.

"Scarlett? Where am I? Why am I so cold?"

Too lost for words, I helped her into my robe. "You came out here, Maya, you were trying to get past the barrier."

"I was?" she asked confusedly. "Why would I want to do that? How did you come to save me?"

I smiled in pain. "I couldn't sleep. Come on, we need to get you back inside." I rose and offered my hand. She struggled to her feet, but couldn't keep her balance.

"I can't!" she cried out. "I feel so weak!" She grasped onto me in support. We were of an equal height, but she was sliding down my side, her arms just as weak as her legs.

"Well," I said, terrified, but trying for logic, "you just made a full transformation, I'm sure that can be very draining."

"I did? I was a full wolf?"

"Yes, and a very beautiful one at that, but we need to get you inside."

I struggled to carry her, for she was incapable of walking now. But keeping her talking seemed like a good idea.

"Maya, have you ever even tried a transformation?"

"No," she replied, still trying to walk, even though I supported her completely. Her feet were flailing about, and if I had been watching rather than participating, it would have been comical.

Our progress was slow, but I bit my fangs down upon my lip and kept going. In the distance I could hear help coming from all directions. The guards were alerted, and lights were on in the school. From behind, I could hear the angry demands for us to stop and turn to face the guards. From the front, I heard equally angry cries at both us and the guards. Wearily, I focused on each step forward. Maya, exhausted, had decided to start talking all on her own. "I tried once, you know, when I was sixteen. I sat alone in my room and willed myself to change into a wolf. For four hours I just sat there. I finally had to give up and go down to dinner. I figured it would just hit me, like puberty, so I haven't tried since, especially after how weak I became last year. I don't ever want to be an invalid again, Scarlett." She still was flailing and we were being caught by both fronts. "Promise me, Scarlett. Promise me they won't make me an invalid."

I looked into her frightened, earnest eyes. "I can't promise, Maya, they have to do what is best for you."

"Then come and break me out. You'll find a way, just promise that."

"I promise I'll find a way to save you, Maya, if it's the only thing of consequence I ever do."

"Oh good." Whereupon she promptly passed out.

There were so many raised voices, I couldn't immediately distinguish what was being shouted at me. Principal Daniels was there, as was Miss Montgomery and a handful of the school staff, two guards I didn't know by name, and, thankfully, Captain Mortensen. While they all shouted for an answer, I sagged with my burden, who was waking up again.

"Silence!" called Captain Mortensen in a commanding voice. Remarkably, everyone listened. "Thank you. Now I'm certain Scarlett has an explanation, and before we can demand that, her companion looks in need of medical attention."

"Oh no, Officer, I'm just fine," said Maya in that dreamy voice that said she wasn't all there.

"We'll see about that. Lincoln, Magruder, carry the poor girl to the infirmary." I followed behind the two guards who now carried Maya. Everyone else seemed to take it that we would all follow Maya. As we grew closer to the school, I realized Marcus had joined our escort. I looked up, startled, as he fell in step beside me, flanking my left as Captain Mortensen flanked my right. I had this sinking feeling I was being led to the guillotine.

The staff of the infirmary took Maya from the guards, but refused the rest of us entry. Several seconds passed by before I came to acknowledge all the expectant faces. My entire store of bravery had been exhausted, and I took several steps back until I could feel my friends' protection.

"Well, Scarlett?" asked Principal Daniels.

"She was sleep walking," I said weakly. "I tried to stop her several times, but she just wouldn't wake up. When she got to the electrical boundary, she said that with a shape shifter's body she could pass through. I finally pulled her away as we were both electrocuted."

The staff exchanged expressions of veiled fear. "Anne, if you could please go close down all outside communications? Martha, if you could make sure no one is awake in the dorms. If they are, please feed them some cookies and milk and send them back to bed. I trust that all of you know what this could mean. If the Board of Directors hears of this, they will descend upon us again, in mass. Captain Mortensen, I trust you and your men will keep quiet?"

"Of course, Jack. We have no more desire to deal with those deadly bureaucrats than you do, but I suggest that to corral this, you need to look no further than these walls."

I looked confusedly between everyone. "I don't get it. What just happened?"

Principal Daniels looked at me with pity. "Scarlett, I know you have grown tired of hearing this, but it is in your best interest if no one explains things right about now. No one," he stressed, flicking his gaze to Mortensen. "Two visits in one year by the Board would be unpleasant for everyone. We have had students try to cross the boundaries, but I believe Maya is the first to do so while sleep walking. It is possibly a side effect to her medication or her natural shift. Has she been known to sleep walk before?"

"I don't believe so," I replied, still dazed. I shook my head a little, only to realize that the entire staff had left to attend some sort of duty. Only Principal Daniels, Mortensen, Marcus, and I remained.

"How did you find her?" asked Marcus. "She isn't your roommate."

I frowned at him. "I couldn't sleep."

"It doesn't matter," said the Captain comfortingly. "You were able to save her. Would a body in transformation be able to pass the barrier?" he asked, looking back at my principal.

"I don't know," he replied. "Before the strengthening of our boarders, it might have been possible. Now? There's enough power running through that field to light an entire city. I don't see how anything could survive a full passage." He looked back at me. "It is a miracle you were not seriously injured, Scarlett."

"Perhaps you should be checked out, just in case?" suggest Mortensen.

"No!" I moved away from them. "I've spent enough time being poked and prodded this year. I'll be fine, and I have a game in a few hours."

"Well, if you're certain, then I suggest you'd best be getting to sleep. I know I have my staff's full discretion. I trust I have yours as well?"

"Of course you do, Principal," said Marcus smoothly. "I'll take her back and if anyone asks questions, we'll be discreet."

"Thank you, Marcus. Good night to the both of you. Oh, and Scarlett?" Marcus had steered me away, and I had to turn back to see him. "Good luck tomorrow."

When we were out of the Infirmary, I groused. "Is anyone ever going to tell me anything?"

Marcus just rubbed my shoulders as we walked. "Someday they'll view us as adults. By then, we'll have nearly been killed no less than fifty times, but in their minds they are protecting us, and if it means no one from the Board shows up tomorrow, I'm all for it." He tightened his hold on me. "They are dangerous, Scarlett, don't forget that."

"How can I?" I asked, rolling my eyes. "You never let me forget. Besides, you'll be here to protect me, won't you? You're always there, and it's rather spooky."

He snorted. "You think it's odd? How do you think I feel?"

I sighed and relaxed my head into his shoulder. "Thank you, Marcus, for being there when I need you."

"Don't mention it." We had reached our respective paths. "Get some sleep, Lettie, you girls lost to Wolfhaven last month. You'll need to make a difference." Chastely, he kissed my forehead before heading off to his own room. Sighing, I trudged up to mine and collapsed on my bed, falling asleep as my head touched the pillow.

Lucky for me it was a home game. Sam didn't even get up until nine, so I was granted over five hours of exhausted sleep. She shook me awake at nine thirty.

"Jeez, Lettie, you look like you stuck your finger in an electrical socket."

I was still exhausted, and all I could manage in response was to raise a hand to feel my fried hair. "What's it like outside?" I asked groggily.

"Raining," Sam replied, sorting through her various piles of clothing until she found her uniform.

Sighing, I pulled myself upright, legs swinging over the side as I did so. "When was the last time we played a game in the sun?"

"I believe a full sun game, no clouds would have to be last September. Come on, griping won't help you. We need to eat something. Man, I feel hung-over."

I rubbed my forehead. "Tell me about it. We didn't do anything we weren't supposed to last night did we?"

"Nah, I've tried the waiters at Hellfire Pizzeria before. They know how old we are and they won't budge."

The revelation that she had tried was a bit much for my pounding skull. Stumbling up, I padded over to where we kept our pain pills.

"What did you do last night?" asked Sam in shock. "Not only do you look like something that was fried, but you are covered in grass stains."

I looked down at myself. "It doesn't matter," I muttered.

"You didn't sneak out last night did you?" She was looking at me with eager enthusiasm. "I didn't think you had it in you!"

"I couldn't sleep last night, and something happened. Can we please just leave it at that?"

Sam's lips curved into a conspiratorial smile. "Of course I can keep a secret."

It wasn't worth my energy to try to convince her away from her own beliefs. It also wasn't worth my time to wash all three feet of my hair. It must have been some shock to make all of it stand on end. Well, I recollected, it certainly was a powerful shock. Pulling my uniform from the drawer I always kept it in, I was quickly dressed. Sighing, I took an entire bag of hair products with me down to the bathroom. First the de-tangler, then the de-frizzer, and, well, I'm sure no one needs to know just how much product went into my hair. When I was done, my hair was shellacked into a tight braid, my teeth were brushed, and I still looked half dead. Grumbling to myself, I went down for breakfast. Curiously enough, I was starving. I piled my plate high with something of everything before taking my seat next to Sam and Jess.

"Where's Maya?" asked Sam in between mouthfuls.

I swallowed hard and nearly started choking. Helpfully, Jess patted my back. "She wasn't feeling well last night. She's back in the infirmary," I finally managed.

"That's horrible! This could be our last game of the season!"

"Don't say that, Sam," rebuked Jess. "We are going to win and we are going to be playing in the title game in two weeks. Optimism!"

The rest of the team gathered around us gave little huzzahs. Sam just rolled her eyes. "Which is why you and Scarlett are team captains, Jess, and not me."

"Well, that and my sparkling personality."

There were a couple of giggles, but we all loved Jess and in comparison to Sam, she did have a sparkling personality.

"Well, for four of us, this is our last regular season game, and speaking personally, we had better win. I don't want to end my last year on a third place finish."

"Me neither," I added. "So, our pep talk before Coach Snow gets us, would be that if we don't win, all of us fourth years will hunt the rest of you down and haunt you for ruining our last year." I smiled sweetly, and only Corey looked worried.

"And believe me, after being haunted in years past, we have some pretty creative punishments," added Sam wickedly.

Sarah, always the quiet one, just snorted into her oatmeal. "Sarah," I whispered across the table in a fake conspiratorial tone, "you're going to give us away."

She just looked up at me and I could see her lips twitching. It took another few seconds for her control to slip. She was laughing outright. "I'm so sorry, Scarlett, I just can't help it! You sounded just like Megan last year!"

"She's right," chimed in Wendy, "Megan and Sash had the same speech as the two of you. Except they did it at night, with sound effects and gruesome details."

"Yeah, but they only took what Lucy and Lara said the year before," added Izzy.

"Who only took what Joanna and Abby said the year before that," I finished with a roll of my eyes. "Hey, it's tradition, so shoot us for following it. Besides, you'll have to continue in our footsteps. Maybe you should actually do some of the threats early in the year. Jess and I contemplated it, but we're just too soft hearted."

There were several snorts to this. I tried to look affronted, but failed miserably. We were in a good mood when Coach Snow found us. "Are you ready?" she asked.

As one we rose, gathered our gear and headed off for what would be my last trip to the locker room.

I wish I could say that the game was intense, and full of suspense. In reality, it was wet, sloppy, and might as well have been over in the first half. Sam, Jess, and Sarah all scored a goal in the first half. Brittany and I scored in the second for a resounding 5-2 victory. In celebration, we all slid down in the mud that lined the center of the pitch. The werewolves were quick to leave, and we were out there for nearly an hour. We had done it! A championship game in two weeks! We all celebrated, getting so filthy our uniforms would take six hours to clean. One mass of brown, dripping hybrids finally worked its way back to the lockers. It felt so divine to take a shower. As much fun as the mud had been, I was freezing and filthy. When I was clean and dressed in my sweats, I went to find my hair dryer. My entire team came with me. It was quite the sight to see thirteen girls blow-drying my hair. It turned out to be just as much fun as the mud had been.

"You know, Scarlett," said Wendy as they all took turns playing with my dried mane. "If it hadn't been for you, we might not have made it to the championships game. We were really suffering there without you."

I blushed and denied her praise.

"No really," said Brittany, coming to braid a section of hair. "You are our captain, and we play better with you around. I don't know how we're going to manage next year without you and Jess and Sam and Sarah and Iz and Liz."

Sarah pushed on Brittany. "The same as we always have. You find a new Captain and you find a way to win, or Coach Snow manically works you to exhaustion. And besides, we still have to play in the title game. We haven't won anything yet."

"You are such a spoilsport, Sarah," said Sam. "So, what's next for us? Are we all going down to Brimstone for celebration or are we just going to go raid the kitchen?"

There was some discussion, but Jess finally made the choice. "Kitchens. We were all down at Brimstone yesterday, and I'm not sure we can find anyone to take us. Besides, I know where Mrs. Baffert keeps the popcorn."

We converged upon the kitchens. Taking with us bags of popcorn, cookies, juice boxes, and anything that looked good. Girls on a diet? Hah! We were on a junk food binge that we might regret tomorrow, but most definitely not tonight.

We all converged on the Group Room, but with no TV, we had to amuse ourselves some more. We played charades, pool, foosball, anything that struck our fancy. Sometime during this all, the room had filled with other hybrids, so we all gathered close to the fire and concluded with a final game of charades. In the midst of all this fun and excitement, I fell asleep in one of the overstuffed chairs, grateful that the last twenty four hours were finally over.

I awoke some time later in my own room. Looking up, I realized Sam was with me and sound asleep. Rolling back over, I too slept the morning away.

"Come on Scarlett, we need to go see Maya," Sam was shaking me awake. "The boys already went to see her yesterday to tell her about the game, but she needs to hear it from us."

When I didn't move fast enough for her, she started throwing clothes at me. "Give off Sam, what time is it?"

"It's one o'clock in the afternoon, now get out of bed you lazy bum."

Faced with no choice, I wearily got dressed in the clothes she had thrown at me. I insisted on my bunny slippers though. I followed her through the hall and down the stairs. The cafeteria was full of food smells, but my stomach recoiled. I did manage to get some hot chocolate as Sam pulled me along, and I basked in the warmth it provided. When we entered the infirmary, the nurse looked coldly at me.

"No outside food or beverage." She pointed one manicured finger at the trash can. Reluctantly, I deposited my ambrosia and trekked after Sam, who clearly knew where we were going.

Maya was back in her old room, looking tired and terribly unhappy, despite the fact that Douglas and Marcus were there. I couldn't help the jaw cracking yawn that escaped me and I curled up next to Maya on the bed, pushing Marcus off in the process. She gently patted my head.

"Did Sam make you get up?" she asked quietly.

I nodded into the blankets.

"You poor thing," she said sympathetically. "I know how much I've wanted to sleep lately. You can certainly relate."

We had a rapt audience, but no one was speaking up.

"So," said Douglas slowly, "what exactly happened?"

I looked up at him, only to see speculative expressions on his and Sam's faces. I turned to look back at Maya, waiting to follow her cue.

"Like I told you, Doug, my medication is no longer working. Scarlett happened to find me and bring me here. There is no great conspiracy."

Sam was looking quite intently at me. "You mean when you came back looking like you'd been hit by a cyclone, you hadn't been out with Marcus?"

Trust Sam to ask the single most embarrassing question imaginable. I buried my face in Maya's shoulder and laughed helplessly. "No!" I answered, still muffled by Maya.

"Don't tell me, Samantha, that you have been under the impression I would take advantage of Scarlett," said Marcus in his silky smooth voice.

Sam just shrugged. "Come on, now, we're not children. You would hardly have been taking advantage. Too bad, though, I was really proud of you Scarlett."

"She saved me!" defended Maya. "That is more than enough reason to be proud of her!"

I was laughing and crying in helplessness. It was so comical and yet so painful at the same time.

"It's all right Maya, I'm not offended. Sam, I'm sorry to have disappointed you." I looked across at her and she seemed slightly mollified.

"Well," she said, as though this was of great import, "I had hoped you were beginning to live on the edge. I'll forgive you for being as boring as ever."

Everyone looked at Sam incredulously.

"You're serious, aren't you?" asked Marcus, slightly stunned.

Sam looked at him with heavy lidded eyes. "Marcus, some of us have different priorities."

"Well," said Doug, "we certainly know what yours are."

She turned to look at him. "It's never bothered you before, Doug."

"It doesn't still, but congrats to Scarlett for saving Maya."

With that, the conversation shifted back out of such treacherous waters. Ben joined us shortly after, and we passed away the afternoon before going back to our own rooms.

TWENTY-ONE

It was rather heartbreaking to go back to school without Maya. We all went back to our original plan and studied with her every evening. It hurt so much to see her there, knowing how she hated it, and not knowing how to get her out. I studied more than I had all year, desperately trying to find a way to cure her.

My studies had some effect on our sessions with Daphne. However, it seemed that every idea I had came up with failure. As much as I was beginning to like Daphne Lennox, the constant lack of successful ideas was wearing me down.

Again, my escape was through soccer. I could forget that one of my best friends just might be dying as we all tried to win ourselves a championship. There was an unprecedented amount of fourth years on the team that year, six in total, and we were all desperate to win. In my three years, we had won once, lost the championship game and missed out on the championship by one game. It was now or never.

The boys, having won their championship, were a bit more relaxed, and they couldn't keep from teasing us mercilessly about our dedication. Marcus was alone in leaving us be. He had joined some of his teammates from swimming on the baseball team. Again, I was astounded at his choice of sport. I realize I will offend a great many people, but baseball was so *boring*.

However, it seems that the lack of excitement I found in baseball worked in my favor. I was able to secure Maya a pass out of the infirmary to come watch one of the last baseball games. It had taken even more work than I had foreseen, though, for Coach Snow, also desperate for a championship as she was every year, had moved us up to two-a-days all week. I had gathered the entire soccer team together and asked them how we could get Maya out and about. Miraculously, Coach Snow agreed to letting us have just morning practice on Thursday.

Sam and I stopped by the office on our way to get Maya. The office held all of our mail and Sam was expecting her course catalog for college. We were both set to go to the same college, but Sam, for whatever reasons, was very keen on deciding classes before school was out. I gathered my mail as well, a letter from my mom and my own course catalog. I opened it as we made for the infirmary.

Sam was so engrossed, she didn't notice when I stopped, for out of my catalog had fallen a postcard. Frowning, I leaned over to pick it up. It was a picture of the onion domes of Saint Petersburg. Flipping it over, I expected to seen Chad's signature at the bottom, but there was none. Totally engrossed, I realized the handwriting was like nothing I had ever seen, and Chad and I had kept up a light correspondence since his leaving for Russia.

> *Scarlett,*
>
> > *My apologies for not writing sooner. As much as I hope you have forgotten all about me, I happened to meet a friend of yours here in Russia. It made me think that for all my selfishness, you might just have been worried as to whether I survived after our encounter. I have, and along with your friend, we are safe here in this frozen wasteland. Again, thank you for your very timely assistance. And say hello to Blake for me.*

There was no need for a signature after that message. Sam had belatedly returned for me. She looked down at the postcard.

"Oh, another letter from Chad? How is Mathias?"

Numbly, I looked at her. "What?"

She seemed confused at my inattentiveness. "The postcard? It is from Chad, isn't it?"

Oh, the need to tell a friend! The safe excuse was right there. No one would wonder at Chad's writing me. No one would ask questions if I didn't share the postcard, but I was so tired of hiding the truth and having it hidden from me. I trusted Sam, I trusted all my friends, but I had been told not to say anything, not only by Captain Mortensen, but my mother as well. In just a few weeks, I could share it all, but my mother's paranoia kept the truth from escaping.

"Yeah, they're both fine," I replied as lightly as I could. "It's just been awhile since I heard, I was surprised."

Sam shrugged. "Well, I never hear from Mathias, so I'm happy to hear it through you. I couldn't live in Siberia. One, I need heat, and two, all those werewolves would be too much for me."

I smiled at her. "Well, unless they were handsome werewolves."

She bumped into me. "As hard as it may be to believe, Lettie, I don't really like werewolves on the whole. Hybrids are okay, there is something else in them I can relate to, but full bloods? They set all my tactile hair up."

"Mrrow!" I waved my hand like a paw.

"That is so mean!" She pushed me harder.

We gathered Maya and took her outdoors. It was a bright May day outside, but in the foothills, it was never hot. I had spent some time in eastern Washington during my summer vacations as a child; Sam had been raised in southern California.

We knew hot. Sam didn't relish cold, though, especially with her werecat blood. Werecats loved heat, and even in human form, they were known to curl up in front of a heater.

The entire soccer team had turned out to watch the game. It wasn't often that we were allowed total freedom during soccer season, and we were all enjoying it. Sam and I settled Maya down near the rest of the team. In the distance, we all secretly enjoyed watching the boys practicing on. They had their final exhibition game on Saturday, so Coach Abrams wasn't about to let them off easy.

Predictably, Sam was in her cheer mode, but early on, she realized there wasn't much to yell for. She sat down with Brittany and they began to discuss the positive versus negative of the players. I looked at Maya, who just smiled.

"Thank you, Scarlett, this is wonderful to be allowed outside. Do you think I can count on the boys getting me out for your championship game?"

"Well, Marcus got you out once, and I'm sure Ben and Doug would hate to be shown up a second time."

"Hmm, I'll have to give hints this week."

"Do they get hints?" I asked, trying to follow the batting order.

"Well," replied Maya calmly. "We all know that if I come out and ask directly, they won't like feeling as though they failed. If I leave it to them to decide, they get to feel special."

I just laughed softly. "I'm happy I could help this time, Maya, but wouldn't it have been more fun to watch the soccer practice?"

Maya patted my arm. "I happen to like baseball."

I shifted to hug her and my mail fell to the ground. We both bent to gather it, but to my horror, she was the one to grab the postcard. "Oh, look a letter from Chad." She flipped it over and I could tell when she realized who it wasn't from. She looked up at me and I just shook my head violently. "But, Scarlett, what is this about?"

I wasn't going to get away with another lie this time. I could beg her not to ask, that I just couldn't tell, but I knew that it would hurt me just as much as it did her. There was this horrible pit of guilt in my stomach, and if I could just share, even with just Maya, maybe... I bowed my head. I couldn't tell one and not the other. Sam deserved the truth as much as Maya, didn't she? But I had promised myself to tell all my friends when we were free of the school. Wouldn't it be wiser to share this secret with just one? Until I could share it with them all? Maya was looking at me beseechingly, as though knowing that I had hidden something before. If Marcus could smell when I lied, Maya must be able to as well. I gathered the letter back from her. Leaning over, I tapped Sam on the shoulder.

"Sam, we're going to get something to eat from the concessions. Do you want anything?"

"No, I'm good." She turned back to Britt, and I led Maya out of the bleachers.

When I knew we were free from any interested listeners, I stopped.

I sighed deeply as I looked at her. "Do you remember that time Marcus brought you to the soccer game and we all went down to Brimstone afterwards?"

"Of course I do. Does this have to do with what happened when you went beyond the student grounds?"

I nodded my head sadly. "There was someone out there, I heard his body's cry of pain in my head and went to find him. He had been attacked by a refractor."

"But the refractors didn't show up until weeks later." The cogs of her brain were working furiously. "You're sure?" she asked quietly. I nodded again. "Then that means they're on our grounds!"

"That's what the electric field is for. It is nearly identical to the one around the Other Realm. I have a passportal from my summer job, and it works here."

"That's horrible! Why would they endanger us like that?"

All I could do was shrug. As much as I had tried to figure that very question out, I was no nearer an answer. "Anyway, the vampire I helped, I promised not to tell anyone about him. My mother was furious when she found out. Furious that it had been necessary, and she is worried out of her mind about so much right now."

"Did you find him like you found Daniel?"

"Yes, it was the same sort of thing. I could hear their pain in my own blood."

"He must be important for you to not tell us." She looked at me consideringly. "I suppose you were made to promise not to tell anyone? Then I'll save you the problem of telling me his name."

I couldn't help the smile that came. "Thank you, Maya, but I always intended to tell all of you when we were gone from school. Everyone who has taken me aside this year has stressed that it isn't safe to talk about it at school. I never meant to always keep these secrets from any of you."

Unexpectedly, she hugged me. "I know, Lettie, you are always trying to help the rest of us. It must have been horrible for you to keep this inside so long. Thank you for telling me."

I smiled crookedly. "Maya, you can tell when I lie. You knew the postcard wasn't from Chad. What other option was there?"

She linked arms with me and we went to the concession stand. "I look forward to hearing all about this in a couple of weeks, Lettie. Every detail."

"Maybe not every detail," I returned. "Surely I can keep a secret or two."

I could feel her repressed mirth. "Maybe, but you know full well Sam will expect more than I would. You can't keep much from her when she gets it in her head to find something out."

My lips twitched and caught on my fangs. "Yeah, I'll have to rehearse what I'm going to say. I'll need to be prepared for the lot of you."

We took our places in line. "I'm just happy you weren't prepared for me. It's a nice feeling to know something more, to be a secret keeper. So, what are you buying me?" Much as I loved my friends, honestly, every once in awhile they could pay.

A week of double practices later, the entire soccer squad was gathered in the locker rooms, washing and just trying to feel normal again. We were all so full of giddy anticipation, it was kind of difficult. That night, when I went to dry my hair, all thirteen of them were there. I put up a hand to hold off the usual drying though. Amazingly enough, I secured everyone's attention.

"I know we are all looking forward to tomorrow's game, and even though we already tried to scare you all into winning last time with no success—I mean, yes we won, but you weren't scared—I just wanted to ask you all to do your best tomorrow. One last time before six of us leave. It would mean a lot to have two soccer championships in one year."

"Yeah," chimed in Sam, "and please save us from the boys if we lose!"

A few giggles escaped. Jess came forward for her turn at the podium, so to speak. "While we might not be as imaginative as our predecessors, I hope you all know that the offer still stands to make your lives miserable in years to come. As everyone who was with us last year knows, it was heartbreaking. Let's not repeat. Now, I know you will all do your best, with no petty squabbling," Izzy and Lizzie discreetly didn't make eye contact with anyone. "So, in the spirit of the team, let's dry Scarlett's hair."

I'm not sure my hair was ever dried faster. If this was a sign of things to come, we were going to clobber Riverdale.

Saturday dawned bright and sunny. Sam and I were giddy as we got dressed, I had to help her find her uniform, again. We were all seated to breakfast as our teammates filtered in. The boys were conspicuously absent, but I figured with so many girls around, no boy dared to squeeze in. We wouldn't have welcomed their presence anyway. We were all gathered on the field before the elves even showed up. Coach Snow, rather surprised to find us where she did, couldn't seem to make up her mind what to do with us.

"Well, I must say that in all my years of coaching I have never seen a season like this one." There were several guilty faces in the team, mine included. "But if you can all continue to play with the same level of intensity you have been these last few weeks, I have to say Riverdale doesn't stand a chance. Now, I'm sure your Captains have already discussed what happens if you lose, but let me tell you what happens if you win. Despite our rather firm policies on travel, which have gone sadly lax in the last few months, I have secured a bus for all of you and your closest friends, to go down to Brimstone after the game. I might even have arranged for discounts at the pizza parlor." Her air of innocence made us all question.

"Coach Snow, why would they offer us a discount? Brimstone missed the playoffs by one game to us." Brittany was, as one of our most spirited, our spokesperson.

Coach Snow smiled with no warmth, in fact I saw a distinct gleam in her eyes. "I don't mean to insult any of you with vampire or elven blood here, but, well, let's just say the vampires are quite willing to help anyone who brings elves down a peg or two. If they're girls couldn't do it, they're still willing to reward anyone who can."

Jess and I met the elven captains at midfield over half an hour later. As I've mentioned before, elves are very stately creatures. There was rarely any warmth when we greeted the captains of Riverdale, but today, there was downright animosity. We shook hands, agreed to abide by the rules, and promptly went to work ignoring our vows for good behavior. Elves are very graceful, however, so we hybrids had the advantage of playing dirty. We could do it and it looked natural. When an elf did it, it just looked wrong. Now, the elven referees were bound to have some feelings towards favoritism, but with all the other factors at work, we really did get away with quite a bit.

At half, we were all just wired up and ready to go. It was still tied at zero, but our energy knew no bounds. Coach Snow made sure that we were all given playing time, a rarity for her. She usually just had her starters play until they died, but she seemed to know how much it would mean for all of us to say we did something. We went back out after half time and our barely repressed energy was unleashed.

Jess back passed to me, and I promptly crossed it to Lilly, who moved it up before crossing back to Jess. Jess played with one of the defenders before arcing it high to Sam who trapped it, controlled it, and shot off towards the goal where Sarah ran in and scored. It was a beautiful moment, but the game was hardly over. We quickly regrouped as the elves started their own onslaught. They crossed quickly and picked their way through our defense until Tina came in with a slide tackle and Wendy recovered the ball. That was the story for the rest of the game. As hard as the elves might try, we were just better. Towards the end, all of the midfielders pulled back to play safety. The elves never made it past our defense after that. When the game was called, well, I can't say I've ever been happier. It was glorious to be on top. To taste victory at the end of a very long road.

When all of the congratulating was done on the field, we went to our friends in the bleachers. Maya had been brought down by Ben and Doug, Marcus had conspicuously remained a bystander, but the way he and Maya had looked at each other, I had the sneaking suspicion he had again been the instigator.

We were so involved in our congratulations that I didn't immediately notice how sick Maya was. She hugged us all, but her eyes were over-bright, and she had to sit immediately back down.

Sam was excitedly telling all of our friends about Coach Snow's bargain, when I finally took in just how exhausted Maya was. I sat down beside her.

"Maya, are you up to going?" I asked quietly while the boys talked with Sam.

She looked at me, and I saw a side of her I had never seen before. My eyes began to well up just at a simple glance. I gathered her to me. "We'll bring you back some pizza. Supreme with no mushrooms, right?"

Sam took Maya's other side, concern tempering her enthusiasm. "Maya, are you okay?"

"I'm just feeling tired," replied Maya. She looked at all of us, for the boys were intently watching her now as well. "You go on without me. I'll be fine." She looked back at me. "You don't have to bring me anything, Lettie, I'm sure I'll be fine to go down myself next weekend."

Suddenly, it struck me that her words were hollow. She was so brittle, and I had been so blind. When I had talked to her about hearing the pained blood of Maxim Rochester and Daniel Livingstone, I had blocked out hearing hers as well. Since she had been taken off her medication she had deteriorated rapidly. In just two weeks she had become a near invalid, the very thing I had promised her she would never become. I helped her to stand, fighting my own tears. "Come on, Maya, I'll take you back. Sam, make sure the bus doesn't leave without me."

Sam looked set to argue. "We should all go with Maya."

Maya turned her soulful eyes to Sam. "No, make sure the bus doesn't leave without Scarlett, Samantha. You can all come see me when you get back. You know where I'll be." I put my arm under her and helped from the stands. Leaving a silent, shocked group behind us.

"Do you want me to carry you?" I asked softly.

"No, and I'm happy it's you, Lettie. You're the only one who would have asked."

"You mean my watchdog isn't behind me?" I asked, trying for some levity.

She glanced back. "He seems a bit indecisive. You know how he can be oddly sensitive. I think, though, that he knows how I feel."

"So you're telling me he'll just follow at a discreet distance?"

She laughed softly, collapsing against me as she did. "Something like that."

I got her back to her room, with a nurse following in at our heels. The nurse immediately began to fret at Maya over extending herself, but Maya silenced her quickly.

"I enjoyed every moment. And I wouldn't change anything about this day. Go on, Lettie, I'll see you when you get back."

"You sure you don't want me to bring you any pizza?"

She laughed softly as the nurse put her to bed. "Believe it or not, I don't want any pizza right now. Save yourself some money for college." A ghost of a smile flitted about her lips.

"Right, save it for when we go to college. Well, I think after tonight I'll be down to less than fifty dollars. That's not such a great start."

"Looks like you need a job."

"Again, yeah, yeah, yeah. I'll be back, Maya."

It was so difficult to recapture the happiness of winning. We were champions after all, but for much of the ride, I couldn't shake the look in Maya's eyes. I felt so horrible for not doing more, but somewhere over pizza, I managed to enjoy myself. She would pull through, she always did. She had to.

TWENTY-TWO

The five of us took the short cut home. The woods that surrounded Hybrid High grew dense closest to Brimstone. Some students were horribly frightened to traverse through the denseness. After all, Brimstone was populated by Immortals, and though most weren't inclined to bother younger Immortals, some liked to pull pranks on us. And, of course, there were always those who proved truly dangerous. Additionally, the attack earlier in the year should have warned at least me away. However, I felt safe with my four friends, and we had daringly chosen to walk home with the lifted curfew and restrictions on travel.

Sam and I walked surrounded by a rotating guard. Douglas, who was still trying to make up for a verbal slip in town about a beautiful waitress, was trying to get Sam's attention. Marcus and Ben were tormenting him. It was amusing to watch as Douglas would walk forward to talk to Sam or try to, and Marcus would walk behind him, either pulling his hair, tapping his shoulder or giving him bunny ears. When Doug would turn to confront Marc, Ben slipped in to torment. Even Sam, working to ignore Doug, was laughing.

We were cresting the final bank, Hybrid High's lights were in the distance, when everything changed. Sounds started coming from everywhere. Marcus quickly moved to protect me, as we all looked for the origin of the noise. Sounds seemed to be coming from everywhere. Above, behind, to the left, to the right. We all had stopped and were craning our necks to find the source. I heard someone behind me and turned. Ben's sharp eyes were shifting everywhere. There was more than one.

"What do we have here, Damian?" The creature behind me was hard to distinguish in the night. The voice was feminine, but the form was nearly impossible to distinguish from the shadows behind.

Another form landed beside her, this one clearly visible as it solidified, a tall, blond man, pale in every aspect. I could hear them sniffing like a werewolf. They glided more than walked. In a fleeting second, the male stood beside me. Gliding a finger down my cheek, he looked at his companion. "Hybrids, my dear Cornelia. Five hybrids."

The female moved towards Douglas. "Let's see, a vampire, an elf," she ran a seductive hand over both boys. She swept up by Sam. "And a werecat."

The male cradled my jaw. "Another half-vampire." His thumb flicked my fangs. He reached for Marcus, but for all the spell they had woven on me, Marcus was not held. He pushed the man away from me, snarling and flashing his fangs.

"What do you want from us?" he demanded harshly.

The female came to comfort him, but there was enough hostility in his stance to force her back. "A werewolf," she said in an aside to her companion.

"A touchy werewolf mutt," replied the male. "We were in the area; we were lost and thought we'd stop for directions." He dropped his voice with a trace of sadness. They were seductive creatures.

"Why not introduce ourselves? Hum? Let us be civil. I am Cornelia and this is my mate Damian. And who might you be?"

"You're not supposed to be here," said Ben coldly.

"Are we trespassing?" asked Cornelia with feigned innocence.

"Perhaps not on school grounds just yet, but shadow creatures are not allowed in the mortal realm. You've gone beyond trespassing."

His words snapped the rest of us from our spell. It also had a frightening effect on the Immortals. Their fury at being recognized made them flash bright, and they suddenly looked more like the refractor I had met. Remembering just what that refractor had saved me from, I began to shake in fear.

"We underestimated you half-blood," said Cornelia, all warmth gone. "Do you wish to turn us in for our crimes?"

There was so much hostility in the words, I took an involuntary step back.

"You let us go, we'll forget we saw you," said Doug quickly.

Cornelia and Damian exchanged glances. Damian looked at me. "This one would tell."

"What would it matter?" I asked, trying to sound calm. "By the time anyone who could stop you was notified, you would be long gone."

"Perhaps," he replied, "but a lesson should be taught."

"It wouldn't do any good to kill us," I stammered. "You're already wanted for your breach of the Other Realm. There is no need to add murder to your charges."

Cornelia laughed, and it was not a kind sound. "You seem so pragmatic, young one. But regardless, you need a reminder, I think. We beings of the shadows have been too long forgotten." She looked at her mate.

"The vampires are the weakest."

It took a second to understand, and in that moment of confusion, they attacked, becoming shadow and smoke. Suddenly human, Damian grabbed me. Again shadow, I was separated from Marcus. I fought, but his unrestrained form moved with me, suffocating me. I managed to glimpse Doug across from me, equally helpless. When they were again solid, I managed my first breath of air.

"We don't wish to kill you hybrids, you are very valuable to us, but you need to know what you deal with. When you live alone in isolation for a hundred years, you tend to become forgotten and forget in return. If not for the elf, none of this would have happened." Cornelia tightened her hold on Doug. "Now understand why we were sealed off from this realm."

Doug fought as she swirled around him. Samantha, claws extended, jumped into the fray. That was all I could see before Damian shifted on me. I had fangs but no powers, and it hurt when he shifted. It was as though my body was trying to shift too. He seemed to be everywhere, there was such pain, but out of nowhere, shadow and I were struck. Marcus tore at Damian, who struggled with his form. I rolled away, but I knew Marcus didn't stand a chance, even if he was showing his wer-traits in some form of balance. I had seen his eyes and they were no longer human. For several precious seconds, he mastered his warring halves, and was equal to the refractor. Just like that, and it was gone. The shadow creature let out a painful sound, and it felt like my body was trying to split in two. Everyone must have felt the same, for we all cried out and covered our ears. I screamed in pain, but a scream did not come out. What emerged sounded like a coming thunderstorm. I was in excruciating pain, but I heard the noise, surprised as I was to feel my vocal cords vibrating, and knew in every way it was opposite to the refractor's weapon. His mouth shut and both he and his mate materialized away from us.

"Vampire isn't the half of it," murmured Cornelia, as they both covered their ears. In a moment, they shifted, becoming light and shadow, and burning a path away in the night.

I turned to look at the damage done to see Marcus on the ground, rolling about in agony. The familiar urge I had to bite him was amplified to a deafening pitch. He was in more pain than I had ever heard an Immortal be in. Ben came up beside me.

"What's wrong?" he asked.

I had to swallow past the bile in my throat. "He's morphing, and it isn't working." I struggled with Marcus, hauling him to his feet. "We have to get him to the infirmary."

Ben took his other side. "Then we'd best hurry."

Marcus was quite physical as he thrashed violently. Ben and I wrestled back as we drug him to the infirmary. I could feel his blood boiling within, battling with himself for dominance. Werecat-werewolf crosses were the most dangerous, as the two creatures were so fundamentally different that the blood would at times try to tear itself apart. The most frightening part of the ordeal as we struggled with Marcus was the fact that he was completely silent.

We were shown into the first available isolation room as the receptionist ran for help. The only noises we could hear were our own labored breathes and Marcus's thrashing. We fell into a heap in the isolation room, but Samantha and Doug were nowhere to be found. Marcus began throwing himself against walls as Ben and I watched in horror.

"One of has to go for help, Ben, we need a doctor."

Ben nodded silently, but was still frozen at the painful spectacle in front of us. The pain of Marcus's transformation was like a screaming in my ears. I knew I had to do something, but my own blood could not make out what. I looked out the door, but no one was coming. The sharp ringing in my ears escalated, and I cried out, and clamped my hands over my ears. This roused Ben, who looked at me.

"Scarlett, what is it?"

"A doctor," I gasped, pressing my hands still more tightly. "Get a doctor, Ben!"

He was indecisive, clearly worrying about me and whatever Marcus might become, so I pushed him out the door and shut it. He looked back at me through the glass, but I gestured frantically for him to leave as I cried out in agony at the sounds in my ears. I turned to look back at Marcus, and I knew, in a second of clarity, what had to be done. I scrambled to him, ducking to avoid his flailing arms. I could feel the blood fighting for supremacy in his veins, and the screaming in my ears, my own blood screaming for me to bite. I sharpened my focus, and I was drawn to him, my mouth opened to emit an eerie crooning noise that calmed both the wolf and cat within him. His blue eyes met mine for one brief second before he threw his head back and emitted a painful howl. I pounced in that moment, biting down on his neck. His arms gripped me as I bit, and I gripped back, as the humming in both our bodies melded for a split second. I drank the blood that was so volatile to him, and in a moment the humming in my ears and the screaming in his veins melded to the rhythmic sound of our hearts. Slowly, I began to feel him calm, I felt his different halves separate and then meld peacefully. The humming in my ears slowly left, but we remained entwined with my teeth still latched to his neck. Several moments slipped by before his throat vibrated in speech.

"I think you can remove your teeth now." His voice was weak, but firm, and I carefully removed my fangs. A few drops of blood trickled down his neck as the wounds began to heal over. Our eyes met for a moment, but what had just happened was impossible to put into words.

"Well," came a voice from behind us, "I see you have finally developed some Immortal powers, Scarlett."

I turned, dropping my hands to my sides, to see Daphne Lennox, standing beside Ben in the open door. Marcus's arms were still around me, but it was more because he was still battling with what to do with his body than anything else. Daphne walked up to us both. She gently pushed me aside and looked at the bite marks on Marcus's neck. She then pressed two sharp fingernails into the pulse on his wrist.

"Impressive," she said, after several moments silence. "You have balanced his blood, Scarlett. It was not a power I knew any hybrid to have. Do you know what this means?"

I just shook my head.

"I would say, Scarlett Wharton, that you are half shadow creature. Only shadow creatures have been known to balance opposing forces as you just did. Mr. Shepherd should be grateful." She turned her imposing eyes to him. She looked long and hard at him for several silent moments. "A fully blended werewolf-werecat. You shall be an interesting hybrid to follow, Mr. Shepherd. I believe you'll be wanting to rest for the next twenty-four hours. Full transformations, like you just experienced, although your body never truly changed shape, are very draining. I am sure Mr. Martin will be happy to take you to your room." Ben came forward to support Marcus as they began to make their way back to their dorm room.

Daphne watched me for several long moments. When she finally spoke, it was with an edge of sadness. "I believe, Scarlett, that you possess the power to tame the blood that can kill us hybrids. I must ask your help, for though I do not fully understand your powers, I believe there are many who would benefit from you. First and foremost, a friend." She left the room expecting me to follow. She turned up a corridor leading to Maya's room. She gently knocked and was told to enter by a voice I had never heard. We entered the room to see two Immortals sitting with Maya on her bed

When I had left her just a few hours ago, I had known she was not well, but never could I have imagined she was so ill that her parents had been contacted. I could not imagine how they had made the trip so quickly. I couldn't have known that they had, in fact, been told to come down when her medication had failed her. It had taken them longer than they liked to make arrangements. Maya managed a smile at our entrance, and her parents turned to look at us as well. Her father was the werewolf, and quite an imposing one at that. Full blooded werewolves can grow to be over seven feet, and Maya's father was one such specimen. Her mother was a fair elf, with ebony hair and inhuman beauty. Daphne stopped two steps in.

"Mr. and Mrs. Duvall, I must ask your leave for a moment. I wish to speak with Maya about something privately. After she has answered, I will ask the same question of you."

Maya's father looked ready to fight for the right to stay with his daughter, but his wife gently led him out, looking at me with something like hope.

Daphne came to Maya's side, taking her hand in her own.

"Maya, I know I have told you for several weeks now that I was no nearer a cure for you. However, it seems that I was looking in the wrong direction entirely. Scarlett has just managed to save your friend Marcus from his rather violent transformation, and I have every hope that she can do the same. Will you allow her to try?"

Maya's beautiful hazel eyes met mine. I could see deep within in her the spark that kept her alive. She looked at me with such faith that I nearly cried.

"I know Scarlett will not hurt me. You have my permission, Doctor Lennox." She smiled reassuringly me. "And you have my faith, Scarlett." She then lay back on the bed peacefully waiting for whatever was to come. Daphne looked at me calmly.

"Let your blood call to you, Scarlett. Your senses will hear her need. I will just be outside the door with the parents. I am not entirely certain Mr. Duvall will agree, so you'd best be quick about it."

I closed my eyes and tried to shut out everything else. For a moment I could hear the humming that had deafened me with Marcus, but I couldn't focus. I looked at Maya and then back at her parents and Daphne on the other side of the door. Daphne nodded at me. Shutting my eyes again, I felt my focus shift. Without sight, I took her left hand and brought it to my mouth. I gently sank my teeth into her wrist, even as I did so the humming turned to a painful scream. I could not open my eyes or take my teeth away. The instinct that screamed in my head told me to hold on no matter how it hurt. I tried to focus for the beat of her heart, that sound that had balanced Marcus so quickly, but it was weak, and her pained blood was so strong. I kept trying, again and again, until I heard her life pulse thump ever so softly in my ears. I drew one last gulp of blood before passing out.

I awoke several hours later in a room much like Maya's. A needle was in my arm, and attached to that was a bag of clear fluid. I groaned to be back in the hospital. My eyes took a moment to focus clearly, but when they did, I saw a form at the foot of my bed that I hadn't seen in weeks.

"Mom?" Those frighteningly similar eyes met mine.

"Scarlett?" She moved without a drop of grace until she was even with me. "Scarlett, my baby, are you all right?"

"I'm fine, mom, I'm fine." She burst into tears as I spoke, and threw her arms around me.

"Oh, my stars, I thought I had lost you, Lettie, and those things we said last summer—"

I awkwardly stroked her head. "It's okay, Mom, don't think about it anymore. I thought we were past that last time. Besides, we are all full Immortals now."

For some strange reason, this just made her cry harder. I was afraid to ask about Maya for fear my mother's tears stemmed from her.

She finally looked up at me, and dried her eyes on my blanket. "I am so sorry, Lettie, I was wrong to say you would never be special, though of course I won't repeat all the things you said, but now you've saved not one but two students, oh, it's just more than I can bear." She let out a fresh wail and buried her face in my sheets again.

"But surely saving people is a good thing, isn't it Mom?"

"Of course," she hiccuped slightly as she looked back at me. "You have the powers for good, Scarlett, and I only wish sometimes I could say the same."

TWENTY-THREE

Maya and I were both allowed out of the infirmary the following morning. Our parents were still with us, as were our friends. I felt kind of like royalty surrounded by a very loyal escort. We were all sitting down to breakfast when the intercoms called us to the gymnasium for an assembly. Still feeling sluggish, I followed my mother to the gym. Our entourage now consisted of nine people, and we sat near the bottom, for both Maya's and my sake.

When we were all gathered and silenced, Principal Daniels stepped forwards to the microphone.

"I have asked you all here today to try to assure your justifiable fears. Earlier in the year, we were alarmed by an unprecedented attack by those beings known as shadow creatures. Five of our students were again attacked by these creatures last night. Now the Board of Directors has not yet acknowledged such, and it will be some time before the Board of Immortals does as well, but it is in everyone's best interest to be made aware now! Shadow creatures are widely recognized as the most powerful of the Immortals. They can blend from flesh and blood to light and shadow in a second. No one Immortal can stand against a fully fledged shadow creature and I cannot stress that fact enough. In the coming days before the end of year, the utmost caution must be taken! Go nowhere without company. Go nowhere without notifying staff. All excursions off of the grounds are now prohibited. I realize I am punishing everyone with this last edict, but we cannot be too vigilant. If we are cautious, we may yet remain unharmed. So long as you remain on these grounds, you will be protected by the utmost protection my staff and I can provide. If you have questions, please don't hesitate to ask. In the following days, we will be having evening classes for the purpose of educating you all on the existence of shadow creatures. As soon as the Board of Immortals decides upon a course of action, we will be informing those ready for graduation of their options. For now, any further questions can be answered by your home room teachers. You are all dismissed."

I just sat there was the bleachers cleared. Teachers were inundated, and Mr. Daniels was doing his best to explain as well. Oddly enough, my mom as well as Maya's parents went to help the teachers explain the crisis. I don't know where the other five of my entourage went, but I was left alone. Slowly, I got to my feet and slid out the side doors. Some students were content with what they knew. Some were fighting over phone rights. I thought to find my friends but everything just seemed so wrong. In twenty-four hours everything had changed.

"Scarlett?" I turned to see Doctor Lennox coming up behind. "Can I speak with you for a moment?"

"Sure," I said, but my mind was still trying to cover a million miles in a few seconds. I followed her into one of the empty classrooms.

"Please, sit," she said as she took a seat herself. "Now, Scarlett, I meant to mention this while your mother here, but I'm sure you will be able to share what I have to say with her shortly. I am not nearly old enough to remember the terror that necessitated the Control, but I have traveled all over this world and heard enough stories to line a library, so I can hypothesize. We are on the brink of something terrible, but I believe that you might just be able to help make it a little better."

"How?" I asked, not really believing her.

"Has anyone ever told you the potential of a hybrid? A fully balanced hybrid, like Marcus, like Maya, is a match for a refractor. Only a fully balanced hybrid has been known to stand against a refractor and win. Your teacher, Anne

Montgomery, is a rare example of a hybrid blending with no assistance."

"Are you asking me to create an army?"

"No," she shook her auburn head. "I do not condone war, and refractors are far too subtle to wage full scale wars. No, I am asking for you to help defend your people. Don't think that refractors are unaware of a hybrid's potential. They sell their talent for power. It was how they gained such dominance, for though you hybrids are rare, your power is frightening to other Immortals. A preemptive strike, and the ability to help countless children who would otherwise die."

"So, I help hybrids in trouble, and in exchange, I give the Immortals a chance to use us?" I was disgusted with the idea.

"Think, Scarlett! If you had not balanced Marcus he would be dead, as would Maya in a few more days' time! You have the ability to save hybrids! Whatever they do with their powers is their concern, but you would be a fool to expect the refractors to let you all go without interest. Some hybrids, your other friends, they were never meant to be more than a cross. Their genetics balanced on their own with a dominant set, but others, like Marcus, are meant to merge completely. You are simply giving hybrids the chance to choose."

I leaned back in my chair, struggling with my unbidden petulance, and a desire to do some good in this world. "And if I help?"

"We would have to leave soon, there are children all across the world who could benefit from your talent. However, I'm aware of your desire to finish here, and, of course, any movement before the Board's approval would only be asking for difficulties."

"Which Board?"

Daphne laughed harshly. "I have no reason to fear the Board of Directors. They do not control me, but the Board of Immortals will be a different matter. I am allowed free range to all Immortal facilities by their grace. I shall have to get you clearance as well. That is, if you wish to come."

I frowned and stared off into space for a few minutes. "I would be helping others like me, right?"

"Yes, and I will try, with what knowledge I have, to help you learn about yourself as well."

I sighed and sat up. "Then, yes, I'll go. When do we leave?"

"You graduate in two weeks, yes?"

"Yeah."

"Then we will aim to leave then. Don't you think you should ask your mother, though? I had meant to, but I simply lost track of the time."

I looked intently at her. "I will tell her, but she will understand. She does what she does to help her kind. She is a very good tracker, and I will be helping my own kind. If you don't mind, I'll tell her tonight."

"Excellent. Very well, Scarlett," she held out her hand. "It will be a pleasure working with you."

When I told my mom, she was ecstatic.

"I've always hoped you would find something that you felt compelled to do. And everyone knows Daphne Lennox. You'll be safe with her."

My mom had to leave that evening. The widespread pandemonium sweeping the neighboring Immortal communities was catching. I didn't know just what she was going to have to do in the days to come, but it wasn't going to be easy or pleasant.

Maya's parents found a room in Brimstone and decided to just wait until graduation. They were too happy to just leave their daughter they thought they were losing.

The six of us were all a little shell shocked in the following days. Everything we thought we knew no longer applied. The Board of Directors came to speak to us two days after our confrontation with the refractors. Rather than lose my temper again, I stayed away. I made a call I had been needing to make, before wandering out into the sunshine filled courtyard.

I was sitting on the rim of the fountain, idly making circles in the water. I knew Marcus was near before he spoke.

"You've been avoiding me."

I looked up and squinted in the sun. "Maybe I've been avoiding everyone."

He sat down next to me and watched my hand. "I understand. Did you go to the assembly? I couldn't find you."

"No, I didn't see the reason to listen to them. Did you learn anything interesting?"

"Not really, but by order of the Board of Immortals, they are beginning to recruit hunters and seekers."

I tensed at the baited eagerness in his voice. I knew separation was days away, but every reminder hurt. "What is a hunter?" I asked as casually as I could.

"Well, a hunter and a seeker work in pairs. One tracks the shadow creature by sight, the other by scent. It's kind of like scouting."

"And you are going to be a hunter?" I asked, looking up at him.

"I think it will be a good opportunity. It pays decently, and I should be able to utilize my newfound abilities. Ben is thinking of being my seeker."

I chewed absently on my lip. "It sounds great, Marcus. In fact it sounds perfect for you."

"Then why don't you sound excited?"

"I guess I just hadn't planned on this year ending as soon as it is. That's all."

"What about you? Are you going to college?"

"No, I called them yesterday and cancelled. Doctor Lennox will be taking me with her. There are other hybrids who need to be balanced. And she can help me find some answers."

He maneuvered masterfully to take both my hands. "How long does she think this will go on?"

I squeezed his hands. "I don't know, she is rather vague about a lot of things. But my mom fears it will be years before all of the refractors are found. She says it seems that they were planning this break out for decades. There was an insurrection nearly twenty years ago, and the power figures wanted out. They refused to accept that they were harmful to everyone else. She's really worried, and I don't blame her."

"What does she think of you going with Doctor Lennox?"

"She's likes it. She says at least she'll know I'm safe. And you? Will you be safe?"

He smiled boyishly. "I'll have Ben with me. I'm sure we'll muddle through, but it'll be six weeks of training before we go out into the real world."

I bowed my head, tears beginning to fall. One hand broke free and he tilted my head up.

"What? No false cheer about being protected by one of your best friends? No warm hearted sarcasm?"

"Oh, Marcus, I'm terrified! They are truly terrifying creatures, and not only am I related to one, but we're all going to be separating and I don't know how to protect you."

He smiled and smoothed a tear away. "You never needed to protect me, sweetheart. That's what I was for. I wish you would come with me, so

I didn't have to worry, but I'm sure we're all over reacting. This could be some great big alarm over a couple escaped Shadow creatures. It will all quiet down eventually."

I tried to smile at his optimism. "What if it doesn't?" I whispered.

"Then you and I will have to run away to Bora Bora and live free of our past."

I gave a watery chuckle. "Bora Bora?"

"Yeah, I always wanted to visit somewhere warm. You'd come with me, wouldn't you?"

I shook him off and stood. "You are absolutely incorrigible, Marcus."

He sprang to his feet and took a hold of me again. "It's what you love about me," he murmured tenderly.

"Did I ever mention love?" I asked archly.

"You didn't have to," he replied cheekily before leaning in to kiss me quickly. He danced out of reach before I could hit him.

"If I ever utter those words, Marcus Shepherd, they will be heartfelt and tender, and I had better be hearing them in return from whomever I direct them at."

He just winked. "Whatever you say, Lettie." And with that he made for the safety of crowds.

There really was no way to have private conversations after the second assembly. The hum of conversation was amazing. As I sat down to dinner that night, I realized that I wasn't even going to manage hearing anyone else's conversation over the noise. Without wondering if my friends would follow, I took my tray outside and sat on the courtyard wall.

I was absently eating and watching the sun begin to set when Maya sat down beside me.

"It's like a rock concert in there," she said, gracefully setting her tray down.

"I never realized just how loud we could all be if we tried."

"I don't think we've ever had the opportunity to find out until now." She finished her tacos before looking back at me. "I talked to Doctor Lennox today. She has offered me a place on her expedition as well."

I smiled. "That's wonderful, Maya. It will be nice to have some semblance of normalcy after graduation."

She offered a smile of her own. "Yeah, the boys are all eager to start their training, and Sam is looking to volunteer with them as well."

"It would fit Sam," I replied, finishing off my dessert. I pulled my legs up under me. "You know, I always knew we'd all have to separate eventually, but it seems so much more different now. Before, it was simply a matter of what schools we'd be going to. Now, it's a matter of survival."

Sam came out shortly after. "Well, aren't the two of you serious. Come on, we're all going to play a quick game of soccer."

"But I don't play," said Maya.

"Neither does Marcus, but it will help get our minds off this waiting. I mean, unless you all want to go and do homework?"

Needless to say, we all went out and played soccer. We played with a Nerf ball instead of a regular one, and ended up with a sort of dodge ball game in the end. When the sun finally set, we all collapsed on the field.

"So, one more week," said Doug.

"Yeah," I replied. "Am I the only one worried about what comes after?"

"Hardly," said Ben. "We'd have to be downright stupid not to be worried. We all saw what those shadow creatures were capable of."

"But they can't all be bad," said Maya, looking over at me.

"No, there was that one that saved Scarlett. And whoever her father is has to be at least somewhat decent," ribbed Sam, poking me to get my goad.

"You know," reflected Marcus after a moment's silence. "I have a feeling that a year ago I could never have imagined being here. Sometimes I feel like I woke up in another reality."

"You kind of did," I said. "I mean, humans are way off in their mythology about us. Even when you were told what you were, is it any wonder you didn't go running in the opposite direction?"

"What's to say I didn't try?" he asked. "But, and don't expect me to ever say this again, I'm happy I came here."

"Don't worry, Marc," replied Douglas good naturedly. "We won't let you forget."

"That's what friends are for," added Sam.

Graduation was by far and away the least of my worries. When it was all said and done with, there was a much bigger problem at hand, but with Maya at my side, we set off for a world so much bigger than our own.

Sneak peak of:

Born to Shadow

*Further Confessions of Scarlett Wharton:
Vampire*

ONE

I am a vampire hunter. And a werewolf hunter. And basically everything in between. If you can think of it, I've probably tried finding it. When it comes to interesting career choices, I think I can safely say I am right up there at the top of the list for conversation starters.   However, I'm not alone in my profession. There are others, some do it for sport, others for government agencies, and some do it to protect others. What makes me different is that I hunt my own kind.

For most of my life, I would have given anything to be unique, to be the Immortal that my mother was. I would never have told her this, and I would have to threaten anyone I did tell into silence for eternity, but I would, hands down, have given anything to be different. Instead, I grew up almost human. I could have gone to a normal school and blended right in. Then I discovered that I actually do have a certain skill set, one that can actually be used to help others, and now I wish I could go back to being normal.

I was born a hybrid in the race of Immortals. Humans know only a fraction about our different species. We like to keep it that way. Over the years a few of our species have slipped out of fairy tales and into mass media movie franchises. Yes, there are vampires, like my mother, there are werewolves, there are also elves and werecats. Then there are shadow creatures, a species that we Immortals have sheltered from even our own kind. And shadow creature, it turns out, is my other half.

Sometimes, life happens in more ways than anyone could imagine. Sometimes, what tomorrow brings could come straight from a novel or the movie screen. Sometimes, it can be as boring as watching paint dry. While my life was hardly movie worthy, it had been months now that I would have been perfectly content to watch grass grow in peaceful boredom. Instead, I was in the middle of Africa and plagued by insomnia. I would love to say that I couldn't sleep because of the blistering heat on the African plains, somewhere between Kilimanjaro and the grasslands of the Serengeti. But that wasn't the case when I happened to travel with the premier doctor in all of the Immortal world. We traveled in style, and that style included individual cooling units in all of the tents.

For six months now I had been plagued with insomnia. Ever since I had left the life I knew behind to venture out into the unknown. Since sleep was no longer an option, I pulled on my shorts and long sleeved top, pushed a hat on my head and went to warm up in the setting sun. Despite common misconception, vampires do not die if exposed to sunlight. Our skin is freakishly sensitive, though, and we burn painfully if we don't apply sunscreen. As I was half shadow creature, I had times where I might not appear whole. The other name for shadow creature was a refractor. Full blooded refractors could shift to light and shadow. In theory, as a half blood, I should be able to as well, but in the meantime, I would settle for not burning or turning involuntarily into a ball of light in the middle of Africa.

"Trouble sleeping?" asked a soft voice behind me.

I nodded, not needing to turn to know it was one of my best friends who spoke. Maya Duvall had been the second hybrid I had ever balanced, and therefore saved. We hybrids have a higher than usual mortality rate due to our dual species incompatibilities. Maya, as a werewolf-elf cross had nearly died before her eighteenth birthday, but was now healthier than ever, and surprisingly tanned. Her werewolf half didn't oppose the tan, and it seemed to override the elven half. Werewolves, despite popular fiction, merely transform into wolves when mature Elves, the stateliest of the Immortals, have a strength unmatched by any other. However, as with all the purebred Immortals, the species rarely intermingled. Maya was one of only half a dozen such a cross that she or I knew of. Her long dark hair and green eyes gave her the ethereal beauty of an elf, but at night, she would sometimes shift and run as a snow white wolf.

"Full moon tonight," she said gently, looking off at the sunset.

"You going to run with the wolves?" I asked playfully.

"Hardly," she replied with a wry smile. "The hyenas around here are not my type, and the cats we're staying with would be hard pressed to let me run free."

We both stared at the small village we were camped outside of. A few of the residents were beginning to stir. Though to the outsider, the village looked much like a traditional Maasai, with brambles all around the edge, it was conspicuous for its lack of cattle. Though the tribe we had come to visit was still very much a part of their landscape, when the first of their kind had begun to change into a cat of the Serengeti, the tribe had turned away from herding and depended instead on the prowess of the newly made hunters.

"Even after we traveled all this way to save one of their own," I said with a touch of snark. Though I had been welcomed warmly, it had rankled to see Maya treated with the same sort of discrimination that so often faced us hybrids.

She shrugged gracefully. Maya didn't do anything that wasn't graceful. "I am still half wolf to them, Lettie, and they are a werecat pride. I'm impressed they let me come at all."

"Huh." She had a point. I just didn't want to acknowledge it. In the past six months, we had visited Immortals in metropolitan areas, but most often, we ended up outside the typical range of human contact. We Immortals liked to stay out of the way of humans, for our own protection as much as theirs. Maya and I had been to the Amazon, the outskirts of Cairo, Finland, China, Mongolia, to name just a few places. And each time, the species we were helping had set the tone. I let out an annoyed snort, and Maya wisely didn't continue to previous topic.

"So," she said after a pause. "Where are we off to next?"

"What makes you say that?"

"Lettie," she said, turning to me with stressed patience radiating from her eyes, "it's been six months. I know what the full moon means to you. We should have the boy found and home tonight, so where to next?"

I sighed, and noticed as our mentor, Daphne Lennox, came out of the tent as well.

"So?" she asked.

I hated being so predictable. Even though I didn't have one of the shifters like the werewolves or werecats in my blood, the full moon still brought a strengthening of my senses. Werewolves and werecats, when they're younger, sometimes can't control a shift when the moon is full. For me, I couldn't block out the others across the globe who cried out in pain and were rarely heard.

"Russia," I replied at last. "If you get me a map, I'll narrow it down.   Cold, though, and more remote than Moscow or Saint Petersburg."

Daphne nodded, almost as if she expected this. "And tonight?" she turned her expression to Maya.

Maya's nostrils flared for a moment, and she alerted north. "About four miles," she said. "Shouldn't be more than half an hour after dusk."

Daphne nodded again. "Good, I'll go find our translator and let the pride know."

As we watched her wander up to the camp of our hosts, I heaved a heavier sigh. "You're the werewolf. Why do I get affected by the moon?"

Maya frowned at me for a moment before turning her expression back out at our surroundings. "Daphne gave me a journal when we started moving around.   It's by one of our ancestors.   She was the first to find our separate kinds. Did you know that shadow creatures are the reason for all the species?"

"Really?   And yet we locked them up?" I asked in surprise.   In America, about a hundred years ago, had come a time known as the Control, when all of the shadow creatures had been rounded up and kept in a high security area in the remote regions of the eastern Cascades. My mother had found it her calling to work at one of the facilities that monitored the high power electrical fields that kept the shadow creatures contained. A freak storm a little over a year ago had breached some of the containment, and it was only then that more than a few of us had learned of just what the Control really meant.

Maya frowned and chewed on her lower lip. Her fangs were a little longer than average, but hardly noticeable. As for me, well, it was harder to hide. "The journal isn't about the Control," she said slowly, weighing her words. "But Jakobella made a point of finding her cousins, who just happened to be some of the first of their kind."

I snorted. "That's kind of funny, you know."

"What?"

"Well, for all the modern media outlets get wrong about us. Jakobella? Isn't that sort of..."

"A combination of Jacob and Bella?" asked Maya with another wry smile. "I suppose it is, but we have dibs on that. She existed over six hundred years ago. She was named for her father, King Jakob."

"She was a Princess?"

"Yeah, but she was stripped of her title and her family was forced to abdicate when she was a child. The government that replaced her wanted to strip the family of everything, but Jakobella refused without the remainder of her family's consent, and so she left home to find them. It seems nearly every branch can trace themselves back, if not to one of the Royals, then to a compatriot of one. When the shadow creatures crossed with the natives, it brought out long dormant traits, and in the German and Baltic regions, the werewolves resurfaced.   In Africa and parts of Asia, the werecats came to be, and from a set of twins came vampires and elves. It seems that particular gene pool was a little uncertain of itself, and the elves and vampires were separated originally only in their desire for blood."

"Wow," I said, my eyes widening despite the sun. "Who knew? Tell a vampire and an elf that nowadays and it'll get you a full grade brawl."

"I imagine the animosity originated then," Maya continued, "when one could control the base urge and the other couldn't."

"Hey," I interrupted, "that baseless urge saved your life."

"I didn't mean any insult, Lettie."   Even when she was upset, her tone was always soft.

"I know," I reached out and put a hand on her to let her know I meant no offense. "But I think this is all a little bit of the pot calling the kettle black. Are you honestly going to tell me as a wolf you've never eaten a bunny?"

She jumped away from my hand in indignation. "I can retain my own thoughts even in wolf form."

I simply raised an eyebrow. Her cheekbones darkened, and she had to look away. She and I both knew that was only true to a certain extent. When we had been in Finland, she'd gone for a two day long run with the local pack.

"It is in a wolf's nature to hunt," she muttered.

"Then why the disparagement towards vampires?" I asked gently. I had grown up around vampires who didn't care for me being different. I had also had more than my fair share of discrimination from the other species. It always blew my poor brain that we were so tribal. If humans ever knew about us, they wouldn't stop from hunting us to extinction, but we seemed content to remain separate rather than stand together.

"I'm just telling facts," she finally answered. "The wolves and the cats, it makes sense why they hunt. There was never any sense in the vampires."

"But it is our nature," I said softly. "It doesn't have to make sense."

"No, I suppose it doesn't. Did you know even elves once shape shifted? Every creature could. Shadow creatures, obviously, to shadow, elves and vampires struggled in the beginning to find one species. Ella said in her writing that if a hybrid took the form of a predator it was more likely to be a vampire in the beginning, but many struggled so greatly with their blood lust that they shifted form between species. Her cousin, Castor, who was one of the first vampires, and the first to truly control it, was a great horned owl. His twin, Helen, who was an elf, was a snowy owl. Ella wrote that when Castor particularly hated himself, his form would shift daily, from bird to bat, anything that could fly."

"Wonder when the bat form took precedence," I wondered.

Maya shrugged. "Not in Ella's time."

"And why," I added. "I mean, bats are mostly harmless."

Maya just shrugged again. "Maybe Daphne has other journals of their descendants."

"Their?"

"Well, Ella's granddaughter was one of the leaders of the Grand Council of Immortals. Which reminds me, Ella herself had something like premonitions. She could see what was happening sometimes moments before it happened. I meant to tell you when I read it, but I just got caught up in everything else. Her grandmother, the Dowager Queen, also possessed something like it, they called it the Sight. You're visions, they're like that, aren't they?"

I nodded, rubbing my head to try and take all of this in. "So it's not uncommon?"

"Oh, it is now. But it wasn't unheard of then."

"Then it just bred itself out of us?"

"I think we forgot," replied Maya, her sharp eyes alerting on Daphne's returning form. "But I think because you're so unique, the talent resurfaced."

"But why the full moon?"

"It's possible you pick up off of Maya," replied Daphne, stopping beside us. Even in the hottest climate, she always looked calm and collected. It never ceased to amaze me how she managed. "She is more affected by the moon and its cycles than any of the rest of us. And we have been traveling together in close quarters for a while now. Since a part of your blood remains with her, it might be that."

I wrinkled my nose and flashed my fangs. "Ugh, so a part of me is with everyone I balanced?"

Daphne had to smother a chuckle. "I'm afraid so, Scarlett. The first few, I think, more than others but if they didn't keep that part, they'd revert back to what they were."

"Goody." I felt violated for no good reason. Suddenly full of restless energy, I bounced to my feet. "Well, are we ready?'

"We can start off now," agreed Daphne. "Our guides are ready."

""What do we need guides for when we have super sniffer?" I asked with a head jerk at Maya.

"So we avoid the snakes," replied Daphne calmly.

"Snakes?" I squeaked.

Maya chuckled and shifted to her wolf form, her clothes dropping around her. She looked up at me, and I could still see the laughter. It was bad enough to be laughed at by a friend, worse when she's in her animal form. Glowering, I took a hold of her ruff, which I knew she was waiting for, and she led me on to my latest victim, or patient. It was all a matter of perspective.

Coming October 2022

Born in Germany, and raised in the Pacific Northwest, L.E. Gibler has been writing for as long as she has been riding horses, nearly 30 years for both. Weaving together work in the real world with finishing a college degree in Communications from Washington State University, she is now working towards opportunities in publishing her fourteen (and counting) finished works.

Each venture into the world of written words is a step closer to realizing a long standing dream, and each story shared is a step in the right direction.

www.ingramcontent.com/pod-product-compliance
Lightning Source LLC
Chambersburg PA
CBHW061052210726
48294CB00001B/116